JILL TRESEDER was born in Ham
in sight of the sea on the Solent
Wales. She writes best in a room
the ocean, and now lives with her
River Dart.

After graduating from Bristol, she followed careers in social work and management development, but since 2008 has focused on writing fiction.

This is her third novel, following *A Place of Safety* (2014), *The Hatmaker's Secret* (2013) and a non-fiction book *The Wise Woman Within: Spirals to Wholeness* (2004).

ALSO BY JILL TRESEDER

A PLACE OF SAFETY

'*Jill Treseder deals with some very profound issues in this book, but as they are woven into an emotional roller-coaster of a plot on an entirely individual level, they never seem to weigh heavy. I was reminded of some of Thomas Hardy's novels in which stories of passion and pain are played out against a backdrop of English countryside with a small but vivid cast of secondary characters. This is a surprisingly gripping, credible love story, and a cracking good read.*'

Christa Laird, prize-winning author of the companion novels for young adults *Shadow of the Wall* and *Beyond the Wall*

THE HATMAKER'S SECRET

'*A beautifully written, intriguing and touching story of the effects of racial prejudice across generations. A compelling and satisfying read.*'

Judith Allnatt, author of *A Mile of River*, *The Poet's Wife*, *The Moon Field* and *The Silk Factory*

'*There is a profound wisdom to Jill Treseder's fiction, worn lightly as befits this subtle, engaging storyteller, but always there, always thought-provoking, and always enlightening.*'

Peter Stanford, writer, journalist, broadcaster and biographer of Lord Longford, C Day-Lewis and the Devil

BECOMING
Fran

JILL TRESEDER

SilverWood

Published in 2016 by SilverWood Books

SilverWood Books Ltd
14 Small Street, Bristol, BS1 1DE, United Kingdom
www.silverwoodbooks.co.uk

Copyright © Jill Treseder 2016

The right of Jill Treseder to be identified as the author of this work
has been asserted by her in accordance with the
Copyright, Designs and Patents Act 1988.

All rights reserved. No part of this publication may be reproduced,
stored in a retrieval system, or transmitted in any form or by any means,
electronic, mechanical, photocopying, recording or otherwise,
without prior permission of the copyright holder.

This is a work of fiction. Names, characters, places and incidents either are
products of the author's imagination or are used fictitiously. Any resemblance to
actual events or locales or persons, living or dead, is entirely coincidental.

ISBN 978-1-78132-491-2 (paperback)
ISBN 978-1-78132-492-9 (ebook)

British Library Cataloguing in Publication Data
A CIP catalogue record for this book is available from
the British Library

Set in Sabon by SilverWood Books
Printed on responsibly sourced paper

In memory of
Kate Charles and Mary Criswick
in celebration of friendship

PART ONE

Francesca

1

Whenever Francesca Fairweather saw a child's swing hanging from a tree, she would be transported to her long-ago childhood garden. She could almost feel the planks of the seat pinching her thighs as she kicked up dust and pushed off with her toes from the gnarled roots of the locust tree.

Legs out straight, leaning back, she'd look up at a sky giddy with the pattern of leaves. She would kick under and crane forward, working hard to get level with the top of the long brick wall. Then she could see across the daffodil bank to the roses her father, Harry, loved to grow and which her mother, Eleanor, loved to pick. She could see the runner bean tunnel and the big bay tree, both places where she loved to hide. She could see the rose arch where she gave dollies' tea parties with pink petal food, and where Mother came and made daisy chains.

Two more kicks gave her a view over the wall to other children, who were allowed to play in the street that was forbidden to her. There was the blonde one she called Pinkie because of her pink cardigan and Pinkie's friend who answered to a screeching call of 'Andrea'. There they were for a moment, vanishing from sight as she hurtled downwards. Back on the upswing she glimpsed that cardigan being grabbed in a game of tag.

Then, bravely, she would stand up on the swing, using her knees to drive herself higher, careful not to look up the sheer face of the house wall to its dizzying chimney stack. There went Andrea, standing on the pedals of her bike to be first to the end of the road.

But Francesca's spying would be interrupted by the creak of the gate and the crunch on the gravel as the gardener wheeled his altogether more plodding bicycle down the path beside the house. Usually he would be singing, 'It ain't gonna rain no more, no more,' but she never stayed to listen. By then, she would have leapt clear of the swing, dodged behind the hedge, jumped down the area steps and into the kitchen, just in time to see his black boots passing the ground-level window. Anything to escape the routine of his questions and her silence, followed by his teasing injunction, 'Don't make so much noise!' to which there really was no answer.

Her most vivid childhood memory took place in that kitchen with her mother.

There is the blue-sweet smell of paraffin and the light is muffled. She can't see the apple tree because of the snow packed halfway up the windows. A murmur of yellow-grey light flickers from the black metal stove teetering in the middle of the room, but that is the only sound. They call the stove Aunt Tabitha because it is tall and thin and prim. She doesn't think there is a real Aunt Tabitha.

Her arms move stiffly in a pea-green jersey, and she's sploshing paint onto big paper, which is spread on newspaper. The table-top is covered in dark green lino and every now and then she pokes her finger underneath where it lifts at the corner. She likes the warm, grainy feel of the wood which is the real table. Mother is huddled over her easel by the door, wrapped in her old camel coat with the big shawl collar. The deep cuffs are folded back to the elbow, and she is painting too.

Then Francesca sneezes. It's quite a small sneeze. But a much bigger explosion comes from Mother.

'Now look what you've made me do!'

The words bounce across the space between them like shots.

'Get out! Francesca, go to your room!'

She clambers down from her chair, grapples with the battered brass doorknob and sets off up the stairs, climbing one steep tread at a time. Coming out of the warm kitchen is like going outside. By the time she gets up to her first-floor bedroom the air feels hard on her face and the tears are icy on her cheeks. But she is a good girl. She knows to stay in her room until she is fetched.

*

The adult Francesca knew this happened in the winter of 1946-7, when she was three years old, and that the kitchen was in the basement with steps down to the door. That was why the light was so eerie, with snow covering the windows and the glass porch over the door. She knew that, next day, her father had dug out the snow that had blown into the area and shovelled a path all the way to the coal shed. She knew he brought back coke and clawed the clinker out of the Beeston boiler which crouched, cold and sulking, in its alcove. The tension, the swearing until the flames eventually took hold, were also familiar to her. She knew he would have brought coal and lit a fire in the sitting room too. What she didn't know, and would never know, was what dreadful thing she'd done. Was it really just the sneeze?

A second memory belonged in the room above the kitchen.

It's shadowy with firelight flickering on the ceiling and making patterns on the iron post of her bedrail. There's something wonderfully cool on her forehead, but under the bedclothes she is slithery inside her nightie. When she wakes she can smell that Auntie Goldie is by the bed, inhales the deep-layered smell of comfort. It's daylight and Auntie Goldie's nose is silhouetted against the wall. Tears are running down her cheek. Out comes a lace-edged hankie. She wipes and dabs and looks round and her eyes are still swimmy.

The adult Francesca knew it was the time when she and Eleanor both had the flu. In those days her bed would be moved downstairs when she was ill, into the snug at the back of the house where a coal fire burned. She knew Eleanor was ill upstairs and that Goldie had come to look after them. It was when her father was still in the Navy and his ship was at sea. She knew Goldie read to her, brought her Marmite sandwiches and played Ludo until Eleanor was back on her feet. Was it a weekend? Or did Goldie take time off work, she wondered. But none of that explained the tears. That was peripheral stuff. Not the crux of the matter.

A third scene was altogether crisper: snow on the ground; the sky blue as a balloon.

*

Francesca is scared. Something not right is happening and she knows to keep quiet. Mother is rushing in and out of the house, carrying canvases into the garden and piling them up. Francesca has to help crumple up newspaper, and Mother stuffs it underneath. She's told to stay well back and Mother puts a match to the paper. It goes up in a great whoosh. Then Mother shouts at her to stay put and rushes back inside. Comes out with her easel and throws it on top. It's sticking up into that fierce blue sky like a Guy on a bonfire. Mother's jumping about and shouting and Francesca's keeping quiet and watching the flames – beautiful colours, brilliant greens and blues. The snow is melting in a big circle all around the fire. Then they go inside and Mother's blowing her nose a lot and says the smoke's got in her eyes. But the smoke went straight up. Francesca watched it.

The adult Francesca couldn't bear to think about the crux of this matter.

Whenever she looked back on her childhood these scenes appeared; three events viewed through the keyhole of memory. They always hung together like beads on a string, but she was never sure of the nature of the thread that connected them.

2

Francesca had just turned ten when she made her first real friend. Zelda's looks were dramatic – black curly hair, dark eyes, long lashes – and she certainly made a dramatic entrance. It was a Monday morning in the spring term. When the new girl walked in behind the class teacher she was actually mimicking Four B's walk, that slightly lopsided stride. Miss Forbes introduced her, and Zelda, instead of shuffling to her place, did an elaborate twirl, curtsied and positively pranced to the empty desk. She didn't appear to notice the titters spreading through the class.

'Is this where I'm to sit?'

Miss Forbes was tight-lipped. 'Indeed.' She eyed Zelda. 'Now...'

But Zelda was busy getting to know her neighbour.

'Zelda, no talking. We are starting the lesson.'

'But, Miss, I was just finding out—'

'Miss Forbes. That can wait until break time. You are here to learn. Now...'

In a couple of days Zelda went from being 'that show-off of a new girl' to becoming the person everyone wanted as their friend. Her skinny brown legs windmilled round the playground in perfect cartwheels. She was constantly surrounded by other girls, laughing or intent on a game, her tangle of black curls always at the centre. When teachers gave her a ticking-off she would toss her hair and lift her chin – a defiant gesture they could do nothing about.

Francesca couldn't take her eyes off this bold stranger who refused to fit in. She hovered on the edge and kept looking back when less interesting friends claimed her attention. Until, one day, Zelda singled her out. Francesca had joined a group which had gathered round Zelda, who was organising a game.

'One potato, two potato, three potato, four,' said Zelda, tapping each outstretched fist. 'Five potato, six potato, seven potato, *more*!' Arriving at Francesca's hand, she took hold of it and marched her away, abandoning the group and whatever game had been planned.

Francesca was alarmed when the first thing Zelda did was pull the ribbons off her plaits (tightly braided by Mother every morning), and even more surprised when she gently teased out her hair until it bounced around her face.

'Lovely,' said Zelda, skipping about at the effect she had created. 'It's like flames. Or a lion. How does it be all different colours?'

Francesca shrugged. 'Just is.'

'Why do you do plaits?'

'Mother says it has to be controlled.'

Zelda made a face and Francesca noticed how a few dark hairs crept across the bridge of her freckled nose so that her eyebrows nearly met in the middle.

'You've got green eyes,' said Zelda.

'Sort of. Ish.'

'What do you mean, sort of, ish? They're green.'

Francesca persisted. 'Today. Sometimes they're grey.'

Zelda ignored this. 'I've got green flecks in mine. Look.' She thrust her face into Francesca's. 'See?'

She did see.

'So you'll be my friend. I'll call you Fran.' And when Francesca just stared she added, 'Will you?'

'Because I've got green eyes?'

'Because you're different,' said Zelda without hesitation. 'Like me.'

Zelda's mother hugged Fran on the first visit to her house, even though they had only just met. She smelled of fried bacon and wood smoke and she was wearing slippers in the afternoon. She told Fran to call her Gaye and sat in the kitchen in an old cardigan, sipping tea out of a mug while Zelda made Marmite on toast. She didn't say, 'Sorry about the mess,' in spite of the toast crumbs underfoot or the dirty dishes in the sink. She didn't say, 'I haven't had time to change,' nor did she tell Zelda a better way to make toast.

'Got that bonfire going at last. Tea for you two? There's plenty in the pot. I must get back to that fire.'

She climbed into the wellington boots which were lying by the back door and pulled on an old tweed jacket. 'Don't forget to feed the cats.'

Fran stared. The most gardening Mother ever did was snipping deadheads off the roses. Dad was the one who sweated away digging trenches and getting muddy. She'd expected Zelda's mother to be different, but not in this way. For some reason she had imagined an elegant Bohemian smoking Turkish cigarettes with a long holder.

'She's always in the garden,' said Zelda. 'It takes her mind off things.'

Fran wondered what things and thought it better not to ask. She guessed it might have to do with Zelda's father who seemed to be permanently away 'on business' and 'abroad'. She'd asked about him once and it was the only time Zelda had ever gone quiet. But Zelda was like a different person at home. Kind of softer, more domestic. It took a bit of getting used to. She watched Gaye feeding the bonfire with a fork which was almost as tall as she was and couldn't imagine her ever playing bridge.

Zelda started towards the door and pointed at a photo propped against a jug on a shelf. 'Plus, she misses him. Rory. My brother.'

It was a wedding snap of a smiling couple, and the bridegroom looked just like Zelda with the same dark curls.

'Me too, actually. It's so blooming quiet with just the two of us. He only got married at Easter. She's very sweet and they come and see us, but it's not the same.'

Fran stared at the picture wondering what it would be like to have a brother. But Zelda was gone, calling her to come upstairs to meet Panther, a huge black cat who was asleep on her bed.

Zelda's first visit to Fran's house was very different. Fran knew it was a mistake as soon as Mother met them at the door.

She looked Zelda up and down. 'Tea in the kitchen, I think,' she said. 'In half an hour.'

Zelda wandered into the drawing room and Fran followed nervously.

'We're not really allowed in here.'

'I'm not even touching,' said Zelda, holding both her hands in the air to prove it.

She stopped in front of the mantelpiece, looking from the porcelain shepherdess at one end to the corresponding shepherd at the other. She pointed her toe, mimicked the pose and simpered. Then she stroked the gloss of Eleanor's rosewood writing desk and peered at her rose pictures, the pair Dad had given her for Christmas.

Zelda made a face. 'They're not like real roses.'

'But they're exact! Every detail, Mother says. They're her pride and joy.' Fran tailed off, indignant, but afraid Zelda would laugh at her. 'Like a photograph. Mother wants to collect them.'

'Exactly. Why not use a camera?'

'There weren't any then, silly.'

'Well, how was I to know that? Anyway, if he could paint that well, why not paint the smell?'

'You can't paint smell.'

'Bet you can.'

And Zelda was gone, taking the stairs two at a time to inspect the bedrooms.

All through tea Zelda was oddly polite, conversing like a grown-up with Eleanor. She didn't talk with her mouth full or put her elbows on the table or tell jokes about their teacher like she did at home.

It happened during the washing-up, the ritual of Eleanor washing and the girls drying and stacking the clean crockery on the kitchen table. Zelda dropped a plate. She was standing just behind Eleanor and she let it go quite deliberately. Fran watched her do it and her mouth dropped open in awe.

'Oh, Mrs Fairweather! Look what I've done! Silly me!' Zelda winked at Fran and stooped to pick wedges of china off the quarry tiles.

Up in Fran's bedroom Zelda stood with hands on hips in front of the window.

'Your mother doesn't like me.'

Fran started to protest.

'And *I* don't like *her*.'

Fran giggled. She felt horribly hot.

Zelda clapped her hand to her mouth. 'Sorree! I didn't mean... I mean she's your mum.'

Then she smoothed her skirt and gave Fran a withering look. 'Really, Francesca, I don't know what you see in that Zelda person. I do think she is a *very* bad influence.'

It was too much for Fran. She collapsed onto the bed next to Zelda, laughing, helpless. In bed that night she relived the scene and her tummy lurched with guilt for being such a wicked traitor. She knew Mother hadn't grown up in an elegant house, though Fran wasn't sure where she'd lived as a child. ('I prefer to say Southsea' meant it was somewhere in Portsmouth.) That's why her things were important to her. But she did wish Mother was a bit more like Gaye.

Francesca didn't ask to have Zelda to tea again. It seemed one-sided, always going to Zelda's, but when Auntie Goldie came to stay she saw her chance to even things out. Her visits were rare since Harry had come out of the Navy and joined a dental practice in the High Street. It was as if Eleanor had less need of her sister, and Francesca missed her aunt.

'What would you most like to do, Francesca, while I'm here?' said Goldie at breakfast on the first morning.

'I'd like to have my friend Zelda for the whole day and stay the night.' Fran held her breath, looking sideways at Mother. What would she say?

Goldie spoke over Eleanor's protest. 'That sounds like fun. Better than being stuck with silly old me.' She patted the bow in her bright blonde hair. 'We'll paint the town red!'

Eleanor was making a point of studying her toast.

'Not silly old you! You're brilliant. Just, I think you'd like Zelda.'

'I'm sure I will. The more the merrier.'

'How do we paint the town, Auntie Goldie?'

'It just means, have fun. Too hot to go to town. We'll paint the beach instead.'

After breakfast Eleanor sent her up to make her bed. She went slowly on the stairs listening to them in the kitchen.

'I have to say, Gold, this Zelda is a little madam. Be warned, if you must insist.' Eleanor clattered plates more loudly than necessary.

'Hark at you, Nell. Anyone would think you were never that age.'

Painting the beach turned out to mean ice cream cornets and fizzy drinks and ducking Auntie Goldie, who didn't mind that all her mascara and lipstick ran. When it came to bedtime she said it was far too hot for them to sleep and took them back to the beach for a last swim.

It was exciting to go swimming in the evening. The air was still warm when they got dried and dressed. They threw pebbles into the little rushy waves and Goldie pointed along the shingle. A huge red moon had risen and was hanging just above the beach.

'Race you to the moon,' yelled Zelda.

They started running towards it, stretching out their hands, convinced they could touch it. But they came to the end of the beach and Auntie Goldie was calling after them.

'Time to go back.'

Fran and Zelda squealed their protest. 'Not yet!' 'Just one more race!' 'Please, Auntie Goldie! Please!'

'I tell you what,' said Goldie. 'We'll have a moon picnic in the garden.'

It felt late and wicked. There was dew on the ground and a chill in the air. The girls pulled on their cardigans and their feet slipped inside their sandals. Custard creams and lemonade by the hollow tree. Lights were on inside the house, where Fran's parents sat, unaware of the revelry. Goldie perched on the swing and drank her lemonade.

'I needed that,' she said with a deep sigh.

Fran squawked when a woodlouse ran over her foot.

'Time for bed,' said Goldie.

In the kitchen they met Eleanor.

'You're late with them.'

'We saw the moon. It was red,' said Fran.

'My mum says the moon is magic,' said Zelda.

'Hmm,' said Eleanor.

'Up you go,' said Goldie, and poured herself more lemonade.

'That's grown-up lemonade,' said Zelda knowingly. They scuttled out the door, giggling and pushing each other to be first, nudging each other up the stairs, tread by tread.

Eleanor's voice came from the kitchen. 'See what I mean, Gold? Too clever by half, that one.'

Fran hoped Zelda hadn't heard.

When Fran and Zelda moved on to grammar school whisperings reached the bridge club that Zelda, and therefore Fran, was mixing with the *wrong crowd*. Eleanor Fairweather put her foot down.

'But, Mother, what's wrong with Zelda?'

'That outlandish name! What do you expect?'

'It's after Scott Fitzgerald.' Fran thought it was glamorous.

'Quite,' said Eleanor. 'That proves my point. And with a mother like that.'

'Like what?' Fran couldn't bear to hear Gaye criticised.

Eleanor was tight-lipped. 'She lets her run wild. And no father…'

'Gaye can't help it if…'

'If she married the wrong man? You make your bed, you lie in it. You make it fit, you trim your feathers, you *accommodate*. And all other clichés which are marriage. You even learn to play bridge.'

Fran blinked. 'But I thought you liked bridge.'

Eleanor turned from the window, looking surprised to see Fran. 'Bridge? Yes, of course I do. Where was I?'

'Zelda's father – he has to be away on business. It's his job…'

'Francesca, there are some things you do not understand. And it's Mrs Turner to you, for goodness' sake. Gaye, indeed. I'm not having you associating with that girl, do you hear?'

Inevitably, Fran caved in. 'I can't come to your house anymore,' she told Zelda.

They were coming out of school one Friday afternoon and Fran had been putting it off all week.

'Whaat?' Zelda stopped dead, dropping her satchel so that Fran nearly fell over it. The river of schoolchildren heading for the gates parted clumsily around them. 'You can't let her dictate…'

'I get sucked in. I don't know…'

Some older boys called out to Zelda and one shouted, 'Who's your carroty friend?' but Zelda ignored them.

'Don't you want to be my friend, then?'

'Of course…'

'Well then.' Zelda swung her satchel onto her shoulder. 'And we can always *resort to Plan B.*'

Fran frowned. They had a hopeless geography teacher who kept forgetting vital handouts for lessons. He was always saying 'we'll have to resort to Plan B' so Plan B had become a catchphrase for resolving all manner of awkward situations.

'Plan B? Didn't know we had one.'

'Well,' said Zelda and took a deep breath. 'My dad is rubbish, basically. Mum thinks he's got another woman. Your mum is a pain. So – Plan B – you and your dad come and live with me and my mum. Simple! You can share my room!'

Fran pictured the quiet order of her bedroom at home vanishing into the chaos of Zelda's glory hole and felt a split second of disloyalty to her friend.

Zelda was already moving on. 'Remember we're going to the flicks tomorrow. Meet you at the bus stop. Usual time.'

Fran meandered home. How could Zelda talk about her father like that? So casually? She couldn't imagine her own father caring for any woman other than her totally impossible mother. He wouldn't even look at Gaye. That thought had her bumping into the lamppost outside the greengrocer's. Harry adored Eleanor, but he was also Francesca's ally, a mediator between her and her mother. He helped her with her maths homework and had even persuaded Eleanor to let her have a bike and ride it into the village. As to her impossible mother – for all she bossed them both about – she would be lost without Harry. Her parents were, well, they were just there. Plan B was brilliant just as long as it never happened.

In spite of Eleanor, summer days were spent mostly at Zelda's house, climbing trees, stalking the cats and planting out seedlings for Gaye.

'I wonder what it's like to see the world from down here.'

Zelda was stretched full length on the scrubby back lawn, watching lettuce leaves disappear into the jaws of her tortoise.

'Pretty boring.' Fran was unimpressed by the tortoise.

'I can see an ant climbing through the grass like it's the jungle. Just think, Fran, we clomp about destroying whole worlds and we don't even know they're there.'

That was the thing about Zelda. She saw things differently; she was never boring even if her tortoise was. Fran couldn't imagine not being friends with Zelda. It would be like drowning.

When they were both fourteen, Zelda went to stay with her London cousins. On the day of her return, Gaye invited Fran to meet the train, a jaw-dropping experience for both of them. Zelda had departed in shorts and an Aertex shirt. Now she stepped off the train in a swirling pink and white polka-dot skirt and painted toenails revealed by strappy sandals with *heels* – low heels, for sure, but heels nevertheless. Could this be the Zelda who never wore shoes in summer unless forced to do so? A charm bracelet tinkled on her arm as she waved, and she carried a handbag in white patent leather to match the sandals. Her mouth gleamed with lipstick, but she chattered on about her holiday as if nothing had changed.

That night Zelda tuned in Radio Luxembourg on her new transistor and made Fran a present of her Shocking Pink nail varnish, because she preferred Scarlet Lady.

'You'll never guess,' she confided in a breathy whisper. 'My cousin tried to kiss me. He's my *cousin* and he's got *spots*. Yuk!'

'What did you do?'

'Told him I'd tell his sister. He had the nerve to laugh.'

Fran hoped the exotic creature Zelda had turned into would still want her as a friend. She preferred the Zelda who tried to get into the mind of a tortoise. But within a day Zelda's nail varnish was chipped and her black curls were once more caked with salt. All the same, she had peeped through a door into another world and brought back what seemed to Fran like contraband.

Eleanor was not fooled by Fran's increasingly lame fibs about where she spent her time and called on her husband. Harry Fairweather sighed.

'What am I supposed to do?'

'Not take Francesca's side all the time.'

'But what's the harm in Zelda? Always seemed a sparky kid to me.'

'Exactly. Sparks will fly. You haven't seen what she's grown into. Mark my words.'

'I mean, Francesca does know…? She is aware? The birds and the bees, and all that?'

'Oh really, Harry!'

Which left him none the wiser. One Sunday after lunch he took his daughter for a walk.

'Now, Frazzle, your mother's worried…'

'Oh, she's got onto you about Zelda! I thought you always used to have a soft spot for her. Tell you what, Dad, why don't we drop by the Turners' and get Zel to come with us? Then you can see for yourself the monster she's supposed to have turned into.'

By the end of the afternoon Harry was thoroughly convinced Zelda was just the sort of friend his daughter needed.

The next landmark in Fran and Zelda's lives was GCE. Eleanor was reassured when Fran passed eight O levels with marks in the eighties and nineties, and smirked because Zelda scraped six, excelling only in Art.

'That girl. I suppose she'll leave and work in Woolworths.'

'She's staying on to do A level Art and Biology.'

'A fat lot of good may it do her. No future for girls in Art. As to Biology…' Eleanor gave a bark of a laugh. 'She'll have babies and have to pack it in. Poor deluded child.'

Fran gaped. 'But I thought you studied Art at…'

'Precisely.' Eleanor stomped off with the secateurs, leaving Fran with an empty feeling in her stomach as she watched her savagely deadheading the hybrid teas. A memory seemed about to shake itself loose and present itself, but evaporated. It was as if she was waiting for a play to start: the safety curtain had gone up, but the scene on stage was never revealed. She was left feeling cold and shaky.

A levels were over. They were lying in the long grass in Zelda's back garden and Zelda was practising blowing smoke rings. A squarish loop of smoke drifted upward.

'Oh there's one! Well, sort of. I could do it when Tomasz was showing me.'

'Who's Tomasz?'

'One of my patients. My favourite.' Zelda sighed and stretched. She had that annoying I've-got-a-secret look.

'Patient?'

'You know. The sailors at the naval hospital?'

Fran laughed. All those shapes wrapped in blankets, sitting on the balcony opposite the seawall. What could Zelda want with them?

'We used to wave to them when we went swimming after school.' Zelda nodded.

'They used to throw us sweets.'

'So they did.'

Fran was getting an uncomfortable feeling. Zelda was always one step ahead of her, but every so often she would take a quantum leap into unknown territory and Fran would be left behind, clinging to what was familiar.

'There's a gap in the fence,' Zelda was saying. 'You could come too.'

All through the last two years Zelda had repeatedly fixed Fran up with dates. She had duly held clammy hands with several spotty boys in the cinema, drunk endless coffees with a Mathematics bore, and been on sailing picnics to the Isle of Wight in foursomes. All to no avail. The only constant in her life was a keen sailor called Eric who was more interested in his boat. They used each other whenever partners were required.

'Why would I?'

'You said you wanted a boyfriend. And, by the way, before you say it, I don't count Eric. Why don't you come?'

'Don't fancy a sailor in striped pyjamas.'

Zelda gave a slow smile and her eyes went slitty. 'He could always take them off.'

'No thanks.'

Zelda shrugged. 'He's learning to walk on crutches.'

'Who is?'

'Tomasz, of course. He's taking his time. They won't discharge him until he's walking unaided. So I've got him for a while.' She passed her roll-up to Fran who took a puff and made a face.

'I still don't like it.' Fran returned the cigarette. 'What's that noise?' A mewling sound was curling out of the rhubarb patch.

Zelda grinned, said nothing.

Fran crawled away and found Zelda's little tabby she-cat writhing on her back in the shade of a leathery green parasol. 'It's Willow. Come here, Zel! She's ill. She's in pain!'

But Zelda just laughed. She didn't even get up. 'She's on heat.' She raised her voice. 'You shameless woman, Willow!'

'What do you mean?'

'Wake up, Fran! I mean, she's randy as hell and she's calling every tomcat in the neighbourhood to come and give her a good shafting. As Ed would say.'

Fran was quiet. Knowing Zelda said things to shock didn't stop them being shocking.

'Why are you so scared of sex?'

Fran pretended not to hear. She dropped down beside Zelda chewing a grass stalk.

'Who's Ed?'

'Someone I know. Hey! That means kittens for Christmas. What fun! You could have one.'

'I can just see Mother going a bundle on that idea.'

'You and your sainted mother. At least you'll be shot of her in Bristol.'

'If I get in. Wish you were coming too.'

'Of course you will. Me? No way. I'm never, *ever* going to take another exam. That's a promise. Anyway, I need to work – now Dad's finally come clean and moved in full-time with the Trollop from Trowbridge.'

'You and your mum, you're more like sisters.' Fran smoothed sun cream into her shoulders. 'But university isn't just exams.'

'You bet. Wild parties. Smoking dope. Loads of men. I guess you're holding out for a brainy one. Just make sure he's decent-looking. And don't go all snooty on me.'

'Course I won't. Anyway, we've got to get the results first.'

'Yeah, well. But if all else fails – and it won't, worse luck for me – there's always Plan B.' Zelda lit another cigarette. 'You know what? Doesn't the sun make you feel randy? Like now?'

Fran wriggled experimentally. 'Don't think so.'

'When it's this hot and it shines right on me there, it feels almost like screwing. Like when you look at a guy and you fancy him and you know he knows it? And you get that feeling? Know what I mean?'

'Not really.'

'I really do despair of you.'

That evening, as Fran was leaving to go home, Zelda stopped her at the door.

'You never did answer my question.'

'What…?'

'And I know you heard.'

'Just because I don't have animals…'

Zelda slowly shook her head. 'How the hell are you going to manage without me to sort you out?'

3

Bristol was another world. Fran's father had studied there himself and was in his element, eager to show it off.

'The first thing you need to understand,' said Harry, 'is that it's on three levels. The business end as I like to call it, with the railway coming in at Temple Meads, the shopping centre, Haymarket, the docks and the wine trade and so on.'

He broke off, changing lanes as he negotiated the laden car through heavy traffic. Eleanor was tense in the front, driving every inch of the way from the passenger seat.

'St Mary Redcliffe thataway.' Harry waved a hand and changed gear. 'Lovely church, worth a look. Fine brasses, if you like that sort of thing. Now, here we go up Park Street, with the Wills Tower at the top in all its Neo-Gothic glory.'

Eleanor cleared her throat. 'It's very fine. Glory is right.'

The mood in the car instantly relaxed. Fran, relieved, happy even, craned forward from the back seat to get a view of the looming Wills Memorial Building and its elaborate tower. She'd seen it before when she came for her interview, but it had been a fleeting visit and she'd been too nervous to notice much. The city was taking on a new identity with Dad's enthusiasm. She'd hoped Mother would opt not to come, but she'd insisted on seeing where her daughter was going to live, which Fran found oddly touching.

'And here at the top, George's bookshop.' Harry paused for pedestrians. 'You'll be spending a lot of time in there – and money, no doubt. And even more time drinking coffee in the Cadena – see? Just there?' He did a double take. 'Oh, it seems to be called the Berkeley nowadays. Hope that's all that's changed. Splendid haunt. This level always just meant the university to me, but of course a lot else goes on. This bit we're coming to is called the Triangle – for obvious reasons.'

It wasn't at all obvious to Fran but she trusted all would become clear later.

Harry waved an arm to the right. 'There's Brights department store. And off up there, most importantly, is the landmark Victoria Rooms, aka the Vic Rooms, theatre and so on, where I believe the Student Union now is. Then there's the BBC in Whiteladies Road, and Blackboy Hill up to the Downs. Don't worry. They'll all be familiar names in a week or two.' He grinned at her over his shoulder. 'The Downs is the third level, the posh bit – big houses, Georgian crescents in Clifton, and so on. You'd like that, my dear.'

He tapped Eleanor's knee as they came to a halt in a queue of traffic, and Fran guessed he'd be taking her on a tour of Clifton crescents before they went home. Fran wondered if she'd ever find her way around. Dad was being overwhelming. She wanted to cover her ears against the overload of information. Now he was off again.

'But the Downs of course, they're great for walks – with Leigh Woods just over the Suspension Bridge. And the men's halls of residence are all up there. Trying to keep you apart I suppose. But we peel off here. Hotwells straight on down – and up there, that's Queen Elizabeth's Hospital School where the boys wear skirts.'

'Really? Why?'

'No idea. Now, I think the women's halls are up this hill here. Yours should be on the left, if I'm not much mistaken.'

Fran's first months in Bristol, compared with sleepy Gosport, passed in a sequence of fast frames. Everywhere she went involved climbing, particularly the hill to her hall of residence. Migrating from the English department in Berkeley Square to the library in the Wills Building, or from the library to settle in the Berkeley coffee bar, involved knifing through the city traffic. This became a daily routine. She'd sit on the periphery of a sprawling group which would suddenly depart en masse, leaving her exposed among the empty cups and cigarette ends, as if the force of all that magnetism had ripped away a layer of her skin. She missed Zelda, who would be in the thick of it, the centre of attention. If only she could be like that.

She wasn't exactly homesick, but it felt like a failure not to be so absorbed in her new life that she never gave her parents or Zelda a thought. Was she the only person she knew who enjoyed writing home? It conjured the breakfast table with Frank Cooper's marmalade and Mother slitting the envelope neatly with a paper knife.

Dear Mother and Dad
I hope you had a good journey back.
The mousy girl in the next room you spotted is called Rowena and plays the recorder. The girl opposite is Russian and never seems to be there.
I have found out where to go for most things. The student union is in the Victoria Rooms, like you said, Dad – and the library is in the Wills Building. At least I'm not doing German – that's at the top of the Wills Tower and students aren't allowed to use the lifts. The English department is in Berkeley Square – top corner, of course! The tutors seem okay but it's early days. I'm getting so fit, what with all that and the hill up from the Triangle. Sometimes I do it twice a day.
I already have a big essay to do on 'The Faery Queene' so I must go and get started.
Much love,
Fran

Dearest Zel
I have a great little room but right at the end of the corridor, so a bit out of it. It's not even quiet as the girl next door plays recorder. It seems to be all she does and she's not even a music student. I think I may go insane. Mother thought she might be a suitable friend – dowdy and wears aggy shoes – so, guess what, I'm not keen. Typical Mother! The Russian opposite – Sofka, I think she's called – is much more interesting, exotic. She sweeps in and out – mostly out – in knee boots and a fur coat. But she's never there long enough to talk to.
The food isn't too bad and apart from mealtimes and lectures

I can do what I like – I don't even have to eat the meals. There's the Refectory in town which is quite cheap and a little kitchen down the corridor where you can make tea and do beans and toast. Some people moan about the doors being locked too early and say it's like boarding school, but you can always get a late pass key. And there's no M giving me the third degree!

Let me know how you get on finding a job.
Loads of love,
Fran xxx

Dear Mother and Dad
I've just met my Philosophy tutor – Mother, you would not approve as he wears sandals with socks – yellow ones even. We are doing the Empiricists which is rather dry and all about perception so, Dad, I won't be able to help you on the meaning of life, certainly not this term and probably never, as Sartre and people come much later in the syllabus when I'll have given up. It's Mill next term. Hope he's more interesting.

By the way I got an A for that essay I was telling you about, so that's a good start.

Mother, I do not spend all my time 'gadding about'. The phone is right the other end of the corridor so nobody can be bothered to come and get me. They just say I'm out. Plus I need to spend a lot of time in the library because of the recorder.
Much love,
Fran
P.S. Thank you for sending my jumper.

Dearest Zel
You'd never believe the Philosophy seminars. I took ages finding the place – down in the basement with all the pipes – so not in an ivory tower, ha ha. At first I mistook one of the students, who's called Edward, for the tutor. He wears tweed jackets and smokes a pipe and looks like somebody's uncle although he's only the same age as us, plus he holds forth like he is the tutor. The actual tutor is this great lumbering guy who always wears sandals with yellow socks.

I thought Philosophy would be interesting, debating questions like 'Why are we here?' But we don't get to do that until after I'll have given up, as it's only my subsidiary subject. We're doing Empiricism which is SO boring. It's all about whether things are still there if you're not looking at them. I ask you! There are windows along the top of the wall in the room where we meet – and guess what? We all had to stand on the table and peer through into the next room to see if the table was still there. You would have wet yourself!

It makes me mad to think we waste time like that and this guy is paid to teach it! They are all so self-important about it, especially Edward. What do they think the table will do? Disintegrate and fly out the window? And come back the moment I peep round the door? Berkeley got round it by saying God was always watching everything. At least I think it was Berkeley. There's even a limerick about it, but, as you know, I can never remember things like jokes.

Better read my Hume now and make some notes so I can hold my own with Edward next time – some hope!
Lots of love,
Fran xxx

My Darling Fran
The girl in the room next door sounds awful and I know what you mean about recorders. My brother played it once and it was dire. Can't you move out of that place? Whatever you say, it does sound like boarding school and you must be missing out on all the joys of student life.

Who the hell is Berkeley and has he got anything to do with the coffee bar you mentioned? Reckon you should be spending more time there than in the library. Sounds like you're getting way too learned for me.

Job hunting is not going well as all the best ones require short-hand and typing and I won't do that although Mum says I could. I'll probably end up on the pick and mix in Woolies.

I hope you're not reading poetry all the time – it always makes you depressed.
Loads of love,
Zelda xxx

Dearest Zel

I finally decided to tackle the Rowena woman and her recorder and asked her in for a coffee. But I hadn't got that far before she went down on her knees and started praying for me and wanting me to join the Christian Union. I'd rather put up with the recorder.

Glad you got the filing job. At least you've got money even if it is boring. My grant came through at last and guess what? I went straight out the bank into the shop next door and bought myself a record player! You'd love it – a Bush, silver-grey, very elegant. But that used up most of the grant so I've got to keep the rest for books and can't afford any records! So you know what you can get me for Xmas! Lucky I'm in Hall and don't have to buy food.
Loads of love,
Fran xxx

Dear Mother and Dad
Just a quick card to let you know my grant came through at last and I put it in the bank. I will try and make it last, but it wasn't as much as I thought it would be.
Fran

Dear Zel
I've sorted the recorder! I got my first record. It's an EP of Eddie Calvert – only 1/9 in the second-hand shop down the road – so not exactly a hit, but a bargain and I do love trumpet. Every time she started practising I put him on and turned the volume up full so I couldn't hear her. After three days of that she arrived at my door in tears. She didn't try the praying and we've agreed times she can play the damn thing and when she can't.
Lots of love,
Fran xxx

Christmas came and went and Fran hardly saw Zelda. She and Gaye had gone to her brother's and were snowed in. Zelda phoned in great excitement that her brother's wife, Beth, was expecting. 'Fancy, Rory a father! I can't imagine it.' It was all she could talk about, and Fran lost interest.

Back in Bristol, the snow meant cancelled lectures, stranded cars and interrupted routines. After one heavy overnight fall Fran waded down to the Vic Rooms in her wellies to look for company and information. The world had gone mad – she was engulfed by multiple snow fights. As she looked for people she knew a cannonball of ice hit her square in the back and toppled her into a bystander with a domino effect. She found herself lying eye to brown eye with a total stranger who rubbed his nose across hers.

'It's what the Eskimos do, isn't it? Very appropriate.'

She rolled off him into deep snow. Her left ear filled with the stuff and a shiver of crystals crept down her neck. The eyes still smiled across at her.

'So, who are you? Apart from being the Snow Queen herself, obviously.'

'Fran. I'm Fran.'

'And who is Fran?'

'I'm a student.'

'Well, there's a surprise. And what does student Fran study, or is that classified information?'

'English.'

'And apart from being a student of English who is uncommonly mean in the use of the English language, who are you? Have you recently left a silent order of nuns?'

'I'm cold, that's all.' It wasn't true but it was all she could think of to say.

'Which is no surprise either. You're lying in a snowdrift instead of on top of my warm body. Come on.'

He stood over her, holding out both hands. As he pulled her to her feet it was an effort not to slither into him for the second time.

'The elusive Snow Queen,' he said, as if defining her.

It sounded mocking but she couldn't see his face as he was beating crusts of snow off his army greatcoat.

Then he leant forward and gently flicked some flakes of ice off her cheek. 'The last time I saw you, you vanished.'

'The last time you saw me?'

'At one of the hops in Freshers' Week. But...'

'The meat market?'

'You said it, not me.'

Fran remembered that so-called dance in the Vic Rooms during her first week: gaggles of nervous girls pretending not to notice the second- and third-year men stalking up and down, viewing the merchandise. How come this guy had noticed her, remembered her?

She screwed up her nose. 'Not my scene.'

'No. One minute you were standing by the door and the next you'd disappeared without a trace. I hope you don't make a habit of it.'

The eyes were still on her, not smiling, just looking. She'd only met him minutes ago but he seemed to know more about her than she did herself. It was frightening.

'I've got to go now. But come out with me? There's a party on Saturday over in Cotham. Meet me here for a drink – in the bar, I mean.' He nodded over his shoulder towards the Vic Room steps. 'If you fancy it. About eight.'

Fran found herself nodding. He smiled and the whole shape of his long serious face changed.

She forgot all about checking which lectures had been cancelled and walked home wondering what to wear on Saturday. She wanted to be someone. But who should she be? Who was Fran? A girl with red hair who didn't behave like her hair was red. Her mother's daughter? Argh. Escaping from being her mother's daughter. Her father's daughter, yes, but what did that mean?

She burned with embarrassment at her hopeless answers to the man in the snow. His question kept repeating in her head as she trudged uphill in the road where traffic had cleared tire tracks through the snow. *How do I be me? How do I be someone like Zelda? Someone people remember and want to be with? Zelda would say, get on with it and have sex and then you'll know.*

I know who I'm not. I'm not the daughter Mother wanted, not mad about fashion, not looking for a man to marry, not into make-up, and I'm saving up for books instead of clothes. People ask what I want to do and I don't even know. Mother always told me what to want.

The exhilaration of the snow had worn off. Her scarf and mittens were sodden and she was just plain cold, her toes hard with the pain of it. She pushed in through the main door of her hall.

What would Zelda say? She'd ask what she was going to wear

to a party where she'd have to take off her coat. She'd say, 'The sooner you get that awful coat off the better.' Okay, so a duffel coat wasn't a fashion statement but it was warm. Wasn't that the point of a coat? She could hear Zelda sigh and say, 'Oh, Fran!' and, 'What are you doing, going out with a guy when you don't even know his name?' But maybe that last voice came from Mother.

That afternoon she wrote to Zelda that she had a date. A reply came by return of post.

Dearest Fran

You are SO annoying! You say you met in a snowball fight and you don't say what happened. Did he roll you over and have his wicked way with you in the snow??!! Probably not, knowing you. Tell me ALL about the date!!

I have given up going out with anyone – they are all so boring. It's more fun playing mah-jong with Mum. And of course we're knitting like mad. Bootees and matinee coats – she does the twiddly bits when I get in a muddle.

Remember to tell all.
Loads of love,
Zel xxx

Fran wrote back that it had 'kind of fizzled out', which was not exactly true.

The party that Saturday was a disaster. That is, Fran's choice of a skirt and her best green jumper was a disaster. Everyone else was in black or denim. She wanted to hide. She found out Dale's name, but he got into a deep discussion about music with a bearded man called Mike and left her high and dry. Who could blame him? She couldn't get with it and they had nothing in common. It was a mystery how a green jumper could stop you talking to anyone, but it did.

She was surprised he wanted to see her again, but that evening wasn't a success either.

She'd wanted to go to Portishead to see the sea, but the Bristol Channel was disappointing. After a freezing walk on the beach they warmed up in the nearest pub. When she fended off his beery advances, he called her more frigid than the weather.

'More Ice Maiden than Snow Queen,' he added.

On the way home he stopped to fill up with petrol. When he got back into the battered old van, he slammed the door and waited.

When he eventually spoke, there was a harsh edge to his voice. 'Just giving you a chance to pay for the petrol.'

He'd paused, waiting for Fran's response, but she'd just sat there with her mouth open. Another slap in the face, but a perfectly fair one. What had she been thinking of?

'You never even say what you're thinking – look at you now!' He waved his hand across Fran's eyes. 'Anyone in there?' He shook his head and forced an exasperated sigh. 'Like I said, Ice Maiden – all those chaste kisses you ration out.'

He started the engine. 'It was nice knowing you. Or not knowing you, as it happens. I might have known – you're just too middle-class for me.'

They drove in silence and stopped at the road to her hall.

'I'm sorry.' She handed him a ten shilling note.

Dale waved it away.

'Go on, take it.'

Dale dropped his head into his hands, then lifted it slowly, scraped his fingernails through his hair. When he spoke the harshness had gone out of his voice.

'Keep your money,' he said. 'But take some advice from an ordinary bloke. Hang loose, have some fun. Life's not just about essays you know.'

Fran would rerun the whole evening endlessly, cringing all over again at how inept she'd been. For weeks afterwards she avoided the Vic Rooms for fear of running into Dale.

Dear Mother and Dad
There was a bit of a drama here at the weekend. Rowena's parents came to fetch her things after she was admitted to hospital. Apparently she took an overdose and is not coming back. I didn't realise she was that unhappy. It is peaceful of course, but oddly I kind of miss her and wish I had been nicer to her.
Love from Fran

Dear Frazzle
I'm sorry to hear about your recorder-playing neighbour, but don't take it to heart. Reading between the lines, it sounds as if she was quite a troubled young lady and it would probably have happened in due course whatever you had done. It would have been patronising to befriend her out of pity. These things are as they are, and I only hope she gets the help she needs and that you can move on.

How are you getting on with John Stuart Mill? I always thought Utilitarianism had a point. Learning not to blame yourself for everything will be more useful than philosophy – especially the kind you have described so far!

Buds are bursting and I'm hoping the ground will have thawed sufficiently to get out into the garden at the weekend.
Yours ever,
Dad

My Dearest Zel
Big drama here on Saturday night. Suddenly there were people everywhere and they got the master key to Rowena's room and she was out cold. The ambulance came and took her away and apparently she was stomach-pumped and is okay. Evidently she took an overdose, but she phoned her brother to say goodbye before she did it. And so he got hold of the warden somehow and raised the alarm. People say she probably meant for that to happen and it was a cry for help, but a close-run thing.

I feel awful that I wasn't nicer to her, but how was I to know? Her parents came and collected all her things. They looked grim and didn't speak to anyone. They say she isn't coming back. So now I'm all on my own at the end of the corridor and even wishing I could hear her beastly recorder.
Lots of love,
Fran xxx

Spring brought a drift of daffodils to the lawn below her window – just like the garden at home. Both her father and Gaye would be out with their spades turning the soil and Zelda's tortoise would be stirring in its box under the kitchen table. Odd to imagine their lives continuing without her. Did they give her any thought? Picture her having a more fulfilling time than she was?

Posters went up in Hall about the university settlement, which seemed to be some sort of community project run by student volunteers. It captured Fran's attention – an opportunity to make a contribution, to make up for what she hadn't done for Rowena. On a day of cold spring sunshine she caught a bus to Barton Hill, the area somewhere beyond Temple Meads where the project was located. It felt like turning a corner and she felt a glow of excitement as the bus careered through the city streets, presided over by a conductor who whistled up and down the stairs and said, 'There you are, my luvvel!' for every ticket he rung up.

Everyone at the settlement seemed to be in jeans and leather jackets and she felt out of place in her warm trousers and stupid fur-lined boots. Whatever sort of contribution could she make to this run-down neighbourhood? What on earth had she expected? They wanted dynamic helpers to run the youth club, which had her backing off in panic, feeling middle-class, curiously middle-aged and hopeless. She was stopped in the doorway by a tall man striding in wearing a duffel coat, corduroys and a university scarf like hers. He took up a position behind the desk, running a hand through his dark frizz of hair, then looked her up and down as he reached for the phone.

'Volunteering are you? We need visitors. A whole lot of old folk have been moved into that block of flats over there.' He waved a hand in the direction of the window. 'All isolated as hell. Fancy one of those?'

Fran nodded. He must be in charge, a third-year perhaps. He had a reassuring presence; a better-looking version of Eric, but much taller and not in the least bit square in spite of the duffel coat. His accent was hypnotic although she couldn't quite place it. American? But not as harsh as the Americans she'd heard. Canadian, maybe. She'd be willing to do pretty much anything he asked.

He flicked through a card index. 'Here we are. Fill in this form. And there's a name and address to take down.' He handed Fran a card. 'Rest is up to you. I'm Palmer. Palmer Robinson.' He shook her hand firmly. 'Put the card back when you're done. Alphabetical order of surname.'

Every time she went to Barton Hill after that on her weekly visits to Mrs Nicholas on a Thursday afternoon she called at the settlement offices on the chance of seeing Palmer, but he was never there. At least her involvement with the settlement gave her something to write to Zelda about.

> *Darling Fran*
> *Spring at last after all the bloody snow, though they say there's more on the way. I'm sitting in the ferry gardens in my lunch break writing this. Mum's going mad in the garden as you can imagine.*
>
> *What on earth is this university settlement stuff? When I said to join something, I meant a club, like jazz or something where you'd meet people and get out. Not to end up visiting old ladies, even if they are sweet. And I hate budgerigars. Couldn't stand having it flying around the room, let alone in a cage. As to kissing it, tell her you can catch something from that. I bet she loves seeing you. It must be awful, only to have a bird to talk to.*
>
> *Mum's still having trouble with the maintenance payments. Dad's being a b***** and refusing to cough up. Fingers crossed we don't have to sell the house. I'm going for an extra Saturday job at The Swordfish for the season. Every little helps.*
>
> *Remember to get out!*
> *Loads of love,*
> *Zelda xxx*

It wasn't until Rag Week that Fran saw Palmer again among the organisers in the Vic Rooms.

'I'll take a tin.' She signed for it quickly before she had second thoughts. She'd go collecting where no one else would think of going – along the docks.

It was an exhilarating day. She had never climbed so many ladders or received so many catcalls, scaling the heights of warehouse after vast warehouse and dragging herself the length of the wharves. Her tin was heavy as she toiled back up the hill. She hadn't understood half the jokes, but the generosity of the dockers was overwhelming and she had never once felt threatened.

Palmer was so impressed he offered to buy her a drink, which turned into two or three, and Fran was light-headed as they left the bar. His hand on her waist holding her close suggested he would soon kiss her. But in the doorway they were met by a group from one of her seminars who obviously knew Palmer.

'Hey, Fran! What's this? Out with a married man? Better watch out there.'

A good deal of banter in the same vein followed and someone asked Palmer how his nappy-changing skills were shaping up. He responded in kind, but was looking decidedly sheepish by the time he turned to her on the steps outside.

'As you will have gathered, I must get on home.' He pecked her lightly on the cheek. 'Congratulations, Star Collector. I'll make sure you get a mention in *Nonesuch News*.'

With that he was gone. She was glad she'd made no mention of Palmer in letters to Zelda, and saw little of her during the Easter vacation. Auntie Goldie had moved into a flat on the harbour and Fran spent a happy week helping her redecorate. She exorcised Palmer by making him into a funny story for the entertainment of Goldie, who thought his name was a hoot for a start.

At the beginning of the summer term Fran was determined to knuckle down and do well in the end of year exams, but events took an unexpected turn.

Dearest Zel

The most amazing girl has moved in to Rowena's room – she's called Verity and is a real music student but she is a pianist and sings and plays the guitar. She has got the most amazing voice. She's so small and fragile-looking you'd never guess she could make that amount of noise, but I like it and she's really careful to check with me before she practises. So things are looking up. She was in digs way out in Westbury and it was costing her a fortune in bus fares plus her landlady was a strict spinster type who didn't like her having any friends round. So she was desperate to move nearer, and didn't mind having a room where someone tried to top herself.

Must rush as I'm going to the Vic Rooms with Verity to meet some mates of hers and I have an essay on Wordsworth to finish first.
Much love,
Fran xxx

Dear Fran
I'm sitting soaking my feet after my shift at The Swordfish. Never do waitressing – it's exhausting and anyway you'd be hopeless – you'd never remember what people ordered.

When are you coming home for the summer? I'm hoping I won't miss you, as Rory and Beth have asked me to go and help after the baby comes. As you can imagine, I am over the moon to get away and see my niece – or nephew if it has to be a boy, which of course Rory hopes. I'm fed up to keep missing you, so I do hope she or he doesn't come too early and stop me seeing you.
Tons of love,
Zelda xxx

Dear Zel
Verity and I are going to share a flat next year. We've started looking for somewhere. I haven't told Mother and Dad yet but it will be much cheaper than living in Hall. Verity wants somewhere she can have her own piano – imagine! And even if there's no room for anything else!

I'll have to stay here flat-hunting if we haven't found anywhere, but do hope I don't miss you.

When I've got my own place you'll be able to come and stay!
Must dash – we've got a flat to look at over in Cotham.
Love Fran xxx
P.S. You'll make a brilliant auntie!

Fran licked the envelope and stuck it down. She almost wished she hadn't invited Zelda. How would it be to have Verity and Zelda alongside each other? Would Zelda fit in?

4

Fran escaped from the dark, smoke-filled room of couples either swaying together or filling the space between them with jerky, self-conscious movements.

The old Cliff Richard hit 'Living Doll' echoed loudly in Fran's ears, fading as she closed the door behind her. Another bum-clutching dance with Eric was more than she could bear. She used to be glad of his company, but tonight he was simply getting in the way.

'Don't tell me you *still* haven't got a boyfriend?' It was almost the first thing Zelda had said on the phone when Fran got home for the Christmas vacation. 'I mean, after a whole term in a flat? No warden. No rules. What have you been up to? Precisely nothing, I suppose! We'll soon fix that. There's this party – and I know some fellas who'll be pleased to see us.' She'd laughed that Zelda laugh and Fran realised how much she'd missed her.

But thanks to Zelda, here she was landed at a party where Eric was the sole person she knew. Zelda was nowhere to be seen and there seemed to be no welcoming 'fellas' either. She paused in the doorway of the kitchen.

'Hallo, gorgeous girl with the flaming hair.' Fran's thoughts were interrupted by a voice that sounded as if it were listening to itself. She turned to see a pair of amused eyes gazing at her from the opposite doorpost. Their owner was propping it up in a casual pose, feet crossed. Straight, straw-coloured hair fell to one side of his high forehead. He was wearing a black smoking jacket over a white polo neck, held a glass in one hand and a Black Russian cigarette in the other. Poseur, she thought.

'You were miles away,' he continued. 'Do you often stand around in doorways casting spells on people?'

'Actually I was after a glass of water. The wine's too sweet. Not much in the way of magic.' Fran hoped she sounded cool and dismissive. Inside she was churning with anticipation.

'Looks pretty magic from here. What is more, I can grant your wish. I can save you from water. Never touch it myself.' The eyes did not waver. Their cool blue matched the sardonic smile.

'How is that, then?' Fran was both unnerved and intrigued by his smooth confidence. How did he manage to turn his mouth down at the corners and smile at the same time? Was she being made fun of? Would he suddenly turn on his heel to find someone more sophisticated?

'Ah, first you have to say the password. I'm not moving from this spot without knowing your name.'

'Fran. Fran Fairweather.'

'Short for Frances?'

'No, Francesca, but—'

'Now that *is* a magical name. Francesca Fairweather. May I call you Francesca?'

'No you may not. I don't like it, never have. It sounds pretentious.'

This was met with a shrug and a carefully blown smoke ring. Fran feared she had been too abrupt.

Music blared suddenly from the door across the hall, this time the pleading refrain of 'Please Don't Tease'.

Eric appeared and she moved aside to let him pass. He opened his mouth to speak to her, saw the stranger watching and closed it again. Pushing his glasses back up his nose, he made for the crowd round the drinks table. Fran noticed the eyes opposite taking all this in.

He moved over to her side of the doorway. 'More room for people to get by.'

The eyes smiled down at her, precipitating an internal earthquake.

'What about granting the wish, then?'

'Follow me.'

He led her through the kitchen into a utility room, shutting the door behind them. It was like walking into a freezer. As a seduction technique she didn't think much of it. But he now lifted a champagne bottle off the windowsill with a flourish.

'Ice cold.' He laid it over his arm and held it out for her inspection with a deferential air. 'Would madam care for a glass? So very refreshing.' He was positively purring.

Fran giggled and held out her glass.

'It's the only drink.' He smiled at her, removing the silver spoon that was suspended in the top of the bottle.

'Why the spoon?'

'Oh, didn't you know? It stops it going flat. Such a useful tip! Not that it's necessary as a rule, but I wanted to save it to share with someone special.'

'Why? How does it do that?'

'No idea, it just does. More magic.' He grinned, carefully pouring and pausing, pouring again, not spilling a drop. Just enough fine hair on the hands. Long straight fingers.

'It's very grand.' Fran watched the foam rise and subside.

'I got it from the mess, cut-price luxury.'

'Mess?' She sipped from the glass he passed her.

'Fleet Air Arm. I'm at Lee.'

'What's your name?'

'Charlie Coverdale. I thought you'd never ask!'

Fran looked down at his suede boots and a warning of her mother's made her smile: *never trust a man in suede shoes.*

'That's more like it,' said Charlie, refilling his glass. 'Now, here's a toast. Let's drink to many more happy evenings.'

Before Fran could drink Charlie curled his arm round hers, bringing his glass carefully back to his lips and holding her gaze all the while. Fran found herself drawn close to him. As she reached to sip the pale, sparkling liquid her cheek brushed the velvet of his sleeve. She inhaled a slightly bitter, spicy smell mingled with the aroma of the bubbles breaking on her nose.

'Now let's get out of here before we freeze to death.'

Charlie topped up their glasses and held open the door for her. As they emerged Fran came face to face with Zelda whose mouth fell open in a very satisfactory way.

'I see you've met Charlie, then!'

'You know Zelda?'

'Certainly do,' said Charlie, wrapping his arms round Zelda and squeezing her to him so she was lifted off the floor. Fran's stomach knotted.

'Fran, this is Ed.' Zelda nodded towards her companion. 'But what are you doing here, Charlie? I thought Tom was coming.'

'Got him to swap duties. Can't resist a party.'

'What were you doing in there, then, Coverdale?' Ed winked at Fran. 'You need to watch him, fast worker.'

Charlie responded by squeezing Fran's buttock in a way that was so unlike Eric's clutchings that it took her breath away.

'When the cat's away, then, Coverdale?'

'We're going outside,' said Zelda, adding in a stage whisper, 'for a smoke.' She winked. 'Want to join us?'

Fran didn't have time to wonder what all the winking was about.

'We're going to dance,' said Charlie. His arm circled Fran's waist and swept her towards the music.

Zelda frowned. 'Fran...'

But when Fran looked back, Zelda shrugged and said it didn't matter. She had such an odd look on her face that Fran wondered for a moment if Zelda might be jealous. *Zelda jealous?* The thought made her lean even more readily into Charlie's smooching.

The phone did ring the next day. As Fran had known it would. As she had feared it would not.

'Meet me at the Lord Nelson,' Charlie said. 'We'll go for a walk on the beach.'

As she approached the pub Charlie strolled out wearing jeans with an Arran sweater and swinging a worn leather flying jacket over his shoulder. Well-polished Chelsea boots clipped down the steps. Mother would be happier with those.

He greeted her with a peck on both cheeks which took her by surprise. 'Can I buy you a drink, or would you rather walk?'

'Definitely walk. I've only just recovered from last night.'

'Dear oh dear. That's what comes of mixing it. I should have got to you sooner with the bubbly.' Charlie pulled on his coat. 'Wicked wind, straight off the sea.'

'Like the jacket.' It was certainly a change from Eric's duffel coat.

'My father's. The one he was shot down in.' Charlie thrust his hands into the pockets. 'That's why I like to wear it. Ed says he wouldn't be seen dead in it. Dad was. That's good enough for me.'

As an interesting story this beat having a father who was a dentist, but equally Fran could not imagine life without her dad. How dreadfully sad to grow up without one. How spooky that a dead person had worn this coat.

'That's quite something,' she said eventually. 'When was he killed?'

'Last year of the war. Hardly remember him.'

'How old were you?'

'Three, nearly four. One thing sticks in my mind. There's this stranger coming through the door and throwing me up in the air. Scary really.' He gave a short laugh.

'So you hardly knew him, that's awful.'

'Maybe just as well. He was a difficult bugger by all accounts. A "bounder" according to my Auntie Win. I liked having his stuff though – I've got the hat and the goggles too, the whole Biggles bit. Loved playing with it when I was a kid.'

Charlie reached into his inside pocket, pulled out his wallet and extracted a small, creased photograph. 'That's him.'

Fran took it and saw the same mocking smile as Charlie's, the same flop of pale hair over one eye. 'You're so like him!'

Charlie took the photo back abruptly. 'What on earth are we talking about all this for? By Christ, it's cold up here. I vote we go back for that drink after all. One of Frank's Bloody Marys will sort you out. And you can tell me how you know Zelda.'

5

The next day was Monday. Fran couldn't wait to tell Zelda all about Charlie. Zelda had landed what she called a 'drear' job in Bull's china shop in Stoke Road. They'd agreed to meet in her lunch hour at the Mocambo coffee bar.

Zelda's opening question brought Fran up short.

'You're not getting involved with that Charlie, are you? When I rang on Sunday your ma said you'd gone for a drink…'

'Certainly am. Well, it seems like it. We met at the Lord Nelson. Went for a walk. He seems keen. In fact, he suggested we all meet up later this week. Hey, Mother never said you—'

'Never mind that. I mean, she wouldn't, would she? Oh dear. About Charlie, I mean. If only he hadn't swapped with Tom.'

'Why "oh dear"? I thought you'd be pleased.'

Zelda licked the coffee froth off her upper lip. 'But what about Amanda?'

Fran sensed she stood at a cliff edge and that someone with a name like a snake was about to push her over. 'Amanda? Amanda who? Who's she?'

'Only his girlfriend. Amanda Smythe. She's away with her family, skiing.'

Fran struggled to keep balance. A scene at the party came back to her: the voice of Zelda's friend Ed, Zelda frowning after her. 'So that's what Ed meant – "when the cat's away". But Charlie, I'm certain he can't still be…'

'I wouldn't be so sure. Ed *might* just have been stirring it. But you need to be aware.' Zelda spooned at her coffee. 'Why don't you ask him and see how he reacts? Now, tell me all about it. The flat. How did you get on?'

Fran wanted to grab her coat and run. She'd wanted to talk about Charlie. Now she could hardly bear to think about him.

Zelda waved a hand in front of Fran's face. 'Wakey wakey!'

'Oh, yes. The flat. But I wrote. I told you all about it in my letters. And you only wrote back once, you cowbag.'

'Ah, but letters aren't the same. And anyway you hardly mentioned any men. Is there one?'

'No. I'd have said.'

'You see! I can tell. There was someone. I can tell by your voice.'

'Oh well, I went *out* with someone. But it didn't come to anything.'

'What the snowball guy? That was yonks ago.'

'Not him. Since then.' Fran quickly reinvented Palmer and made him more recent. 'But he was a womaniser.'

'And Charlie isn't?'

'Shut up, Zel. Anyway this one was married.' That silenced her. 'Tell me about the job. I thought Bull's sold hardware.'

Zelda made a mock yawn. 'They do. But I'm in China and Glass. Lots of dusting to make it look sparkly. Ladies wearing lots of powder who watch me like hawks, hoping I'll break something. Terrific.'

'See why you want to move on.'

'Anyway, tell me about the flat.'

'I've got some photos.' Fran scrabbled in her bag. 'That's the view from my window.'

The flat was in a square of run-down Victorian terraces and her room looked out on a tree and some grass in the central garden. Zelda seemed unimpressed.

'That's the phone box in the top corner, where I rang you that time. We queue up every Sunday to phone home at the cheap rate.' Sundays were great, with half the square out there, smoking and chatting to neighbours. 'I usually cheat and reverse the charges, but sometimes it's better to run out of money – if I think Mother's going to have a go.'

'What about your flatmates? Would I like them? Or are they too brainy?'

'Verity plays piano and sings – I told you all about her – and Morag is so Scottish you can hardly understand her sometimes. She's reading medicine, wants to be a gynaecologist.' Fran passed another snap. 'There they are in the doorway. Verity taught me how to make gravy.'

'Gravy!?'

'Yeah, I was surprised. She doesn't look like that, does she? She thought it would be bonding. If we all cooked a roast together. Plus she wanted to impress her boyfriend. It wasn't bonding at all, not at the time anyway. Morag stormed out over the gravy, but we're all good mates now.'

'How very domesticated! I thought students all lived on baked beans and joints – and I don't mean leg of lamb.'

'We probably would if it wasn't for Verity.'

'So this Verity has got a boyfriend. What about…'

'Yes, Verity has – he's doing Engineering. Morag's more into causes than men.'

'Maybe she's the other way inclined…'

'No sign of that.' Fran's heart wasn't in it. She was too worried about Charlie and bloody Amanda. 'Most of her mates are men – medics like her.'

'So you get to meet them, then.'

'It's not like that. They just muck in.'

'Fancy you! Living in a flat. It's weird to imagine. I'm dead jealous.'

It took a few days and several nudges from Zelda before Fran asked Charlie about Amanda as he walked her home from the pub. Her knees shook as she pronounced the name.

'Oh, Amanda, yes. You've heard about that.' He waved a hand dismissively. 'Past history, you know.'

Fran searched his face in the light from the street lamps and decided she could breathe again.

He pulled her close. 'Nothing to worry about there, my little love.'

Nothing to worry about. That was enough to allow Fran to fall asleep that night in a bubble of more than usually wild imaginings. She returned to Bristol, complete with a photograph of Charlie in uniform and tales of her dashing new boyfriend.

Verity and Morag did a bit of eye-rolling about the uniform, but they were clearly happy that their slightly oddball flatmate had come to life.

Morag mocked the cliché in her Glaswegian accent when a dozen red roses arrived on Valentine's Day.

'My love is like a red, red rose.' It might not have done Burns justice but Morag only had to ask for a piece of toast to make it sound interesting. When she went on about her causes, Fran usually lost the words in listening to the voice. If I sounded like that, she thought, I'd be an interesting person.

Verity was clearly impressed. She waved her Valentine's card from rugby-playing Mike. 'All Mike can manage – and decidedly dubious taste! You'd better borrow a vase. Sadly I don't need it.'

Later that week Fran pressed several of the quickly withering petals into the pages of her Yeats. *Tread softly because you tread on my dreams.*

Her dreams were intact and all was right with her world until Dale Weaver became a regular visitor at the flat, Dale of the humiliating evening a year ago. Fran groaned to discover he was a friend of Verity's. Hardly surprising, as they were both music students. Sod's law said that Verity was his accompanist for several key exam pieces, and they needed to practise together.

'Why do you always want to know when Dale's coming round?' said Verity. 'Fancy him, do you?'

'You must be joking. I want avoid him, that's why. Can't stand the man.'

'Didn't know you even knew him. How come?'

'I...I came across him. When I first arrived.'

'He didn't go and try the mattress trick, did he?'

Fran managed a laugh. 'Certainly not.'

It was common knowledge that Dale kept a mattress in the back of his ancient van. He maintained this was to protect his cello in transit, and certainly he'd cut the foam so the case fitted into it. But it was also well known that other shapes filled it in the absence of the instrument. Dale's mantra was that his cello was the only woman he was faithful to.

'He's a very talented cellist you know,' said Verity. 'On track to a brilliant career, they reckon.'

As if that made any difference. Fran was not impressed.

'Okay, you wouldn't know it half the time, but even so.'

Dale usually visited on a Tuesday evening, and Fran would either go out or hole up in her room, writing an essay. But one Thursday, she'd just arrived home and was boiling the kettle when she heard the notes of a cello. Deep, resonant, soaring – all at the same time. Like liquid chocolate. It was a stunning sound, so stunning that she didn't notice the music had stopped. When Dale greeted her from the doorway she spilled boiling water all over the worktop and onto her hand.

'Run it under the cold tap,' said Dale. 'Usually works.'

'Oh, it's fine. Only a splash.' Fran made for the door with her mug.

'Hey, not so fast. Don't I even get the time of day?'

He was leaning back against the cupboard, thumbs tucked into the leather waistcoat he always wore, which he said had belonged to his grandfather, watching her with a twist of a smile. Arrogant? Mocking? Or both?

'Good evening,' said Fran, immediately cringing at how stiff she sounded. Playing into his impression of her. She expected him to laugh but he didn't.

'Look, I'm sorry if I upset you that time. I was wound up and you... I guess I misjudged you. Well, Verity tells me you and she are good mates, so...'

'So I can't be as bad as all that?'

'Something like that.'

'You really know how to apologise!'

Fran made another attempt to get past him to the sanctuary of her room, but he put a hand firmly on her arm.

'I do really think you should put it under the tap. It looks very red.' He led her and held her thumb and forefinger under the running water.

She was trapped. He smelled, not unpleasantly, of leather and garlic and she could feel the heat of him through her jumper.

'Would you let me take you out? See a film? To make amends?'

She shook her head. 'I have a boyfriend. I really don't want...'

'It's only the flicks. And yes, I know about him.'

'How?'

'Verity showed me the photo.' He held up a hand as Fran protested. 'She was only putting me in the picture.' He grinned. 'Nice flowers. Very gallant.'

'Blimey! What else...'

'Nothing else. What I would say...' Dale broke off, staring straight at her. 'Hell, you're – well I don't have a word for it. Let's just say, "I Want to Hold Your Hand".

The burst of song, as he squeezed her fingers, sounded unnervingly Beatle-like. They both laughed and he glanced away, looking almost embarrassed.

'That's not at all what I meant to say – but you are a bit of a honey. You do know that, don't you?'

Fran pulled her hand away. Bit of a honey, indeed...

'What I *was* going to say, as a mate, a humble bloke, is if you really want to save yourself for this pilot guy, then fine. But in my experience those arrangements hardly ever pan out. You'll save yourself, whatever that means, and then find he's off chasing some skirt and it's all been a waste of time. But it's your life.'

Fran gritted her teeth. 'Thanks for the first aid. It does actually feel better. And thanks for allowing me my life.'

Holding herself carefully together, Fran made it to the door and started across the passage.

'I think you forgot something.' Dale held out her mug of coffee. 'Just don't bank on him waiting for you.'

The encounter with Dale unsettled her. Why should what Dale said make any difference, she asked herself as she set off down Kingsdown Parade to a tutorial. She told herself she was Charlie's girl. But not only did the dreaded Amanda keep getting in the way, but so did the question of sex. As if on cue, halfway down the terrace, a man in the usual dirty mac lurched from the porch of a boarded-up house and exposed himself. She startled sideways. It had happened before.

51

The street seemed to be a favourite haunt of flashers. Mother would be appalled if she knew the sort of area she lived in.

Was she afraid of sex? Was she really frigid? Certainly she was terrified of getting pregnant. Just the thought of her mother's face was enough to explain that one.

What if she took that risk away? She played with that question the length of Alfred Place as it started to drizzle. What would Zelda say? Why couldn't she be like Verity and just go along to the University Medical Service and get herself fixed up with the pill? She couldn't do it at home, but it would be easy enough here. You didn't even need a wedding ring.

She was so absorbed in that idea that a van hooted her as she stepped off the pavement at the Royal Fort. She wasn't short of information. There was endless talk in the flat of contraception, abortion and all things gynaecological. Morag was incandescent about the thalidomide scandal and evangelical about the need for women to have access to legal abortions. It was all a bit much, to be honest. 'To hell with sex,' she muttered as she started up the stairs to the English department.

Easter was a disappointment. At home Fran was having a difficult time with Eleanor who kept taking to her bed with a migraine. Usually this was a ploy to keep Fran at home, administering water and aspirin, but Fran was noticing a difference. She complained less and seemed in real discomfort.

Even worse, Charlie was only available for two evenings before going off on exercise. At least he told Fran he'd booked dinner for his last evening.

'Special place. Just the two of us,' he said, kissing her hair.

On the first night, the usual foursome piled into Charlie's old Riley which he drove as if he were flying a plane. Fran loved the smell of its leather seats and the walnut dashboard. After cruising around and failing to find the party Ed had promised, they ended up at the Lord Nelson.

'Clock the new barmaid,' whispered Zelda as they pushed open the door to the public bar. 'She only started last week, but she's bringing them in alright.'

The pub was certainly crowded with a fringe of single men standing at the bar. Charlie and Ed had to push their way through to order drinks. Fran craned her neck but could only see the top of a blonde head.

She nudged Zelda. 'That's some beehive!'

'Wonder how long it takes her to backcomb that lot.'

'Oh, blimey!' The bodies had momentarily parted enough for Fran to glimpse a billowing cleavage alongside Charlie's profile. There was no doubt where Charlie was looking.

'See what I mean?' Zelda lit a cigarette from the stub of the old one. 'Quite a honeypot!'

But when they came back with the drinks Charlie kissed her ear and ran his hand around her buttocks in a way that put all thoughts of over-endowed barmaids out of her mind. All evening he kept giving her the sideways smile that made her insides melt, and she missed the frowns and eyebrow-raising exchanged by Zelda and Ed. All she wanted was to cuddle up to Charlie for ever and ever. The thought that in two days he would be thousands of miles away was unbearable.

'It's bloody impossible to hear in here,' said Zelda as they jostled together at the back of the bar. 'Let's go down to the beach.'

Fran agreed, hoping for a chance to talk to Charlie on his own. She saw a gentler side of him when there was no Ed to impress or Zelda to flirt with.

They scrunched down the shingle and stood watching the inoffensive little waves that barely shifted the pebbles.

A half-moon emerged from the clouds and Fran picked up one of the boat-like shells she'd been collecting since childhood and fingered its smooth mauve foredeck. 'Look at the moon on the water.'

'Fran...' said Charlie. He picked up a flattish stone, bent and flipped it across the water in an attempt at ducks and drakes. It skimmed and bounced twice and vanished. 'Bugger.'

'What were you going to say?'

'Say? Oh, nothing.'

'Tell me about the exercise. What's it about?'

'That's a bugger too.' And he went on to tell her about how he loved flying at night and of his fears about flying over water.

'And that's what you'll be doing. Aircraft carrier, didn't you say?'

He nodded and she squeezed his hand. 'You're different when we're on our own. We talk about things.'

Charlie grunted and lobbed another stone into the sea where it plopped loudly in the stillness. 'You don't. You're still so buttoned up – in every sense...'

Fran felt slapped in the face. 'What do you mean?'

'Well, it beats me how you... I mean, you're a pretty girl, and all this stunning hair... Everything in the right place.' He made an hourglass shape with his hands. 'And yet you're so, kind of...cool, I suppose. I mean, when are you ever going to let me... You know what I mean.'

'I thought we... I thought you said you respected... Don't you ever think of anything else?'

Charlie groaned. 'I don't mean to be crude. But all this groping and finger stuff. It's just that, well, it seems to be all you want, but it leaves me all steamed up and you don't exactly do anything for me. I mean, you could...' He glanced at her blank expression. 'Oh, never mind. But well, you don't seem to care. After all, Fran, I *am* going away.'

'I do care. And I would. I do want to. And I told you why. But there's nothing I can do...'

Charlie laughed harshly. 'Is that so?' Then he looked round at her and groaned again. 'But I do fancy you something rotten.'

He took her face in both his hands and turned it to kiss her. She fell for that every time.

'I love you, Charlie.' Fran buried her face in his shoulder, which made it easier to believe his clumsy words were a declaration of love.

'And I love you too.' He slid a hand inside her jumper. 'Let's get back to the car.'

His squeezing of her nipples led to a more than usually passionate kiss and, what with that and the several unaccustomed gins she had downed, Fran began to get the hang of what this sex thing was all about. All of a sudden she wanted it. She wanted Charlie. He was going away. It was her chance. She kicked off her knickers.

'Fran! Oh, jeez!' Charlie grappled with his buckle.

'Charlie!'

As Charlie grasped her buttocks they were interrupted by Zelda and Ed bouncing into the front of the car.

'Dammit! Fuck it!' Charlie spluttered upright. 'Don't I ever get my car to myself?'

They apologised, but were slow to back off and the moment was lost. Fran sobered up in an instant at the sight of his snarling red face and pushed him away.

'No, I couldn't. Not now. Not with them...'

Charlie drove home in a fury, cornering into her road on two wheels.

Dinner the following day turned into drinks in the saloon bar of a smart pub in Lee.

'Sorry about dinner. I've got a special extra briefing about the exercise. Can't get out of it. Just the way it crumbles, cookie-wise, I'm afraid.'

Her future dismissed in a trite saying, or so it felt to Fran, in spite of Charlie's promise to write. She expected him to divert to the beach on the way home. All day she'd been arguing with herself. Would she do it or wouldn't she? She was too cross with Zelda to discuss it with her. But he kept glancing at his watch and drove straight to her house. When he dropped her at home, he stayed in the car blowing kisses until she closed the front door. Dear Charlie. Knowing he'd be doing a three-point turn, she ran to wave from the front room window, but he'd gone. He must have driven straight on, into the village. How odd. She tried not to remember that Amanda's house was down that way.

Eleanor was not well the next day. As Fran filled hot water bottles, she kept thinking of Charlie setting off on exercise. She wished they'd done it. That would have bound him to her. Bugger Zelda and Ed blundering in. The phone rang as she placed the bottles, one for Mother's icy feet, one for her tummy.

'Oh, it's you.'

'Of course it's me,' said Zelda. 'What happened last night?'

'Nothing. Not that it's any—'

'You're mad at me. Sorry about the other night. Sorry to mess things up, accidentally on purpose.'

'On purpose? But why? Just as – well, you know, we were...'

'That's what we were afraid of, me and Ed. You see...'

'You've changed your tune. You were always on at me to...'

'Look, Fran, you're my mate. I don't want you in trouble, hurt. Any of that stuff. And I did hear a rumour. Okay, might not be true. But Charlie and Amanda were spotted looking in Hugg's window. You know, Manfred Mann and all that. They were looking at *rings*.'

'How could they be? What with the other night, we were so close. We're okay, me and Charlie. It can't be true.' Fran quickly shut out the mental picture of the empty road, where Charlie was not turning the car. 'And what do you mean, Manfred Mann?'

'Mike Hugg, he's their drummer. I thought everyone knew. I suppose they just could have been dropping by to see Mike. I think Amanda might have gone out with him for a bit. She'd want to keep up the connection now the band's so famous. That would be her all over. So okay, maybe that's all it was. If you say so.'

'I do, really.'

'But don't bank on it. Don't say I didn't warn you.'

'Anyway, I never got round to asking you about the new job? I thought you were looking a bit down yesterday.'

'You never said.'

Fran felt a pang of guilt for neglecting her friend. 'Well, there wasn't much chance...'

'You were too wound up in Charlie, you mean!'

'Of course Charlie. But Mother too. Like I said, she's not well – again. Oh, Zel, I can't believe he's gone. I'm going to miss him so much. Anyway, what about the job? HMV, didn't you say in your letter?'

'It's okay. At least I'm in the High Street. See more people. And there's music all the time. Sorry about your ma. That's a bore. You sure she's not putting it on? She has been known...'

'Doesn't seem so. Not really.'

'Well, I hope she picks up. But I'm bored, Fran. Bored with Ed. Bored with Gosport. Nobody ever talks about anything remotely interesting. I'm even thinking of applying to art college.'

'That's a bit of a turn-up.'

'Truth is, Fran, I'm a bit lovesick myself.'

'But you just said you were bored with Ed.'

'Not Ed. Tomasz. I told you he went back to Poland in January? All healed at last, his leg. I thought I'd have forgotten him by now. But I miss him.'

'I didn't realise how… Will he come back? Or could you go there?'

'It's behind the iron curtain, Fran. I don't think so. Anyway, he hasn't even written.'

Charlie did write, but his letters turned out to be a disappointment. Florid handwriting galloped across the paper filling an impressive number of pages while saying very little. What he did say was technical: wind speed ratios, flying conditions and weather patterns. What did she care about how big the aircraft carrier was? His smooth-talking gift of the gab did not transfer to paper. Instead of loving phrases, there were terrible puns and smutty innuendos and he always signed off 'Don't do anything I wouldn't do', which caused Fran to wonder what exactly he would do.

Fran told herself she was lucky he was writing at all and turned to Keats for romantic nourishment. The summer would be when it all came together. She must be patient. Meanwhile she would get herself fixed up with the pill. Or should she wait for Charlie to propose first?

6

'Fran! Great to see you. What a blessing! For goodness' sake, can you get that daughter of mine out of her room? She's taken to her bed, smoking like there's no tomorrow. I tell her, she'll burn the house down.'

It was the summer vacation, and, to Eleanor's irritation, Fran had shot off to the Turners' on her very first morning at home, eager to talk about Charlie and her hopes for the future. Gaye stopped her in her tracks at the kitchen door.

'What's wrong? What…?'

Gaye switched off the kettle. 'Don't ask me. She'll tell you. Men! That's all I have to say. Here, take tea up and prepare for an ear-bashing.'

Zelda's room reeked of stale cigarettes and grubby clothes. She was sitting on the windowsill in her dressing gown, red-eyed and smoking.

'Heard you coming and dragged myself out of my pit in your honour.'

Fran handed her a mug of tea. 'You look grotty. What's happened to your hair?'

'Gee, thanks. Great to see you, too. Just haven't washed it, that's all.'

'Nor much else by the stink of this place. What's happened?'

'I'm not telling you a word until you stop behaving like your mother and give me a hug.' Zelda stubbed out her cigarette and held her arms wide.

Fran inhaled the sad smell of her and wanted to weep. 'Sorry. It's just you're – not you. Go on. Tell me.'

'Tomasz. That's the whole story really. I got a postcard last week. Said he was coming. Turned out he never went to Poland like I thought. He was in London all the time, the bastard. I could have *seen* him, Fran.'

'So when's he coming?'

'That's it. That's the whole thing. He didn't. Said he was coming on Monday. Five whole days ago. Didn't turn up. Not a peep out of him. What's going on, Fran? What have I done to deserve this?' She took a drag and exhaled slowly. 'Only moped about for months. Then I'm over the fucking moon, only to drop to earth like a fucking burst balloon.'

Fran was at a loss. 'Haven't you phoned him?'

Zelda rolled her eyes. 'Not without a number. No address. Nothing. It's as if he doesn't really exist. As if he's deliberately setting out to drive me insane. And he's bloody succeeding. Why would he do that, Fran?'

'How do I know? I've never met the guy. What a bummer. Something must have happened.'

'What could possibly have happened that he couldn't let me know?'

Fran thought of hospital, death, prison and said nothing.

'Yeah, I know what you're thinking. Don't think it hasn't occurred to me. One minute I'm raging at him for being a total bastard and the next I'm convinced he's in some morgue.'

So it went on until Zelda said, 'You've lost weight. Nice dress – shows you off. Bet your ma hates it. I suppose you're going to tell me you've landed a totally gorgeous hunk who's been shagging your arse—'

'Shut up, Zel! You are *so* crude. No, just looking forward to seeing Charlie.' Fran continued in a rush, taking her chance. 'He and Ed are coming round tonight to take us out. I thought you'd know... But I guess...'

'Oh, hell. Ma did say something. Ed, eh? Haven't seen him in an age. Tonight, you say? Shit.'

'You don't have to come.'

'You mean you'd go with both of them?' Zelda slitted her eyes. 'You would! But knowing you, you're thinking safety in numbers, not threesome.'

'Zel!'

'Only joking. But hell, I'm not letting you steal Ed off me. Didn't know he was still interested. He may be my only hope.'

'Well, you can't come like that. Get in the bath, wash your blooming hair, find something—'

'Okay, okay. Here, be a love, take these down and tell Ma I'll be out tonight. She'll give you a medal for getting me out of bed.'

Charlie fell on Fran that evening and kissed her with such ferocity and at such length she had to push him away and come up for air. He was on his own in the car, Ed having made other arrangements. This boded well for time alone together, but to Fran's disappointment, they headed straight for the Lord Nelson.

'One of my oppos – birthday bash. You don't mind do you? Can't really miss it.'

Fran gave an exaggerated sigh and followed him into the bar where a transformed Zelda was waiting with Ed.

'First round's on Paul,' said Charlie. 'We'd better make it doubles all round.'

Fran was further disappointed to see Sandra, the blonde barmaid, behind the bar.

'I thought she might have moved on by now.'

'No such luck,' said Zelda.

'You're looking brilliant, by the way. How does it feel on the inside?'

Zelda made a face. 'I'm fine. Hanging in there, just as long as you don't ask.'

Zelda's hair was glossy again and she looked as sexy as ever in skin-tight jeans and a black T-shirt. But although she laughed a lot, it was a brittle sound, not her deep belly laugh.

Sandra was flirting outrageously with Charlie. She flirted with all the men, but it seemed to Fran as if Charlie was singled out for special attention. Sandra would toss her peroxide hair so that her earrings tinkled and then look at him from under her lashes as she pulled the next pint. Charlie fell for it every time and at one point, when it got very busy, he went behind the bar to help out. Even Ed started protesting.

'Give it a rest, Coverdale. We all love Sandra, but what's Fran supposed to do while you're carrying on like that?'

But Charlie was drunk and told Ed to mind his own fucking business while continuing to fondle Sandra's bottom every time she passed. Fran tried to laugh it off but felt like ripping the earrings out of Sandra's pretty little ears.

'She's so blatant!' she said to Zelda as they shared the mirror in the toilets. 'Can't he see what she's up to?'

'Of course he can. You're missing the point. Sex isn't about being subtle.'

'Sex?'

'Well, that's what he's after. Get real, Fran.'

'Zel! He wouldn't! It's just flirting, you said so yourself.'

'She's permanently on heat, that one, and he's on the scent. He's drunk. He can't help himself.'

'He wouldn't. He's just not like that.' Fran concentrated on her lipstick as if the strong red outline would stop her world falling apart.

'Fran, just don't be so trusting. He's just a bloke. Either give him what he wants and have a good time, or move on before you get hurt.'

'He loves me. He wouldn't hurt me, he respects me too much.'

Zelda gulped pointedly. 'You do say the weirdest things. Why d'you make him out to be a saint? I don't know where you get it from.'

'You don't know him like I do. I see a side of him no one else does. He opens up to me. Just because Tomasz has let *you* down.'

'That was below the belt. Just when I'm trying to forget and act normal. Don't say I didn't warn you.' Zelda rolled her eyes and snapped her bag shut. 'Anyway, I think we should get that Charlie home before he gets in a fight. I've never heard him be that aggressive before.'

Back in the bar, Fran gulped the gin Ed had bought her. Charlie was nowhere to be seen. She began to feel hot and swimmy and couldn't focus on what Ed was saying. She felt the need for some air and made her way in the direction of the gents and the door to the garden. Maybe she would meet Charlie and he would come out with her.

As she walked unsteadily down the corridor, low voices and a stifled laugh came from what looked like a storeroom. She stopped because the laugh sounded just like Charlie's. There was the noise of scuffling and then silence, and, as she was about to walk on, grunts and a strange little cry. Her stomach turned over and her palms pricked with sweat as she moved toward the door. It was not quite closed. As she pushed it open she could hear more sounds. The strangely familiar tinkle of something metallic, panting, a rhythmic rubbing. She looked round the edge of the door.

At first she could see very little as the only light came in from a street lamp through a small window at the far end of the room. It fell on Sandra's blonde hair, which was bouncing as if she were on a trampoline. She seemed to be jumping up and down on a table, but as Fran's eyes adjusted to the dim light she could see Sandra had her arms and legs wrapped around a dark figure. Her short legs in their fishnet stockings crossed at the ankle, gripping like a vice, one stiletto heel stabbing toward Fran. The other had capsized on the floor. Below those ankles, pale buttocks pumped in time with Sandra's bobbing beehive, pale legs braced against the table. The leather belt Fran had given Charlie for his birthday was still uncoiling on the bare boards. The panting was reaching a crescendo. Fran gasped, and Charlie half turned, loosening Sandra's grip and dropping her back onto the table. Fran turned, rushed down the corridor and out of the door where cold air met her hot face. She vomited beside the dustbins.

Fran opened one eye. It fastened on the dress and cardigan she'd dropped on the floor the night before. Treacherous clothes which had shed the magic mood in which she'd put them on, failing to protect her and failing to enchant Charlie.

The stupid sun was falling on his photograph and giving him a halo, so she closed her eye again.

'Francesca! Fran...'

She pulled the pillow over her head to drown out whatever message was floating up the stairs. A rap at the door followed and her mother's neat footsteps approached the bed.

'Francesca, driving practice. Now. It's ten o'clock and I'm feeling better this morning, but I haven't got all day.'

So no migraine today. Just when it would be convenient. 'I can't... I don't...'

'But you will.' Mother retreated. 'If you want to pass that test.' She banged the door after her.

The clothes reeked of stale cigarette smoke and vomit. It must have splashed.

'The smell of betrayal,' she told Charlie's inane grin and slammed him into the back of the drawer with the old grey knickers she kept for her period. She took a slim mauve packet from the front of the drawer and, in the bathroom, popped each tiny pill out of its foil into the toilet bowl.

Eleanor was at her sharpest.

'What gear is that supposed to be?'

Fran, still in top, lurched to a stop at a roundabout. 'Sorry.' She shifted into first and made a kangaroo start into the path of a lorry emerging suddenly from the right.

Eleanor gave an exasperated sigh. 'You haven't done that in a while. Whatever's wrong with you this morning?'

It was a rhetorical question of course, but the answer would have been 'everything'. Completely bloody everything.

'Right. Go straight down Military Road and turn right at the end. We'll do a circuit over Ann's Hill Bridge and back. Unless... We could go on down Forton Road and cut through Spring Garden Lane? No. Too much, the way you're driving today. Forget that.'

'Okay.' Oh, God. Busy Saturday morning. Too much even by the short route.

'Plenty of local traffic. Watch out for pedestrians – parked cars and so on. Should wake you up.'

'I feel just in the mood to run someone over.'

In her peripheral vision Fran saw Eleanor's head flick round.

'You shouldn't joke about such things. Tempting providence.'

Headlines ran through her head. 'Student runs amok in High Street. Families killed. Children maimed'. And then: 'I was looking for me ex,' she is quoted as saying while being led away to be sedated.'

Concentrate. Concentrate. She moved down through the gears and stopped smoothly at a zebra crossing. She felt Eleanor relax. Poor Mother. She was a good driver, better than Dad, and Fran knew sloppiness pained her even when it wasn't dangerous. A couple with a pushchair and a jaunty dog muddled across the road.

'They got away with it. Nice dog.'

'You *are* in a strange mood.'

But she wasn't asking why. Mother never asked. Why would you, if you didn't want to know?

As they approached home Fran thought she saw Zelda arm in arm with a man walking down the road to the sea. She was too busy turning right to take a second look.

'Looked like that friend of yours,' said Eleanor. 'Wrapped round another man.'

'Mm, maybe.' Who was it? Certainly not Ed. Too tall.

A light rain was falling as Fran reached the Turners'. Gaye was in the garden, hoeing, with a basket of freshly pulled spinach on the path.

'Fran, darling! I didn't expect to see you. I hear you had a rotten time last night.' She drew Fran into a damp, earthy hug. 'Charlie didn't behave well, I gather.'

It was the first mention of Charlie's name and Fran was cross that she still wanted to weep. 'Bugger Charlie. I never want to see him again. I was such an idiot. Zel kept…'

'But it still hurts. We're all idiots, sooner or later. When it comes to men, that is.' Gaye threw down the hoe and picked up the trug. 'Come on. Tea? Answer to all life's ills.' She led the way into the kitchen.

'I thought I saw Zelda. With someone…?'

'Yes. Oh dear. I fear she's not having a good time either.' Gaye filled the kettle and struck a match.

Fran watched the blue flame lick up round the edge of the kettle and settle underneath it. 'Who was it? Not…?'

'Yes. Tomasz turned up. Out of the blue, yesterday evening. He was waiting here on the doorstep when I got back from the cinema. He didn't say much to me, except that his father had died, which is why he didn't come when he was supposed to. I think it's bad news, Fran. I suspect he's going back to Poland.'

'Didn't Zel say?'

'She was ranting on about Charlie when she came through the door. But when she saw Tomasz, they just went straight up. All she said was that she'd taken you home, that you were tucked up in bed. This morning, she came down to fetch coffee. And when they got up they went straight out. But look…' Gaye pointed to the porch. 'There's his bag all packed ready.' She shrugged. 'But I'm only the mother. I have to guess.'

'Rubbish. She tells you everything.'

'Eventually.' Gaye made a face and poured boiling water into the teapot. 'She may be going with him for all I know.'

'Uh? To live? She wouldn't. Would she?' Lose Zelda? On top of Charlie? It was more than Fran could bear. She sat down, holding the edge of the table, feeling its solidity.

'Might do. If she really loves him.'

'I guess I should go. They might soon be back.' But Fran couldn't move.

Gaye pushed a mug across the table. 'It'll sort out. You too. I know you don't want to hear this. But you really do have your whole life ahead of you. And you're well shot of that Charlie.' She raised her mug. 'I drink to women. And to hell with the other lot.'

Fran stared into the brown liquid. Gaye was right. She didn't want to hear that. But it was better than Mother's tart comments.

Fran sat tight at the back of the kitchen when the pair returned. Tomasz shook Gaye's hand long and hard, serious eyes looking into hers. He struggled to find words while Zelda hung back in the porch, not helping. Then he slung his bag over his shoulder, embraced Zelda briefly and strode out. She followed and watched at the gate until he had disappeared.

'Where do I start?' Zelda flopped down at the table. 'I can't even bloody cry anymore. He's going back. Turns out he's been working his socks off in London all this time, to send stuff back – money, food, stuff they could barter. To his family.'

'He's got a family? Oh, Zel…'

Zelda's eyes darkened. 'His mum and dad. I may be going soft, but I do actually believe him. And what else can I do anyway? And now...' She grabbed the packet of cigarettes and Gaye tossed her the box of matches. 'His dad just dropped dead and his mother needs help. She's not well herself. Some lung problem. He's got to go back. Look after her, the land. It's the only way they eat. Growing stuff. So there goes the love of my life. Out the door.'

Gaye met Zelda's eyes across the table and Zelda sighed. 'Yeah, we talked about me going too. But he doesn't really know what's going on there. It's difficult. He said, "How can I take you when I can't promise to even feed you and keep you safe?"' Her eyes filled with tears and she brushed them away impatiently. 'It's easy for me. Think what he's got to face.'

Fran had no words. Her own pain seemed paltry in comparison.

'And it doesn't help to be Jewish.' Zelda turned to Fran. 'You probably didn't know – I mean, we don't practise or anything. It's through Mum's family. He didn't say so, but I got the impression his own family wouldn't go a bundle on that. And the trouble is, I *look* Jewish.'

It was true. Zel did look Jewish, now Fran came to think about it. 'So? What...?'

'I don't understand the half of it. But the regime – it's communist. Jews have been known to disappear – even since the war. We don't know how lucky we are.' Zelda exhaled and looked across at Fran through a cloud of smoke. 'No, I couldn't believe it either. Not when he first told me. But then he told me some of the stories. Horrendous.'

Zelda stubbed out her cigarette and dropped her head onto her arms, her shoulders shaking. Gaye had left the room. Fran put a clumsy arm round her and they wept together.

Zelda was the first to emerge. 'You're making my hair all wet. What a bloody pair. You know what, Fran? You were right. About trust and sex and all that. Tomasz was really hurt I was out with someone else. That I might have been having it off with someone else while he was away. Not that he asked and I certainly wasn't telling. But I think he kind of guessed.'

'But when he didn't write or any...'

'He's a very traditional person. And in his family you do things properly or not at all. He was ashamed. Because he couldn't afford to take me out, buy me anything. I tell you, Fran, it's another world. Survival. And I was living such a…well, trivial life compared to him.'

'We take it all for granted, don't we? And there's…'

'At least you're studying. You've got a purpose. I've just been having a good time, except not, not really. All sad underneath. And you know, Fran, if I'm really honest, even if he'd agreed to take me – could I have done it? I'd be so scared…'

'You? Scared? I can't…'

'Leave Mum? Maybe never see her, or my brother and my niece, ever again? Be cold and hungry and scared all the time? As well as not speaking the language. Even being with Tomasz. Would I have been able to risk all that? And then not cope, and me and Tomasz end up hating each other?'

'You'd have coped,' said Fran, but she went home with a different view of her friend.

Harry met her with a long face.

The migraines that had been plaguing Eleanor had led to a series of investigations and tests.

'Your mother's had her diagnosis. She has to have a hysterectomy.'

Dread words. Nobody mentioned the big 'C' word, but they all knew it was lurking behind every question, every plan they made.

'Nice Frazzle's here to take the load,' said Harry. 'You can be around to help your mother, can't you? And get some studying done at the same time?'

'That will keep her out of mischief.' Eleanor laughed but Harry didn't join in.

In the kitchen, Harry said, 'I'm having lunch with Don – you know, your mother's surgeon? There are forms I have to sign. We go back a long way – medical school. I know it's naughty, but I'll pull any strings I can to make life easier for her.'

Meaning, increase her chances.

'Meeting him next week. See if he can give her priority.'

Dad would never normally do such a thing, on principle. Once again her woes really didn't count for much. She threw herself into shopping, cooking, cleaning and washing as much to ease her father's concern as to give her mother a rest. No need to look for a job, no time to think about Charlie, but hardly any time either for the essays which needed writing. And always the fear that closed in at night. Eleanor might be a difficult mother but she was the only mother she had. She was surprised at how much she felt for her when the pain hit and all Mother wanted was to curl up with a hot water bottle. It was like when she was very little, except the roles were reversed.

Harry needed attention too. All Eleanor wanted to eat was soup: Heinz cream of tomato; or mashed potato – no lumps, Francesca please. One evening she bought her father's favourite pork chops, but she'd forgotten it was the day of the lunch with Don.

'I'm really not hungry.' Harry sounded preoccupied.

'Big lunch, was it? Never mind. We can have them tomorrow.'

'Big lunch? No, sandwich and a pint. That awful pub in Lee.' Harry disappeared into the larder and emerged with a bottle.

'What's up, Dad?'

Harry never drank whisky. What had Don said about Mother's condition?

'Dad? What did Don say? Wouldn't he book her in early?'

Harry poured half a tumbler of Scotch and gulped it neat. 'Oh yes, he said he would. No problem.'

'Then what? Was there something he wasn't telling Mother?'

'Telling your mother? No, no. He said not to worry. Her chances are really good – we caught it early. He's pretty sure it's benign. Can't be sure of course until…'

'So what's this about?' Fran took his glass, sipped and made a face.

'Filthy stuff. Hits the spot though. Don't be led astray by your old dad.' He turned suddenly aside as his eyes filled with tears.

'Dad?'

He blew his nose and stuffed the handkerchief back in his pocket. 'Take no notice. Talking about things. Got to me. Cans of worms, cans of worms.' So saying, he disappeared to find Eleanor.

The precious time doing *The Times* crossword when Eleanor had gone to bed early was not the same that evening. Fran found she was getting more clues than Harry. Every time she looked up, he was staring at her, and even his high-speed anagram habit had stalled.

'Come on, Dad. There is something. You're holding out on me. That Don…'

Harry blinked. 'Nonsense! Would I do that, Frazzle? No, just tired. Thought I'd enjoy seeing the man…reminisce and so on. Didn't turn out like that. The past is the past.' He sighed and stretched. 'Sorry, brain's not in gear. Think I'll turn in.'

She watched him gather himself out of the armchair and walk unsteadily to the door. She'd never thought of him as old before.

He turned with his hand on the doorknob, the porcelain knob painted with flowers Eleanor was so proud of. 'You'll see to the fire and so on? And, Frazzle, don't worry.'

Which she did of course, adding Harry to the pot of worries which included Eleanor, Zelda, and the situation in Poland. A seething stew of anxiety knotted her stomach and built behind her eyes. And always, when she shut her eyes, the picture of Charlie's pale buttocks haunted her.

'I think I know what we have here.' Dr Jenkins packed away his stethoscope and rubbed his grey moustache.

Fran watched from the sofa, eyes half closed against the sunlight streaming in from the bay window of the drawing room. She was exhausted from coming downstairs to save their ageing GP the climb. At least he wouldn't be prescribing the vile M&B, the thick, bilious yellow liquid that had made her retch as a child. Medicine had moved on. It would be tablets. Anything to take away the pain in her head.

'You, young lady, have a classic case of glandular fever.'

Fran heard a tut from Eleanor.

Dr Jenkins perched on the edge of a chair and started writing on his pad. 'Some antibiotics for that throat. And you say aspirin isn't touching the pain? So some stronger painkillers. There we are.' He passed the prescription to Eleanor. 'Plenty of fluids, juice, water. The fever will gradually drop, not to worry. Eat normally as soon as you can swallow. And complete rest. I doubt you'll be up to doing much anyway for a few weeks.'

It didn't seem to occur to him that Eleanor wasn't currently capable of doing anything much either. The date of Eleanor's operation was fixed for early September, only a week or so away. Fran had been hanging in there, feeling worse each day and guilty that she was wishing her poor mother into hospital.

Eleanor came back from seeing the doctor out. 'That's what they call the kissing disease,' she said, but without her usual venom. 'Goodness knows what you've been getting up to with that friend of yours.'

Fran was too weak to protest. What she had been 'getting up to' since that fateful evening was looking after Eleanor. Her throat was too painful to talk. It was a relief to have an excuse to stay silent.

Eleanor frowned and placed a blissfully cool hand on Fran's forehead. 'Still burning. But he said not to worry. Well, now I suppose *I* shall have to look after *you*! Why on earth didn't you say you were so poorly?'

Fran shrugged. It was all too much, but there was satisfaction in seeing Mother worried, hearing what she knew was meant as a thank you and a sorry. She even went straight off to the chemist with the prescription instead of waiting until Harry got home.

But Eleanor really couldn't cope. The stairs defeated her, and at the weekend Harry insisted on calling Goldie, who insisted he bring Fran to her.

It was a surreal drive. Fran lay, swathed in blankets, on the back seat, swimming in and out of a drugged sleep, aware of a frieze of green passing which took the shape of buses, trees and hills. There was the drone of Harry singing, the roar of engines and eventually Goldie's voice as she enfolded her. 'Come on, Fran sweetheart. Oh my, but you're hot! Let's get you tucked up.'

7

Goldie rocked her gently, repeating over and over 'Fran sweetheart' like a lullaby, and the smell of face powder and *Evening in Paris* brought a memory of the tiny sapphire-blue bottle Auntie Goldie kept on her dressing table. It felt as if she'd come home, but as she breathed in she was overwhelmed with tears and a great sadness. It really was an odd disease.

Goldie made jellies and soups and always seemed to know what she needed. No demands. No tensions, no Charlie, no Mother. Fran started to recover.

'No temperature for two days now,' Goldie said one morning, throwing open the window that looked across the harbour entrance. 'Time for a talk. You don't get a fever like that for nothing. And don't believe a word of all that "kissing disease" nonsense.' She chuckled. 'Which is not to say you haven't been kissing. I should hope you have!'

It was easy to tell Goldie all about Charlie. She even told her about Sandra. And noticed afterwards that she stopped having the nightmare where Sandra was thrusting her cleavage into Fran's face and jangling her earrings while she, Fran, tried to eat a bowl of cornflakes and fly a small aeroplane. Goldie didn't judge. She didn't even judge Charlie.

'He'll regret it. But that won't be any of your business. A lucky escape, though it might not seem that way.'

Increasingly, it did seem that way. A letter came from Verity, forwarded from home. She was full of a concert she'd given and a wedding she'd sung at. It would be good to see Verity again. Harry brought her books and her brain managed some reading. But attempts at the essay defeated her and Goldie found her in a deluge of tears.

'Too soon to be working. You need to get out in the sun now you're better. Enjoy yourself.'

'How can I enjoy myself with no Charlie, and Zelda so miserable and Tomasz struggling and Mother off to hospital and even Dad…'

'All the woes of the world on your shoulders. Oh dear, oh dear!' Goldie lowered herself into her armchair. 'Now, sweetie, you're young and pretty and intelligent. I know what it's like to be knocked sideways in love. Believe me. And I never had your looks or your brains. But I made a decision. There's a saying, in Latin I think it's supposed to be. But roughly translated it goes, "Don't let the buggers grind you down."'

Fran couldn't help smiling. Auntie Goldie looked so serious.

'Not funny, sweetie. It's a good motto if you take it to heart. *Que sera sera*, and all that jazz. Be your own person. Make your own luck.'

Fran shrugged and blew her nose.

'It's the hormones, Fran sweetie. Can't rush these things.'

When news came through that Eleanor's biopsy showed there was no malignancy, they celebrated in style. Goldie produced a bottle of champagne and put it in the fridge.

'One of my beaux brought it one time. I was keeping it for a rainy day, but it'll be just the ticket. Let's get spruced up, make an occasion of it.'

She even changed her frock and insisted Fran wear the new green and yellow skirt she'd bought at the Landport.

'Are you sure it's not too short?'

'Go on! You're young – and with legs like those? Why not?'

They sat on the balcony in the evening sun and drank to Eleanor.

Goldie raised her glass again. 'Here's real pain to my sham friends, and cham-pagne to my real friends!'

Fran giggled. 'I like that. I'll remember that. Not that I'll have the chance…'

'You're tipsy already, my girl. Here's to the future. Yours in particular. They'll be queuing up to take you out. And there must be one young man in Bristol who'll gladden your heart.'

Fran found herself back home sooner than she wanted, but her return to Bristol was delayed. Eleanor had made a good recovery from her operation and was due to transfer to the small, local hospital in Gosport to convalesce.

Harry came on the phone to Goldie, distraught. 'Nell refuses to go to the War Memorial. Says it's just down the road and she might just as well be at home. As she very well knows, I booked leave specially but that's not for two weeks. She can't seem to grasp that.'

Goldie muttered about 'that sister of mine' and how Eleanor was missing the point and making life difficult for everyone. 'And don't think you're going, Fran sweetie.'

'Of course I'll go. After all, she is my mother.'

Goldie glared. 'You'll be back to square one. She won't be able to do much – you know that, don't you?'

Fran knew exactly what she was in for. She was better, but tired quickly and was still prone to bursting unexpectedly into tears. But Mother was Mother and they'd muddle through.

Zelda was on the phone the moment Fran got home.

'Your dad said you'd be back. Must see you. I've got some amazing news. I just can't wait to tell you. I guess you're allowed out?'

'No, I can't leave her, Zel. She's really weak and she's not allowed to lift anything. You come here.'

'She won't eat me?'

'She's mellowed, Zel. We're getting on really well. Anyway you probably won't see her.'

Fran took Zelda down to the kitchen and Zelda firmly shut the door before striking a dramatic pose as if she was about to take flight. 'Guess what?'

Fran shook her head.

'I'm pregnant.'

'You're *what*?' Fran stared at Zelda with huge eyes.

Zelda danced about. 'Go on. Tell me you're thrilled.'

'I can't take it in. How you can be so pleased. What did your mother say?'

'You know Mum. She takes things as they come. She just said, "We'll manage together and when you're fed up with being here with me, then you can find your own place." She even said she'd babysit so I can get a job and be independent.'

'Your mum is amazing.'

Not for the first time Fran found herself wishing Gaye was her mother, and felt guilty for wishing it.

'She's just Mum. I've always wanted a baby.'

'Really? Did you? I always just thought you were mad about sex.'

'Well, that too. But deep down... I suppose that's what it was all about.'

'Aren't you scared?' Having a baby, a child to look after, was about the most terrifying thing Fran could imagine. 'Did you mean to get pregnant?'

'Course not.' Zelda rolled a pencil up and down the table. 'I mean it wasn't a deliberate "here I go, let's make a baby". But then again I wasn't that bothered either. So maybe, in the back of my mind, I did.'

'So what about art school?'

'Oh bugger that. Don't need it anymore. That was only about looking for some sort of purpose. And now I've got one. I'll carry on at HMV as long as I can and save up.'

'And he doesn't know? Tomasz? You won't tell him?'

Zelda hesitated. 'Tomasz. No, I won't tell him. It's probably his.'

'*Probably?*'

'Can I trust you? To keep a secret absolutely and for ever?'

'Sounds like when we were kids. Cross your heart and hope to die. Sorry. I promise.'

'I'm serious. It could just as easily be Ed's.'

'I didn't think you and Ed...'

'I know. Just good friends. Yes, that's how it was in the summer. But then, I was so pissed off when Tomasz didn't turn up. And, well, one thing led to another. In the back of Charlie's fucking car. Pardon the pun.'

'And then Tomasz. I mean, both of them?' Fran felt foolish and nauseous.

'Don't look so shocked. Sex is no big deal. I just do it. I enjoy it. Like chocolate fudge cake.'

Like Sandra, thought Fran, and shut the thought out immediately.

'At least I used to.' Zelda shook her head vigorously. 'I know what you're thinking. No, not like a certain barmaid of our acquaintance. It's not like that anymore. Not since Tomasz came back. Like I said, I really loved that guy.'

Eleanor didn't need to overhear this conversation. She was kept regularly informed of the gossip by her bridge crony, Maude Penfold, and it was no time at all before this juicy morsel reached her.

'She'll let it go for adoption, of course? I'm surprised they've not kept it quiet.'

Fran sighed. 'No. She wants the baby.'

'And that crazy mother of hers is letting her I suppose. The child will be a bastard of course.'

'I don't think people think like that anymore.'

'Believe me they do, and believe me, that child will suffer.'

Fran was silent, seething inside, and sad Mother had not mellowed enough to accept Zelda at last. On the plus side, the news seemed to energise her and the old fighting spirit was back in her eyes. It was the end of the companionable time they'd been having.

'Mother thought you'd go for adoption,' Fran told Zelda.

'Of course she did. I bet that's not all she said.'

They were hunched up on the beach, throwing pebbles at a half-submerged post.

'You know what?' Fran selected a stone and flung it at the target. 'I sometimes think she enjoys finding people doing things wrong, things she disapproves of. She seems to get a kick out of tearing people to shreds.'

'I don't know why you don't break loose and lead your own life.'

'I'm scared of her, that's why. Pathetic isn't it? That's why I won't sleep with anyone. Afraid of what she'd say if I got pregnant.' She paused. 'It's the first time I've admitted it.'

'It doesn't surprise me. She's scary. Anyway you can always borrow mine.'

'Thanks. You know, I don't think she even likes me.'

Zelda spun round. '*Likes* you?'

Fran was silent. Zelda shuffled across the shingle and put her arm round her.

Fran chewed her lips. 'Loves me maybe. In her own kind of way. She was pretty cut up when I was ill. Is that possible? To love someone without actually liking them?' She kicked at the pebbles.

When Harry's holiday started, he was keen for Fran to stay on and get some rest. But she couldn't wait to get away from Eleanor, from her pregnant friend and from Harry's strange manner. He would be perfectly normal for most of the day and then would switch off and be cold and distant, particularly to Eleanor, which was most unlike him. She even felt protective of her mother.

'There's nothing wrong with *you*, is there?' she asked over the washing-up. 'Ever since you saw that Don....'

Harry laughed. 'Would I go to a gynaecologist to find out about me? Come on, Frazzle. There is absolutely *nothing*.' He gave her a big hug and she felt reassured.

Zelda came with Fran to the Harbour station when she went back to Bristol. It was several weeks past the start of term, and the warm September weather was over. A strong northerly wind was funnelling down the harbour and they snuggled together in the stern of the ferry.

'Got something to show you.' Zelda rooted about in her bag and waved a newspaper cutting. 'This might come as a bit of a shock. Brace yourself.' She unfolded it and smoothed it onto Fran's knees.

A photograph. A wedding photograph. Unmistakably Charlie and something frou-frou at his side. Fran opened her mouth but no sound came out. Her throat was dry. She couldn't swallow. All that stuff Zelda had told her about looking at rings in Hugg's must have been true.

'When?'

'August. So you see, he married Amanda like he was always...'

Fran held up a hand, shook her head. She didn't need it spelled out.

'But the really interesting thing is…' Zelda turned the cutting over and pointed to the running header. 'See? The *Petersfield Herald*. Not local. I saw it when I was over at my brother's. Which is why your mother hasn't been waving it in your face. Married from her grandmother's apparently. And why?'

Fran shook her head.

'Tells me one thing. They wanted to keep it quiet, not draw attention. And yet they wanted a proper wedding. Registry office would have been too furtive. Anyway they're churchy folk.'

'But why?'

'She's up the duff. Her and me both. But she's going to regret it and I won't.'

'She looks smug as a guinea pig.'

'Guinea pig! That's good, yes.' Zelda puffed out her cheeks and snorted. 'A guinea pig with a bun in the oven.'

Zelda doubled over laughing and soon Fran was laughing so hysterically that she was able to cry and conceal how much she cared until she was safely on the train.

8

Fran slid the key silently into the lock, but as she pushed the door, the familiar smell of fried bacon and damp brought with it the sound of voices. The door gave its usual groan and Verity erupted from the kitchen, hugging her in the vice grip of her bony little frame. No hiding place. No slipping into her room and falling into bed.

The newspaper cutting had done for her. On the train she'd gone over and over her last meetings with Charlie in the light of his wedding two months later. Obviously it was what he had intended to tell her about. Had he been too much of a coward or was he having second thoughts? Except of course, if Zelda was right and Amanda really was pregnant, second thoughts would have been irrelevant. She imagined him torn between his duty to Amanda and his love for her, Fran – a Charlie so distressed that he got drunk and Sandra took advantage of him. Deep down she knew it was all rubbish and the action replay of the scene in the storeroom haunted her once again.

Verity grabbed her suitcase and flung it into her room. 'Good timing! Tea's just brewed.'

'Here at last!' Verity announced Fran's arrival as if she'd just produced her from the black trilby perched on the back of her head.

Morag and, of all people, Dale waved enthusiastically and Morag pulled the extra stool out from under the table.

Dale was the last person Fran wanted to see. After the episode with the scald and the cold tap they'd made an unspoken truce. She'd got used to having him around and even enjoyed his presence, his jokes and the curries he came and cooked from time to time. But he mustn't know about Charlie. Even if he didn't actually say I told you so, he'd be bound to think it.

Morag was speaking, making a narrow shape with her hands. 'My god, Fran, you've shrunk! You're wasting away.'

'She's been ill. Didn't I tell you?'

'Yeah, but you made it sound like flu or something, Verity. I didn't realise how…'

'Glandular fever. Not how I'd have chosen to lose weight, but it's one advantage.'

'Infectious mononucleosis, commonly, very commonly, known as the kissing disease.' Morag took off on the medical ins and outs.

Dale had said nothing. Fran was aware of him watching her, sipping his tea. Now he interrupted Morag's list of symptoms.

'The kissing disease. Well, at least that says something for your social life. Lover boy came up to scratch, did he? Did you—'

Verity cut in. 'We had bets on you coming back with a ring on your finger.'

Fran gulped her tea. Too hot. It caused a sputtering which neatly covered the threat of tears.

'So how was Charlie?' Verity was persistent as ever.

'Oh, fine. We had great times. He's off in the Far East now.' It might even be true for all she knew, and it would take care of Charlie for the time being. 'What have you all been up to? I know all about Verity – blimey that bistro! Clifton too, of all places. I'll never eat out again after what you said goes on in the kitchen.'

Verity laughed. 'That's nothing to what Morag's got to tell.'

Morag had been working in a mother and baby home on the outskirts of Glasgow.

'General dogsbody, cleaning mostly. But what an eye-opener! Gruesome stuff. Kids too young to be mothers given just enough time to bond with their bairns before they have to hand them over for adoption. Heart-rending. One girl in particular – she wouldn't hand over her babe – completely went to pieces. I'll never forget the look…'

'But couldn't she change her mind?'

'Nope. Too late. She'd signed on the dotted line. The pressure, the bullying – no, it's not too strong a word – to get them to sign, you would not believe. Imagine yourself at fifteen or sixteen.' Morag ran her fingers through her hair as she looked round the table. 'They're so isolated, with no support – and no one tells them their rights. I wouldn't want to be a child care officer, carting babies off to foster parents with the mother being sat on – literally, no kidding.'

Fran couldn't help thinking of Zelda and how lucky she was, and of Amanda who'd had Charlie to come to her rescue and do the decent thing. Had she really set out to nab him by getting herself pregnant? She wouldn't be the first. But what a desperate measure.

'But I suppose, from the adopters' point of view…' Verity was saying. 'They need some certainty. They don't want the mother suddenly taking their baby away.'

'True. But what bothers me in all this is who's thinking about the bairn? You just have to hope it's the child care officer. My point is – and I won't rant, I promise – so many of these babes never needed to be born. It's all very well for couples who want to adopt, but it can be ruinous for those girls. But there's hope, a light at the end of the tunnel, now Labour's got in.'

'How will that…?'

'Bodes well for the abortion lobby. I reckon they're going to make big changes. You see.'

'You were well out of it on polling day. Morag was so mad – too young to vote.'

'And I'm twenty-one next month, would you believe? Missed it by a whisker!'

'But the socialists managed without her, so we all got rat-arsed, celebrating.' Verity tapped out a cigarette. 'As to this idiot,' she jabbed a finger at Dale, 'he only took a job on a building site.'

'Why shouldn't he?'

'Why? His hands, his precious hands! Lose a finger and then where is he?'

Dale shrugged. 'Best money around. Plus being outside. Excellent tan.' He pulled up his shirt to show off a flat brown belly. Tendrils of black hair disappeared into his jeans.

'Put it away!' said Verity, who could never expose her pale skin to the sun.

'It was good company. Lots of rufty-tufty blokes. And no worse than you smoking and risking your voice.'

Dale turned to Fran. 'And you? Did you get anything as mundane as a job?'

It sounded sarcastic, putting her right back in the spoilt middle-class mould of their early date.

Verity frowned at him. 'Dale!'

Fran took a deep breath. 'Not between looking after my mother with cancer and my best mate who got pregnant and her man had to go back to Poland. Oh, and being ill myself.'

She glared across at Dale who held up his hands. 'Out of order. As ever.'

Which she ignored, while taking it as an apology of sorts.

Verity cut in. 'I thought you said in your last letter your mum was okay?'

'Yes, she is. But we didn't know that for ages. Dad's been in an awful state. Not himself at all.'

'No wonder you look so exhausted.'

Dale stood up. 'I'd best be off. Do some practice. Did we say we were meeting later? At the pub?' He looked round the group. 'Morag, yes? Fran?'

Fran saw her chance. 'I'm knocked out. Early night. Sorry to be boring.'

As soon as Dale had gone Verity and Morag rounded on her.

'So what really happened with Charlie?'

Fran looked from one to the other. She saw curiosity and concern, all ready to turn to pity.

'Well, if you really want to know…'

But she couldn't do it. Couldn't spew her humiliation all over the table. Couldn't forego the status having a boyfriend had given her. Couldn't cope with their pity. Couldn't face the condition of being 'available' and all the games that went with it: the sizing up, the trying out on painful dates with fellow students. Not to mention working out where to sit in lectures in order to avoid the disasters and not to look too keen on the next guy in your sights.

'If you really want to know, we went on lots of picnics, drank in lots of pubs and drove about in Charlie's car.'

'And caught GF snogging in the back?'

'Something like that.'

Verity sighed. 'If you say so.' She took her mug to the sink and emptied the teapot. 'I'd better do some practice too, before we go out.'

Morag put a professional hand on Fran's forehead. 'Mind you don't knock yourself out. You look wiped.'

It was nearly a week before Fran found herself ambushed by Verity and Dale in the Berkeley between lectures. They were sitting at a table at the back and she didn't see them until it was too late.

Fran set down her coffee. 'Filthy day.' She pushed her bag under the table, aware she was avoiding eye contact with Dale.

Verity put down her cup. 'Fran, when are you going to tell us what's wrong? We all know there's something…'

'There isn't anything.' Fran's eyes skittered over the tabletop, the sugar bowl, Verity's cigarettes.

'Look, we're worried about you, and there's not much we can do if you won't talk to us.' Verity lit a cigarette and inhaled deeply, the blue vein at her temple showing as she watched Fran expectantly. 'It's what friends are for.'

Fran said nothing and fiddled with her teaspoon. She could see their distorted images reflected in the bowl, a pair of tiny people miles away. That's how the world seemed these days.

'Isn't it enough? All the things I've told you?'

'Your mother's better, your friend wants the baby, you've recovered. So, no,' said Verity.

Fran had thought she'd be fine in Bristol, away from the scene of Charlie's crime. But it hadn't worked out like that. Even so, she reckoned she'd been holding up brilliantly since she'd been back, joining in, saying the right things. Evidently not. They'd rumbled her.

Now Dale was speaking. 'You can't go on shutting people out forever.' He leaned forward, trying to get Fran to look at him.

She could see his pale face through her hair, thin cheeks drawn down in concern. She longed for him to make a joke and to see those lines shift to bracket his wide smile. But he continued to gaze intently at her. She concentrated on counting the number of black tiles in the design on the floor.

'I'm not shutting anybody out!' she heard herself almost shouting.

Dale shrugged and gathered his books. 'You know where I am,' he said in a low voice as he left the table. Fran lifted her head to watch him cross the café with a characteristic flick of his dark ponytail, the skirts of his old army greatcoat sailing behind him with the energy of his stride.

'Well, I feel pretty shut out,' said Verity quietly.

The pattern of tiles swum out of focus. Fran grabbed her bag and made for the toilets. She stayed there long enough to be sure Verity would have left for her next lecture.

She might have known she'd never pull the wool over Verity's pale blue eyes. It was like living with your own personal lie detector. She'd been fooled by Verity when they first met. That flower face and fragile build that made her look so vulnerable. She was so tenacious, so uncompromising. She respected her, but there was such a thing as overdoing it.

When she got home Fran opened her Yeats at the page where she'd pressed the rose from Charlie's bouquet. Its faded petals reminded her of a blouse her History teacher used to wear, spinster-coloured, dusty and dead. 'So much for dreams,' she said aloud and slammed the book shut.

That evening Verity knocked and entered simultaneously as Fran struggled to prepare for a tutorial on *Middlemarch*. 'I saw your light was on.'

'I'm really...' Fran started.

'I know. And I'm really not giving up.' She looked round the room. 'I see there's no photo anymore. Fran, I know and you know, and I know that you know that I know. So why don't you just spit it out?' She curled her legs onto the chair and sat back, waiting.

Something caved inside Fran. And, strangely, it was a relief. She told Verity the whole story, including both Sandra and Amanda.

'Christ Almighty, no wonder you're traumatised.' Verity was vibrating with indignation by the time she'd finished. 'I'd be demented. No kidding. Enough to put you off men for life.'

'You can say that again. But I feel such an idiot.'

'And your best friend got pregnant? At least you didn't. My mum would go ballistic if that happened to me.'

'Mine's going ballistic about it and it isn't even me!'

'But I guess I'd keep it. I couldn't get rid of it, whatever Morag might say. And then Mike would "have to" marry me.' Verity made quote marks in the air. 'Be thoroughly *bourgeois*, as Morag would say. Not an ideal way to start…'

'So no sign of him popping the question, then?'

'Not a snowball's. Too wrapped up in his rugby and his drunken mates. Anyway, fair dos, I've got my career to think of.' She stretched. 'How come that mate of yours is keeping the baby? Won't it be difficult with no man around?'

'She's got the most totally amazing mum. Plus she's always wanted a baby – not interested in a career. She's bright enough, but she never was academic. Hey, Verity. Promise me one thing? Don't tell Dale. About Charlie, I mean. He'll have a field day with I-told-you-sos. Even if he doesn't actually say it.'

'You're right off track there. I won't tell him – but you've got him wrong. That's the last thing he'd say – or think.'

Next morning Fran packed *Middlemarch* and her notes into her bag. She stopped on the way out the door, went back, grabbed her Yeats off the shelf and shook the withered flower, every leaf and petal, into the waste paper basket. Then she shouldered her bag and swung out of the flat.

9

April was Fran's favourite month. The sun had shone all day, there were daffodils in gardens and blossom breaking on cherry trees. Christmas had not been fun. Zelda had been away and she'd spent a dutiful time with her parents and Auntie Goldie, trying not to think about Charlie. But the Spring term had been going well, and she was really enjoying her work. This evening she was coming home late from Jenny's, a new friend she'd made in her tutorial group. Fran had got an A for her *Beowulf* essay and Jenny had wanted to read it and take notes.

She was so busy thinking about her good week that it was some time before she registered she was being followed. At least, there were footsteps behind her. Not necessarily following, but she realised they had been there for some time. In the narrow cut-through road they sounded a hollow counterpoint to hers, echoing off the stone walls as if in a vault. When she crossed over they crossed over. And when she turned right onto Fremantle Road they turned right and kept on coming, closer now.

Her stomach contracted and heat rose into her throat. She told herself it might be coincidence. But her body knew different. She could hear her heart thumping as loudly as the footsteps. She quickened her pace. Her pursuer started to run. She turned the corner. There was the phone box on the corner of the square. She sprinted towards the oblong of light, the fanlight above her front door. In sight of home!

Too late. A weight like a giant haversack arrived on her back. She was immobilized, clamped. She opened her mouth to scream, but nothing came out. *Help! Help! Verity! Morag! Help!* she yelled in her head, but was utterly silent. She staggered to remain upright. On her back a pounding, the jackhammer of the man's penis ramming and slamming into her backside. There was a lamppost a few feet away. She summoned all her strength and used the momentum of the thumping to shift her feet towards it. She grabbed it. She could hear a car. Was it coming this way? It was approaching fast, down Kingsdown Parade. If only the driver could see her. She gave an almighty two-handed heave on the lamppost and swung herself into the road. *Please, please. See me. Help me.* Headlights hit her full on, but swung away round the square.

It was enough. As soon as the lights fell on him her attacker was gone. She was weightless, running, unlocking her peeling front door, shouting for Verity, sobbing into her arms.

'Of course you must go to the police.' Morag joined the conversation from the kitchen door as she headed out to the anatomy exam that had been dominating all their lives for weeks.

Verity had administered the last of her damson wine the night before and had tipped Fran into bed with a hot water bottle in the early hours. Now she was trying to persuade her to report the assault.

'It's vital you go. He could do it again and the next girl might not be so lucky.'

Fran shuddered. 'I can't go on my own.'

'I can't go with you this morning. Like I said, it's piano trio. I can hardly not be there. Prof would do his nut.'

'Me neither. Big exam – as you know. Sorry, hen, but I've really got to go.'

'Of course. Go on! Don't be late.'

'I'll be thinking of you.' Morag banged the front door behind her.

She wouldn't be thinking of her, of course. Her head would be full of all those bones. But it was comforting all the same.

Verity stretched, her eye following the solitaire diamond on its platinum band that sparkled on her ring finger. It was a characteristic gesture of hers ever since Valentine's Day when Mike had gone down on bended knee. Fran found it an annoying habit.

'We'll go this afternoon. All you've got to do is tell them what happened. Anything you remember…'

'I don't. It was dark. How's it going to help?' Fran hugged herself to stop shaking.

'I'll wear these monsters.' Verity put on her hated new glasses and immediately looked less blonde. She stared at Fran. 'But I can't leave you on your own.'

Fran shrugged and tried to smile.

'I know. Idea. Get dressed and I'll take you round to Dale's. Pick you up there after trio. See if he's there. If not you'll just have to come with me and listen.'

The thought of Dale wasn't as reassuring to Fran as Verity obviously assumed it would be. But it was true, she didn't want to be alone.

Dale was at home and said, 'Of course,' and made her coffee. He was more reassuring in person than Fran had expected. She nursed the hot mug and relaxed a little.

'I could take you,' he said as he lifted his cello into its case. 'I don't have to be anywhere until this afternoon. Get it over with?'

Fran considered. Surprisingly, the idea was not alarming.

'Might be better with a male,' he added.

Fran scribbled a note for Verity. As they were leaving the flat, Dale turned back. 'Just a mo.'

Fran heard rustling and he re-emerged wearing a suit jacket over his black polo neck instead of the usual baggy sweater.

'I'd like to think it wouldn't make any odds,' he said. 'But I know different.'

Dale knew where the police station was, which was a good start. He never lacked confidence, but his unfamiliar jacket lent him a useful gravitas. The desk sergeant even called him sir.

'See what I mean?' Dale said, as they took their seats in the waiting area.

The interview was worse than Fran had imagined, but it was worth it. For one thing she had at least done something, the only thing she could, to fight back. And, it showed her another side of Dale, who stayed with her throughout the ordeal. She hadn't bargained for the uncontrollable shaking that took over her whole body as soon as she had to describe what had happened to her. All Dale did was put a hand on her back.

When she thought about it afterwards, Fran knew she couldn't have coped with anything more. But that slight pressure, that warmth, had been the most comforting thing ever.

He took her straight to the first pub on Whiteladies Road and bought her a brandy. She knew he couldn't afford it, but he wouldn't let her pay.

'Purely medicinal. That wasn't so bad, was it?'

Fran made a face. 'I can't thank you enough. Couldn't have done it without...'

'Rubbish. Anyway, why wouldn't I? We're mates.'

'I guess I was lucky with that policeman. At least he seemed to believe me.'

'Bit patronising – but yes, could have been worse. When he asked you what you were wearing I was beginning...'

'Glad it wasn't a mini. He might have thought...'

'That you were asking for it. Wouldn't be at all surprised.'

'But think how much worse it would have been if I *had* been wearing a mini. He might have...'

'Don't even think about it. You weren't and he didn't.'

Dale put an arm across her shoulder. 'You're still all trembly. Get that down you. Then we'd better get something to eat.'

All Fran wanted was her favourite pork pie with English mustard in the Refectory, washed down by several cups of black coffee. Dale let her buy the same for him. Then he insisted on walking her home even though it was broad daylight and told her to have a bath and go to bed.

The bath was the best thing. She lay back in the warm water and closed her eyes. Instead of the lamppost and the dark shapes of trees in the square she saw Dale's face in this new gentle mood. Instead of the pounding weight on her back, she felt the light pressure of Dale's hand. He'd been such a good friend, put the whole incident into perspective – 'The guy's sick. Think of him as a poor old pervert. Just don't walk home alone at night.' All the tensions between them had dissolved and she felt happy she wouldn't be avoiding Dale anymore.

The shaking had stopped and she was relaxed after the bath, but she wasn't ready for bed. She lit the gas fire in the chill of her room. Music was what was needed. She'd only been able to afford two LPs so far, the Beatles' *Rubber Soul* album and Bob Dylan's latest, which she'd bought primarily for the cover. The Beatles didn't suit her mood so she fell asleep to the Dylan, which caused both Verity and Morag to raise an eyebrow when they came home later. It was known to be a favourite of Dale's.

'I wondered whether you might like to come to London with me this weekend?' Dale stopped Fran in the doorway of the Berkeley. 'Thought it might take your mind off things, change of scene.'

'London! That's an idea. That would be fun.'

'Don't bank on it. I have to go see my folks. Think about it, let me know.'

'The only thing is, my best friend at home – you know, Zelda? I think I told you, she's expecting. Due any day now. I said I'd go down for the weekend when she's had it.'

'Like I say, let me know.'

Fran phoned Zelda that evening. She was depressed.

'How much longer? The blooming head's not even engaged, so they say. I tell you, Fran, I'm having an elephant. No, go ahead, enjoy yourself, go to London, have fun. Don't mind me. Only joking. Mum says I'm impossible. Of course, go.'

Zelda didn't even ask who she was going to London with.

Fran had heard about Dale's mother and her chronic depression. There was never any mention of his father. Did she really want to go? Trouble was, she had no friends in London, and she didn't fancy visiting art galleries on her own, or window shopping with no money. She imagined the place peopled with men in grubby raincoats. Perhaps it wasn't such a good idea after all.

But Verity grinned and said, 'No worries. Just go with him. It'll be fine.'

'You're looking pleased with yourself.'

Dale was grinning like a kid when he picked her up.

'Why wouldn't I be? You're coming to London with me.'

Fran grunted and slammed the door.

'But there is something else.' He turned a knob on the dashboard and music filled the van. 'I got the radio fixed. Brilliant, eh?'

'Great. How come?'

'Mate of mine in Barton Hill. Owed me a favour and I bumped into him last week.'

'Oh! Do you go to the settlement, then?'

'Nah. Don't go in for that patronising stuff. No, I worked at the garage down there over Easter.' He pulled out from the kerb and looked sideways at Fran. 'Have I just put my foot in it? First of the day? Do you go down there?'

Fran nodded. 'I only visit an old lady.'

'No harm in that. Bet she loves it.'

Fran remembered her very first instinct to run from the settlement offices. Maybe it had been a reasonable impulse after all. Did Mrs Nicholas feel patronised? Was that the price she paid for a bit of company?

'No, it's really that Palmer bloke I have issue with. Ever bump into him? Thinks he runs the show down there. Which he doesn't.'

Fran swallowed hard. 'Yeah, I met him.'

'All his socialist principles are a total sham. His family only own half of Northamptonshire. And I gather that's not as big an exaggeration as you might think. All very feudal.'

'Really?' Fran struggled to put Palmer in this new context.

'Yep. The degree's just for show. He'll be off to run the estate when he graduates.'

'How do you *know* all this?'

'My mate. The one in Barton Hill. His mum used to be Palmer's landlady. He got all the lowdown. Fascinating. He's married to the Honourable Double-Barrelled Somebody-Somebody.' Dale slowed for traffic lights. 'And you know that kind of mid-Atlantic slur he puts on? It covers a very plummy accent, apparently. You should hear Brian take him off on the phone to his folks.'

'I thought he was Canadian.'

Dale shook his head. 'No. Just crafty.'

Fran looked away at passers-by, hoping Dale wasn't noticing the flush she could feel on her cheeks. Did Palmer really put that on?

The drawl she had found so attractive? She felt doubly an idiot, but hell, it was all past history.

'What deep thoughts are going on in that head of yours?'

'Wondering if my old lady feels patronised.'

'You're not a patronising kind of person, so probably not. It's the whole situation that's patronising – like how come she needs you to go and see her in the first place.'

'Oh well, that's because she was moved out of her house into this flat and she misses her neighbours and seeing people coming and going and kids playing, etcetera, etcetera...'

'Exactly. So it's a housing problem. Or planning. Social engineering, if you like.'

'But she loves her flat. It's warmer, easier. She just doesn't like being up in the air in a load of concrete. Even though it's not a tall block.'

'Don't get me started on tower blocks. Biggest mistake... Anyway, you're the sticking plaster.'

'Thanks a lot.'

'You know what I mean. You can't do anything about the real problem, but you make her – and everyone else – feel better. But better than no sticking plaster.'

Dale always made her see things differently. She'd often sensed an oddness about how she came to be visiting Mrs N. It vanished as soon as she was with her because they'd struck up a genuine friendship out of an artificial beginning, so she'd never analysed the feeling before.

Dale fiddled with the radio as they crawled through heavy traffic. 'It's ironic, really. I was just thinking about Palmer. When you look at what happens with tower blocks – all in the name of healthy living, my arse, and clearing overcrowded slums –when I think of the greed that's actually behind all that – the developers making a packet and so on. Then the feudal setup looks suddenly benign, much as I hate to admit such a thing.'

'I see what you...'

'Sorry. I said I wouldn't get on that hobby horse. Here, can you get that station tuned in?'

Fran twiddled the knob fractionally to get rid of the hiss,

wondering if her middle-class mind would ever tune in to Dale's way of thinking.

'You'll see the alternative today,' he was saying. 'And that's not pretty either. That's if you come with me. But you don't have to. I could always drop you off. You could go to Carnaby Street and be part of swinging London.'

'Think I'm a bit square for that.'

Dale laughed. 'You'll be bored rigid, I warn you. But Ma likes a bit of company, a bit of a party.' He turned up the volume and they sang along to Cilla Black belting out 'Anyone Who Had a Heart' as they made their way out of town and onto the road to Chippenham.

Mrs Weaver was clearly surprised to see Fran and fussed about lighting a fire in the front room, but Dale insisted they stay in the back where the grate was already banked up with glowing coke.

Fran had imagined a thin, nervy, chain-smoking woman living in an arty kind of chaos. The street of run-down terrace houses fitted, but she was not prepared for the tidy front garden and net curtains at number seventy-two, nor for this rather plump, motherly-looking woman. She felt both disappointed and reassured.

Dale was immediately set to work fixing various things – a dripping tap in the kitchen needed a new washer and the curtain rail had come loose in his mother's bedroom. Fran was grateful to be asked to hand things to Dale as he worked, although she could see it was unnecessary.

When the jobs were done his mother produced ham and tomatoes and a Battenberg cake and Dale helped her make tea and lay the table in what seemed like a familiar ritual. How strange to see Dale apparently so at ease in such a domestic setting.

Afterwards he said he must visit their neighbour and was gone for what seemed like hours. Mrs Weaver's conversation returned again and again to the subject of Dale and his achievements: going to university, being musical.

'But he's a good lad. Always sees to everything when he comes.'

'He's very practical. I'm not much good with things like that.'

Fran's attention wandered, taking in the knick-knacks and frills of this very conventional room, trying to imagine Dale growing up in it.

'Used to worry me, having a kid like that. You know. What they call gifted. Seemed a responsibility. But I couldn't do anything. Not with his dad.'

They both stared at the orange and brown swirling carpet.

'His dad tried to beat it out of him.'

Fran looked up, startled.

'Tried to beat the music out of him. Pathetic – said it made him a poofter. I dare say he never told you that.'

Fran felt the colour rise into her face. 'He's never talked to me about his father.'

'I guess he wouldn't. They didn't get on. And then I became a burden to him.' She stopped and eyed Fran. 'I dare say you know that.'

'He did say you hadn't always been well.'

She gave a harsh laugh. 'Understatement of the year, that is. But he's never missed coming, never cut himself off. Not ashamed of where he comes from.'

'Of course not.'

Another harsh laugh. 'He's never brought a girlfriend before.'

'Oh, I'm not his girlfriend. Just a friend. He thought I'd like the trip.'

'He's gone next door. Good neighbour, she was. Couldn't have managed without her. Used to take the kid in. When he was a babby. Dare say he wouldn't have survived without her. She'd hear his father coming up the street and tap on the glass. Baby'd go out the window as the old man came in through the door.'

'That must have been hard.'

'Hard? It broke me up. We fell out, her and me, when he got older. Always wanted to be in there with her, he did. Wouldn't have that. Didn't want to lose me own kid. But we do speak now. Life's too short.'

Fran was relieved when Dale returned. It was uncomfortable being told so much about him. It felt like eavesdropping. When they left the house Fran saw the curtains move next door. Dale evidently saw it too. 'Come on. You've got to meet Woods.'

Fran was introduced on the doorstep to a fierce-faced woman in men's trousers. She shook hands firmly and Fran noticed her fingers and the front of her greying hair were yellowed with nicotine. Bright, darting eyes flicked over Fran and softened as they rested on Dale.

'I'd ask you in, but I'm on me way out. You take care of 'im.' Woods laid a hand briefly on Fran's sleeve.

Dale smiled back at her. 'I take care of myself.'

'Believe that, you believe anything.' They both laughed but Woods looked sad about the eyes.

'She's like a second mother to me,' said Dale as they drove away. 'Ever since I was, what? Seven? Something like that. Turned up after school one day. I was looking for something to eat and there she was holding out a paper bag. "Like toffees?" That was all she said and we were mates.' Dale grinned and pulled out into the traffic on the main road.

'Where was your mum?'

'Another trip to the funny farm. It had happened before – more than once – but since Dad left, Ma had been doing well. We got along okay, just the two of us. At least this way I'd be on my own. No skipping out of the way when Dad came in drunk. No beatings. But I wasn't on my own. Woods took over.'

Dale swore at a driver cutting him up.

'"You'd best come back to my place for yer tea," she said. I'll never forget the taste of that shepherd's pie and tinned peas. Ma never cooked anything like that.'

He was smiling to himself almost as if Fran wasn't there. She said nothing.

'She sat me down by the fire and told me stories. She was a clippie, so it was mostly stuff about the folk on the buses. I was mesmerised by the way her cigarette stuck to her lower lip. Never fell off. Funny the things you remember.'

He laughed. 'Oh yes. She was always saying "Where's me fags?" so I learnt to notice where she'd last put her Woodbines, and she always cuffed me round the ear when I fetched them – but gently. She used to leave me breakfast – that was new. And the key was on the string if she wasn't home when I got back from school.' He paused as he swerved for a cyclist. 'She took me on her bus once. One Saturday. Sat me up the top at the back, out the way. There she was, my Woods, up and down the stairs in her uniform and her badge, ringing up tickets, full of banter. Pressing the bell – "Hold very tight, please." I was so damn proud of her.'

They pulled up at traffic lights and Dale shook his head and turned to her. 'What the hell am I telling you all this for? Boring old stuff.'

Fran protested but Dale hardly said a word after that. He'd said something earlier about staying over and sleeping in the van, but he seemed to have forgotten all about it. Fran gave up trying to start a conversation and went to sleep.

When he stopped outside her flat Dale dropped forward onto the steering wheel, wrapping both arms around his head. He groaned. 'I'm sorry. I should never have taken you there. What a fucking awful weekend. And I forgot all about what we said we'd do tomorrow.'

'It wasn't awful. I liked meeting them, seeing where…'

'Don't. You don't have to say that stuff. It's depressing and that's all there is to it.'

'Well, I didn't find it depressing.'

'You didn't grow up in it. Once upon a time it was a good place. They wrote books about it, for Chrissake. The good old East End community spirit and all that. And it did exist, alongside all the drunkenness and violence. But now. Nothing left, and two old birds sitting it out amid all that graffiti.'

Fran was silent.

'I'm always like this after I've been there. Sorry.' He banged his hands on the steering wheel. 'I ought to take you for a curry to make up for it, but it's probably too late and I haven't got any money anyway.'

'You don't have to make up for anything. And I've got some baked beans.'

10

Finals were over and done with. Fran had found herself a job at the BBC in Whiteladies Road, starting in a week. Freedom. Plenty of time to go home for a rest and to catch up with Zelda and her baby girl.

The visit started well. Harry arrived at the station to meet her in a sky-blue Morris Minor.

'It's yours. A combined degree and very belated twenty-first birthday present. Just to make sure you didn't pass your test for nothing.'

She hugged him, stunned and delighted. Her big birthday had barely been celebrated the year before. She'd kept quiet about it in Bristol, and Eleanor's illness, Charlie's absence and subsequent behaviour had put a damper on the whole thing. Only Goldie had marked it spectacularly by sending her a cheque for a hundred pounds.

'You've worked hard. It was your mother's idea, in fact. Thought it would give you some freedom. And we might see you more often. She always said you were a good driver. It's a bit elderly but it's in good shape – and all taxed and insured for the year. By then maybe you'll afford to do it yourself.'

Fancy, Mother!

'You can drive home if you like. See if you can remember how.'

She did remember, and the gift lightened the mood when she got home. Eleanor made much of her and all was sweetness and light.

Seeing Zelda and meeting baby Tamzin was not so easy and not as Fran expected. Zelda was oddly distant, in another world, absorbed in breast-feeding, unable to talk of much else.

'Pretty name, Tamzin. Where did that come from?'

'Well, you know I told you I wasn't certain whose baby it was? When she was born it was perfectly clear. She just reminded me so much of Tomasz. She's got his eyes. You remember his eyes?'

'I really don't remember what he looked like. Are you still in touch with him?'

'Nope. He never knew. I've got a few things of his, a photo, in case she ever wants to know.'

Zelda wouldn't say any more. Fran was nervous about holding the baby and failed to enthuse. All the things she'd been eager to tell her friend seemed to run away down some kind of drain in her mind. She came away bitterly disappointed.

At home, the glow of her arrival quickly wore off. With Harry at work and Eleanor busy with her own routines, Fran was bored and depressed. She couldn't stay. She didn't belong anymore. She couldn't wait to get back to Verity and Morag and take them for a drive. She told her parents she needed to prepare for her new job. Well, she did need to buy some respectable clothes. She didn't tell them she was to be a lowly filing clerk. Why spoil Mother's pride in the fact that her daughter was working at the BBC?

Back at the flat it was disappointing to find Verity was away for the weekend and Morag still hard at work. She still had exams to come, and being a medic, several more years to complete. Fran decided to give the flat a belated spring clean to give Verity a surprise on her return. Every time she passed her bedroom window, the sight of the little blue car parked outside gave her spirits a lift.

11

Verity was dead.

Fran had rarely left the flat since she heard the news. Most evenings, as she and Morag sat over cold coffee among dirty dishes, Fran expected Verity to walk in, protesting about the state of the place. Even now, in the van with Dale looking like a stranger in black trousers and a formal shirt as they drove mostly in silence to Oxfordshire, the idea kept recurring that they would see Verity when they arrived.

'Hope you can map-read,' Dale had said. 'It's somewhere near Banbury.'

Only when she saw Verity's mother walking unsteadily into the church did reality begin to hit home. Fran had met her once after a concert in the Colston Hall, a vivacious blonde often taken for Verity's elder sister. Today she looked more like her grandmother, grey and shrunken in her black clothes.

Fran stared at the coffin, trying to imagine Verity inside it, trying to make sense of how that came to be. Death was instantaneous, it was said, and she wondered about that too. How did anyone know? Verity had dived into a calm sea and hit a rock under water. An idyllic weekend in Cornwall with Mike, a celebration at the end of finals, had turned into horror.

And there was Mike, supported on either side by equally hefty rugby-playing mates, all three of them openly weeping as they processed behind Verity's parents, following the coffin out to the graveyard.

Morag had refused to come. Said she didn't do funerals and

wouldn't explain further. Fran knew she had to be here and now she understood why. Every detail she witnessed brought her nearer to grasping the truth: she would never see Verity again. Standing with all the other mourners round the grave she glimpsed the glint of the brass plate on the coffin through a gap between black coats. As the box was lowered on straps, it tilted slightly towards her and she saw the name, VERITY ROSE, the final evidence her friend was going into the earth. All that light being swallowed by darkness.

She and Dale didn't stay long at the wake. Waitresses in white aprons circulated in a room filled with antiques and porcelain, a room Eleanor would approve of. They joined the group from the Music department who had gathered outside the French doors, smoking and looking awkward in their formal clothes. Verity's mother came out and told them to help themselves to sandwiches, but she turned away quickly as if she couldn't bear to see them, living and breathing on her verandah. The rest of the older generation ignored them, behaving as if it were a cocktail party. Fran was relieved when Dale raised an eyebrow and nodded towards the door.

They talked on the return journey as they'd not been able to before.

'Goodbye, my friend,' said Dale. He loosened his tie as they passed the churchyard on the way out of the village.

Fran gave a little wave. 'Bye, Verity.'

Dale slowed for a roundabout. 'I wish one of us had been asked to say something.'

'I couldn't have. I can't think of anything worse.'

'It's just the whole focus – in what her father said – was on her piano playing. No mention of her voice. Whole facet missing.'

'I suppose so. She did have an amazing voice. Not that I…'

'Oh, it was outstanding. Really. If she'd gone for singing she'd have been at the Royal Academy. No doubt. But her mother drove it. "My daughter, the concert pianist." What was that all about?'

'She was a pianist herself, wasn't she? What she understood, maybe?'

Dale nodded. 'I suppose. But she's got ears, for Chrissake. Verity's an excellent pianist…*was*. But not in a class on her own. And Mike, solid bloke, but he doesn't have a clue about music.'

'But he was proud as hell. Now he's crashing about like an animal in a cage. Trying to get out.'

'But the cage is inside his head.'

'God knows how he's going to cope.'

Dale shook his head. 'How does anyone?'

'You were quite in love with her, weren't you?' Fran surprised herself by asking the question.

'In a kind of way.' He glanced across at Fran with a half-smile. 'But it was always the music. Nothing physical. Even before Mike.' He gave a short laugh which might have been saying, *if you believe that you'll believe anything.*

It set her wondering if Verity had had sex with Dale in the distant past. And what did it matter if she had? She drifted into a doze, aware of the rumble of the road surface and of the engine noise shifting pitch with the gradient. As they slowed through a village she was aware of Dale's profile, his hand on the gear lever and of warm Cotswold stone giving way to the comforting roll of tree-clad hills before she slipped back into sleep.

She woke to Dale's hand on her knee. 'Hey, map-reader, are we on the right road? I've been miles away. Could have missed the turning to Cirencester.'

Fran peered out as she groped for the map which had fallen on the floor.

'No. We're fine. I remember those trees.'

'How are you going to cope?' Dale resumed their earlier conversation as if there had been no gap.

Fran shrugged. 'No idea. I've got my job. Should have started last week. I couldn't. And there's results to wait for…'

'I was thinking, you could probably have Verity's job – if you don't fancy the BBC. At that gallery place on the Triangle.'

'The Arnolfini. Yes, I suppose. But no, I'd feel like I was pretending to be her. I'd like the pictures, but it would be boring, seeing all those people rushing past and no one coming in.'

'You could read.'

'But I don't need to read anymore.'

'What, never?'

'Don't be daft. But I feel a few trashy novels coming on. Just at the moment I don't even care about results. I mean, what the hell does it matter? Exams and stuff.'

'Career? The future? Life goes on.'

Fran sighed. 'But I don't have a passion like you and Verity do. Shit. Did. But you're going...'

'Sure, it makes it easier for me. This time next week I'll be in New York. Off in a couple of days – back to London, say goodbyes. All that stuff. Thank Christ the funeral was in time.'

'Can you stop? I'm desperate for a wee.'

Dale pulled in to the next gateway and they both climbed the gate into the field and went in opposite directions.

'You need it, don't you?' said Fran as they set off again. 'A funeral, I mean. To...well...to feel the burn, make it real. I did.'

Dale nodded. 'Me too.'

'Would you have come anyway?'

'Yes. No. Who knows? Kept asking myself that before the date was fixed. Glad I didn't have to choose.'

'Verity would have said go!'

'Yeah. She was so excited about the Juilliard. She'd have said, "I'm dead and you mustn't keep those guys waiting." Oh Christ. She was just such a fucking good friend.'

They both sniffed and wiped their eyes and fell silent. Fran thought of the weeks ahead, of herself and Morag in the neglected flat, of Dale's imminent departure for the States. It was too bleak for words.

As if in sympathy the heavens opened as they crested a hill and they drove on to the dismal slap of the windscreen wipers.

Dale peered up at the dark sky. 'Reckon she's telling us to get a grip.'

'That would be just like her. I'm glad it was sunny for her though. She fixed that too. Oh God, I sound like it was her blooming wedding. She. Was. Not. Even. There.'

'Oh, but she was. Don't you think?'

'I guess. Laughing up her sleeve. Whatever that means.'

'Mm. Nothing worse than a burial in the rain. All dripping yew trees and black umbrellas.' After a pause Dale added, 'At least we don't have to face the lovely Joanna in a big hat.'

'What? What're you talking about?'

'Mother of the bride? She'd be unbearable. Gushing all over the place.'

'Dale, what a horrible thing to say.'

'I know. I am horrible.'

'She's a lovely person and she's devastated…'

Dale grunted. 'The whole smug edifice of middle England, middle class-ness blown apart…'

'That's vile.'

'And true. I know it's vile. But you know how it gets to me. That house, all the trappings, the whole bloody manicured village. I mean, it was quite grand, you have to admit. But it didn't do them any good, did it? Under all that pretension they just crack like you and me.'

So I'm on your side of the class divide these days. Aloud she said, 'They're just people, Dale. And the things are just things.'

He gave her a sideways smile. 'I know.'

They were approaching the outskirts of Bristol. If only she didn't have to go back to the flat. She couldn't face being alone. Nor could she bear to have to tell Morag about the day.

Dale spoke into her thoughts. 'Come back with me? Stay over at my place? I don't want to be alone.'

Dale let her into his room and fixed up the striped blanket which served as a curtain over the window.

'If you put the kettle on, I'll fetch us something to eat.'

He turned to go as Fran burrowed in her bag for her purse.

'My treat – but with any luck this will be free.' He tapped the side of his nose with a finger and vanished.

She'd only been to Dale's a few times before. The whole place reeked of garlic and spice from the Chinese restaurant downstairs, but the rent was cheap and he could practise whenever he wanted, a necessity denied by previous landladies. Books stretched along one wall on planks held apart by loose bricks, and sheet music and LPs were stored in an arrangement of orange boxes stacked precariously one on top of the other. Another orange box served as a table. There was a battered leather pouffe, an upright chair, and an old armchair.

On a rickety bamboo cupboard beside the bed a notebook and pen was lined up neatly. Next to it was a photograph, framed in passepartout, of a middle-aged woman in a floral overall. She was standing against a brick wall, holding a huge black cat and laughing into the camera. A long thin face with a big nose and glasses, recognisable as a younger version of the neighbour she'd met on the visit to Dale's mother. Fran was oddly touched by the picture.

The last time she'd been in this room had been embarrassing. Dale had offered to lend her his recording of Dylan's "Mr Tambourine Man" and had specifically told her to come round the next afternoon for a coffee. He'd hardly greeted her when she arrived, muttering that he was busy composing or transposing – some musical thing she didn't understand. When she made coffee he ignored her and let his go cold. The album, *Bringing It All Back Home*, was lying on the floor. Eventually she tore a page from her notebook and made a cartoon drawing of Dale as Mr Cello Man with his profile in place of the scroll and arms emerging from the body of the cello to play the instrument. She scribbled a few words and left, leaving the note in place of the album. He'd never made any reference to it.

Now she realised she still had the LP. Would he want to take it to America? Should she offer to buy it off him? Before she could find answers Dale was back with a paper bag already patched with oily stains.

'Chicken chow mein, pork balls, even some prawn sesame toast. All free, like I said.'

'How d'you manage that?'

'Mrs Wong has a soft spot for me, thinks I need feeding up. Plus it's late on a Monday night. Not likely to get any more takers.'

Dale cleared a pile of manuscript paper off the orange box, unpacked the bag and produced chopsticks.

'I can see you've never used them before.'

'Never had Chinese before.'

Dale whistled through his teeth and showed her how to balance the sticks between her fingers, but she couldn't achieve a mouthful.

'Go on, use fingers. Sometimes I wonder where you've been all your life.'

She persisted with the chopsticks but was defeated by the noodles.

Dale took pity and fetched her a fork. 'I've got something I've been saving. Must be drunk before I go. Just the thing for a day like today.' He pulled a bottle from behind a pile of books. 'Best Kentucky bourbon. Cuts the grease like nothing else.' He poured it into two tumblers.

He was right. The whiskey scorched down her throat and offset the gooey batter of the pork balls. Wonderful.

'The best bit is not having to wash up.'

All the same Fran took her fork and the chopsticks to the sink. 'You know that's a whole half hour I haven't thought about Verity. She always had to wash up, wouldn't let us leave it for the morning.'

Dale's hands held her waist, pulling her away. 'You can leave things here.'

'It makes me feel almost guilty. I don't mean not washing up. I mean not thinking of her. Silly, really.'

'I was thinking the same. How quickly life takes hold. The need to eat – I was ravenous. Like we're saying, "Don't take us with you. We need to live." Something like that.'

She could feel the heat of his breath through her hair.

'But then again, I'd give everything to have her here right now.'

'I keep thinking she'll be there when I get back to the flat. Like she'll be wondering where I've got to. I ought…'

Dale's arms slipped further round her waist. 'Relax. Turn off that blooming tap. Those chopsticks must be cleaner than they've ever been. Come.'

He sat her on the end of the bed. 'Let's have some music.'

He slid a record out of its sleeve and placed it on the turntable, lifting the arm and lowering the needle carefully.

'I've still got your album – the Dylan. I'll bring it back…'

'Shh. No, keep it in memory of me.'

The hiss of static gave way to a sound that filled the room like wind in a tunnel.

'Brahms. This will be soothing. Verity loved these sonatas. You'll have heard them in the flat – we used to play them together, especially this first one in E minor.'

He shared out the remains of the Jim Beam and sat close beside her, raising his glass. 'To Verity.'

They clinked and drank.

'You're shaking.'

It was true, as if the music had loosened some vital tie which usually held her together.

'I can't help it. I don't know what's the matter with me. Well, I do know, but I can't…I can't stop. I don't… Oh, Dale, I don't…' She was sobbing as she hadn't since being sent to bed as a child for a crime she didn't understand.

Dale held her close and stroked her hair and her back for what could have been hours but which maybe was only minutes. When she pulled away she saw his face too was wet with tears.

He passed her glass. 'What a pair. Drink up. What you need is a massage. Relax you. I'm pretty good at that.' He held up a hand. 'And it doesn't have to lead anywhere. Only if it's okay for you.'

She hardly registered what he was saying and was only too glad to be free of her clothes and stretched between cool sheets in his bed.

What happened next was a miracle, his touch somehow moving with the rhythm, with the weaving of piano and cello, so it seemed she was being massaged by the music. It was as if his hands were breathing for her and she drifted halfway into sleep.

When she surfaced again Dale was rolling out her spine like dough, making it longer and longer. Her body felt heavy and fluid as if spread like thick honey. After a while she was aware the heaviness was not just the depth of her relaxation, but the weight of his body on top of her. His chin nuzzled her neck, and his tongue licked her ear.

Then she felt suddenly light and cold as his weight lifted off her. She heard him turning the record over and music filled the room again. She shivered as he rejoined her and slid his fingers the length of her spine. When he turned her over and kissed her she had never felt so open and loving, as if she were in love with the universe. She could feel him hard against her thigh. More than anything she wanted him inside her. She realised she had been in love with a Dale for a very long time. How come she had never noticed?

He laid his cheek against hers. 'Is this okay? Do you want this, Fran? Because if you don't, I'll get up this minute.'

She moved against him. 'I want you, Dale. I really do. Now. Come on.'

His sigh turned into a groan as he pressed the heel of his hand into her pubic bone, finding her wetness with his fingers, making it flow. She cried out as his hand moved away and arched her back. He started to enter her, pulled away.

Go on, screamed Fran inside her head, *you can't stop now.*

But Dale was scrabbling in a drawer beside the bed. Of course, a sheath – she should have thought of it.

'These buggers are a pain. Always ruins the moment. But worth it.'

She could smell the rubber, and yes, the moment was ruined. Not by the French letter but by that little word, 'always'. She knew, of course, but it was the worst moment to be reminded of Dale's many women.

Then he was back, heavy and warm. He kissed her mouth and her breasts and the moment was saved. He moved gently inside her, gradually moving deeper, working at the resistance he found with a grunt of surprise. She lifted her pelvis, pulling his buttocks towards her, hardly noticing the brief sharp pain of the rupture. She came in a long, noisy crescendo which drowned his climax, and they sunk together into a sweaty sleep, her back curled into his stomach, his arms wrapped around her.

In the dawn Fran slid out to the toilet on the landing. Returning, she stood at the door of the room taking in where she was in the dim grey light. Dale's waistcoat was hanging over a chair, the rest of their clothes in a heap on the floor. His cello leant in a corner, its curves draped in purple silk. Was she really here? Had she and Dale really made love? She unhooked the window blanket from its nail, and held it across her as she peered out at the pavements of Cotham Hill. Nobody stirred.

Dale lay on his back, his arms flung out. She wriggled back under the covers and they snuggled into each other. Sleepy noises, her head on his chest. Bodies warm, pungent, fitting together, his heartbeat in her ear. His arm came round her back, rolled her on top of him. A grunt and a lazy sigh later and she was straddling him, smiling down as he opened sudden wide eyes.

'Jesus! I thought I'd died and gone to heaven.'

'Shh!'

As she leaned forward her hair brushed his face. He caught her breasts in his hands and strained his mouth upward. Then she broke free, grabbed his hands to steady herself and rode him, faster and faster, her breasts bouncing as the first rays of sunlight fell across his face. The old bed creaked as he joined her rhythm. Then he was trying to break his hands away but she held them fast.

'Fran, Fran! No more johnnies! And how the hell can I withdraw if you're on top?'

'Who cares!'

Later he sat on the edge of the bed and stroked her hair. 'It's all flaming in the sun. Beautiful Fran – and that was beautiful. I always thought you were amazing – you would *be* amazing, but, even so, you took me by surprise. And there was another surprise. I'd no idea.' He nodded towards the stain on the sheet. 'Your first time. You never said…'

'Bit embarrassing. At my great age. And I didn't want to scare you off. Actually none of that's true. I never even thought of it.' Which, to Fran's surprise, was the truth in spite of all her previous agonising over whether and when to 'do it' with Charlie. Thank God she hadn't.

Dale grinned. 'I guess that's quite an honour, then.' He kissed her lightly on the cheek. 'One thing I do have to say – you're a fast learner. Christ! You are the most…the most magnificently sensuous woman.'

'I am?'

'You know you are. How could you not know what you did to me?'

'Easily.'

'Know it now.'

'So you've changed your mind.'

'Uhh?'

'Thinking I was frigid. You remember?'

'That callow youth! What did he know? Zilch. But you always were someone apart, special. Not like the others.' He paused, staring at the floor. 'I have to ask, was it okay? Was it…?'

'It was…better than anything I ever expected. That's a bit tame. But I can't put it in words.'

'Me neither.' Dale stood up. 'But I might manage notes. Might it be something like this?'

He sat with his cello between his legs, adjusted the tuning, closed his eyes for a few moments and started to play. The notes began to fill the room, pouring across the floor until she was floating on sound and the vibrations opened and stretched her senses like the massage he had given her the night before. She was hardly aware when he stopped playing because the music was still moving in the room, still raining down on her.

'Like that?'

'Yes. Like that. What was it?'

'I just made it up.'

'Wow!' was all Fran could manage.

'I'll call it Francesca.' Dale put the cello in its case and started to pull on some clothes. 'I've got to go. Sorry to rush, but I've got a load of stuff to do up at the department. And, Fran, you do know, don't you? This can't go anywhere. My music, the Juilliard… Christ, that sounds crass, after what we just had, but…'

He stopped and gazed across at her.

'Of course. I know you're going. Nothing's stopping that. You and your cello… If I don't know that by now…'

He grinned, wobbling on one leg to pull on a sock.

Fran leapt up from the bed.

'I'm going. I don't want you to leave me here. It'll make me sad.'

On her way home Fran passed strangers who smiled at her. Although it was a dull day, the shops, buses and cars pulsed with light – as if she were seeing the world in colour after living in a black and white movie. The trees seemed fresh-washed.

When she reached the square she stepped up into the garden, past the phone box which had become the place where she heard about birth and death: Gaye telling her Zelda had a baby girl; phoning Verity's home with Dale after she failed to return from the weekend and still wasn't there when Dale came to collect some sheet music. She could still hear Dale's voice after the call: 'But she's on track for a first. She can't be…' Yes, Verity and Dale, it was all about the music.

She stood under her tree, the only tree, which was opposite her window and pulled down a leaf from an overhanging branch. She held it to her cheek, feeling its coolness, breathing in a transfusion of green energy, then examined it, noticing the pattern of veins and the haze of fine down on the underside.

How different her only two experiences of making love had been. In the one she had been as open and yielding as a buttercup to a bee, in the other streaming with light and fire – powerful beyond anything she'd ever known. She grinned, her body soft inside, and made for the flat, ready to face the absence of Verity, wondering how she could be so happy and so sad at the same time.

12

The summer drizzle was chilled by a sharp wind funnelling down Blackboy Hill from the Downs, causing pedestrians on their way to work to clench their elbows to their sides and button in their faces. Fran threaded her way grimly towards the BBC.

Dale had departed for London en route to New York. She'd offered to help him pack up.

'No need,' he said. 'One box of books. One box of records, one bag of clothes. One record player, one cello. It'll take me about half an hour to get that lot in the van. No stuff. Can't do stuff.'

They'd met for a farewell drink. All she could think of was wanting him, but his mind was already in America. Had their magical night ever really happened? As he was leaving he pressed something into her palm and closed her fingers over it.

'I found this. Used to belong to my grandmother. Amazing woman – played the fiddle like a demon, in the pub every Saturday night. Thought you might like it.'

And he was gone. No tearful farewell, no hug. As if they had never been lovers. She'd opened her hand to find a tiny hare, the sort you find on a charm bracelet.

Her life had fallen apart. All the people who mattered were gone. Such pain and such joy and now nothing. No Verity. No Dale.

She and Morag had nothing to say to each other without Verity. And Zelda was lost to her too. The filing job was dead boring, even if it was the BBC, and this damn weather wasn't helping.

Head down she pushed her way through the glass doors, shook

the rain out of her hair and made for the stairs. On the first-floor landing, laughter burst from a door followed by a tall, loose-limbed man who nearly knocked her over.

He stopped in his tracks and stared at her. 'Good God! Good God!' He stepped back, apologised and disappeared up the next flight, muttering under his breath. Fran frowned after him and shrugged.

In the canteen at lunchtime she noticed him sitting alone at a table in the far corner and chose a seat round the corner, out of sight. Before long she was aware of someone hovering at her elbow.

'Excuse me, I wanted to apologise for my behaviour this morning. It must have seemed rude.'

She laughed. 'Just a bit odd. You looked as if you'd seen a ghost.'

He stood uncertainly, turning over the coins in his pocket, looking down at her. With his mousy schoolboy haircut and grey flannel trousers, he reminded Fran of old photos of her father in his student days.

'Well, aren't you going to tell me? What it was all about?'

'I'd rather not tell you here. Would you have a drink with me this evening?'

'The mystery deepens. How about The Blackboy?'

Fran was glad to have somewhere to go after work. Geoffrey, not Geoff, with a G, not a J, as he had introduced himself, was not bad-looking in an old-fashioned sort of way. He hadn't seen the joke when she'd told him her name was Fran with an F and Fran not Francesca. But in any case, she didn't want a relationship. No one was going to replace Dale. But she could do with some company.

The pub was nearly empty and she bought herself a half pint under the gaze of two old men at the end of the bar and took it to a corner table. When Geoffrey arrived, he came straight over and sat down eagerly, then leapt up again, nearly knocking her drink off the table.

'Sorry, sorry. There I go again.'

Eventually he was settled with his pint, his legs packed safely under the table.

'So what's the story?'

'Please don't laugh.'

Which was guaranteed to make her want to. She pursed her lips and caught her glass as his knee jolted the table again.

'I went to a fortune teller.'

Fran gritted her teeth.

'She told me I would meet a red-headed woman. Showed me the picture. There she was, sitting on a kind of throne with all this red hair.'

He lifted his big hands in an expansive gesture and she grabbed her glass although this time there was no need. He took a long draught of his bitter.

'That's it?'

Again the hands held wide as if he had explained everything.

'What? You mean when you bumped into me you were thinking I was the red-haired woman on the throne?'

Geoffrey nodded.

'But I can't be the only redhead in Bristol.'

'You were the only one at the top of the stairs at that moment.'

'No throne.'

'Doesn't stop you being a queen.' He spoke softly and colour flooded into his face like wine filling a glass.

Uh, uh. How corny was this going to get? 'But you were in a state before you saw me. You shot out of that room.'

'Well, I made the mistake of telling one of my colleagues about the reading and he thought it was hilarious. He told me... Well, what he actually said was that I was too much up my own arse. And I was a bit put out. I was on my way out, when he said I should go find myself a woman. And I rushed out of the door and bumped straight into you.'

Fran raised her eyebrows and shrugged. Geoffrey clearly thought they were in some way fated to meet. 'Just because some woman in Portishead with a shawl over her head tells you about a red-haired woman, it doesn't mean we are meant for each other.'

'How did you know she was in Portishead?'

Fran groaned. 'I didn't. It's just the sort of place a fortune teller would hang out.'

'We're telepathic, you see.'

'Nonsense.' Normally she would have been intrigued by this story, but there was something about Geoffrey that was making her uneasy. 'What made you go?'

'Saw an ad in the newsagent's window. Nothing going on in my life. You know the sort of thing.'

She knew the sort of thing all right, but was not about to say so. She attempted a teasing tone. 'So she had a crystal ball and all the works, did she?'

'Oh, yes.' Geoffrey stopped short, seeing her face. 'You promised you wouldn't laugh.'

'I didn't actually.' She relented at the sight of his earnest face. 'Go on. Tell me what she did.'

'It was a different rate according to what you had. I had the full works – crystal ball, hand reading, tarot cards, personal item…'

'And how much did she want to know about you before she started?' Fran was determined to be cynical.

'Nothing. That was what was so impressive. She didn't even know my name. She said, "You're my five o'clock, that's all you are to me." And then told me things about my life she couldn't have known. Except she did.'

Fran looked at her watch.

'Don't go. I've done nothing but talk about me. I don't know anything about you.'

'Actually you haven't told me much about you either. But you've explained your strange behaviour and now I really have to go.'

'There's no need to be scared. Really. I wish you'd stay.'

She hesitated.

'There was something else she told me.'

'What, then?'

'Something she saw. In the crystal ball. She saw a big letter F. Kept seeing it she said, very clearly.'

'I need another drink,' said Fran.

Fran woke to a room full of light. She pulled the covers over her eyes, noting the pain in her head and the foul taste in her mouth. She'd sat up half the night with Morag over a bottle of cheap wine. Morag was mad about a chauvinist doctor at the hospital, Fran was secretly sad about Dale and they were both still missing Verity. Now the sun was making a brash pathway across her bed where a soothing full moon had been earlier. She fetched water and swallowed aspirin. It

113

was Saturday. She'd wait for the post and then go out before Geoffrey turned up to take her on one of his walks.

She'd seen him a few times in the weeks since their first meeting. A hesitant friendship had developed, once Geoffrey had stopped exclaiming with wonder at every coincidence as if they were destined to be together.

What she wanted was a letter from Dale. An address, any kind of news. It would be a long wait, she knew. He'd told her he didn't 'do' letters. She could, of course, write to him at the school. A friendly, newsy, well-wishing note. She'd tried it. She couldn't write such a note.

She padded out to the kitchen and put the kettle on. Last slice of bread. No sign of Morag, so she put it in the toaster. Did Dale ever think of her? Or was she just another of his women, however much he'd said she was different? If only she could talk to Verity, who'd known him better than anyone. Zelda had never met him, and anyway, their lives had diverged. Hers seemed to have come to a dead end. Zelda had her baby. Dale had his music. What did she have? A boring job and a guy who bought her canteen coffee.

As she scraped the marmalade jar, the mail slapped onto the mat. She sifted it quickly for an airmail letter. Nothing. But the last envelope was addressed to her. She recognised the flowery handwriting and took it to read in the sun.

Dear Fran
It is so long since we had a chat and your old aunt is missing you. I feel badly I did not keep in touch after our last time together. The fact is Nell wasn't too pleased about it, heaven knows why. Am I such a bad influence?

As you know your mother and I do not always see eye to eye – which will probably not be a great surprise to you. You are a grown-up now and I think I can say these things.

I am still loving my flat on the harbour. Wish I'd moved years ago. It suits me down to the ground and I'm pleased to be away from the traffic – it had got so busy.

Well, I have been thinking about you a lot and decided it was silly not to get in touch. I didn't want to have regrets later.

You are my only niece and we used to have good times together. Maybe we can again. Of course you must be very busy, but if you want a break, there's always a spare bed here for you.
Love and kisses,
Goldie
P.S. I think it's time we dropped the Auntie, it makes me feel old.

Fran held the letter in her hand as she chewed her toast. She liked Goldie's frankness, the comment about Mother – 'don't always see eye to eye'. She could imagine Goldie chuckling as she wrote it.

13

Standing at the bus stop the following Monday, Fran found herself gazing at a display of tampons in the chemist shop window. A whole set of thoughts and feelings crystallised at the sight of the pyramid of neat blue and green boxes.

It was an age since she had bought any tampons. The nagging anxiety which she'd been pushing away for days, weeks even, could no longer be ignored. A rash of heat brought her out in a sweat in spite of the cool breeze. She was pregnant. She'd rationalised about being irregular. She'd told herself that Verity dying and Dale going was enough to disrupt anyone's cycle. She'd made increasingly desperate calculations while constantly checking her underwear. But her body knew the truth.

There was nobody to turn to. Morag would be right in there with her rampant feminism and all the latest news of the pro-abortion lobby. It was the last thing she wanted to hear. She avoided Geoffrey. There was only one thing on her mind and she couldn't talk to him about it.

She had to be sure.

Visiting the surgery was an intimidating prospect, but in practice she found the process straightforward. No one eyed her disapprovingly.

When the test proved positive her heart gave an unexpected leap. But after that, panic and unanswerable questions closed in. Should she tell Dale? If only he was still here. Would she keep it? What would he think? What would Mother say? How on earth would she cope if she did keep it? If she did nothing she would end up with responsibility for a small creature who would be utterly dependent on her. The thought made her sick with terror. She'd been given a number to ring if she wanted advice and counselling, but how could that help?

After work she walked and walked, but she couldn't outstrip the fear. It seemed outrageous to destroy a life that had sprung from the night with Dale which she still held as a sacred memory. Yet the responsibility for that life was overwhelming. And all the time the sense of urgency grew as she imagined the tiny being growing inside her.

The next day she stayed at her desk in her lunch hour until the place was deserted, pulled out Goldie's letter and dialled the number at the top. The moment she heard her voice, tears pricked her eyes, unsteadying her words. Could she come for the weekend?

'Not this weekend, sweetie. I'm spoken for. An individual I met at a whist drive. Taking me to the races, set to win myself a fortune.' Goldie chattered on.

When would she be free? Would it be too late? Then she was going on holiday. But no, she had the dates wrong. The weekend was free after all. It was fixed. Fran found herself crying with relief. As she replaced the receiver she felt she was being watched. Geoffrey was standing in the doorway.

'At last. You've been avoiding me. I thought we were friends.' No flicker of a smile.

She couldn't deny it. 'Things on my mind. Been very busy.'

He nodded slowly. 'I can't get you out of my head.'

'Excuse me.' One of Fran's colleagues came back from lunch.

For a moment Geoffrey seemed about to bar the door, then he stepped aside, came and stood over her. His obsession made her uneasy and she agreed to meet for a drink to get rid of him. She must use the opportunity; make it clear this was a friendship and no more.

Geoffrey was waiting with their drinks at a secluded table. He started talking before she sat down. 'Why the tears earlier? I saw.'

Fran shook her head, shrugged the question away.

'I don't want to intrude, but how else do I look after the girl who's been sent to be my soulmate? And, as you know, it is decreed that I am to look after you.'

Fran sighed. Was he serious? His eyes were smiling at her, but kindly. He made a helpless circling with his hands. What was disarming about Geoffrey was that he knew he was being ridiculous, yet he carried on regardless.

'I only want to help.' He touched her on the arm.

The warmth of that simple gesture melted her. It seemed so long since anyone had touched her. Her tears flowed, washing away her defences along with the careful preparation. 'I'm pregnant.'

Geoffrey stared at her as if she'd announced she was the lost Princess Anastasia. Finally he spoke. 'But it can't be me.'

Fran choked into laughter. 'Hardly! Even if you got pregnant through kissing, it couldn't be you. Didn't anyone ever…'

'Don't mock your *friend in need who's a friend indeed*.' Geoffrey was dead serious.

She gulped her drink. What the hell did he know about all this that could be remotely helpful? 'There's nothing you can do.'

'I think there is. Something we can do together at least.' He put his hands together and Fran thought he was about to suggest a prayer.

'Oh yes?' She was ashamed at how heavily sarcastic she sounded. After all, he was only trying to be nice.

'We can get married.'

Now it was Fran's turn to be speechless. Was he mocking? No. Was he so naïve he thought this was remotely possible? Was he quite simply as mad as a hatter? 'I can't take that seriously.'

'It is meant absolutely seriously. It all makes sense now. This is why we were supposed to meet. This is my destiny. Your knight in shining armour.'

'A very present help in trouble.'

'I didn't know you were religious.'

'I'm not! I don't know where that came from. And that's just it – you don't know the first thing about me and you are suggesting we get married. You are actually stark, staring bonkers, aren't you?'

'I don't have any details worked out. Naturally I was not expecting—'

'Details! What details? Jesus, I need another drink.' Fran moved impatiently towards the bar.

He raised his voice. 'I don't think you should. I've read it's not a good idea, especially in the first months.'

She walked back to the table and banged her empty glass down in front of him. 'Perhaps you'd like to tell the whole pub? I'll have you know, I'll be the one who decides what I'm going to drink!'

She grabbed her coat and stalked out. She'd call in at the off-licence and see what inspiration came with getting drunk. Gin. That was the answer. Why hadn't she thought of it before? A bottle of gin and a hot bath. Wasn't that the way to get rid of babies? It was worth a try. The route took her past Dale's old flat. There were proper curtains drawn across the window now.

She thought of the striped blanket and of Dale as he had been that morning, lying half asleep as they started to make love. When they made their baby. Their baby. She could hear the sound of his cello as he played that amazing piece – the piece he called Francesca.

When she got to the off-licence she carried on walking. It was unthinkable. Every bit as unthinkable as marrying Geoffrey. She shuddered at the thought of drowning Dale's baby in gin. Roll on a sane weekend with Goldie.

Goldie welcomed her with her with ice-cold Pimm's and coronation chicken. 'I thought we were due a little celebration!'

After the meal they sat on Goldie's balcony in the sun, drinking coffee and watching the steamer leave for the Isle of Wight.

'So what's your trouble?' said Goldie.

'Trouble?'

'Of course. I can see there is one. You may as well tell me. I can keep a secret and it's what aunts are for.'

'I have this ridiculous man wanting to marry me. He hasn't even kissed me and he wants to get married.'

'That's unusual for a young man these days. In my day a beau might have held back, but nowadays…'

Fran smiled inwardly. With Goldie, a past admirer was always a *beau*. Someone of current interest would be an *individual* until he became established enough to earn a description, such as the entertaining Mr Cooper, the culture vulture Mr Vernon and so on. Next she'd use their first names, but no Sids, Berts or Freds were allowed. It was Sidney this and Bertram that and only Goldie could roll Reginald off her tongue to make it sound exotic and seductive.

'It's not so much holding back. I don't think he *wants* to really.'

Goldie's carefully pencilled eyebrows shot up. 'Why do you think he wants to get married?'

'He thinks we're meant to be together.' Fran couldn't say any more.

They watched a yacht under sail slipping back into harbour on the rising tide, silent except for the flurry of wind at the edge of the foresail. The figure at the helm looked up and waved and Goldie raised her glass in reply.

'Well, if that's all, it's no problem. I could have sworn when you rang up you were going to tell me you were pregnant.'

Fran felt Goldie's eyes upon her as the heat rose up her neck and flooded her face.

'You just have to send him packing. Unless of course you fancy the fella, in which case you may need to give him a few lessons.'

How come she could tell Geoffrey when she couldn't bring herself to tell Goldie? Telling Geoffrey had been a bit like telling someone on a train whom you don't expect to see again. Which was all the more reason not to marry him.

Goldie kept returning to the subject of Geoffrey. She would not pooh-pooh the fortune-teller and suggested a shy man might be worth his weight in gold. Was he good-looking? What did he do? Was he generous? Did he have a sense of humour?

'Oh, for God's sake, Goldie! Shut up!'

Goldie stopped in mid-sentence, the eyebrows shooting up.

'Oh, Goldie, I'm sorry…but…you see…'

'I was right wasn't I?'

'Of course you were blooming right. What the hell am I going to do?'

'You're going to have a nip of my special medicine and you're going to go to bed and get a good night's sleep and we'll talk about what next in the morning.'

*

Fran looked past the harbour entrance and out to sea. The stars were bright and she wondered if they were as bright in New York. Was Dale looking out at the same stars? Of course he wasn't. It would still be daylight in America. Damn Dale for not being here. Damn Dale for not writing.

How could she possibly talk about the baby to anybody but him? How could she think of not telling him? It's just as much his baby as mine, she thought. He'd be furious not to be told. He had a right to know. Then they could work out what to do together.

She'd write immediately when she got back and mail it express. She could go up to the Royal Fort and get the address from the music department. It was obvious. Why hadn't she thought of it before? Fran felt a great weight lift from her and she slept more deeply than she had in weeks.

Goldie was less enthusiastic about Fran's strategy. 'A man with a career? In the US of A?' she said, making it sound like a royal appointment. 'I just wonder how such an individual might react.'

'But he has a right to know…'

'Rights have to be earned.' Goldie examined her nail varnish. 'A bird in the hand is worth two in the bush.'

'Meaning?'

'When it comes to husbands. If this Geoffrey is willing to care for you both… It's happened before. And, well, I'm just saying, I'd keep your options open.'

'So you think I should go ahead and have it? Keep it?'

Goldie got up out of her chair and walked to the window. It was so long before she spoke that Fran wondered if she'd heard.

'Only you can decide. But then again, it's the worst time to be making decisions. When you're afraid and your hormones are playing games with you. I don't like the idea of abortion, but you've got to be sure you want a real baby before you go ahead. This won't be a nice quiet doll to remind you of your beau. It'll be a real, live, hollering bundle of troubles. But if you do go ahead, then keep it. Whatever you do, don't let anyone persuade you to give it up for adoption. That's the worst possible thing you could do.'

It was the longest and most serious speech she'd heard Goldie make.

'I tell you what,' Goldie continued. 'You were telling me about your friend Zelda. Why don't you go and see her while you're here? Talk to her. Change a few nappies while you're about it?'

But Fran couldn't face Zelda just yet. 'It's a good idea, Gold. But I just want to get that letter written. I'll see Zelda another time. And anyway, like I said, I promised to go and see Mother and Dad. Can't do everything. And no, I won't be telling them. Not yet.'

14

As Fran sat down with her parents to a lunch of cold roast beef and jacket potatoes, Eleanor smiled across the table. Her eyes had a dangerous glitter. 'I heard from Betty Marsden last week. Joanna's getting married in the spring – to the Payne boy. They're having the do at the Country Club. Coleslaw?'

Fran attempted a light-hearted tone. 'Funny. She always said Bill Payne was boring, but I had a feeling she'd end up marrying him.' She helped herself to Harry's robustly sliced cabbage salad.

'And the Wises are having a marquee in their garden for Annabel.'

'Uh huh.' Fran felt her throat constrict and the heat rising from her stomach.

'Annabel. She's getting married in July.'

'Yes, you said. Still Jeremy, I suppose?' Fran cut the fat and gristle off her meat and pushed it to the side of her plate.

Eleanor eyed Fran's pile of stringy rejects before she replied, 'Oh yes. You don't seem very interested.'

'Don't I?' Fran rolled her eyes in Harry's direction and he gave a barely perceptible shrug. She wished she hadn't come. She was being confronted with the enormity of revealing her situation to them, or more exactly, to Mother.

Eleanor glared at Harry and changed tack. 'How is your social life these days, Francesca?'

Actually I'm pregnant by a penniless musician who's escaped to America and I'm considering having an abortion, but I can't afford it. 'Not a lot going on, really.'

'I'd have thought you'd meet a lot of interesting people at the BBC.'

'Oh, it's a fine place to work.' There flashed into Fran's mind an image of Geoffrey drooping in the doorway of her office.

'If I were you, I'd be looking about. You don't want to leave it too long.'

'Leave what too long, Mother?'

'You know perfectly well what I mean.'

'Let the poor girl be, Eleanor.'

'If you really want to know, I have had a proposal – in the last week.'

Harry paused and looked up, then continued to massage a drop of red wine thoughtfully into the polished surface of the table.

Eleanor's fork stopped in mid-air. She smiled, almost coy. Fran pictured her greeting her next bridge party with just this expression. *Why did I have to tell her that?*

'Well? Who is he? Why have you not told us before? Why are we not meeting this young man? We need to see if he is the right one for you.'

'Mother! I'm not marrying him.'

'Well, I think we have to see about that.'

'We? *We?*' Fran nearly choked on a particularly chunky piece of cabbage stalk.

'What is his name?'

'Geoffrey Henderson, if you must know.'

'Where does he come from? What does he do?'

'He's a production assistant. Lives in Clifton. No idea where he comes from, Billericay maybe.'

'Oh dear! You're not...'

'Oh, Mother! Joke! I don't know where he comes from. He may have mentioned Watford, come to think of it.'

'It's no laughing matter. And you can take that smirk off your face, Harry.'

Harry pulled a serious face.

'When will we meet this Geoffrey?'

'Probably never.' Fran wished she'd never mentioned Geoffrey.

'Now, that is a very silly attitude. Your father and I are here to help.'

'I don't need any help.' Fran heard her voice crack. She cleared her throat and sucked wine into her mouth. What an ambush words were.

'Leave it, Nell.' Harry wiped the table with his napkin, then flicked the stain out of sight onto his lap.

Her father rarely used Eleanor's old nickname. It silenced her, and Harry went on to talk about the arbour of old-fashioned roses he was establishing in the garden.

On an impulse Fran stopped at Zelda's house on the way out of the village. She knocked on the kitchen door and waited, but there was no reply. She scribbled a note with her new phone number on a scrap of paper and pushed it under the door.

The phone was ringing as she arrived home. It was Zelda.

'*So* sorry to miss you. Why on earth didn't you let us know you were coming? We were only walking on the beach.'

'I didn't know I was coming until I did.'

'Great you've got a phone at last. How come?'

'Morag had it put in. She needs it these days – for when she's on call at the hospital.'

'We'll be able to talk at last.'

Zelda was chatting on as if there had never been a gap in their friendship.

'You don't write anymore. I've no idea what you're up to. Tell me, tell me.'

She sounded just like the old Zelda. She was horrified to hear about Verity.

'I almost felt like I knew her. You talked about her so much. You must miss her.'

Fran perched on the kitchen windowsill next to the phone. She couldn't tell her about Dale over the phone.

'It helps I've got a job. At the BBC – no, you won't be seeing me on telly. Just a lowly filing clerk.'

'Don't tell me you need a degree for that. I used to do that. Are there some hunky men there?'

'Not exactly. I mean, I expect so, but...'

'You sound a bit down. Well, I suppose you would do, but what else is wrong?'

Fran swallowed. 'The job's boring…'

'That's not all, is it? Fran? *Tell* me.'

'I think I'm pregnant.' It was almost as if she could see the words escaping down the telephone into Zelda's ear. 'Actually, I don't just think it.'

'You're sure?'

'It's confirmed.'

'Oh, my God! You of all people. Have you told…? Are you going ahead with it?'

'I'm not sure, Zel. That's the problem. I'm not like you…'

'Who's the…'

'I can't talk about that just now.' Fran stood up and paced the length of the phone cord. She could hear Morag in the bathroom.

Zelda took the hint. 'If you want any help…you know. Let me know. And, Fran? Can I just say one thing? You won't think I'm poking my nose in?'

'Go on.'

'The only way it works is to be selfish. You have to think – this is your life. Is that what you want? That and nothing else, 'cos believe me, there won't be much else. Not for ages. If you're selfish it will be okay. And that's for the baby too.'

'Right.'

'You okay, Fran?'

'Yes, I'm fine.'

'Like hell you are. It's big, Fran. Ring me again tomorrow. Best after seven, Tamzin should be down by then.'

Fran put down the phone and went straight to bed, attempting to get down on paper the words to Dale that had been forming in her head on the drive home. She wrote and rewrote it, scribbled out words, wrote over the top and finally dropped it on the floor. It was as good as she could make it. She would sleep on it, read it again in the morning, then copy it out and post it on the way to work. She fell into a deep sleep.

She was on the way out of the door when the postman arrived. An airmail letter. She held it in her hand, side by side with her own letter with Dale's name on it, ready for the address. She fingered the red and blue flashing round the edge and turned back into the flat in slow motion.

> My very dear Fran
> Sorry it's taken me so long to write. You may not believe it but once my feet touched the ground I've been thinking of you lots.

Fran's heart made a ridiculous leap.

> This has been breakthrough time for me. A new dimension of playing. I always knew it was there, like a secret drawer in a box. It is what always drove me, right from school. But I only ever achieved more of the same. Practising and practising and only getting a better technique, more brilliant expression. But this is different, Fran. I can't explain. It's the same old cello, same bow, same me. It's something like I tried to express when I played to you that morning – I almost touched it then.
> How? Reuben – my teacher – said stop practising! He said go sit under a tree. He said lie on the grass and watch the clouds, really watch so you forget where you are. I did that for one practice a day and he would say, 'You are still practising, my friend.' So eventually I dared to stop altogether. Hard after all those years, the guilt! After a week it happened. I felt it when I played for him. But when I'd finished he said nothing. In fact I thought he was asleep. I started to pack up and go. But as soon as I stood up he said, 'Sit down, young man. You took me to a place of meditation; let us continue there together for some minutes.' And we sat there in silence. Since then we start each lesson with meditation. He's telling me to practise again, but less than before. He says I've practised enough to last a lifetime.

Fran smiled and hugged herself.

> Dear Fran, are we still friends?

She stared out of the window and bit her lip. Friends?

> *D'you know, I nearly asked you to come with me? I'm glad I didn't. Not because I wouldn't like you to be here, but because you would be a distraction and I would neglect you and you would be miserable. I couldn't manage all that right now. My focus has to be total – on Reuben and on playing my way into that hidden place. The door has just opened and I have one foot inside. I'm not such a fool as to think the door can't close again if I don't take it seriously.*

She put the letter on the table to stop it shaking about. *Bugger Dale and his bloody career. Distraction? Neglect me? What does he think he's doing right now?*

> *We musicians lead protected and artificial lives. At first I was impatient of it. It felt escapist, elitist – and you know what I think about that! But now I see breaking this kind of ground isn't possible if you allow in distractions. And believe me there are plenty out there on the street. I have a room like a cell and I'm happy.*
> *Dear Fran, please write that the Berkeley and the Vic Rooms are still there, they seem in another world.*
> *Love Dale*

Fran sat motionless at the table. Tears ran down her face. To stop herself shaking she gripped her elbows across her stomach and rocked back and forth. Every now and then she banged her head on the table until she came to rest it there and was still. Eventually she was roused by an ambulance siren screaming into Fremantle Road. She rolled her head to one side, seeing the blur of thin blue paper close to her eye. She crumpled it slowly, sat up, looked at her watch. She was late for work, half the morning gone. In a sudden surge of fury she ripped up the envelope addressed to Dale, dropped the pieces in the bin and rushed out the front door, colliding with Morag coming home from a night shift.

'What bit you, hen?'

'Dale.' The word shot through her teeth before Fran could stop it.

'I thought as much. That man!' Morag stepped into the hall. 'When's it due?'

Fran swung round. 'I don't know what the hell you...'

Then she saw Morag's ginger freckles puckered in concern.

'I've known for ages. I'm not blind and I do know what to look for.' Morag put a hand on her arm. 'Look, I don't want to intrude. And I'm not going to rant. But if you want any gen, just let me know. You'll need two psychiatrists, yeah? And I do have some useful contacts. It'll cost, mind, but...' She shrugged. 'And, Fran, best of luck.'

'Thanks. Yes, thanks. But I don't think... I'm sorry I...'

Morag waved away her protests.

She went to the room where Geoffrey worked. He was bent over his desk, annotating some papers. She touched his shoulder. He started to jump up.

'No. Don't get up. Geoffrey, I came to say, I will marry you.'

'Fran!'

He looked up at her, eyes popping like a goldfish she used to have.

'That's all just now. I'm going, I'm late.'

She started to turn away, but her world started strangely to shrink to the size of his eye, surrounded by a blackness that swallowed it.

When she came round she was lying on the floor surrounded by a circle of Geoffrey's colleagues who had witnessed her announcement.

'You fainted,' said one of them unnecessarily.

Geoffrey ordered a taxi and in no time she was walking into the doctor's surgery on his arm. The doctor signed her off work for a fortnight and prescribed rest and TLC.

'And that is what you shall have,' declared Geoffrey.

He wanted to take her to his flat but she insisted on going home. He sent her to bed and went shopping. When she woke there were tulips on her bedside table and smells coming from the kitchen. It was both strange and comforting to have him there. He was desolate she didn't own a garlic press, but soon arrived with a tray.

'Sole à la meunière for Madame!'

The food was simple and beautiful, a feast for the eyes. Potato delicately creamed, peas neatly heaped, a rosette of tomato, not a bone in the fish. Fran ate it gratefully and wondered how she could ever cope with such perfection.

She slept again, aware Geoffrey was clattering crockery in the kitchen. He arrived at her bedside, concerned, earnest, wanting to talk. He propped her up on pillows and stood, clasping and unclasping his hands.

'I don't want us to misunderstand each other.'

'You mean, you didn't really want to marry me, or you've changed your mind now you've discovered I'm a total slut and don't possess a garlic press?'

'Don't mock. I mean we need to talk about what this step into marriage is going to mean.'

'Geoffrey! You're sounding like a vicar. What's got into you?' Geoffrey might sometimes be ridiculous but he'd never before been pompous.

'I've been cogitating.'

'Oh my God! Come and sit down and spit it out.'

Geoffrey sat down at the far end of the bed. 'I was thinking of a deal between us. Whereby…'

Fran raised an eyebrow.

'Look, you want support for the child you are carrying? Well, you do, don't you?'

Fran nodded.

'I want a wife.'

'Just any wife will do, will it?' What the hell was all this about?

'No. Certainly not. You know I've been mad about you ever since I nearly knocked you downstairs.'

'But that was before you knew I was pregnant. Why would you want to take on someone else's child?'

'Because I want to protect you and support you. I really do believe that was why we met.'

Fran was silent.

'But I'm not stupid. I realise you don't love me.'

Geoffrey gave Fran a sideways look, ran his hands through his hair and cleared his throat. 'That's why I need to say I do want a traditional wedding.' He paused and looked at the carpet. 'You know, in church. Love, honour and obey. White dress. Marquee. You know the sort of thing.'

'Not really my style. Especially now. I mean, I'd feel a hypocrite.'

'More than you would anyway?'

Fran made a face. The remark went home. Being so wrapped up in her own troubles, she'd underestimated Geoffrey.

'I knew it wouldn't appeal to you. That's why I was nervous about this conversation. It's about my family. My father mostly. He's a builder, turned developer, pulled himself up from nothing. Made a packet. Married class, as he would say, and built this dream house in the country. He'd want the best.'

Fran laughed. 'It would suit my mother alright. Sounds as if they'd get on well.'

'My mother too. She's always on at me to bring home girlfriends, keep my father happy. She's a gentle soul and he gives her a hard time.'

'And the baby?'

'Well, the usual thing. It'll come early and even if they guess you were pregnant when we were married, they won't mind by then. My dad, he sees himself as starting a dynasty, wants an heir who'll carry it on. I'm the only child.' Geoffrey went quiet, staring out of the window. 'It's a bonus really. He'll have a bit of respect for me when I take you home.'

What was that about? Fran kept watching the tree branches swaying outside the window.

'The baby's father… You'll want to know…'

Geoffrey held up a hand. 'Stop right there. I prefer not to know. Not my business.'

Fran bit her lip. 'If you say so.'

'So the deal is, the child is mine. You must promise never to tell anyone different. You need security for your child, a husband to keep your parents happy – you see, it's not just for me.'

She nodded, kept watching the tree. 'And you?'

'I agree to support the child. And we stay together while it grows up – security, stability. That's what kids need.'

Fran was silent again. Geoffrey sounded more confident. He'd lost the look of the dog that wants to be stroked, but expects to be hit. She bit the bullet and raised the question of divorce and custody. Geoffrey looked hurt and swallowed a lot. It didn't seem to occur to him that the marriage might not work out. But he agreed she would have custody of the child if it all fell apart.

As soon as Geoffrey had gone home, Morag banged on her door and burst in.

'Who is this *perrson* who's been in the kitchen? What's going on? You never mentioned *him* this morning.'

Fran explained a little. 'I was wrong about Dale, you see.'

'You mean it's this Geoffrey's?'

Fran nodded, not yet comfortable with the lie.

'A likely story.'

'We're getting married.'

'Oh, bollocks in hell, Fran, you never! Marry someone who washes the cutlery *before* using it?'

'He didn't?'

'Aye, he did so. God, I wish Verity was here to talk some sense into you. Or Dale. Can't you get hold of Dale?'

Fran held up her hands. 'No, I can't. I won't. And like I say, it isn't...'

'Okay. I'll back off. But just say if I can help. In any way.' Morag opened the door. 'I'll say this for him, he's cleaned up the kitchen a treat.'

15

'I cannot do this!' Fran shouted to the ceiling, to the pale sky, to the ghostly tree outside her window. She was sitting bolt upright in the bed having woken in the dawn, extracting herself from a nightmare that did not want to let her go. Slowly she remembered scenes from the previous day and the unlikely contract she was making with Geoffrey. It did not feel like her life, but it was clinging to her like sticky cobwebs, while she struggled with how she was supposed to feel.

'Damn you, Dale Weaver. I need you, Dale. Why can't you bloody *be* here?'

Hours later she woke again, damp with sweat, dry-mouthed, feeling nauseous. She stumbled through to the kitchen for water, noticed a letter on the mat, took it back to bed. Unusual for her father to write.

Dear Frazzle

It was a treat to see you on Sunday. I hope all is well with you. I sensed there was something troubling you underneath your casual casting off of lovelorn suitors. Take no notice of all that ridiculous talk of your mother's. She just wants the best for you, although she has a strange way of going about it sometimes.

I enclose a cheque, a bonus for getting your good degree. Better you choose what you want. I've left it blank. This is in case you are in need of a larger sum of money. I trust you not to take advantage and I don't need to know how you spend it. There are some things fathers and daughters don't discuss. However,

if you need help with the necessary contacts and can't find them in Bristol, I can provide them. I also want the best for you and just for the record, I happen to believe girls should have careers if they want them and that marrying for love is the way to go. It worked for me, whatever you may think.
Yours aye,
Dad

Dear, dear Dad. What timing! Clever old thing, not saying anything, noticing everything. She wished she were a little girl again, being rocked in his arms after she woke, screaming, from a nightmare. If only. Wiping her eyes, she read the letter again, gazing out of the window. It meant she really did have a choice. A parentally approved choice. And hell, that was still important to her. Was Morag awake yet? Should she wake her? Get those contact numbers? Or see the GP first?

She knocked on Morag's door – no grunt of reply. She peered inside and saw an empty bed. Morag had already left while she was asleep.

She dressed and tucked the cheque into her bag. She wrote a note for Geoffrey, left it on the kitchen table and set off in the direction of the surgery.

Fran walked purposefully, head down, and was surprised to be interrupted by a voice and a soft hand on her arm.

'Missy? You remember me?'

It was Mrs Wong, Dale's former landlady. Fran hadn't noticed she was passing the entrance to his flat.

'You young man, send in post. You see.' She waved at Fran to stay where she was and dived into the shop, soon returning with a picture postcard. She beamed with pride, and handed it to her.

'You read. Say nice things. Kind young man, remember Missy Wong.'

Fran reeled to see Dale's handwriting so unexpectedly, in such a context. The message was brief and thanked Mrs Wong for her kindness in looking after him. The picture was of the Statue of Liberty.

'Amelica,' Mrs Wong was saying. 'He pray in Amelica.'

Fran frowned, thinking it highly unlikely Dale was doing any praying. But Mrs Wong was stretching out her right arm and drawing it backwards and forwards across her body in an exaggerated bowing movement. Light dawned.

'Oh yes, he's playing in America.'

Mrs Wong nodded, smiling in delight. 'His play is beautiful. I like. Is good boy.'

Fran nodded.

'You say him, is nice picture? You thank him?' She nodded vigorously until Fran promised to pass on the message.

As Fran said goodbye, Mrs Wong put her hands together and bowed, holding her postcard as if it were an offering and smiling happily.

She was absurdly touched Dale should think to send Mrs Wong a postcard and even more touched by the pleasure it obviously gave her. He clearly occupied a special place in Mrs Wong's heart.

At the surgery Fran took her place in the waiting room.

The smell that had wafted off Mrs Wong brought back Dale's room – their feast of Chinese food, the thrill of him inside her on that sunlit morning. Her own wild spontaneity which had felt so good, which she must now pay for. It was no good being angry with Dale. He had simply done what he always said he would do. It was her responsibility. She must take it.

Dad had given her the means. He wanted her to have a career like Dale and Morag. Like Verity would have had. A proper future. But what career? She had no vision of a career, a future that was proper. What did it mean? What could you do with an English degree? She sure as hell wasn't going to teach.

She rummaged in the bottom of her bag until her fingers closed over the tiny hare Dale had given her. Then she went to use the toilet and walked out, back onto the street.

She cut down Woodlands Road to Park Row and headed for Christmas Steps and a junky antique shop that sold second-hand books, china and glass and a few pieces of jewellery. She'd often found birthday and Christmas presents for Zelda here and had a flirty kind of friendship with Adam, the cadaverous owner. He greeted her warmly and found her a silver chain fine enough to thread through the loop on her hare.

'You realise this is silver?'

'Is it? No idea what it's made of.'

'I'll give it a polish.'

As usual, Adam invited her for a coffee and as usual Fran refused. She surprised him with a farewell kiss on the cheek and came away pleased with the feel of the silver hare making a secret bump under her jumper which she touched from time to time as she strode along. It made her feel safe.

She called in at the bank in Queen's Road, made out her father's cheque for the amount she had paid for the silver chain and queued to pay it in at the counter.

When she got home she found a note on the kitchen table alongside the one she had left for Geoffrey.

> *Where are you? I'm worried sick. I've gone to look for you. Phone the office and leave a message if/when you find this note.*
>
> *A girl called Zoë or Zena or some such phoned, sounded quite unhinged. She was rather rude. Wanted you to ring her.*

Fran picked up the phone and rang Zelda's number.

'Fran, I phoned and this strange guy was there. Who on earth...?'

'Never mind him. What you said, about being selfish? Just tell me some more about how it works, what you meant.'

'I meant that when you make a decision like that, it's overwhelming, right? You're saying, will this tiny being inside me live or die? No one can decide things like that. So you have to say, okay, what about *my* life? That's the only thing you can know about. Deep down, do I want this? Can I cope? Do I want it with my whole selfish being? Because it's no good wanting it with your romantic "I'm a hero" being. That would end up shit for you and the baby.'

'That's what I thought. Oh, God, Zel. I've been in such a dither. This morning I was all set to go for an abortion... No. Listen. I'd be free to have a career. Then everything became clear. I don't *want* a career. I can't even think what that would be. So I've stopped dithering about. I've made up my mind. I'm getting married.'

Silence at the other end of the line.

'Zel? Are you there?'

'Yeah. Yeah. I'm just...you took my breath away. Is it that guy I spoke to?'

'Geoffrey. Yes.'

'Is it his?'

'Yes, Geoffrey's. Of course.'

'But, Fran, how come...? I mean, getting married, Fran? I could help you. We could help each other.'

'No. I'm too conventional. Is that pathetic? I don't care if it is. It's the only way I can do it. I'm not like you. I need a man. That's where Geoffrey comes in.'

'I rather thought he came in a bit earlier. I mean it *is* his...?'

'I *told* you. Of course.'

'And you're sure about being selfish? About the baby I mean, not getting married. Describe it. Tell me how it feels.'

'As if my life depends upon it.'

'Ah. Yes, that's how I felt.' Zelda carried on with endless questions, then announced she was coming to visit. 'I can't bear not to see you. Mum's off work, she'll have Tamzin. Tomorrow. I'll be there and I won't take no for an answer.'

She wants to check him out, thought Fran. She'll have a surprise.

Next she set about writing to her father. She debated whether to acknowledge the between-the-lines message of his letter. Eventually she wrote:

I'm going to be married – to Geoffrey. I've thought it through endlessly and I do know what I'm doing. I'm sorry if it isn't what you would have wanted. I'll be in touch about it soon. Do your best to smooth the way with Mother when the time comes. Now I have taken the plunge she's bound to find a reason why the Hendersons, whether from Watford or Timbuctoo, are NO GOOD.
Lots of love,
Fraz
P.S. Thank you for being psychic and generous and trusting me, and not just with the cheque.

She addressed the letter to her father's practice.

Finally she left Geoffrey a message that he was on no account to phone or come to her flat before midday tomorrow.

Next day, on the stroke of twelve, Geoffrey burst in, full of indignation and protest.

'Rest was what the doctor said. You can't just go off without letting me know.'

'I had to sleep. A lot's been happening. I appreciate your concern, but it's not an illness you know, being pregnant.'

'What about the doctor's advice? And, by the way, who the hell was that girl on the phone?'

Before Fran could reply the doorbell rang and Geoffrey opened it on Zelda who said, 'Oh, you must be Geoffrey,' and pushed past him to gather Fran into an extravagant hug.

16

The house was ugly – the bricks too bright and sharp, the pointing harsh, like the stick-on paper on Fran's childhood doll's house. The pillared porch was too big and the windows too small. The whole building looked embarrassed to be so exposed to its neighbours, which stood around the little close like red-faced matrons at a church fete. It would be years before the baby weeping willow on the front lawn would be big enough to soften the façade. Fran hoped she'd not be there to see it.

The wedding had been embarrassing too – an occasion which Geoffrey wanted, Eleanor masterminded and Fran endured. Geoffrey's parents wanted to pay for a lavish affair at their house. Eleanor was outraged and won hands down. Fran had to admire the way she swept Ted aside, but it did her no good. Eleanor was no more interested than anyone else in what the bride wanted. Harry was Fran's only ally. Dear old Dad. He'd given her arm such a squeeze as he gave her away, as if he really couldn't bear to do it.

Meeting Geoffrey's parents had been painful.

'Didn't know you had it in you, lad,' said his father in front of Fran, looking her up and down. A crude remark, but an honest gaze, a steady smile.

Mavis Henderson, squat in Crimplene and still with the startled look of a newly done perm, wrung her hands and whispered, 'You'll have to excuse Ted. He's very direct.'

After what Geoffrey judged was a decent interval, he'd told his parents *a little Henderson* was on the way. Why did he have to put it like that, making it into a lie? Ted opened champagne and once more looked at his son with new respect. They must move to a house in the country with land and good neighbours. This child should have freedom and horses and go to a good school. It sounded like Jane Austen. He would set up a trust to pay the fees, better put the boy's name down right away. Fran asked, 'Supposing it's a girl?' But they all ignored her. When no one was looking she poured the orange juice Mavis had brought into a hideously matching begonia and filled up her glass with fizz. Ted could go jump in his artificial lake.

'How about one of those big Victorian semis in Redland?' said Fran, realising she must think upmarket. But Ted looked past her.

'Or a Georgian townhouse on the Downs?'

Ted frowned. 'Old houses. Nowt but problems. New build for my son and heir.'

He threatened to build them a house himself. 'Not as grand as this place, but along the same sort of lines.'

Fran shuddered. What a horror to live in a mini version of Henderson Hall.

But a developer colleague of Ted's was building an exclusive estate in Dorset.

'There's a bonus,' said Ted with some pride. 'It's neo-Georgian. That'll appeal to your taste.'

A further bonus was the job Ted secured for Geoffrey with an estate agent in Dorchester. 'An offer we can't refuse,' said Geoffrey. Which was not how Fran saw it.

So here she was, ensconced (for that was the word) in number two Corner Close – or Pseud's Corner, as Zelda had instantly christened it. She was standing in her through-lounge watching her neighbour at number four cleaning her windows and listening to Nancy Sinatra belting out "These Boots Are Made for Walkin" from the transistor radio in the kitchen. She had twins asleep in identical cots upstairs, a freezer full of Marks and Spencer's food and a Peugeot estate for transporting her offspring. Geoffrey wouldn't even keep her beloved blue Morris Minor for driving to work. 'Not the right image,' he told her and bought a cumbersome black saloon.

*

'You didn't say you had twins in your family,' Mavis had said in the hospital.

'We haven't,' said Fran. 'Not as far as I know.'

Mavis narrowed her eyes, but Ted just said, 'There's got to be a first time.'

They'd disagreed about names. Fran wanted a single syllable after the tyranny of Francesca. When she suggested Kim and Dan, Geoffrey translated them into Kimberley and Daniel.

'Absolutely not! They are totally different names.'

During the night feed she gazed down at her daughter sucking vigorously. 'What would you like to be called?' Zoë, was the instant response in Fran's head. Zoë. Well that was very clear. She looked at the tiny girl with new respect. She liked the name and it was the closest thing to naming her after Zelda. Zoë and Dan. Daniel was okay too. A happy compromise. She phoned Zelda and told her about the Z.

Eleanor was appalled that Fran planned to breastfeed. They had such an odd conversation. That strange look when Fran asked, 'Did you feed me?' Startled almost.

And then, 'Good Lord, no!' As if it was something for animals. 'We were only too glad to have a bottle.'

Fran certainly couldn't imagine Mother breastfeeding. Far too intimate. *She doesn't like babies. She didn't like me.* It was obvious.

Eleanor managed to slip a disc, which meant she was unable to help Fran when she came out of hospital. Oh dear, said Geoffrey. Thank God, said Fran. She rang Goldie. She'd always wanted to ask her but convention – and Geoffrey – dictated her own mother should be called upon first. Goldie was inexplicably reluctant. The more Fran begged, the more adamant she became. It would not be right, Eleanor would be upset, she was no good with babies, her cat could not be left, her knees were playing up.

Spare me from Mavis, thought Fran. But Mavis said she couldn't leave Ted.

Motherhood did not come easily to Fran. The worst time was when the twins were asleep – if she ever succeeded in getting Zoë and Dan off at the same time. She'd stand at the window in a state of paralysis gazing at the garden or, like today, wondering about her neighbour. So much she must do before they woke up, before Geoffrey got home.

Eventually she would creep into the utility room and heave a load of evil-smelling nappies out of the bucket and into the washing machine – thank God for the washing machine – only to hear their first wavering cries as she set the programme going. Then she was released. She would rush to the kitchen and wash dishes at high speed as the wailing reached a crescendo, feeling a matching wave of guilt and panic rising into her chest. Finally she would gallop up the stairs and gather up the hot little bodies, wiping their snotty faces, hushing them gently and kissing them in remorse.

Eleanor phoned to see how she was managing and tears burst out of her.

'Are you crying, Francesca? Oh, I expect it's the hormones. I expect...'

'I'm frightened, Mother.'

'I'm not at all surprised. Children are frightening – and you've got two of them.'

She made it sound as if it were Fran's fault she'd had twins.

She rang Zelda for Tamzin's first birthday.

'She's getting so grown up. I'm beginning to see there's a future again.' Zelda started rattling on about her plans to find a place of her own and a father for her next child. It took Fran's breath away the way Zelda bracketed these together.

'I might train as a therapist,' Zelda went on. 'But you know me, Fran. One minute it's acupuncture, the next it's reflexology and then I'm on to herbs. But it would all go well with working from home. I'll wake up one morning and I'll know. Don't you find that?'

Fran was silent, choking back tears.

'Fran? Are you okay? Oh, God, I've been nattering on about me. What's...?'

'I don't know what's wrong with me. I don't get anything done.'

'Well, hey, you've got a handful there. Can't be much time...'

'But there *is* time.' She pushed at the dust on the dark-stained windowsill. It frilled like the edge of a doily. 'I just stand and watch the grass grow. Until they wake up. And then I'm frantic.'

Zelda told her relaxing was more important than housework.

'But I'm not relaxed. I'm bloody paralysed.'

Zelda said, 'Hmmm,' and that she was on her way. She brought life and warmth and Tamzin into number two Corner Close. Fran felt the knots in her stomach relax. Zelda understood. She enjoyed the twins. To her they were not a scary package to be handled like some kind of time bomb. But Zelda did not understand the same was not true of Geoffrey. She went about opening windows which Geoffrey would close, left dirty dishes which Geoffrey would wash and disregarded the twins' rigid routine which Geoffrey had established. Fran's knees turned to jelly the first evening he came home to unbathed twins.

'Daddy's turn to bath you,' Zelda greeted him, winking at Fran and handing him Dan before he'd had a chance to find his slippers. She poured herself and Fran a drink and read Tamzin her bedtime story while Fran fed Zoë.

Zelda showed her the twins as individuals for the first time. 'Sure they need a routine. So do you. But at least let them have a say in it. Stagger it so you can handle them separately. It might take longer but I think you'd find it easier. And for God's sake, get Geoffrey to do more.'

Zelda's other mission was to get her out of the house. 'And I don't mean coffee mornings. Bugger coffee mornings. You need the wide open spaces and there are some fantastic walks around here.'

Kitted out with baby slings and a backpack they walked nearly every day in all weathers. Zelda showed Fran a countryside she'd barely noticed before.

'See the woman shapes everywhere!' Zelda pointed across the valley to the undulating hills on the other side. 'Look how she's lying there, lovely round belly, long thigh. Get it?'

Fran did get it and she loved it. In the months and years that followed she was to grow strongly attached to this feminine landscape with its intimate valleys, long sweeps of curving downland and wooded knolls. The ancient settlements and sacred sites added to her feeling of awe, and the wide stretch of the skies compensated to some extent for the distance from the sea, which she sometimes ached to see.

Geoffrey couldn't wait for Zelda to leave. 'Life's a continual picnic with her around. I just can't stand the mess anymore.'

He watched them preparing for a walk and complained they never used the pram.

'We're not going to the park,' said Zelda.

Then Jez arrived. It was the final straw for Geoffrey.

Jez was the new man in Zelda's life. Fran had already met him when he dropped Zelda and Tamzin at the beginning of their stay. Geoffrey had been at work. Zelda admitted her search for a place to live and a father for her next child had begun to converge. Jez wasn't interested in donating his sperm and moving on – he was happy to make babies, but only on the condition they live together. He thought they could probably afford to buy a cottage in Cornwall and had continued his journey to explore the property situation in the far west.

One evening during the bedtime routine, the sound of a throbbing engine and the crashing of gears announced his return. Zelda and Fran watched as Geoffrey went out to meet Jez, who strode from behind an ancient blue Dormobile, all six foot four of him flexing inside a scarlet tracksuit, crinkly black hair catching the sun. Geoffrey took a step back and visibly wilted. Jez beamed and shook hands. At the same moment Tamzin toddled out of the front door in her nightie, shouting, 'Da-da, Da-da.' Zelda and Fran grinned and returned to the bathroom with the twins.

As they went to bed that night Geoffrey turned on Fran.

'Well, Jez is a bit...'

'A bit what?'

'You never told me he was black.'

'It didn't seem important...'

'It just would have been nice to know. Not that I... He's got a lot of... I don't know what the word is. Well, ebullience. I suppose you need it to cope with that Zelda.'

'You've never liked Zelda, have you? Ever since that first time in Bristol.'

'She's just so...well, different. Wasn't Tamzin's father some foreigner too?'

'Polish. Anything wrong with that? And Jez was born in London and brought up in Reading, by the way.'

'So he told me. No, nothing wrong. Just, you know, different.

And I can't think how they'll get on in Cornwall. Pretty insular, the Cornish. They can be quite hostile, I'm told.'

'Oh, Jez has got a way with him.'

'Yes,' said Geoffrey slowly, 'he certainly has,' and he disappeared to the bathroom.

Zelda packed up the next day. 'I can see Geoffrey can't stand us being here, and I don't want to make it worse for you when we leave.'

Fran wondered what she meant.

'When Jez was playing with the twins, Geoffrey looked as if he might explode. It's a man thing. And of course he's jealous of us – you and me, I mean. He probably has fantasies we're going to abduct you in that dreadful old van of ours.'

Which were exactly the words Geoffrey had used to describe the Dormobile when he'd made Fran promise not to take the twins in it.

'Actually I *would* like to kidnap you and the twins, if you must know. I can't think what possessed you to marry the man.'

Fran hugged her. 'I can't thank you enough.' Zelda had shown her how to love her babies. 'I know now, they won't break.'

'Never again,' said Geoffrey as the van turned out of sight. But Fran didn't hear. She was too busy wiping her eyes.

Everything changed after Zelda left. Geoffrey stalked about restoring order like a tomcat marking his territory.

In bed that night, instead of saying a tentative 'Shall we…?' and accepting her excuse of being tired, he simply turned off the light and climbed on top of her.

'Marital relations' Geoffrey had called it in the beginning, but she'd teased him out of that. From the start he insisted she tie back her hair. Couldn't cope, he said – it was too much for him. And it was better if it could happen in the dark. At least then she didn't have to manage her face as well as her body. He was a competent lover, well-endowed – like a horse, she noted with surprise the first time she saw him naked. He would shaft away with vigour and always cared about whether she came. Only rarely, on summer nights, did she see the look of disgust that passed across his face as he rolled off her.

Tonight was different. He showed none of the usual consideration, but shoved himself into her abruptly and moved in a kind of frenzy until he was done, exiting equally abruptly. He didn't even say goodnight.

Next day Geoffrey started a new routine – asking Fran for details of what she planned to do every day. He phoned her from work and complained when she wasn't where she'd said she would be. One morning she told him she was going to the sea. She said it casually over her shoulder as she switched the kettle on. Geoffrey said nothing, but when she came to load the car she couldn't find her car keys. In the evening he walked away when she told him about the keys. Later she found them on the normal hook.

On the next day of good weather she didn't announce her intentions and took off for the sea, equipped for a whole day out and leaving him a note about her change of plan, as any wife would.

It was a sparkling September day with a pleasant sea breeze. The little seaside town was quiet and the beach deserted. Fran spent hours walking and gazing while the twins gurgled at the sky and the seagulls and slept peacefully while she sat on a rock and ate a pasty.

A woman in a red coat appeared, walking along the shoreline. Every few paces she bent and picked up a pebble or a shell. Sometimes she threw it into the sea, sometimes she turned it over in her hand, transferred it to her pocket. As she came level she looked up and walked towards Fran. She was a young woman with smooth, pale skin and wispy hair. Her face was expressionless as she looked at the sleeping twins.

'Are they your babies?' Her voice was childlike.

Fran nodded, brushing flakes of pastry off her coat.

'Can I hold one?'

'They're asleep. No, I wouldn't want…'

'I could always wake them up.' A hand moved towards the pram.

Fran jumped up. 'It's time we went home.'

The woman gave a high-pitched laugh. 'You're afraid I'll take one…'

'We have to go.'

'…because you've got two and I haven't got one.' Tears ran down the woman's face. Her voice rose in pitch but didn't falter. 'I wouldn't hurt them, you know.'

'I'm sure.' Fran could hear her voice lurch as she released the brake and turned the pram, impatient with the pebbles that trapped the wheels and slowed her down. She felt a hand on her shoulder.

'Dear little babies.'

Back on the promenade Fran turned and looked down to the beach. The woman was still staring after her, the red coat flapping in the wind. She lifted a hand, let it fall, turned back to the sea. Fran loaded the car, sweating. It took longer to drive home. There was more traffic, none of it in a hurry. Fran could not get the woman out of her head. Was she mad, or just sad? What might have happened?

She needed to be home before Geoffrey, with the twins safe and sound in their own living room. She tried to overtake and had to drop back sharply to the blare of an oncoming lorry. Geoffrey was already standing on the drive. His jaw was tense and he didn't smile. She clipped the flowerbed as she parked and her knees shook as she stepped onto the gravel. He said nothing, just stared at her, his eyes glazed, not a flicker.

'We went to the sea.' She tried a bright smile but her voice cracked.

Still no sound, no movement. Then Geoffrey looked at his watch. 'I was leaving half an hour before I called the police.'

'The police? Are you mad?'

The twins, apparently, were not old enough to go to the beach; she was irresponsible, childish in her need to see the sea. 'Anything might have happened.'

'Like what? Look at them! Is there anything wrong with them?' An echo of 'dear little babies' caused her voice to falter and she bent into the back of the car, murmuring, 'Thank you, thank you,' to her children for being contented and happy instead of screaming their heads off.

Once inside the nursery she leaned against the door and breathed deeply, the three of them safe in their domain. She sometimes felt the carpets in the rest of the house were sucking up the air, but this room had never been carpeted. It was full of light and air.

Sinking into the sofa, she pulled off outer layers of clothes: her own, Dan's, Zoë's. All three of them descended into the deep release of feeding time. Her mind emptied and she was carried along on the wave of routine that brought the babies into their cots. She stood gently patting Dan's back, which soothed him into sleep, watching Zoë, who preferred to lie on her back and follow the pattern of the butterfly mobile above her head.

Downstairs, Fran paused in the doorway of the living room with its neutral Wilton carpet, pale linen covers and a husband with his head in his hands. How had she come to be here, among this furniture, with this apparent stranger?

'So what was all that about?'

At the sound of her voice, Geoffrey slowly lifted his head and turned to face her. His eyes seemed to look through her.

'I love you,' he said in a monotone.

Holding her in an unblinking gaze, he began to cross the room like a sleepwalker. She flinched as he stepped up close. Slowly he raised his hand, then brought it down, splaying his fingers and dragging them through her hair and down her cheek.

'You are mine,' he said in the same flat voice.

As Fran turned sharply away he gripped her wrists and held her in the doorway. She winced with pain.

'Do you hear me?'

Fran nodded.

'Remember.'

She nodded again. 'You're hurting.'

Geoffrey looked down at their hands as if unaware of what he was doing and slowly released her. He straightened up. 'I didn't say goodnight to the twins.'

Fran blinked at the sound of his normal voice. She leaned against the doorframe, watching his receding back, rubbing first one wrist, then the other.

Later Geoffrey apologised. He said he cared so much for them all, promised they would visit the sea at weekends. Her knees stopped shaking. Her ridiculous fear of the woman on the beach receded with his words, just as his anger had magnified it.

That night in her dreams she was in a glass box at the top of a staircase. A pale-faced woman flew up from the stairwell, pressed her face against the glass, laughing, then turned into a seagull and disappeared.

Geoffrey's strange turns recurred every few months after that. She told no one and learned to handle them by practising silence and invisibility.

Just before the twins' fourth birthday she went to lunch with a friend and stayed on for a cup of tea. Geoffrey was on the forecourt when she got home. She waved merrily and his stony glare was as unexpected as a blow.

'You knew where I was. Pat's for lunch. Stayed for a cuppa. She was filling me in about the school. There's a playgroup they could go to… Get to know… What's wrong?'

'Lunch, yes. It's five fifteen. I won't have it. And, for the record, I am not having them going to a so-called playgroup. They stay home with you until they start school.'

'I take *my* children out to lunch and stay to tea, and that's a crime? My God, Geoffrey, we can put men on the moon, but you're still living in the last century!'

The colour went from Geoffrey's face and he turned on his heel and went inside.

Next morning after he had gone to work she found she and the twins were locked inside the house. He'd turned the key in the deadlocks on both outside doors.

She phoned him immediately but couldn't get through. She rang Zelda.

'Jesus Christ! You have to leave! You could come to me but we're moving, packing up as I speak. Jez has hired a van.' Zelda sounded excited. 'The cottage I told you about has all gone through. Come and stay – as soon as we're settled.'

Fran was reduced to going home to Eleanor. She called a locksmith and packed her bags.

17

Fran skidded into the house with her bags of goodies and unpacked them carefully onto the kitchen table. Don't rush and mess up, she told herself. Plenty of time to make cakes and paint eggs before heading off to fetch the twins from their boarding school.

This year, unusually, Easter was early enough to coincide with the twins' birthday, so she'd stocked up with a mega load of eggs, of both the real and chocolate varieties. A large chocolate egg each, plus small ones for hiding in the garden. They might be twelve, but the traditional egg hunt was still a must. Hens' eggs to paint for the egg-rolling ritual on Cadbury Hill (which they used to believe was made of Dairy Milk) and for two cakes: one with Smarties for Zoë and one with Maltesers for Dan. Zoë had decreed years ago it wasn't fair that they had to share a birthday cake just because they happened to be born on the same day. There were two Raleigh Chopper bikes – the latest must-have craze – hidden in the garage: red for Zoë, blue for Dan, in spite of Geoffrey's ridiculous idea that they share one.

She turned on the oven and set the mixer creaming margarine and sugar while she clattered about in the cupboard to find two matching cake tins. They were still young enough to fight if one had a bigger cake than the other. Where had those years vanished? Their birthday again and here she still was, in this existence with Geoffrey, having achieved what he called a *modus vivendi*. Ironic, that he described their life in a dead language. Sometimes she regretted coming back all those years ago. But it had seemed like the lesser of two evils at the time.

Going home to Mother was never going to have been easy, and it had been a painful few months. Mother gritting her teeth all day, and at night the rumble of Dad's voice in the next room calming her down. One day a week Goldie came over. What a disaster that had been. The twins adored her and she them. She'd gather them on the sofa and read to them. 'Dreadful cheap books about animals dressed up as people,' Mother would say, tight-lipped.

Fran greased the tins and sifted them with flour. Then there had been the toy radio fiasco. She grinned at the memory. Mother had bought Zoë and Dan a Fisher Price wind-up radio that played 'Happy Birthday' which they fought over until Fran had to hide it. Goldie promptly set herself to scour Portsmouth in search of another.

'Found it in Handley's at last,' she announced the following Thursday. 'I had to find one that looked the same but played a different tune.'

Fran was touched but Mother rolled her eyes and blinked a lot. 'Whatever does it matter what it plays? Why do you always have to make such a song and dance? Personally I think it's ridiculous for them to have one each. They have to learn to share.'

'If it gives them fun, that's what matters. They'll learn to share soon enough. You never had twins.'

Eleanor looked daggers at her sister and left the room.

Fran sighed as she broke eggs into the mixture. What had got into those two, Mother and Goldie? Always those venomous looks and Mother disappearing upstairs for hours. Even Dad couldn't diffuse the hostility. If anything, his presence had increased the tension. It had all been exhausting and this loving family of hers eventually drove her back to the relative peace of her loveless marriage. Geoffrey had agreed to marriage guidance but it hadn't lasted long. The counsellor was far too astute.

Theirs was an odd relationship, but then again, no worse than some she knew of. His strange turns were rare these days. She just kept on trucking. Zelda, she knew, found it incomprehensible. Zelda, who wasn't even allowed to come and stay. They rarely saw each other, making do with an hour or two when Zelda was en route to see her mother.

'Crazy! I can't even see my best friend for heaven's sake,' she said aloud, switching off the machine.

Flour, cocoa powder and that would be it. Why couldn't she say, Easter, birthday and that will be it, me and the twins out of here? How would she ever escape, and into what? Damn, not quite enough cocoa. She stopped measuring by the spoonful and shook the tin into the bowl on top of the flour.

Hell, she did miss Zel; they'd be having such a laugh doing this. Instead of which she was stressing about getting it right and not leaving the kitchen in a mess. Time! What was the time? Okay, two hours to the school if the traffic wasn't bad, two hours back. Fudge time for talking to the teachers.

Cakes cooking. If she left as soon as they came out of the oven she'd still get back with the twins before Geoffrey got in. She was so looking forward to having them home. Some life about the place. Candles! Did she have twenty-four? Or would she have to stop on the way?

As she dived into the back of the larder in search of the tin of cake decorations, she heard the phone. Damn! That was all she needed. She grabbed the tin and dumped it on the kitchen table as she galloped though to the hall to pick up the phone.

Mother. Of all times for her to make one of her rare, inexplicable calls. She was speaking in a strange staccato.

'Francesca?'

'Hello, Mother.'

Then silence.

'Mother?'

'Francesca?'

'Yes, Mother.' She was losing patience with this.

'Francesca… Your father. It's your father. On his way to work. He's, he's…' A long pause. 'Dead. He's dead, Francesca.'

Fran froze as the skin all over her body registered the shock. Her brain would not take it in. Everything in her erected a steel wall against the possibility that the news might be true. Words would not come.

Mother's voice came again, strange and cracked. 'Are you there? I've been trying to get you.'

'Yes, I'm here.' The sound seemed to come from a long way off. 'I was shopping. How, Mother? Where was he? What happened?'

'I told him he should stop. Too much work. Francesca, they killed Harry.' She sounded slightly crazy.

'Mother, tell me...'

'In the street. Walking from the car park. Dropped down d... Outside Lloyds Bank. What will we do, Francesca?'

'I can't... I don't know... What?' Fran focused on the piece of garden she could see through the window where next-door's tabby cat was stalking a blackbird.

'Will you come? The police won't leave until someone comes.'

The picture of police sitting with Mother jolted Fran into action. 'Of course I'm coming.' What about Zoë and Dan? 'But, Mother? I have to pick up the twins on the way. You'd better get the Penfolds over. Until I get there.'

She stood in the hall holding the telephone receiver and watching the bird which seemed to be eying the cat, judging the time. It stabbed the grass with its yellow beak and yanked on the elastic of a worm, teasing it out of the earth before flying off. The cat stretched and settled to clean itself. The telephone line was droning in her hand. Fran stared at the handset, replaced it in its cradle and walked stiffly upstairs.

The headmaster let her use his study to give the twins the news. Dan didn't say a word. He slouched past her into the back of the car, hunched and silent. Zoë sat in front, asked a lot of questions, cried a bit and talked about her next cello exam.

When they reached her parents' house Zoë looked round in alarm at Fran as she hugged her grandmother. 'Grandma's shrunk,' she whispered. Dan disappeared. Eleanor clung to Fran like a frightened child.

John Penfold went with her to identify the body. It was the hardest thing she'd ever had to do. John talked all the way home. Words strung between them. She was supposed to bat them back but she missed every shot. She had no inkling of what he said.

When she got in Eleanor was sedated and sleeping. No sign of Dan. Fran went looking for him in her father's study. The room smelled of Harry, of leather and old tweeds with a slightly antiseptic tinge which always hung about him. In his chair she felt held by its curving arms, by the wall of books, by the familiar prints of old Portsmouth, the photos of his days in the Navy and the view of the garden path leading to his workshop door, blistered with peeling paint. Of course. That's where Dan would be. They'd spent hours in there doing woodwork. Harry had taught him to carve and to use all his tools. Best not to interfere.

She picked up the phone and dialled her home number. Geoffrey launched into a tirade. He'd come home to a kitchen scattered with dirty bowls and cakes burnt to a crisp in the oven. She held the receiver away from her ear. What did all that have to do with her?

'Smoke everywhere. You could have set the house on fire.'

'Geoffrey. My father. Dad's dead.'

There was an abrupt silence at the other end. 'I'm sorry, Francesca. I'm so sorry.'

He meant it. She knew he meant it. He was a good man.

Zoë put her head round the door as she rang off. 'Gramps was Dan's special person, wasn't he?'

Fran nodded. She looked at her daughter and had a moment of recognition. She felt glad and sad and jealous, and so did Zoë.

When she made her way out to the workshop Dan was cleaning Harry's tools. They were laid out on the bench gleaming with carefully applied oil.

'They were in a mess. He always said he didn't look after them properly. Left that to me.' Dan put the oil aside and started wrapping the chisels in a roll of soft cloth.

'He would be so pleased.' Fran felt tears spring to her eyes and she squeezed Dan's shoulders in a half-hug. 'Dan…'

'Don't. I can't. I'm okay here. Just leave me be.'

Goldie came to stay the night before the funeral and Fran was irritated to hear her and Mother arguing. They stopped talking when she came into the room. She supposed they were ashamed. Couldn't they for once, for Dad's sake, get on like they used to?

Next morning there was a strange episode when Eleanor rushed out of the kitchen door and started throwing stones into the buddleia tree where a blackbird was singing. She was shaking when she came back in and Fran poured her a brandy. They got through the funeral with Fran supporting Eleanor on one side and Goldie on the other.

Harry's death was like an eclipse of the sun. They'd spoken on the phone most weeks. He'd always sensed what she needed, always cheered her on. Through all the dark times he'd steadily beamed upon her a reflection of self-worth. He'd *loved* her. It was as simple as that. He'd loved her unconditionally as he'd loved Eleanor. And the two of them were feeling the cold now he was gone.

18

The sun was still low in the sky when Fran set off to Cornwall. It threw an image of the car onto the opposite bank as she climbed out of the village, as if her shadow were leading the way. It was years since she had come away on her own. She felt both excited and anxious, as if there was something important she had forgotten to do.

Geoffrey had been visiting his parents frequently since Ted's recent hip replacement and he'd suddenly decided to take the twins to see them at half-term.

'Dad's fed up with not getting about. It'll be a diversion – and anyway, he wants to see how they're shaping up, now he's been paying school fees for nearly a year.'

Ted had insisted on his promise of a private secondary education in spite of it being for two instead of one. Fran didn't see the need, but they'd found a school she was happy with and the twins jumped at the idea of weekly boarding. Zoë had far better facilities for her music than she would have had at the local comprehensive. She'd taken her cello to Hertfordshire and planned a recital for her grandfather. Fran hoped he wouldn't fall asleep.

Yes, it was fair enough Ted wanted to see them. The odd thing was, Geoffrey hadn't insisted she go as well. Even odder, he hadn't objected to her taking the opportunity to visit Zelda. He really was doing his best since Harry died.

The early promise of a fine day had vanished. A dark weather front threatened as she crossed into Cornwall and headed towards Launceston. Black clouds slammed doors on chambers of light in the sky. Over and over, a rainbow slung a perfect arc, framed by the windscreen, only to be doused by another heavy rainstorm. A constant battle was being played out between sun and rain.

Zelda lived near Penzance and Fran hadn't penetrated so far into Cornwall before. It really was another country, without the rolling openness and towering trees of Hampshire or the inviting intimacy of Dorset. Fine architecture was scarce, but the scale of the squat cottages fitted into the landscape. They were unpretentious dwellings, hunkered down into the stony earth, sheltering from the winds that swept across the peninsular. Bodmin Moor stretched bleakly on either side of the road with a take-it-or-leave-it quality. With the passing of the storm, a clear light came off the sea that was never far away.

Now she was off the main A30, heading down narrow lanes with deep banks bursting with bluebells, pink campion and spears of foxglove. Scraggy thorn trees shaped by the prevailing wind grew out of stone walls and the smell of damp moss, bracken and earth gusted in on a warm breeze. The downhill gradient grew steeper, there was moss growing along the middle of the lane and the sides were broken up. Potholes became more frequent. In the bottom of the valley she forded a shallow stream, and just as she began to doubt the directions, the lane bent uphill to the left. After a few hundred yards a turning to the right was marked by a bunch of purple ribbons tied into a hazel bush. *Nice touch, Zelda!* Fran changed into bottom gear and nosed into an unmade track where the wing mirrors brushed the new bracken on either side. Abruptly at the top of the hill she emerged onto open grassland with the sea to the left, the row of coastguard cottages ahead and a rough hillside rising behind them.

Zelda was waiting. She rushed out and hugged the breath out of her. 'Oh, Fran. Your dad, you loved him so much. I can't begin to imagine…'

'Don't start me…'

They clung to each other and wept until Fran broke away. 'Where's your loo? I'm bursting.'

When she emerged she said, 'I just thought. Remember Plan B? No Plan B now.' She grinned and wiped her eyes.

'Blimey. Plan B! That takes me back.'

'How's your mum?'

They edged back easily into each other's lives, as if the years had not intervened.

'Brilliant place you've got here. Amazing view.'

'Amazing weather too. You get more of it here, in your face all the time. It's so good to see the flowers – everything's mud-coloured all winter.'

Zelda and Jez had eventually bought the cottage next door and had knocked the two into one.

'That was a lucky break – we'd be a bit squashed otherwise, now we're six.'

'And I haven't seen Flora, not since she was a baby!'

'She's very excited about meeting you.' Zelda grinned across at Fran. 'So good to have you here. Tell me what you've been doing to make life bearable with that creepy man you insist on living with. I'm surprised he let you out.'

'He's not that bad. He means well.'

'Was never my impression. But never mind him. What about you?'

'I read a lot. I walk a lot. The house is immaculate. And I work part-time in the Sue Ryder shop. Geoffrey won't let me get a proper job.' She held up her hands. 'I know, I know. And yes, I'm bored out of my head. I thought about the Open University. But I don't want another fucking degree!'

Zelda described the co-operative of parents she was part of, all home-educating their younger children.

'It's such a journey to the nearest primary school. They'd have to get up stupidly early and then be exhausted by the time they got home. And not a brilliant school anyway. Tamzin and Tom get the bus into the comprehensive in Penzance. Josh and Flora only have to walk down the lane and across a field to the farm. And of course getting involved with the animals is a bonus.'

'And you take it in turns?'

'I do two whole days and a couple of mornings with them. Usually. It's reasonably flexible and really rewarding. Are you hungry? I made some soup, carrot and coriander.'

Zelda put the pan to heat on the stove. 'Let's have some music. How about this for a bit of nostalgia?' She snapped a cassette into the machine and turned up the volume. 'Bread and cheese okay with it?'

The nasal harshness of Dylan and the twang of the harmonica filled the room.

'Love that jingly-jangly bit,' said Zelda.

Fran shivered. 'I didn't know you were a Dylan fan.'

'I'm not really. They're Jez's. He's got them all, all the obscure stuff. This is a compilation he made for me. What he calls the pops. These ones I love, you can keep the rest.'

They sat down to eat, Zelda telling Fran of her tentative plans to study complementary medicine. She interrupted herself when the next track came on. 'Always makes me feel randy, this one.' She paused, spoon in mid-air. 'Hey, what's up?'

'Just reminded me of someone.'

'Who? Tell, tell!'

'Just a friend, nothing to tell.'

After lunch Zelda made a pot of coffee and rolled herself a cigarette. She lit up and exhaled slowly. 'So who was he then? Your Dylan-lover?'

'Like I said, just a friend.'

'Come on, Fran, you've gone all quiet.'

'Well, he was the first guy I slept with.'

'Love at first sight?'

'No, nothing like that.' Although of course she had imagined herself to be in love with Dale for a while.

'But you did love him. What happened to him?'

'I didn't realise… I've never spoken of him since. He went to the States. On a music scholarship. It's all so long ago. He played the cello.'

'Like Zoë. That's right, isn't it? Yes. When was that?'

'Just before I met Geoffrey.'

'Oh! Right.'

Fran looked sharply at Zelda who looked down the garden, watching smoke curl away from her.

'Did he love you?'

'I don't think so. Though I guess I thought so at the time.'

They fell silent. After a while Zelda said, 'Can I ask you something? This cellist, is he the father of the twins?'

'I was afraid you might have got some crazy idea like that. They're Geoffrey's.'

'Oh well, I've always known that isn't true. That time in Bristol when I came to stay. It was obvious to anyone with half their senses you two had never shared a Mars bar, let alone a bed. And you're no good at lying.'

'Oh God, Zel. I don't want to lie anymore. Equally I can't tell you. A promise is a promise.'

'You didn't tell me. I guessed. So it was the cellist. Why the mystery?'

'Never thought it fair, not when he doesn't know himself.'

'Ahh.'

They both fell silent again.

'Actually, I did tell you about him. Funnily enough. Years ago. Remember the guy I met in the snow? That was him.'

'I remember. It fizzled, so you said.'

'Not exactly. We clashed, fell out. End of story. Until he tipped up in the flat as a friend of Verity's. And one thing led to another. In fact it was because of her... It was after her funeral that we slept together.'

'So why didn't you tell him?'

'Didn't want to ruin his career. Sounds feeble, but he was obsessive – brilliant too. It wasn't just any old career.'

'And your life wasn't just any old life.'

'I know that now. But then all that stuff happened with Geoffrey, and it seemed the obvious way out. Better for all of us. I wrote and told him I was getting married. He didn't write again after that. I sent Christmas cards for a couple of years in the hope of keeping in touch. But he didn't. And so that was that.' Fran paused and blew her nose. 'And now I'm feeling really bad because of Zo and Dan. Promise me you'll never tell.'

Zelda promised. 'Tamzin's been on about her father lately. And of course I've got no way of contacting him, even if I thought it was a good idea. But precious little to tell her either, which is more to the point.'

Would she ever have the courage to tell Zoë and Dan about Dale? At least Tamzin had always known her father was Polish and had a whole country and culture to focus on. Would the twins want to go looking for Dale? The only place she knew about was that street in the East End. It was probably bulldozed long ago and she didn't remember where it was anyway.

She lay awake that night, worrying in the early hours about the confession she'd made to Zelda. It had all set her thinking about Dale for the first time in years. It was as if being here, away from Geoffrey, allowed Dale back into her consciousness. When she fell asleep she had restless dreams and woke early in a sweat.

She crept out and found her way along the cliff path and down to a rocky cove. An oystercatcher took off in scissoring flight as she stepped onto the pebbles at the back of the beach. Hers were the only footmarks on the sandy foreshore which was arrowed with bird prints. She found a comfortable boulder and let her thoughts unravel as she watched the waves roll and crash on the rocks. Harry always said the sea was healing, and that if you grew up in the sound of it, you'd always need to seek it out. He was right. She'd been without it too long.

How long was it since she'd heard from Dale? Ever since she'd got married. All the twins' lives.

How did I not tell him about the pregnancy? I did it for his sake, didn't I? Or was it for mine? I don't think I knew then, and I'm still not sure now. Did we love each other? If I'd told him it would have really tested that, opened up cavernous feelings, the risk of discovering the truth. The tide surged against the cliff, throwing up spray. *Do I still love him? Does he ever think of me? Oh, you stupid woman, what do you imagine?* She rubbed her almost numb legs and climbed back up to the coast path.

When she got back the house was empty. A note from Zelda told her to make herself at home. She made coffee, turned on the tape player and let the sound of Dylan fill the room. She felt a tingling euphoria that set her dancing wildly round the furniture. But euphoria flipped into tears and she ended up on the sofa, sobbing into the cushions, longing for Dale, until the tape clicked off. In the silence that followed, she was forced to face the glaring truth that she could not stay married to Geoffrey. The sound of children's voices in the garden had her running for the stairs and the privacy of her bedroom.

⁎

The following morning Fran woke with a feverish cold that developed into raging tonsillitis. All the glands in her body seemed to have come out in sympathy with her throat, her head throbbed and her limbs ached. She asked about Zelda's doctor. Zelda made a face.

'I don't care what he's like. Just want some antibiotics to knock this on the head.'

'Oh, he's very nice, excellent as doctors go. But, yes, he's bound to give you antibiotics. That's what I was dubious about.'

'Why?'

'I don't think you're in a fit state to go into all that now. But they're bad news, destroy your immune system. I can have a homeopath or a herbalist come to you instead.'

Fran shook her head and insisted on the devil she knew. Zelda agreed, on the condition she'd see the homeopath when she was better.

'What's the point of that? I'll be better.'

'Don't argue, it'll make your throat worse. And no, you won't be better. There's a difference between getting a cure and being healed.'

Fran was baffled but too ill to argue. It took three days for the effect of the drugs to kick in and during that time she was forced to relax, to become dependent. She wept frequently between sleeping and sipping the herbal potions Zelda prepared. When she was recovering Zelda drove her to the house of her friend Maggie, the homeopath.

'She's a very experienced woman. A doctor before she studied homeopathy, not to mention a massage expert. She's also a healer and I've asked her to give you a very thorough going over. So be prepared for anything. Be honest with her. No point in not. Totally confidential of course.'

'What do you mean, a healer?'

'Healing hands, spiritual healing. Don't worry, nothing spooky. I don't understand it either. Ask her.'

'I notice you didn't tell me all this when we made the appointment.'

'I'm not daft. I wanted to be sure of getting you here. See you in a couple of hours or so.'

'A couple of hours?' Fran gaped. But in fact it was nearly three hours later when she found Zelda waiting for her in Maggie's kitchen.

Maggie was a slight, unassuming woman of about fifty with greying hair tied back in a plain rubber band. Fran had a moment of disappointment, as if she had expected at least a halo from someone called a healer. Maggie was someone she simply wouldn't notice in the checkout queue at the supermarket.

'I feel I'm making a fuss,' Fran started. 'Mother would say I was making a song and dance.'

Maggie raised her eyebrows.

'Now that I'm better, I mean…'

'A song and dance? That sounds a fine thing to make. A fine healing process. And anyway, sometimes we need to make a fuss, as you put it. When it comes to living your life. How you live it.'

'Living my life? I never thought of it that way. It was always so negative when…'

'So – redefine it. As a joyful thing, a life-enhancing thing. After all, you only have one life. It's a brilliant place for us to start.'

Maggie went on to ask outrageous questions, yet Fran answered them because she wanted to know the answers herself. Maggie's quality of attention was different from anything she had ever experienced. She felt heard for the first time.

When this process came to an end Fran expected to collect a prescription and leave. But Maggie smiled and said they were only just beginning. Fran lay on the massage table covered with a light layer of fabric. Pillows appeared magically just where she needed them. Music of a kind she couldn't identify filled the room. A bird sang outside the window. She closed her eyes, feeling her limbs becoming heavy. How long she was there, and what Maggie did, Fran had no idea. She woke to hear her own voice shouting out, her legs and arms thrashing about. Maggie's voice was calm and her hands held her.

Afterwards, Maggie said, 'That's great. You've come a long way today. As to what it means, only you can know that. It will become clear to you as time goes on. You've started out on a journey today, the journey of healing. You can continue it as long as you want. It can be a lifetime. Or you may think what you did today was far enough.'

Fran was silent. She felt out of her depth, suddenly foolish.

'You respond very well. Your body wants to do it, to heal itself.'

'From the tonsillitis, you mean?' Even as she said it, Fran knew this wasn't just about a sore throat.

'The tonsillitis is just a symptom. There's so much you're holding onto. Not saying. Some things that happened long ago. But you're ready to release some of them. It's a choice you have.'

'I don't understand. How do I do that? What are they?'

'When things happen to do with the throat, it's often about secrets, pretences, or things you dare not ask for. Not being able to voice things. Women hold on to so many secrets. And they rarely ask for what they really want.'

'Sometimes they don't even know,' Fran heard herself say. 'I was a very silent child. Except for the nightmares, that is.'

But that reminded her of Harry who used to comfort her and rock her back to safe sleep. Her tears flowed.

'You're doing so well,' said Maggie and passed her a box of tissues.

Some voice in her head was telling her that what Maggie said was all 'a bit far-fetched'. But somewhere else, deep in her body, it all made perfect sense.

'One thing I can say for sure,' Maggie was saying, 'you will carry on having this tonsillitis until you speak your truth, whatever that is. And when you do, the infections will stop.'

'Really?' Fran was wide-eyed.

'But of course. The body will not be silenced – and the body and mind are not separate. There is a kind of alchemy that happens. Don't worry, it'll all make sense to you in time. I'll put you up a remedy. I'm pretty sure I know what's right for you now. And I'd like to check back with you in a week or so when it's had time to take effect. Now, take it easy today. You may feel quite strange. Light-headed, queasy even. You may just want to fall deeply asleep. Let yourself do it. This work is exhausting and your system is tired anyway.'

Fran thought it strange she called it work, but changed her mind later in the day when she was overwhelmed by a tiredness greater than she had known since giving birth. She slept deeply and woke in the spell of a dream.

She is a dream-child threading through a field of sunflowers, all with their backs turned towards her. Their stems prickle her bare arms and when she passes each one she turns and looks up into the radiant face to soak up its smile. She meets a woman with blue beads in her hair who lives in the stem of the sunflower in the very middle of the field. Blue-bead woman greets her and flies her up and up into an auditorium suspended in the clouds. She can hear a voice of unearthly beauty singing and filling the sky. It is herself singing and she is walking up between the rows of seats to a roar of applause, and being met by a man in blue robes who is, and is not, her father.

Later, when she described it to her, Maggie said it was an angel dream. 'Angel dreams are special. Not like ordinary dreams. They take you into another dimension. It's like they can dream you a path – a song and dance even – to follow into the future. They let you know you are protected.'

'Is that like a guardian angel?'

'Something like that.'

On her last night they went to the local pub for Zelda's friend Lyn's birthday celebration. Zelda promised Fran she'd be welcomed and would enjoy the music, which turned out to be prophetic. The pub was tiny with a low ceiling and a log fire at one end of the bar. The musicians were setting up in the family room and a number of men with long hair and cigarettes were in and out of the door bringing in more kit and sorting out a mass of microphones, speakers and leads which spilled over into the bar area.

Fran shivered at the draught and sipped a warming whisky. The seat by the fire was occupied by a bear of a man who stood up, towering over her as he ushered her into the chair with a shy smile. He made his way to the drums, peeled off his sweater and for a moment she thought he was wearing an elaborately printed shirt. But the blue and green design moved with his muscles as he bent over each drum, his ear to the surface, adjusting the tension. His arms and all she could see of his chest in his black singlet were a mass of tattooed leaves and tendrils spiralling around birds and flowers.

The other musicians moved into position. A short middle-aged man with a collapsed face and a beer belly was on bass guitar. A younger man in patchwork trousers with a froth of sandy beard and a gold earring took up an acoustic guitar, and a lean older man in denims with lank grey hair and a roll-up jammed in the corner of his mouth seated himself behind the keyboard. Final adjustments were being made, jacks were poked into sockets, leads were being untangled and pints of bitter were balanced in easy reach on the tops of speakers. A packet of Rizla and a lighter were propped against a No Smoking sign. Then the tattooed giant gave a roll on the drums and Sandy Beard grabbed the microphone to wish Lyn a happy birthday.

The band was good. The keyboard player was no longer laid-back, his fingers like rubber, scrambling over the keys. Mostly Fran watched the drummer, who played in a state of meditation, his serenity only broken by a frown of concentration or a laugh shared with the bass player.

A tall, angular woman took up position behind a standing microphone. As they swung into the next number a sonorous voice cut through the chatter at the bar and hushed it. 'Summertime and the livin' is easy' rolled effortlessly round the stone walls. Fran was enthralled. The singer was no beauty but she had a strong face with a big nose, scruffy blonde hair with the roots showing and a spiky fringe. Her clothes seemed to have been thrown together out of the ironing basket and wellington boots poked from a long denim skirt with beads round the hem.

At the interval, Tattoo Man chatted to her while he waited for a refill. His name was Steve.

'That's what I want to do when I grow up,' she heard herself tell him.

'Don't wait to grow up. We didn't.' He waited for her to laugh and gave a slow smile. 'Which instrument?'

'The singer. She's amazing.'

'Oh, Patch. Yes, she's something else. You can have a go tonight, you know.'

'Oh no! I can't sing.'

'You'll be in good company. There's usually one or two can't wait to make fools of themselves.' He stopped abruptly, looking troubled. 'Not that you'd...'

Fran laughed. 'Don't worry. I'm not going to.'

He looked straight at her. 'Life's too short not to do what you need to.'

When Steve had gone Zelda joined her.

'Jez does a lot of work for him, he's a builder. No good taking a shine to him though.'

'Oh? Married is he? Nice guy.'

'In a manner of speaking. He and Roy are an item – the bass player. They think they keep it deadly secret because Roy's afraid of losing clients. He's an accountant. But everyone knows and nobody cares as long as he gets the books right.'

Fran laughed. 'Ho hum. Life's a bitch. Not that I was…'

'Oh come on, Fran! There's no use denying it. I could see… And he was just enjoying it so much. He's a devil, that one!'

'You're incorrigible.' Always the same Zelda. She hoped Steve wasn't eavesdropping. 'Well, I did quite fancy him. But I'm not available. Obviously.'

Zelda rolled her eyes. 'Time you did something about that.'

Fran shrugged and sipped her whisky.

In this wild place, watching Steve and his mates make music within these ancient walls, she was seduced by the sound, tempted into believing anything was possible. The evening wore on. She met friends of Jez and Zelda, food was passed around and then she found Steve at her elbow.

'Your turn now,' he said with a sly wink at Zelda, who winked back.

Fran clutched at the bar as he tried to steer her away, but little bursts of cheering erupted round the pub and she saw the singer called Patch detaching her mike and holding it out.

'What's it to be?' That was the keyboard player who had a Welsh accent.

'I really can't…'

'Rubbish. That's what I used to say,' said Patch. 'Go on. First song you think of.'

'"Carolina Moon"?' As soon as she said it, she thought, hopelessly old-fashioned.

But Patch was grinning and nodding. 'Great choice.'

'I know the words – it was my father's favourite song.' He used to belt it out while making sandwiches for Sunday supper, but she didn't dare think of that now.

Patch relayed her whisper to the keyboard player, announcing it to the room. Steve gave her a thumbs-up. There was no turning back.

She appealed to Patch. 'Help me?'

'Sure.' Patch bent towards her and put an arm round her waist. She heard the opening bars, Patch hummed a note and she echoed it. The keyboard player and Patch exchanged nods and they were away.

She was aware of her pale trickle of a voice beside Patch's tidal wave of sound. It was crazy to be doing this to her barely recovered throat, but it felt released, not strained. Her voice cracked at one point, but she knew, with a tiny bubble of elation, that it suited the song. After that she lost consciousness until there was a sudden silence followed by a roar of applause. Sweating and shaking, she was propelled back to her seat. Someone handed her a pint, someone else a whisky.

'Jesus Christ,' said Zelda. 'That was bloody amazing. I didn't know you could sing.'

'I never could. It was Patch really.'

'I'll have you know I dropped out after the first few bars,' came a voice from behind her.

Zelda nodded. 'Sure she did.'

Steve raised his pint in her direction from behind his drums. 'I told you – life's too short.'

19

Next day Fran bounced downstairs.

'I've never felt better!'

She found herself dancing round the kitchen with Tamzin. Flora ran to join in while Josh rolled his eyes.

'It's your endorphins,' said Zelda. 'Chemicals in the brain. You know.'

'No, I don't know. What are you on about?'

'When you have a high, like last night, it releases chemicals that make you feel good. Not just feel good. Helps healing, makes it easier to learn…'

Josh rolled his eyes again and he and Tom chorused, 'Happiness is better than drugs.'

'I guess your mother's mentioned these end-whatsits before then?'

'Just once or twice.'

'Like two million times a week.'

'You and your healing stuff.' Fran took a mug of coffee from Zelda. 'When are you actually going to do it, then? You said years ago you wanted to be a healing-type person.'

'She's doing a correspondence course,' said Tamzin.

'Except she never corresponds,' came a shout from the utility room.

'Tom, don't put that football shirt in with the rest. It runs.'

Tom came back into the room. 'There you have it. That's typical. She's always so bothered about the washing or cooking stuff that she never finishes her assignments.'

'We have to eat! You all…'

'But we don't have to grind the wheat to make the flour to make the bread. You could just buy Mother's Pride and be done with it. For example.'

Zelda explained about her foundation course. 'I'll do professional training when the little ones are older.'

'Promise?' said Tom.

'If I don't have another baby.'

This was greeted by howls of horror from the boys, shrieks of excitement from Flora and a sigh from Tamzin. 'You know, Mum, you're a hopeless role model.'

Zelda shrugged. 'I am who I am. Anyway I'm far more interested in Fran's new career.'

Fran felt foolish and excited all at once. 'Hardly a career, Zel. You know, I felt, when I was singing, as if – this probably sounds stupid – but I thought, this is who I am meant to be.'

Zelda hugged her. 'You've got to do something with that voice. There must be groups around you could sing with.'

'You must be joking! Can you imagine what Geoffrey would say if I announced I was off singing in pubs?'

They both cackled at the thought.

Fran was quiet for a moment. She'd been doing a lot of thinking since her session with Maggie. 'A lot's got to change when I get home. Not ready to talk about it yet. But big stuff. It's time I took control of my life.'

Josh kicked Tom and grabbed his trainers and the boys started to move off towards the garden.

'Hey, don't go,' Fran called out. 'Something I wanted to ask. I'd really like to bring the twins down here some time. That's if…' She looked over to Zelda, who beamed. 'I just wanted to ask you guys if you'd show them around?'

'Sure,' said Tom.

Fran looked at Tamzin. 'Zoë's younger than you of course but she's pretty sparky. They come between you and Tom. Dan can be a bit… I don't know really. Reserved, I suppose.'

'S'okay. He can tag along if he feels like it. Or not.' Tom headed the football he was carrying back into the utility room.

'Does he support Liverpool?' was all Josh wanted to know, and made a pitying face when she told him West Ham.

Zelda grabbed her arm. 'Hey, why don't you just come and live down here?'

'Crazy idea! But don't think it hadn't occurred to me. It makes me feel so alive – the sea, the land… Oh, I don't know… I can't describe… Anyway, it's out of the question.'

'Oh, yeah? Out of the question, eh?' Zelda nudged her hard in the ribs. 'Like singing, I suppose.'

Fran hardly noticed the drive home. The journey in her head was all-absorbing. Automatic pilot brought her back to Dorset along roads edged with May blossom, cow parsley and buttercups, but re-entry into Pseud's Corner was not going to be so easy. She felt like an entirely different person from the one who had driven away.

She made a diversion into South Cadbury and parked alongside the church. A climb up Cadbury Hill would give her time to get into the right frame of mind, whatever that might be. It was a favourite place where she'd walked many times alone and with Zoë and Dan. They'd brought picnics in the summer and tin trays on the few occasions when there had been enough snow to go sledging. When she reached the top of the path she sat for a while on the roots of the guardian ash tree as she always did.

She needed to sort out the jumble in her head. More than once she'd thought of telling Harry, talking it all over with him, before she remembered there was no Harry anymore. Life's too short, Steve had said. Dad's life had been too short. Cut off in sight of retirement, before he had the chance to reshape his rose garden, dig a new asparagus bed. And think of Verity. She hardly got started on her life. In a way she owed it to them to make the most of hers.

First she must leave Geoffrey, undo the pact they'd made in Bristol over twelve years ago and claim her life back. How could she have left it so long? Next came the pressing question of whether or not she should contact Dale. And why? Would she be doing that for herself or for the twins? She knew instantly it was for herself – but it begged the question of the third issue: telling the twins the truth. When would she do it? And how?

One thing at a time, she told herself. Get free of Geoffrey and she'd be able to see more clearly. How would Zoë and Dan take it? He might not be their biological father, or even a very brilliant father, but he was the only one they had ever known. She mustn't underestimate that.

And of course the first thing they'd want to know was who their real father was. Oh, shit. It was one thing getting turned on by a song, wallowing in the memories. But the real thing, her relationship with Dale – what was it exactly? It had been a friendship, certainly. But that had evaporated the moment it turned into something more.

Not quite true. After all, he had written – a letter to a person he trusted, that sort of letter. Was their love-making just for comfort after Verity's funeral? Could it have been more if he'd stayed? Or was it no accident they'd left it to the last minute? Both of them scared of finding out what it could have become?

Fran stood abruptly and set off up the steep slope and along the high ramparts, bracing herself against a stiff breeze that threatened to throw her off balance and down into the ditch. *What a shrivelled person I've been all these years. What sort of a mother? It's been all I could do to survive half the time, to hold my own in Geoffrey's comfortable prison. Think of Zelda, she's got it right. It's not perfect but it's all rough and tumble. Like it was at her house when we were kids. I always wished my mother was like Gaye, imagining what it would be like to run away and live with them. And I've ended up just like my mother. Well, maybe not quite. But scared just like she was. Zelda's lot, they all communicate. Too much some of the time. But we don't, hardly at all. And I want the twins to know something different before it's too late.*

And what of Dale? Dale as reality, a person who was living and breathing and playing his cello somewhere in present time, not just in 1965. He'd always been there, but only as a ghostly presence alongside Verity. She'd never allowed herself to really think about Dale. Not since the decision to marry Geoffrey.

'I betrayed him,' she said to the sky. *It was easy enough to kid myself he went off and left me pregnant. But he didn't. He was following his dream, his whole purpose he'd been working for forever, since he was a little boy in that godforsaken street in Wapping. Then we made a baby. And I didn't let him know. He had a right to know. Why didn't*

I tell him? Scared of being rejected? Terrified in fact. It was safer to keep it all in my control, tight and tied down. Tied down to Geoffrey. Maybe I was even afraid Dale wouldn't *reject me. Maybe I'd have been just as scared if he'd said to come to New York. Have a baby abroad? Anywhere but in freezing cold England? Oh no, much better to stay here, married to someone I don't even like, being* not *supported by my totally uptight mother.*

She paused to gaze across at Glastonbury Tor, imagining water stretching to that strange and mystical place, setting off in a boat on a quest to Avalon. 'Time I got home,' she muttered aloud. *And I haven't even thought about the singing.* She remembered her angel dream. *I have to do it. I'd never felt so alive.* She laughed out loud. *Dale would be so surprised. If only he'd been there. His Fran with a microphone, and the whole pub listening. Only not his Fran. I wonder who he's with now. Married? Kids? Or still on the loose with a load of mistresses? Did he make it? Or is he just playing in some orchestra, bored out of his mind?*

She walked on towards the entrance to the circle. Suppose the singing was just a one-off? Suppose she could never do it again? Suppose she could only sing one song? That she only had a voice when her throat was sore? She paused at the top of the track and walked back to the ash tree. She leant her forehead against the grooved bark. 'Let it be real,' she murmured, pressing one hand against the trunk.

When Geoffrey came in she fixed them both a drink. It was not her first.

'We need to talk.' They both spoke together.

Geoffrey inclined his head. 'You go first.'

She took a deep breath. 'I think we… I mean I, have come to the end of the road. You remember how we talked about it? Way back then, in Bristol? You said I was under no obligation to stay married to you. Don't get me wrong. I think we made a pretty good job of it. Being parents, I mean. Especially you. Not easy when they weren't yours. But now they're older and I have time to look at my life, I find it isn't enough. It may sound corny, but I need to discover who I am. And I'm sorry, I can't do that with you. I want to leave you, Geoffrey, I want us to separate.'

Geoffrey had turned away and was looking into the dark garden.

How would he react? Would this trigger his old behaviour? She stayed near the door. Her bag was still in the car, keys in her pocket. Just in case. Slowly he turned, shrugged his shoulders and looked into his drink, swirling the bowl of the glass in the palm of his hand. 'I'm sorry you feel like that, Francesca.'

Fran eyed him. Why so unctuous? she wondered. Where was the possessive, controlling Geoffrey she knew and feared? He'd been more relaxed in the last few years, but even so… Would she find herself locked inside the house in the morning?

'I regret this, I really do. That it should come to this. But so be it. Far be it from me to go back on my word. Did it come to you in Cornwall? When you were staying with that Zelda?'

'Don't start on Zelda! Nothing whatever to do with her.'

Geoffrey smiled. 'It hasn't been easy for me either, you know.'

'You didn't have to marry me.'

'I thought we got married to give your baby – or, as it turned out, babies – a father, security.'

'And to keep your father happy.'

'I was obsessed with you. It was you I wanted.'

'Not me. You were obsessed with a picture, a Queen, a tarot card. Your *idea* of me. And you tried to pin me down, imprison me. With your conventions and your house and your roast dinner on Sundays and sex only when you wanted it.' She'd gone too far, waited for the dangerous look in his eye.

'So I wasn't good enough? Did it ever occur to you, it might be you? Always so distant, so take-it-or-leave-it and I'll-put-up-with-it-if-I-must. No more babies, you said. Did it ever occur to you that I might want a child of my own?'

'You never…' Rubbish. Of course he didn't. Or did he?

'And what do you think it feels like to make love to your wife when she *really* looks as if she's lying back and thinking of England?'

This was where he would stride across the room and pin her to the wall. But no. Instead they were interrupted by the telephone. He was monosyllabic during the call: *yes, no, fine, I'll see to that*, and so on.

'That was about the conference,' he said afterwards. 'I won't be back until Sunday after all. Damn nuisance. I won't see the twins. You'll tell them, will you? Best if you tell them.' He dithered in the doorway.

'We'll need to work things out. When I come back. Need to go and pack.'

'There was something you were going to tell *me*.'

'Oh. Well. It's not that important. In the circumstances...'

So. Just like that. Tell the twins. She'd done it. Or had she? Geoffrey didn't go to many conferences and he seemed particularly preoccupied with this one. Fran was only too happy to have the task of telling Zoë and Dan on her own. But she was wary, puzzled. What was going on in his head? Was he just bluffing? Laying a trap?

The twins were at school until the weekend. Meanwhile, the one thing she could do was start to track Dale down. She started by ringing the music department in Bristol, but the person who might help was off sick. She succeeded in getting the number for the academy in New York and calculated the time difference. It was a long shot. Would they keep track of former students? Would they have a forwarding address? In the afternoon she called the operator and waited to be connected to the Juilliard.

A secretary answered in a harsh accent. Yes, they did keep details of past students, but that far back? She had no immediate access. Fran could not be sure of the year he left which was also problematic. However, she would research her '*in*-quirry' and phone back. She phoned back within the hour. Dale had gone to Paris from New York but by now he might be in Moscow. She gave Fran the number of a member of staff who was thought still to be in contact with Dale, but who would not be available until the following week.

At the weekend Zoë was full of a concert trip to London the school were organising.

'Mummy, I *must* go. Miss Henshaw says it is not to be missed. She says the soloist in the Elgar is *the* up-and-coming player of the century.'

Zoë kept thrusting the leaflet and form under Fran's nose. But Fran was too preoccupied with tracing Dale.

The question of when to tell the twins about her and Geoffrey was answered over hot chocolate round the kitchen table when Zoë asked about his conference. Fran found herself telling them of her decision.

Dan greeted the news with silence. Zoë stuck her lip out and started to cry, angry, demanding to know why.

Dan nudged Zoë out of her tears, mouthing at her.

Zoë frowned. 'Her?'

'Yes, *her*. You know.' Dan turned to Fran. 'It's because of her?'

'Who? What her?'

'Because of that woman in Hertfordshire. That's why you're leaving him, isn't it?'

'What *are* you talking about? Woman? What woman?'

Dan looked at Zoë. 'That woman I saw him with. We both saw.'

The truth of what Dan was saying arrived in Fran's stomach but her mind still resisted.

'I saw them. When he dropped us off at the swimming pool. The desk was upstairs and there was a queue. I was looking out the window, waiting. And there he was, walking across the car park with this woman.'

'That doesn't mean…I mean, she may just have been a friend…'

'Arm in arm they were. And I'm just thinking, who's she? – when they stop for a snog. Gross.' He gestured with two fingers down his throat. 'Then they got in Dad's car and drove off.'

Zoë was talking between sobs. Evidently, she too had seen them get in the car but hadn't wanted to believe the rest of Dan's story. But then she and Dan had seen him with her again in the early hours when they'd been awake talking about Grandpa Ted.

'It was the same woman. The same shape. She looked like she'd been poured into her suit.'

'You mean she was at the house?'

Zoë nodded. 'Her car was parked round behind the garages. Dad walked her round the corner, came back on his own, then this car drove off down the drive. I hate him. He's vile, gross!'

Fran bit back a ready agreement. 'It was careless he let you see, that he had her at the house when you were there. But we all make mistakes.'

'You don't mean it, Mum. I can tell by your voice.'

Fran suggested tea and Dan insisted on making it. She hadn't known Dan like this, solicitous of her, since he was a little boy.

'What's her name?' Zoë had dried her tears and was eating custard creams with her tea.

Dan shrugged. 'How should I know?'

'Sandra?' Fran wondered where that came from, then remembered the long-ago scene with Charlie and the barmaid.

'That'll do. Sandra Suit – she was kind of stuffed into it, that thing she was wearing, with little fat legs at the corners.' Dan spoke with venom.

Zoë shrugged. 'Whatever.'

'How dare he do that to you, Mum.'

She couldn't say she didn't care – and she didn't, almost – it would feel like betraying her children. Zoë was visibly simmering.

'You okay, Zo?'

Zoë slammed her mug onto the table, splashing chocolate everywhere. 'No. I'm bloody damn not okay. I'm not having everything messed up by some suit woman.' Her voice cracked. 'Tell Daddy to come back and stop being so silly.'

'But I don't want Daddy to come back.'

'Then you're just as bloody silly, Mummy.' Zoë's crescendo dived into sobs and she dropped her head onto the table, dark curls trailing in pools of chocolate.

When Fran put an arm across her shoulders she shrugged it away. Zoë, always a Daddy's girl, was feeling more betrayed than she was herself.

'Shut up, Zoë.' Dan clenched his fists.

Fran saw tears in his eyes as he took his mug to the sink and washed it furiously under a fiercely running tap. She went to hug him, but he too pushed her off.

When he finally turned off the tap and upended the mug on the rack, he turned and leaned against the worktop.

'So why are you…?'

He was screeched down by Zoë. 'I don't want to know.'

'Like I said, shut up, Zo. Mum?'

'Yes. Okay, to get back to where I started. I'm not leaving Dad because of Sandra Suit. Because I didn't know about her. Obviously.'

'Is it because of us? Is it something…?'

'Whyever? Whatever made you think that? Of *course* not. I'm leaving him because of me. Because I'm not happy. I don't know what I want, not yet, but it's something very different and I have to be on my own to find out.'

'On your own? What about us?'

'I didn't mean you. I'll be with you two. Of course I will. Most of the time anyway. When you're not at school. Or staying with Dad.'

'We don't want to stay with Dad.'

'You probably will want to. When you're used to it. When you've met Sandra.'

'I don't want to get used to it. I don't want to meet Sandra.'

They both spoke together as they used to when they were small, often saying the same thing in chorus. Dan was worried about having to see Sandra Suit, Zoë more concerned about school and music lessons.

'I don't know what's going to happen about everything. And you might have to do some things you don't much like. But I promise you, nothing will happen without us talking about it.'

They exchanged looks and shrugged. They seemed to be calming down, but they had enough to cope with. Too soon to talk about the house being sold.

'I tell you what. We'll have a holiday. How about we go down and stay with Zelda? As soon as you break up.'

'With her kids?' Zoë looked dubious.

'Of course. You remember Zelda brought them for lunch that time? Must be at least a couple of years ago. On her way to see her mum.'

'They're all different colours,' said Dan.

'That's one way of putting it. You wouldn't remember Jez, their dad. You were tiny when he came to stay. His family came from Nigeria as students. So that's why…'

'Oh yeah – Tamzin moaned because her skin's really pale and she had to have sun cream and the boys didn't, and she said it wasn't fair.'

Zoë laughed. 'Hey, I remember – Dan?' Together they chanted, 'Vanilla, Fudge, Chocolate!'

'What?'

'Don't look so shocked, Mum. It's what they called themselves. Tom said. When they went to school down there, and they were the only ones who weren't white.'

Fran was brought up short. How could she not have thought about all that? Was that behind the home-schooling? Years ago Geoffrey had predicted problems – *you hardly ever see a black face in Cornwall* –

and just because Geoffrey had said it, she'd been perverse and ruled out all difficulties in her mind. She hadn't even asked Zelda.

'That must have been tough. And of course, Jez isn't Tamzin's father. He was a Pole.'

Zoë giggled.

Dan rolled his eyes. 'A Polish person, stupid.'

'You'd like Jez, he loved playing with you when you were babies.'

Groans and shrugs from both of them.

'The bad news is that Josh supports Liverpool – he didn't think much of West Ham. But there's a beach five minutes' walk away. Yes, of course you can take your cello.'

Everything in her life seemed to be shifting and flowing. The news of Geoffrey's affair explained why he'd been so relaxed about separating – she'd handed it to him on a plate. But what a toad, not to come clean! She was shaken about being deceived and furious with him for being so careless around the twins. On the other hand, his behaviour left her unexpectedly on the moral high ground.

When she phoned the number in upstate New York, a man with a mid-European edge to his drawl announced he was Reuben Meyers. Dale had been a star pupil. He looked on him as the son he never had. He would go far. Yes, he had been in Paris, then Moscow and now he was in Germany. What a barbaric place to be! He was not too sure about this Tortelier Dale rated so highly. Dale should be in Vienna; there he would have culture. Yes, he could give her an address, the one in Paris. He always returned to Paris. But it would be no good writing there just now because Dale was supposed to be on tour. No, he did not have the itinerary. But would it not include the cultural centres of Europe? Maybe he would be coming to Vienna and coming to his senses and deciding to stay there.

Bemused, Fran put the phone down and sat at the kitchen table over a coffee wondering what to do next. She was frustrated at every turn. Maybe the message was that she should not contact Dale. She found herself staring at the concert flyer Zoë had thrown down in exasperation on the table before she went out. Her parting shot had been, 'You're different since you went to Cornwall, Mummy. You don't do what I tell you.' She really must make a decision about this school trip.

Fran gazed at the programme of well-known classics. Who was this soloist with the big reputation? A cellist she supposed, since it was Miss Henshaw who was praising him to the skies. Zoë was increasingly favouring cello over piano studies and had passed her last exam with distinction.

Her eye stopped at one name. A sensation like ice-cold ants crept over her scalp. The soloist was billed as Dale Woods Weaver. The 'Woods' bit was a surprise but there couldn't be two Dale Weavers in the cello world. It seemed he was playing at the Festival Hall for the first time since returning to his native country.

Fran grabbed the form and saw it was the last day for inclusion on the trip. She rang the school, praying to a god she didn't believe in that it wasn't too late. Her luck seemed to be turning. It happened that Miss Henshaw herself was in the office to check the applications. Yes, there was a place available. Yes, Zoë really should go; she showed such great promise. Fran heard herself volunteering to be an accompanying parent. She had always avoided going before. Miss Henshaw was delighted with her offer. Zoë was ecstatic when she came home and was gobsmacked Fran was coming too.

The coach was full. Fran sat next to another mother who chattered comfortably about gardening, oblivious to Fran's absent-minded responses. Zoë was in the back with her friends, Dan was back at the school and Geoffrey was in Hertfordshire, in the arms of Sandra Suit, no doubt. Good luck to him.

She breathed deeply as trees and fields slipped past in a fog of steamy glass. She touched the little bump under her shirt which was the silver hare, her talisman. When she started the search for Dale she'd burrowed into her box of earrings and found it where it had been since her wedding day. Superstition? Reassurance? Who cared? It gave her courage as the enormity of what she was doing began to take shape in her consciousness. She was taking her daughter to see her father play in a concert. In this she was deceiving both Zoë and Dale. Neither of them knew of the other's existence. She could hear her daughter's voice from time to time, carrying forward from the back of the coach, exclaiming, excited. Like a lamb to the slaughter. She shook herself for being melodramatic. All the same she felt guilty.

Sitting in the auditorium waiting for the concert to begin Fran felt she would break into a million pieces if anyone touched her. It was particularly difficult to be surrounded by nudging, giggling, whispering schoolchildren and the gardening mother who kept rustling a packet of peppermints. Fran clutched her handbag which contained a letter addressed to Dale and puzzled about how and where she should deliver it. She'd already asked Miss Henshaw whether she planned to go backstage. Miss Henshaw had looked shocked and said it wasn't a pop concert.

Dale didn't feature in the first half of the programme and Fran was detailed to supervise children in the toilets during the interval. She couldn't believe the things they talked about from cubicle to cubicle and turned a blind eye to make-up being applied and passed around. The lights were going down as she shepherded the last stragglers into their seats.

She sank into hers as the conductor was clapped on stage and was taken by surprise by the thunderous applause that greeted the tall, spare figure with close-cropped dark hair who followed and took a bow. He was engrossed in tuning his instrument before she recognised him. It was certainly Dale, but what a different Dale. A poised, smoothly groomed Dale. Fran searched for the word to describe this new vision. Elegant. That was it. Dale had turned into someone who was elegant. Disappointment gripped her stomach. For a moment she thought she might be sick, he felt so alien to her. She struggled to gain control of her burning body. Then the cello came in with the opening passage of the Elgar concerto. All movement in the auditorium ceased. Fran gazed at the source of the sound and then glanced along the row to where Zoë was sitting. Her daughter's eyes were shining and her mouth slightly open, mesmerised by the figure on the platform. Fran felt the tension in her crackle, a triangle of energy stretching between herself, Zoë and Dale.

Here we are. A family, and I am the only one who knows it. The electricity feels so strong it could scorch me. I wonder if my presence and my knowing triggers any kind of awareness in either of those two? They look alike. Can't everyone see it? That always disturbed me when she was little. She reminded me so much of Dale it was hard to look at her sometimes. There's plenty of fizz going on between Zoë and Dale, in one direction of course. Is it all admiration of his playing? It helps that he's bloody good-looking of course. Suppose she did get to do a master class with him in a few years? And fell in love with him? What a thought. Worse still, he could fall for her. It happened. Oh my God! The sooner I get this sorted out the better. Is that just jealousy? No! Hell, maybe. Well, yes actually. But some good old-fashioned mother instinct too. Whatever it is, that scenario mustn't happen.

Fran was transfixed for the next half hour, hardly stirring between movements, not hearing the few children who started to clap and were quickly hushed by their more knowledgeable neighbours. At the end of the concert she hurried out, oblivious of what might be expected of her, pushing her way up the gangway with none of her usual hesitancy. She made her way to the box office. No, the lady had no contact with the musicians. She indicated a side door and suggested she find an attendant in the office at the end of the corridor. Fran careered down the corridor and nearly bumped into a uniformed official emerging from a side passage. Could he help madam? Yes, he did attend the musicians. Yes, it would be his pleasure to deliver a letter to Mr Woods Weaver. Should he give a name? Fran shook her head, pressed the letter into his hand with an urgency he could not mistake, turned and charged back the way she had come. As she cannoned out of the door into the foyer Fran nearly collided with Miss Henshaw and muttered about taking a wrong turning.

'Are you all right, Mummy?' said a voice at her elbow. 'I called out to you at the end, but you didn't hear me. You nearly pushed an old lady over on your way up the steps.'

'Did I, darling? Oh dear. But wasn't it wonderful?' Fran hardly knew what she was saying.

Zoë saw tears shining in her mother's eyes and hugged her tight. 'Mummy, it *was* wonderful! And I just know I have to learn from that man! I'm so glad you understand!'

Fran was far from understanding anything and her daughter's words came back to her in the early hours of the morning, setting her on a roller-coaster of unmanageable feelings.

20

Fran had promised to spend the following week with Eleanor, sorting through Harry's papers and clothes. It was a tense and difficult time. It wasn't the fact that Mother did so little to help that got to Fran. All the fight had gone out of her and it was disconcerting not to be constantly criticised. The only time they relaxed was over a drink in the evening.

'What we need is a Navy-strength G&T,' Eleanor would say, handing her a tumbler which was three quarters gin – a good time to tell Mother her news.

There was no need to mention Sandra Suit – or Carys, as she'd discovered when Geoffrey returned from his 'conference'. He'd been embarrassed, but not at all contrite about what the children had seen. 'They need to grow up a little,' was all he'd said. Smug. The nerve of the man.

'Geoffrey and I have decided to separate.'

'About time. Never liked the man. But I suppose he was useful.'

'Mother! I thought you'd be upset. What d'you mean, useful?'

'Taking on the twins, of course. You didn't think anyone believed they were his, did you?'

Fran had rarely felt so foolish, so wrong-footed. Clever old Mother. 'Did Dad…?'

'He was the one who spotted you were pregnant. Wouldn't let me interfere. Said you had to work it out for yourself.'

'You mean you talked about it? Back then?'

'Of course we did. What do you imagine…?'

Fran's gin appeared to have evaporated. She poured them both another, feeling an odd, mixed emotion. Betrayed almost. Jealous? Yes, jealous. Ridiculous.

'Anyway, I'm probably going to move to Cornwall.' She sat down heavily, realising this was probably true. An idea had crystallised. How bizarre that Mother should be the first to know.

'Near that Zelda, I suppose. I never could keep you apart. You'll like that.'

Fran went to make supper with a good deal to think about.

When she got home she took the stack of mail on the doormat into the garden to read in the sun. It was good to be outside after turning out stuffy wardrobes. She'd make the most of it before she had to start packing up. Just so long as this weather wasn't the start of a heatwave like the drought of two years ago. She never again wanted to see Geoffrey going to work in shorts. It caused her a pang to think she'd probably never see him going to work at all. But the pang was short-lived.

There was a thick envelope from Geoffrey setting out the terms of their separation. Headed paper. Proper ink. Fountain pen. Ted was 'generously insisting on continuing with the school fees'. Geoffrey obviously thought this beyond the call of duty. The letter continued in formal tones. Geoffrey was working for his father. The term 'estate manager' made her laugh out loud. Estate, indeed. The house would be going on the market, but not with 'undue haste'.

'Pompous prat!' Fran stuffed it back in its envelope and chucked it on the grass.

The rest of the pile looked like bills and junk mail. She made herself sort through it. And there it was. A handwritten envelope. A tiny rectangle of hope.

It was a few brief lines scrawled in biro on the page of a notebook. Dale was so pleased to hear from her. The 'so' was underlined heavily. He'd tried calling her but she was never in. He was playing in Bristol, at the Colston Hall. What better place to meet after all these years? Would she meet him after the concert in the foyer? If she wasn't there he would try phoning again.

She leant back and turned her face up to the sun. It was strangely comforting that during the painful week in Hampshire the phone had been ringing in this house and Dale had been wondering where she was.

The crowd in the foyer was thinning. Where would he appear from? Fran had hardly been able to hear a note of the last piece for wondering what it would be like to look at him up close, talk to him, touch him. Then there had been that encore. Dale had returned from the wings and instead of taking up his cello, he had walked to the front of the stage. He leaned into the audience, scanning the rows and spoke.

'This next piece has never been performed in public before. I wrote it for a friend who I am hoping is here tonight. It's called "Song for Francesca".'

Fran felt a glow spread through her entire body, causing her eyes to sting. People in the audience had started looking about them curiously as Dale spoke. One or two near to her noticed her confusion and smiled. She smiled back, wiping the wetness from her face with her hands.

'I'd recognise that hair anywhere,' came a voice from behind, and Dale was there, with an arm round her shoulders, then holding her away and looking at her long and hard.

They walked, talking of the concert. Fran exclaimed about the encore, her shock and delight. Dale grinned back, pleased about his surprise for her. He repeated, 'Francesca, Francesca...' and each syllable hung on the air.

She had worried interminably about how to tell Dale about the twins. Should it be straight away or later? How do you make such an announcement? Now she was with him her worries fell away. She was sure the right moment and the right words would be clear to her. Dale had booked a small restaurant not far away. He was greeted by the maître d' and, as they followed him to their table, Fran noticed a quality about Dale she couldn't identify. He'd never been gauche but now, alongside his new elegance, he had a confidence that almost amounted to a swagger.

For a while questions demanded to be asked and answered, questions that all had a subtext of 'How has your life been without me?' She questioned him about his career, where he had been, how he had achieved such success.

'One thing led to another. Lots of hard work. And here you have before you an international star.'

She hoped he was being ironic, self-mocking, but she wasn't sure. 'What's with the double-barrelled name?'

'It's the thing. They're all doing it – John Shirley-Quirk, Richard Rodney Bennett, Brian Rayner Cook. Remember him at Bristol? It's the image of success. My agent insisted. Like it or not.'

'Yeah, I do remember Brian. He came to lunch once. Verity cooked roast pigeon. I don't think any of us had eaten pigeon before.'

'Ah, Verity. You must have missed her.'

'Certainly did. Still do. Anyway, why Woods?'

'You remember her? Ma's neighbour?'

'Of course! Your second mother.'

'My agent wanted something posh, but I said Woods or nothing. Glad I did it. Woods was so chuffed. Said it made her feel important, like she was up there on the stage with me.'

Fran nodded. This was more like the Dale she remembered. 'How's your mum?'

'She died. A year ago last January. Overdose finally worked.'

'I'm so sorry.'

'Woods thought she'd failed me. But it was bound to happen sooner or later. She'd saved her so many times. I told her it wasn't her job to keep Ma alive for me.'

They both fell silent. Then Dale grasped her hands across the table.

'There I go – banging on. What I want to know is how *you* are? How did you find me? Was it chance?'

She wanted to say, it was our daughter who brought us together. 'Sort of. Sort of not. I'd started to try and track you down, but the concert…' She hesitated. 'The concert was chance.'

'If you believe in chance.' He smiled his big, warm smile and she noticed the lines it made were just a bit deeper than they used to be.

'Dale…'

'Fran. The big question for me is difficult to ask. I wasn't sure I'd ask it until I saw you. But my feelings haven't changed. Not one bit. You wrote me that you were getting married…'

'You never replied!'

'I couldn't. I was devastated. I knew I had no right to be. But there was nothing I could have said to you at that time. I kept feeling murderous. I couldn't wish you happiness and all that junk. Because I didn't want you to be happy, not unless it was with me. That sounds so fucking mean, but it was how it was.'

She found herself gripping his hands and relaxed her hold.

'Will you answer me? Are you still married and happy? If you are I need to know right away, before I start hoping.'

'We've separated. I was never happy. It wasn't that sort of marriage.'

Dale's eyes lit up. 'I'm sorry you weren't happy, but I can't help being glad as well. Maybe we can spend some time together? After my tour? You could come to Paris. I miss Paris. London's so heavy, especially in this heat. I could buy you clothes, show you the city, take you to the opera…'

Fran flushed, indignant. Buy her clothes? As if her own weren't good enough? 'Dale, there's more to it than that.'

'There's someone else? Another man?'

'Other *people*, Dale.' Why did it always have to be a man? 'I've got a life too, you know. Plus, I have a new career, a life to make…'

She hardly had time to register surprise at referring to her new career before Dale interrupted.

'Make a new life with me…'

She held up a hand, both annoyed and relieved he wasn't interested in the career. 'There's something I need to tell you. The whole reason for meeting…'

'Go on. I'm listening.'

'I have two children. Twins.' She paused, her throat tightening, heat throbbing up her neck and into her head as if she would suffocate rather than continue. 'They are your children, Dale.'

Silence. Slowly she looked up. The light of joy had left his eyes and was replaced with a darkness that frightened her. 'Say something.'

'I…I… What can I say? *My* children? Are you sure?'

'Of course I'm sure!'

'Of course. Yes. Sorry. But I can hardly believe… It's too much to take in.' He waved away the waiter. 'Why didn't you tell me? Why now?'

'I was going to tell you, back then, but you made it very clear you weren't wanting to be a father…'

'But not to even tell me!'

Fran bit her lip.

'So why now?'

'They're of an age when they need to know. I wish I'd been able to tell them from the word go, but that wasn't how it was.'

'Wasn't how it was?'

'My…husband… We agreed. He wanted them to think he was their father.'

'So this – husband person had the say-so over whether my children knew I existed?'

'Dale, I didn't like it. But it was the agreement I made. Now I have control and I want to change that. But I couldn't tell them without talking to you first.'

'So that's why you came looking for me.'

'Not the only reason.'

'How can I know that?'

They both fell silent. Then Dale called for the bill. They'd hardly touched their food.

'I'm sorry. It's too much. I need to be alone.' Dale gave her a last look and stalked up to the desk to pay.

Minutes later she felt the draught of his coat sweeping past and listened to his footsteps fade without faltering.

If only she'd told the twins about Dale before meeting him. It was all the wrong way round, as it turned out. His reaction clouded the issue. She couldn't tell them about it. On the other hand she had a better idea of the sort of person Dale had become. He hadn't exactly rejected them, but surely, if he wanted to see them, wouldn't he have contacted her by now?

That weekend Geoffrey rang to say he wouldn't be coming to the school concert. Zoë had quickly forgotten her rage against her father and had insisted with a flounce, 'Of *course* I want Daddy there.' Now she would be hurt all over again. Fran's anger spiralled out of control. Geoffrey responded coldly.

'I won't be coming because they are not my children. You made it clear you have dispensed with my services and in any case I have my own child to think about. Yes, Carys is pregnant. Don't trouble with congratulations.'

It was the last straw. She hung up without replying.

Zoë was standing in the doorway with her adoring-Daddy face on. Fran gave in to the urge to wipe it off.

'Well he's not coming. He says he's not coming because he's not your father. And he's not. Never has been, never will be.' Fran was surprised to find herself shouting. She clapped her hand over her mouth, but Zoë was gone. There was the slam of her bedroom door. Fran thundered up the stairs after her.

'Zo! Zo! I'm sorry. I have to talk to you.'

'Go away.'

Fran sat on the landing until her words and knocking were drowned out by loud music. What had she been thinking of? All that careful thought about when and how to tell the twins out the window in a second of fury. She spent the next two hours listening for sounds of Zoë emerging, waiting for Dan to return from swimming with friends.

'Dan, I have to talk to you.'

'Mum, it's too hot. Just let me—'

'Now, Dan. Seriously. I've got something really difficult to tell you. And it's got to be now.'

Dan flopped from a great height into a chair and looked bored.

'Dan, I've been wanting to tell you both for some time. It's time you knew the truth, but it's really hard to say. All these years you've known Dad as your father. In fact, he is not your father. He's been like a father to you, but now…'

Fran ran out of words. Dan was wide-eyed. Just as she thought he might swear or cry he laughed.

'That explains why he never liked me.'

'Dan! Of course he did.'

'Not really. Zo was his favourite and she milked it for all she could get. Now I don't have to worry about that anymore.'

'And I never knew. That's awful. I let you down… Oh, Dan.'

Dan shrugged.

'And today I have done something really awful. Big time. I need your help with Zo. She got to hear this news in a dreadful way and she's holed up in her room. Won't speak to me.'

'What happened?'

'It was totally my fault. I got so wound up by your father – Geoffrey, I mean – on the phone that I shouted it at her when I hung up. Shouted at her that he wasn't her father.' Fran winced.

'See what you mean. She's bound to be upset about it anyway. Silly cow,' he added with brotherly concern.

'Would you go and dig her out? Get her down so I can try and explain it better? Explain to both of you.' And to herself she added, 'Like Zelda would do it.'

'What's to explain?' Dan took the stairs two at a time and Fran soon heard the two of them talking.

Zoë thought there was plenty to explain. When she'd finished raging and weeping and she'd hugged Fran and had her tears wiped away, she wanted detailed answers to endless questions. Eventually she gazed at Fran, glanced across at Dan and left a theatrical pause. 'So, if not Daddy, who *is* our father? Did you already tell Dan?' A rising note, ready to accuse.

'He didn't ask.'

Zoë rolled her eyes.

'One thing at a time. That's enough for one day.' Before she finished speaking Fran knew this was ridiculous and even Dan protested. She had to tell them.

At first Zoë wouldn't believe her. 'You're making it up. Like you used to give us sugar lumps after the medicine. You *know* I thought he was wonderful.'

'Don't be such a dipstick. She'd hardly make it up! What'd happen when you go "Daddy, Daddy" all over him and he's never clapped eyes on Mum before?'

Zoë glared at Dan. 'Well, it would explain why I'm so brilliant at the cello.'

'Always the modest Zo. Write and tell him that and he'll run a mile.'

Fran couldn't help smiling. Dan was so right.

'So you were at university with him? Wow!' Zoë paused, thoughtful. 'Were you madly in love or was it a one-night-stand?'

Both, thought Fran. 'Neither,' she said. 'First of all we were enemies, then really good friends. And it turned into something else...' She stopped, hearing her voice crack. 'But then he had to go to America.'

'Why didn't you go too?'

'Because...'

'Give Mum a break, Zo.'

'Because, because. He was very single-minded.'

'What's single-minded?'

'All he wanted was to be a brilliant cellist. And he is.' Fran paused, took a breath. 'Look, I'm not very good at this. Not like Zelda. But one day, I promise, I'll tell you more about it.'

'When can we see him?'

'We can't contact him until his tour's over. September, then he'll be in London.'

'How do you know that?' Zoë didn't miss a trick.

'Well, I did see him briefly. After a concert.'

'Did you tell him about us?'

'It wasn't the right moment.' Technically it wasn't even a lie. She couldn't tell them that a second father in one day didn't want to see them.

Zoë narrowed her eyes. 'So when will you?'

Fran swallowed. 'After the summer holidays. If we haven't heard.'

Zoë groaned. 'I can't wait that long.'

Zoë, as ever, had been quick to recover. Dan had gone quiet.

'There's going to be plenty to do. Dad...I mean Geoffrey, is selling this house. We have to find somewhere to live.'

'Can we live in London and I could—'

'No, we cannot!' Fran glanced at Dan. 'Anyway, you two – I need to say, I'm really, really sorry about all this. I just haven't done any of it very well—'

Dan cut in. 'Don't say it!'

'What?'

'Well, you keep saying you're not like Zelda.'

'Well, I'm not. She's so much better at...'

'Of course you're not. You're you. We'd rather have you, even if you do mess things up. Wouldn't we, Zo?'

Zoë came and hugged her.

*

Two days later a note arrived. She tore it open.

> *Fran*
> *Tell the twins what you will. But don't count on me to see them. I might, I might not.*
>   *As I told you, I'll be back in Paris at the end of the tour – in case there's anything else you think I ought to know about.*

There followed the address in Paris Fran already had from Reuben Myers.

The bitterness of that last line haunted her, so she couldn't bring herself to read it a second time. Anger carried her through the days, until Zelda told her to ring Maggie.

21

In spite of Geoffrey's assurances of no undue haste, news came within a couple of weeks that he had a buyer for the house. Fran panicked. But Maggie laughed. 'At last. The final thing falls away.'

In spite of her panic Fran felt a weight lift, as if she had been looking out through grimy windows and woke up to find someone had cleaned them. She remembered the day she had moved into Corner Close, and how depressing it had been. It occurred to her that she had adapted to it more efficiently than she had realised. In spite of her shakiness she could feel the relief of being free of that house and all it stood for.

After a week packing boxes, she set off for Cornwall. Zelda was always pressing her to visit and she hoped to rediscover the energy of her first visit. With that in mind, she stopped before she reached Zelda's and climbed up to the headland.

Bracken scratched her legs – not many walkers came this way, and most of them were rabbits. The honey smell of gorse was blown away as she emerged onto the cliff top and dropped to her knees on the spiky grass to peer over. She breathed in salt air and stretched out, feeling her body relax into the earth. As she gazed down at the movement of tide against land, her perspective flipped into a different dimension of time and space; she was seeing that land mass continuing under the sea and joining France, Europe, the rest of the world. Of course she'd always known their island didn't float apart like a sandwich on a plate, but in that moment she felt the connection not just in her head, but in her bones. It made her feel infinitely unimportant. The huge decision she was about to make seemed trivial in the whole scheme of things. It didn't matter what she did.

The realisation was both reassuring and disappointing. But, as she considered it, another understanding cut in. The connection meant that she was part of a joined-up system, that what she did was therefore significant, it *would* make a difference. Her integrity, as part of that whole, was important. Thoughtfully, she got to her feet and made her way back to the car.

'I've come to house-hunt,' she told Zelda, as soon as she arrived.

She had another agenda as well. She must keep communication open with Dale. So far she'd been unable to reply to his note. She might come over as too angry or too grovelling. She absolutely did not want to approach him from that sort of place. By the time she'd walked out to the headland a few more times a letter had formed in her mind.

> *Dear Dale*
> *You wrote that I should get in touch if there was anything else I thought you should know.*
>
> *There is. The first thing is that I told the twins. The second thing is that they have names – Zoë and Dan. You can work out how old they are.*
>
> *The third thing is that they were pleased. Dan more because he is not the son of my ex-husband than anything else, Zoë because – I'll come to that.*
>
> *The fourth thing is that they would like (Zoë more than anything in the world) to meet you. I am dubious about this because I don't want them hurt.*
>
> *The fifth thing is something I did not want to tell you, but Zoë is keen I should. She is a cellist – takes it very seriously, is said to have promise. She dreamed of doing a masterclass with you after the concert at the Festival Hall, before she knew anything about fathers/not fathers. I didn't want to tell you in case you think it is the main reason behind this letter. Nor do I want it to be the main/only reason you are interested. Equally I cannot deprive her of her birthright any longer, if indeed it is available to her.*

The sixth thing is that I know I betrayed you and I am deeply sorry. I truly thought I was doing the right thing by all of us at the time. I have often thought since that I was wrong. I don't want to excuse myself, but equally I need you to know it was not a decision I made lightly.

The seventh thing is that I have moved – see address – and am making a new life for myself. I am happy and so are Zoë and Dan, as far as I can judge.

Yours in peace,

Fran

Once she had posted it she started house-hunting in earnest, visiting all the agents in Penzance and becoming steadily more disheartened by the lack of anything possible in her limited price range. The only option seemed to be to take a winter let of a holiday cottage and hope something came up before the next tourist season. She returned home for the weekend to pack more boxes with Zoë and Dan.

'Commuting between Dorset and Cornwall is no joke,' she told Zelda when she got back. 'I'll be glad when it's the holidays. Are you sure you can cope with all of us staying? I mean, at this rate it could be for ages.'

'No problem,' said Zelda. 'Especially in summer. They'll all live on the beach and sleep in the garden.'

The following week Jez came in bringing news.

'There's a cottage for sale, down the Kendiggy Lane. Quite close to the sea. Needs a lot of work. Hasn't been lived in for years.'

'You mean Pascoe's Place?' Zelda sounded surprised.

'Is that the one up above Wrecker's Cove, where those luscious primroses were?' asked Fran.

Jez nodded. 'It's been empty all the time we've been here. No one seemed to know who owned it.'

'But the roof's all fallen in.'

Jez laughed. 'Sure, it's a bit of a mess. But the roof only went in the gales earlier this year. With any luck there won't be too much lasting damage inside as yet.'

'But it's a ruin!'

'Not as bad as it looks, I'm told.'

Fran was still coming up with snags. 'There isn't even a road to it. You have to cross the field and go down that steep little path. It was like a river bed in the spring.'

Jez looked straight at her. 'Do you actually *want* to find a place to live round here?'

Fran burst into tears. 'Yes, yes, yes. But I dare not believe it. That place is somewhere I've looked at and fantasized about. I just don't get that kind of luck.'

'Well, it's only an idea. But you'd better get your act together and investigate sharpish. Before the news gets out. I heard about it on the grapevine, so you've got a distinct advantage.'

'You might not want me living that near.'

Zelda laughed. 'Of course we would.'

Jez gave her a long slow smile. 'Bloody sight better than having you cluttering the place up here, crying all over the shop.'

Fran eyed him and grinned. One of the things she liked about Jez was that however upset and oversensitive she'd been over the months, he never stopped gently teasing her.

Jez went on. 'And by the way, it *has* got a track down to it. It runs off our lane and comes out on the other side of the house. It's just so overgrown you can't even see it.'

Next day she set off early across the fields. Jez was going to bring a builder friend home after work to have a preliminary look at the cottage. She wanted to see it first on her own. She crossed a broken stile and climbed down into the deep lane on the other side, pushing brambles aside and brushing against dog roses and cow parsley. A wren flitted in and out of the hedge just ahead of her. The path led on to the cliff above Wrecker's Cove, but just before the rocky descent to the beach there was a gap in the bank which must once have been a gateway to the cottage garden. Fran pulled a stick from the hedge and beat at the nettles which choked the entrance until she could step through without stinging her bare legs.

It was like closing a door. The sound of the sea, which had been getting louder as she walked down the path, was abruptly shut out by the high banks surrounding the site. There was no wind where she stood and the sun had already warmed the enclosed space. Tamarisk and brambles predominated with a ground cover of glossy-leaved periwinkle interspersed with clumps of orange montbretia. A gnarled apple tree bent close to the ground on what must once have been a lawn, now slippery with moss and clover. The cottage occupied the far eastern corner of the plot protected by the rising hill at the back.

She made her way towards it, surprising some rabbits and startling a pheasant that squawked away over the high bank. The walls were all pretty much intact and seemed to grow out of the earth they stood on. A deep fissure ran down the western wall from the chimney stack to the ground. The roof had caved in at that end, but was still in place on the other half of the building. Fran tried the iron latch on the front door. It lifted and the door gave way when she pushed it sharply. Was it safe to go in?

The flagstone passageway was panelled up to waist height with what looked like oak; unpainted, weathered grey. A door led off the hall on either side and a flight of stairs went up straight ahead. It was pleasantly cool inside, in spite of the musty smell. She pushed open the door on the right to find a room that ran from the front to the back of the building. On the back wall there was an iron range, and a pine table stood in the window opposite with a broken bentwood chair leaning drunkenly against it. On the table was the stub of a candle and a grimy blue and white striped mug. Fran stood at the table looking out to sea and was grabbed at that moment by a determination to live in the cottage.

She didn't attempt the stairs, which were draped with cobwebs and had missing treads. The room on the other side of the hallway was derelict. The ceiling had fallen in at one end and was open to the sky under the collapsed roof. Swallows had nested in the corner and bird droppings crusted the floor.

It couldn't have been more different from Corner Close, and to her it already felt like home.

Jez's builder friend turned out to be Steve the drummer, whose particular skill was stonemasonry. They sucked their teeth and shook their heads for over an hour until Fran was near despair.

'Nah. Like I said,' said Jez eventually, 'place looks worse than 'tis. Structurally, it's okay. We can fix the rest.'

Back-of-envelope calculations continued back at the house over a few cold beers.

Steve's carpenter was John, who doubled as the local taxi driver. Tim, who sometimes played saxophone in the band, was the electrician on the team. Jez would do the plumbing. Steve was juggling other work in order to make an early start, because of Fran's connection with Jez and because he had taken a shine to her at the gig.

'You had guts that night,' he said. 'Patch tells me we've got to get you settled ASAP, so you two can sing together.'

She felt the tide turn. The purchase of the cottage went through amazingly quickly and, through Zelda's friend Lyn and the local grapevine, Fran found a job as a dental receptionist in Penzance. The twins were happy to stay at school for the remaining weekends of the term to save the constant travelling. When work started on the cottage she went there every day to talk to Steve and his boys, all slow-spoken men who made no haste and took pride in their craftsmanship. Zelda persuaded Josh to help her and Fran clear brambles to make a vegetable patch. Fran spent all her free time outdoors, digging the rich, peaty earth, swimming and walking the cliff path to get to know the coastline. She even sang with Patch and the band in a couple of summer gigs put on for tourists. Steadily she began to feel a part of the place as her life moved into a new rhythm.

Zoë and Dan came for the summer holidays. She'd been drip-feeding the idea of moving to Cornwall and resistance had given way to curiosity. But in spite of the envy of friends at school they were still wary. To Fran's surprise Dan hit it off with Tom straight away. They were so different. Tom, although younger, was taller than Dan and had his father's muscular frame. He was extrovert and sporty, while Dan was slight and quiet and had become more and more withdrawn as they'd packed up the house.

But Tom appreciated Dan's understated sense of humour and the way he thought about things before he said them. They were both keen to earn some money and started work as labourers for Steve. Fran watched Dan's physique fill out steadily as the boys did the heavy work at the cottage and on other local sites, digging and clearing, fetching and carrying. Dan's confidence grew and at supper he would relate stories about their day with a few words and a deadpan face, which made the whole table fall about with laughter.

Zoë was always the last one to laugh on these occasions. Did she resent the way Dan fitted in? Maybe she just missed having Dan to herself. Zoë was preoccupied with the prospect of meeting Dale. Obsessed was a better word. She was determined to impress him and spent hours playing her cello in the room she shared with Fran.

'I thought Zoë would share with Tamzin,' said Zelda. 'Give you a room to yourself.'

Fran shrugged. 'She'd feel she couldn't practise when she wanted. It's okay, I don't mind.'

Fran was more bothered Zoë might seem stand-offish. At night she was always asking when they could go home. Once she'd said, 'At least when we live here we'll have our own house.' Fran couldn't decide whether that was progress or not.

Zoë rarely came on picnics or trips to the beach although Tamzin never failed to ask her. When she did join in, she talked incessantly about Dale and how brilliant he was.

'Shut it, Zo. We've heard enough,' said Dan on more than one occasion. Was he upset or just embarrassed? He never mentioned Dale himself.

Fran knew Tamzin wanted to find her own father, but was reluctant to talk about it. The situation seemed fraught but Zelda laughed it off. 'They'll sort themselves out.'

Although she knew Fran had written to Dale, Zoë became impatient to send another letter arranging a meeting.

'It's August already,' she said at supper one day. '*Please* won't you write again?'

Tamzin looked up, 'You *are* lucky.' She hesitated. 'I mean, to have an address to write to.'

Zoë turned on her. 'Lucky? Not if she won't write to him.'

Tamzin pushed back her chair abruptly. 'Yes, *lucky*. But you don't see it. I'm fed up with you nagging like a spoilt brat, and going on and on about your genius father. And being so unfriendly and not joining in. And making an atmosphere.' Tamzin shot out of the room.

In the silence that followed Tom gave Zoë a filthy look and followed Tamzin. Zelda and Jez exchanged glances and said nothing.

Flora was round-eyed, elbowing Josh, who continued eating stolidly. Zoë stared at her plate. Fran knew how much she looked up to Tom. Dan was avoiding looking in Zoë's direction.

When Tom reappeared later he spoke to Zoë, who had stuck her head in a book.

'Personally I don't care if you join in or not. But has it ever occurred to you what it might be like for Tamzin? With her father, I mean?'

Zoë looked up grudgingly. 'How d'you mean?'

Tom leaned back against the door frame. 'Well, if she goes looking for *her* old man, all she's got to go on is a town in Poland, a rather common surname and the fact that they had some smallholding twenty years ago.' He paused, bouncing the door gently against the wall with his foot. 'She doesn't even know if he's still alive.'

Zoë shrugged and bit her lip. 'That's not my fault.'

'Of course it's not. I didn't say it was. Think about it, that's all.'

There was a pause before Zoë started to speak. Fran dreaded to hear her prima donna whine, but her voice had a harsh, brittle tone.

'I know you all think I'm a spoilt brat and my music's all a big pose. But has it ever occurred to *you*,' and here she looked straight at Tom, 'what it might be like for me with *my* father? I grew up all my life thinking someone was my father and all the time he wasn't at all. And then he buggered off anyway. And my music just happens to be more important to me than anything in the world. Or any*body*.' She glared around and stood up. 'I think I'll just go and talk to Tamzin.'

Fran said nothing, fearful of what Zoë might be about to say to Tamzin but determined not to interfere. Zelda made a face and Jez just said, 'Happy families, eh?' and carried on washing up.

That night Zoë said, 'It's funny, Mum. Tamzin doesn't want to talk about her dad because she's afraid he doesn't exist or she won't find him or he won't want to see her. She's afraid it will break her luck to talk about it. And if she keeps quiet it will be okay. And that's exactly why I *need* to talk about mine. To make him real. To make it happen. Isn't it weird how people are so different?'

Next day Zoë moved her mattress into Tamzin's room and mealtimes became less strained.

*

Zoë's reward came unexpectedly the following week. Without warning, Dale appeared in reception at the dentist's as if he'd come for a filling. No suit – which suited him better. Jeans, black T-shirt, leather waistcoat. Surely not the same one?

He'd phoned the house from the railway station.

'Your friend Zelda told me to come here. She said to tell you she won't tell the twins I'm here. But she did invite me to supper.'

Fran wished she hadn't postponed washing her hair, but at least she knew she looked good in the green cotton frock. They weren't busy, so it was easy to get the afternoon off.

As they walked into the gardens of nearby Penlee House she fingered the waistcoat. 'It's not...?'

'The same one? Yes, it is. Only wear it now on special occasions.' Dale looked sideways at her. 'For luck,' he added.

'I thought you were still on tour.'

'I am. Just snatched a day. Back tomorrow.'

He was full of remorse and apologies, and he wanted to meet the twins. Fran was both pleased and wary, wondering why he had taken so long, what had changed. Her stomach churned as they walked and talked, each asking questions and giving factual replies, skirting round the feelings.

His introduction to the twins was hugely helped by the presence of Zelda and Jez and their family. There were no awkward silences and Josh dived straight into the big question before it could become the elephant in the room.

'What's it like to meet your children for the first time when they're already teenagers?'

Dale replied that it was terrifying and exciting in equal measure – and that piece of ice was broken.

Zoë was a little subdued at first, overawed perhaps. No bad thing. Dan was watchful, listening. They both seemed engaged and Dale played it well, with no attempt to be matey. When Tom reminded Zoë it was her turn to wash up and said he hoped she didn't think she was going to get out of it, Dale stepped in with the suggestion that the three of them wash up together. Dan was indignant but agreed, and Jez laughed and said there was nothing like washing up as a bonding exercise. Fran resisted the temptation to join in or eavesdrop and left them to it.

She looked back as she left the kitchen and felt a strange pang to see their three backs gathered round the sink. Jealousy. That's what it was. It was what she wanted, but it would take some getting used to.

She went up to her room to stare out at the sea surging and breaking on the rocks at the outer reaches of the cove. And Dale. Would he stick with it? Or would he take off again, back into his own world when he found out what hard work teenagers could be?

She pressed her forehead against the cool glass. If Dale did stay around, what did she want of him, and he of her? Was he a threat to her independence? She'd always had a habit of letting people take her over. Zelda, for a start, after Mother, that is. Zelda always called the shots. And Charlie had always been in charge of their relationship, even if his strings were pulled by Amanda. Even Verity always wanted to take over and sort her out. Then Geoffrey, of course, who'd tried to lock her up in the process.

Surely Dale would be different? She had so many images of him walking away. Striding out of the Berkeley all those years ago, going off to America, and, more recently, leaving her in the restaurant in Bristol. 'Who knows,' she said to the window and watched her breath obscure the view.

Dale met her as she came downstairs. He squeezed her shoulders in a half-hug and said she had two brilliant children.

'We have, you mean.'

He nodded. 'It's beginning to sink in. They say it's okay for me to see them at school, take them out for the day. But you'll have to write to the headmaster and fix it up.' He hesitated. 'That's if you're okay with that.'

'Of course! That's progress, that is. Zoë's idea, I guess? Yes. I'll see the headmaster about it when I take them back.'

'They told me about your cottage. How about you show me?'

Perhaps it was a mistake to take him to see the cottage, but she couldn't resist the urge to show him her project. It was only half finished with bare plaster walls but Dale was enthusiastic. They wandered into the garden and ended up making love under the apple tree to the hush of the sea in the cove below. She hadn't intended that to happen, but she'd been ambushed by her body. The hunger was overwhelming and their limbs drew them together as if magnetised.

'Just for old times' sake,' she insisted as they flung clothes aside.

They rolled together on mossy cushions of grass, laughing and inhaling pungent herbs and sap. He was on top and inside her in one movement and they came, quickly and together, in a glorious tumult of sweat and cries. Afterwards they lay watching the sky through the leaves as it deepened into twilight.

'Not just for old times' sake?' he said.

She squeezed his hand but said nothing. She couldn't deny her feelings, but she was so afraid of losing herself.

He spoke of her visiting his new place in London and went quiet when she said she couldn't bear the thought of London and that her life was in Cornwall now.

'In any case, I've got a gig tomorrow. I'm singing with Patch and the band – the one we talked about at supper.' Once she would never have said that to Dale, the great musician. It felt good. 'In any case – first things first – you've got to get to know Zoë and Dan.'

22

Fran heard the cello on her way up the stairs, but was unprepared for the surge of heat, light and sound that knocked her back as she opened the door. Huge sash windows on two sides of the room threw rectangles of light onto the bare boards, turning them the colour of hot fudge. Phrases of music sawed along the floor and vibrated up through the soles of her shoes. Stray notes curled up to the ceiling, recoiled off the glass. The heat shimmered with the smell of incense and oranges. Dale was sitting diagonally opposite her in the shadow provided by the corner of the room. A fold of flame-coloured silk hung from the back of his chair. He was bent over the cello, naked, absorbed, and Francesca reflected how this sudden cameo captured and revealed him. He was lean and tanned and with his close-cropped hair, his profile reminded her of Etruscan athletes in Italian friezes.

It was strange to find him here in rural Dorset, of all places. He'd been down to Penzance again to hear her sing with Patch, but had been oddly reticent about what he was doing in London. The main thing was that he was keeping up with Dan and Zoë and had already visited them at their school. A few days ago she'd received a postcard inviting her to 'see what I've found' and directing her to this studio above a barn on a farm in the middle of nowhere.

Dale looked up as she closed the door, continued playing to the end of the passage, and stood the cello in the corner. He picked the orange sarong off the chair, unhurriedly wrapping it around his waist as he came forward to greet her.

He held her shoulders firmly and kissed her warmly on both cheeks.

'Like the sarong.'

He laughed. 'Usually it belongs to the cello, but in this weather…'

'You're so tanned.' He looked amazing – as if the heat wasn't enough.

'I've been outside a lot – helping Mike in his market garden. In touch with the earth, as Mike would say, for the first time in my entire life.'

'Mike?'

'You know, that friend I told you about? From Bristol? He saw me on the programme at the Winter Gardens in Bournemouth, got in touch and we had a drink after the concert. He told me about his place here and I didn't take much notice. Not until I realised where Zoë and Dan's school was. Too good to be true that he had a room to rent.'

'So you're living here?'

'When I don't have to be in London. What do you think?'

'It's stunning. How long do you plan on staying?'

'As long as Mike and Anne will have me. It's not like my own place, but it's all I need. Camping stove, shower through there.' Dale gestured to the vast, bare room, took glasses from a shelf and ran the cold tap at a sink in the corner. 'In a way it's better. At least when – if – Dan and Zoë come for a whole weekend. Mike says they can sleep in the house – less thrown together, less pressure. His kids are younger, but they get on okay.'

'They've been here, then?'

Dale laughed. 'Sorry, yes. It was our little secret. They weren't to tell you about it and I have to report back on what you think. I'm glad they didn't tell.'

'Cunning. I was going to ask how you were getting on with them, but I guess I don't need to.' Fran wished she felt more pleased than jealous.

'One swallow doesn't make a summer. Long way to go. But okay-ish. No worries.'

He handed her a glass of water, giving her a long look. His little finger brushed her index finger as she took it.

'You're wearing my favourite dress. Come and sit down.' He indicated a battered leather sofa placed before a window and squatted in one corner.

My only dress. She sank into the squashy cushions at the other end.

'Loved your gig – you've got a great voice.'

'Really?' She felt absurdly pleased. 'Patch is a great teacher – in a low-key way. I've even started writing a few lyrics – stuff about the sea, Cornwall.'

'We could end up being a team.'

Fran laughed. 'Who knows?' She really doubted that. 'And your music – how does it fit with being here? I thought you couldn't cope with the country. The sticks, you said when you came to Penzance. There can't be much scope here for international concerts.' She waved towards the long view down the valley to wooded hills beyond.

'I'm composing. At last, Fran. I've always wanted to, but whenever I've had the chance it came to nothing. I'm getting it together here.'

'That's fantastic. Is there interest? Do people like it?'

'I've never lived in the country before. It's growing on me. As to the composing, *I* like it, that's all that matters. Nobody knows I'm doing it, no one out there anyway. No pressure.'

Fran nodded. 'Was that your own composition you were playing when I came in?'

Dale laughed. 'I wish! No, that was Saint-Saëns. Said I'd work on it with Zoë, so I thought I'd better do a bit of practice. She's good, really good.'

'And you and her?'

'As far as I can tell, okay. We talk mostly about music, but I don't sense the reserve in her that I do with Dan.'

'I'm not surprised. He's got a long way to go. Don't take it personally – I mean, it wasn't your fault he didn't know you. He can't work out whether to be more angry with me or with Geoffrey.'

'I think Geoffrey is winning on balance. On the basis that all men are the pits. Including me, of course.'

'That's what worries me. The whole thing has given him a bit of a problem with role models.'

Dale gave a slow smile. 'He'll sort himself out. No need to analyse it to bits. I was dead short on male role models, as you put it, and I survived.'

'I just wish I could talk to him. But he's shut himself off.' It was strange to be talking with Dale in this way about her children. Their children.

'You can't make him. Neither can I. When they come here, he'll know where I am. The easy thing would be to spend too much time with Zoë. So I plan to hang out where he is from time to time.'

'Which is where?' Dale knew things about Dan that she did not.

'Oh, he likes woodworking...'

That she did know. 'He used to love carving with my father. They were close. He...'

'Yes, he told me about his grandfather. Anyway, Mike's doing a lot of carpentry, building a new kitchen. And I'm doing a bit of carving. Always liked it at school. It got me down there in the workshop with Dan. Mike put his oar in. He was quite helpful, for all his earnestness.'

'Do you, well...enjoy it? Getting to know them?'

'What do you think?'

'I guess you do.'

'I'm off back to Paris in November – just for a few months. Long-standing commitment. Back in March. So I'm hoping to get them here for a weekend or three before I go. Good idea?'

Dale stretched his arms and looked across at her. 'You know, I've thought so much about what you did. It's difficult to imagine being you. But I guess I'd have done the same. I don't think I would have wanted me for the father of my children.'

'I was more confused than anything. Didn't know what I wanted. Certainly had no clue what kids needed. All I did know was you didn't want that responsibility and I couldn't rely on you. I had to get on with it.'

'I know, I know. I was very arrogant. My career. Music above everything else. I was very single-minded.'

'Don't artists have to be?'

'Yes. Yes, they do – if they want to do anything significant. But then again, what is significant? I thought I knew until you turned up with that news. Children! I had children. Now *that* was significant. It was like the world stopped. And when it started again, the rhythms were all different. Nothing I'd done before made sense anymore.'

'I hadn't realised. It wasn't the impression you gave.'

'I guess not. No, it took a while to kick in. But why do you think I came here? I took a flat in the Barbican. I went there to measure up for curtains and so on. And I sat on the acre of beige carpet in that empty space and thought, what do I do with two thirteen-year-olds here? Teenagers and designer living? Not a good mix. We'll sit and look at each other. We won't know how to talk to each other and they'll end up hitting the London drug scene. I thought, get out of here. Do something different.'

'This is certainly different.'

'I reckoned they'd need freedom and the city wasn't the place for that – especially when they weren't used to it. Not streetwise, not like I used to be.'

Dale paused, his eyes smiling into hers as he stretched his legs out until his toes nearly touched her dress. Long, narrow feet, straight toes with a sprinkling of dark hairs on them. Her hands itched to hold them.

Dale was speaking again. 'When I saw Mike he was very direct about my lifestyle, the fans and so on. Attacked my vanity. Bloody rude, I thought at the time. But spot on, as it happened. I'd got hooked on my image. In fact, in a funny sort of way, it was meeting him that made me decide to come and see you, take the plunge with the twins. Then when I realised they were at school round here – well, you know the rest.'

'I don't remember Mike at Bristol.'

'Music department. I used to kip on his floor between digs. A not-very-brilliant pianist. Went on to teach. But he got himself a life. Market garden, wife, kids. I suddenly found I envied him. Having kids changed his life, he said.'

'But I didn't know you wanted children like that.'

'Nor did I. In fact I didn't. Not then. If I'm honest. Though I do now.'

'So what made you come? To Penzance, I mean?'

'You don't get it, do you?'

'Get what?'

'It was *you*, Fran. It was you I wanted. Always wanted. Once all the glamour wore off and the hard graft set in. It was you I played for all those years. You I wrote for. You. You. You.'

Fran stared. 'Me?'

'I was furious with you when we met after that concert at the Colston Hall. It wasn't just because you hadn't told me about the twins. It was that you ignored me. You weren't flattered. You were more concerned about your kids! I mean, I understand that now. But then! How dare you! It took me a while to realise I'd got so arrogant, so used to adoring fans. It was something my teacher Reuben warned me about. I can hear him now, "Now you get the fame, my boy, take care. It is the music that matters, not you. You have to get the ego out of the way."'

'I can just imagine him saying that. He sounded a very wise old bird, that time I phoned him.'

'He is. Yes, I forgot you spoke to him. And in fact Zoë said something very similar – that brought me up short, I can tell you. When she came to Bournemouth – you know the Winter Gardens concert when I got some tickets for the school? She was shocked by the fans. She said it would take away from the music.'

'Well, well. I am surprised.' Fancy Zoë having the insight – and the guts to criticise Dale.

'Anyway, what I'm getting to is this. Both Woods and Reuben – a likely partnership! They both told me to get myself a woman.'

'Any old woman?'

'That's the whole point. I said to Reuben, "What happened to 'Don't get tied up with women'?" which is what he always used to say. And he said, "Have nothing to do with women in general. But when it comes to *the* woman. That is something quite other. *The* woman is not to be missed."'

Fran snorted and Dale held up a hand.

'He also said, "For me, she had always been there and I had not noticed her."'

Dale crossed the room and fetched his wallet. 'You see, you were always there, Fran.' He pulled out a square of paper which he unfolded and smoothed over the leather, careful where the creases had worn into holes.

'Look. A man being swallowed by a cello. Remember?'

Fran stared. It was her pencil sketch, faded to a ghost, the one she had left when she borrowed his album. Softly, she sang the opening lines of 'Mr Tambourine Man'.

Memories of that morning in Dale's room flooded back. 'And you did. You did play me a song.'

Dale nodded.

'I can't believe you kept it. All those years.'

'I guess I thought if I kept it, I'd find you again.' He folded it again and put it away.

Fran thought he'd not made a lot of effort to find her, but bit back the words.

Dale leaned over and took both her hands. 'You remember that first time in Bristol? I watched you go, you know. From my window. It was all I could do not to run after you, ask you to come to America with me.'

She pulled away her hands.

'What I am trying to say is, I knew I was in love with you then.'

'Oh, Dale!' Fran leapt up and walked away to the window. How different her life might have been. 'Why? Why didn't you?'

'I was scared. Terrified it would spoil the dream, dilute, divert... I don't know what the word is.'

Fran was silent.

'And you were so, well, off-hand before I left.'

She swivelled round, indignant. 'Me? Off-hand? I could only think about you, about that night. I was desperate for you to at least acknowledge it. That you thought it was special. But I was scared to be pathetic, clinging to you because you were the first person to fuck me.'

'That sounds so bitter!'

'It's how I felt then, and for a long time I can tell you. But I sure as hell wasn't going to let you know how much I cared.'

'Wish you had.'

'And if I had? Would it have made any difference? I don't think so. You were so ambitious. You forget. So single-minded. And rightly so. Look where it's got you.'

'It's got me to sleeping at Mike's place all over again, still single, still lonely, a stranger to my children—'

Fran interrupted. 'Famous, rich, composing and with a huge fan club, strings of women who are dotty about you.'

'Fran, they are not you. What's fame and all that? It doesn't make you happy. It's you I really want. Always did, although I didn't know it.'

'That's easy to say now.'

Dale groaned and walked slowly over to the sink, put his head under the tap.

The way Dale had been looking at her made her want him so fiercely that she had to turn away to the window. She could hear the water running, splashing, and Dale gasping and spluttering. Her face was burning, sweat trickling between her breasts. Since the evening in her garden he had respected her 'just good friends' agenda – he'd taken the sleeper back to town after her gig. She imagined he did not even think of making love. Whereas, ironically, she did. All the time. Her whole body, every pore, wanted Dale's body. And her spirit was hungry for the love he was holding out to her. Why was she deliberately being contrary, nasty, arguing against it? It wasn't just the bitter memories. Dale had achieved his ambition. She was just discovering she had one. She desperately wanted to give it space.

The sound of the cello filled the room again. He'd given up. Perhaps she should leave. But he was playing her tune and she let it wash over her, still standing at the window unable to move. She didn't hear him put the cello down. First she smelt the incense on his skin, then felt the velvet dampness of his hair on her cheek, his arms around her.

'I'm sorry, I was a cow...'

Dale turned her face and stopped her words with his mouth.

'I love you, Fran Fairweather, and I don't mean to lose you a second time.' He kissed her again as she started to protest. 'I'll wait for as long as it takes.' He scooped her up and carried her to the bed, laying her down gently and standing silhouetted against the light, naked and alight with sweat.

Fran held out her arms, smelling her own muskiness in the tent of her dress as Dale lifted it over her head.

'No underwear!'

'Too hot.'

'Too good to miss.' Dale set about nosing and licking every inch of her body, hushing her impatience, stilling the hands that wanted to pull him into her. When he did enter her, she came immediately, tumultuously, in every tingling cell of her being.

They lay together, slithering and entwined, murmuring, remembering, laughing softly.

In the shower she said, 'Our bodies are so good together.'

'Meant to be.'

'Maybe.'

'No pressure. And I do realise, by the way, about your singing. You've got to do it. Ever since I heard you. But it doesn't have to be either/or. Remember what I said. Not losing you again, love of my life.'

Fran threw back her head to fill her ears with water.

PART TWO
Eleanor

23

The sky was that heavy grey with a tinge of yellow which might bring snow, the remaining light fading fast. Eleanor shuddered and pulled the heavy brocade across the window, shutting out the weather, all that encircling gloom. It felt like evening already.

She moved around the room, switching on lamps to warm the walls, putting another log on the fire. She hesitated on her way to the drinks cupboard as the clock in the hall struck four. "Sun's over the yardarm," Harry used to say. Never before six o'clock, of course, but dammit, the sun must be over the yardarm somewhere in the world.

'Just a little stiffener,' she murmured as she poured two fingers of gin into a cut-glass tumbler and added tonic.

She sat by the fire and poked it into life, savouring the moment she liked best in the day.

But after a few moments she was up again, glass in hand, to straighten a picture. That row of Redouté roses, it was vital that all the frames were exactly aligned. They looked ridiculous otherwise. It was the formality that saved them. Not proper pictures. Accurate, detailed, flat. No heady smell, no thorns, no browning petals and all those tight buds which would never burst into flower. She took another gulp of gin. They were faultlessly elegant in their gilt frames; understated, stylish. Not art, but part of the décor.

She stepped back and sipped her drink. What that wall really needed was flamboyance, colour. Something bold to bring the room to life. One or two of her paintings. The ones she destroyed, or some she might have painted later. Except she never did.

'Why don't you take up painting again?' That's what Harry had said when Francesca left home. As if it were a hobby, like knitting. Harry just had no idea. Never had.

She'd never forgotten that night in the kitchen when Harry came home. Such a day she'd had. So exciting. That picture had possessed her. It had come like a visitation, a vision, and the paint had just flowed onto the canvas. Underneath her focus and concentration there had been a little crackle of anticipation. She would show Harry when he got back and he would be astonished.

She'd been so intent on her picture, bracing her elbow on the ledge of the easel to gain perfect control, flicking those fine strokes of paint into one corner. She could see it still. Then the child sneezed. Eleanor had forgotten she was even there. Her arm had startled upward and all that delicate brushwork was ruined.

He'd been late of course. All that snow, trains delayed. But she'd heard the slam of the front door, his footsteps down the stairs to the basement.

All he'd said was, 'Where's Francesca?' He'd grabbed her hand when she didn't answer. Taken the paintbrush away. And then he'd been away up the stairs, yelling something about the house being like a morgue.

Well, of course it was cold, what with the coal being at the bottom of the garden and not being able to get out the back door for the snow filling the area steps. Hardly her fault if the child was fool enough not to get under the blankets. She'd been fine of course, but Harry had made no end of fuss. Such a song and dance.

She drained her glass. She'd not been ready for it. Motherhood. Hadn't bargained for what it would mean. Eleanor the Unready. Unprepared, as ill-advised as that Ethelred. Funny what you remember from school. What sticks and what doesn't. Nothing useful of course. No one teaches you to be a mother. She hadn't been prepared or advised at all. But censored, shot down in flames by her gentle husband. The first time she'd seen him angry. Such a hoo-ha. So she'd made a break. Couldn't trust herself with anything but a complete break. No more painting. Except for walls. Turned her flair towards the house, making a home. Not the child's fault of course.

'How about the other half?' said Harry's voice in her head.

'I don't mind if I do. Just a splash,' she replied out loud, heading back to the cupboard. After all, she didn't want the tonic going flat.

She raised a toast to the curtains. 'Here's to you! Eleanor the Elegant.' She pivoted and held out her glass towards the row of demure rose prints. 'Queen of Redouté and magnolia emulsion.'

She sunk back into the armchair and stretched her feet to the fire. 'You did a good job,' she told herself. 'A darn good job.'

24

More and more curtains were enveloping Eleanor in swathes of darkness. It was as if she were waiting in the wings to make her entrance but curtain after curtain lifted without revealing the stage to the audience. They hovered above her head, stale with the dust of the years.

She had felt particularly suffocated by the heavy drapes with the covered buckram tie-backs that hung in the drawing room at Goldney Villa. When they were delivered she was so proud of the dark green velvet falling from ceiling to floor, double-lined, trimmed with gold braid. The first fabric she had owned which she hadn't sewn herself. They could be seen from the road and she revelled in them as she walked up the steps to the front door. Archie said they were grand in the blackout, and because of that they used the room all the time instead of being cosy in the breakfast room. You could have had a hundred chandeliers blazing in the room and not a chink of light would have shown.

When Archie was gone they towered over her, threatening to fall and smother her. She saw how grandiose, how pretentious they were, and they mocked her in her isolation and loneliness. She remembered her mother's remark when they were new, that you could make blackout curtains for half the street with them. She smiled her secret smile. Her pride wouldn't allow her to cut them up. They represented her escape. And whatever horrors she had already survived and whatever hardships were yet to come, nothing could alter the fact she had escaped.

Eleanor went to pour another drink but the bottle was empty. A beautiful green, that bottle. The same colour as those velvet curtains. She took it to the kitchen, washed it carefully and polished it to a fine shine. Pity to throw it away. Better put it with all the others.

'My bodyguard,' she said, closing the larder door. 'All gleaming in the dark.'

25

Eleanor breathed out as she heard footsteps move away from her. Who were these people who kept interrupting the silent movie playing inside her head? Why were they dressed up as nurses? She wanted to finish the conversation with that Archie Thorne.

'Thorne in your flesh' was what Archie used to call himself when all the love and then all the pretence had gone out of their marriage. She could smell him now, coming in reeking of spirits while she pretended to be asleep, climbing in beside her, naked and hairy. He'd push up her nightdress and pin her wrists above her head.

'I'm a Thorne in your flesh!' he would shout as he thrust into her.

Then he'd withdraw, lunge forward and swing that thing around above her face, smelling of the inside of her.

'See what a long Thorne it is! All the better to prick you with!' Then he'd be back inside her. 'You hate me, lass, but you love this!'

Which was true.

'Who'd have thought it, our Nellie loves a bit of rough,' he'd say as he rolled off her into sleep.

In the morning he'd tell her he'd been busy making money for her. Then without fail: 'Nellie loves money and sex, but money most of all.'

How she hated being called Nellie, and how he loved goading her with it. He despised her, she knew, because she fell in love with Mr Archibald Thorne, the wealthy, immaculately dressed business associate of her employer, and had fallen out of love with Archie, the drinker and gambler. Archie and Nellie. That's how they came to be known. No longer Mr and Mrs Archibald Thorne. The people in those circles didn't recognise them anymore, not since the debt collectors appeared. Archie was supposed to be her escape route from poverty and she'd never forgive him for dragging her down lower than before.

She was lucky to be named Eleanor. It had a certain ring about it that floated above the drudgery and gave her hope that she was destined for higher things. Eleanor Rose. She escaped the fate of her younger sisters who were given flower names of increasing awfulness. After her came Lily Marguerite, then Violet Daisy and finally Marigold May. They were known as Nellie, Lil, Vi and Goldie – the Wilkins sisters, sounding like a music hall turn.

When Eleanor got married, her sisters were dazzled when her father-in-law, who was in the motor trade, gave her a car for a wedding present. He brought it to their house the day before the wedding, a gleaming black Bentley with a bonnet that went on forever. All the neighbours came out to see the girls climb in to go for a ride. Then he took Eleanor off on her own for a driving lesson.

Archie himself did one good thing for her – he encouraged her to paint when she was bored at home all day. She'd excelled at art at school and now he bought her paints and canvas. He himself liked a traditional still life or a vase of flowers, several of which he framed. When they had guests he would point them out, referring to 'my wife, the artist' as if it gave him a veneer of culture. It left Eleanor free to work on the abstract themes that filled her head. Painting became her escape and her passion.

Eleanor soon discovered Archie's money came from his skill at cards. When he first started losing he joked she brought him bad luck. But the jokes turned into accusations. Verbal attacks escalated into violence when he was drunk. Eleanor started to check where he went at night. The Bentley was easy to spot parked at the back of pubs notorious for gambling, usually with a lad paid to keep an eye on it. Which was how she came to be there on the night of his death.

The lad that night happened to be Ricky Thomas, a boy she'd been at school with. He was known locally as Dicky Ricky because he was what her mother described as a shilling short of a pound. Eleanor saw the Bentley down a side street by the Mother Shipton with Ricky pacing up and down and wringing his hands. She asked her taxi to wait and went to ask Ricky what was wrong. As she approached he grabbed her arm, his mouth and eyes working frantically in opposite directions.

'Bott-el, bott-el,' he shouted and dragged her toward some dustbins in an alleyway.

'Fight! Fight! Bott-el!' Ricky's voice took on a quavering note and he mimed boxing with feeble fists. Archie was slumped against one of the bins surrounded by shards of broken glass. A jagged half-bottle lay nearby in the gutter. The whole scene looked like something out of a movie.

'Help me into the car with him,' she told Ricky.

They heaved the dead weight of Archie onto the back seat. Eleanor wrapped her scarf round the wound in his neck and bunched up the rug to soak up the blood.

She pressed a note into Ricky's hand. 'Pay off the taxi, see, down there, the taxi in the road?'

She held his face in both hands as she had seen the teacher do at school and turned it so that Ricky looked at her. Then she tried again. 'Taxi? Okay? Pay the driver.'

Ricky nodded.

She still held his face. 'Then go straight home and don't tell anyone. Secret? Understand, Ricky? Secret. These are for you.' Two more notes into his other hand.

He understood that all right, pocketed them and made off down the street toward the taxi, looking back from time to time to make sure he was getting it right.

Eleanor drove Archie to the hospital where he died a few hours later without regaining consciousness. Eleanor told the truth about how she found him but made no mention of Ricky.

Scandal was unavoidable. The police started a murder inquiry with more than their usual energy. They were used to casualties from pub brawls but Archie was better known and better off than most victims. Ricky's presence at the scene was uncovered and he became the prime suspect. His arrest so enraged local people that a deputation headed by his mother and grandmother marched on the police station and demanded his release. The view of all who knew him was that he might be daft as a brush, but he wouldn't hurt a fly and was frightened of his own shadow. Eleanor herself defended him with a passion that surprised even herself.

It was clear from the start that there were those who knew who killed Archie, but ranks closed. As the investigating officer explained with much apology to Eleanor, it was not always clear-cut.

'I'm not suggesting your husband could have killed a man, madam, but it's often a matter of luck, so to speak, as to who ends up dead in a case like this. Six of one and half a dozen of the other, as you might say.'

Eleanor kept her own counsel on the matter of whether Archie might have killed a man, and counted herself lucky in a strange kind of way that things had turned out as they had.

Eleanor had to return to work. She was fortunate to get her old job back with Annabelle's Exclusive Fashions.

To her little sister, Goldie, she said, 'I told him I'd only come back if he gave me a raise. I'm the best cutter he's ever going to get in this godforsaken town.'

'Why don't you sell the car?'

'You've got to have style, Goldie.'

'Wicked waste of petrol, Ma says. They say you won't be able to get any soon anyway. It's going to be rationed.'

'Lovely car. Beautiful car,' said Eleanor to the nurse who was taking her pulse. 'You should always have a good car.'

The nurse said she had a Mini Metro and Eleanor gave her a withering look. 'You've no idea. Absolutely no idea.'

26

Eleanor was feeling serene today. She could see blue sky out of her hospital window, which made her feel young again – those heady days when she had men at her beck and call. Like the evening she met Harry.

She left the party early, as the only eligible man there was too shy to approach her. She was adjusting her hat in the driving mirror when she saw the young man in question walking towards her car. He had evidently followed her. He looked a little gauche, possibly because the sleeves of his jacket were a quarter of an inch too short, but he had pleasing features, thick sandy hair, a direct gaze – altogether a handsome face. He approached with a long stride. Eleanor wound down her window.

As he drew almost level she turned her head halfway towards him.

'You'll have missed the last bus,' she said into the air just ahead of him, watching from the corner of her eye.

She offered him a lift, looked up at him when he stammered acceptance and knew she had captured him.

'In the Navy, I guess?' she said as he closed the passenger door.

He nodded, offering his hand. 'Harry Fairweather.'

She didn't say much on the way to the dockyard. She didn't have to. Glancing sideways, she could see he was having his work cut out just sitting there. She could feel him appraising her, the car, her driving. She didn't want to scare him off.

'Gently, gently, catchee monkey,' said Eleanor to the cleaner who was pushing a mop under her bed.

*

To thank her Harry invited her to a cocktail party on board which was more than she had hoped for. It would all be plain sailing from here. He took her card and tucked it into his inside pocket.

As she drove away Eleanor smiled to herself at Harry's confusion. He'd be even more confused when he read her card.

Mrs Archibald Thorne
Goldney Villa
29 Mayfield Avenue
Portsmouth
Hampshire

He wouldn't have been expecting a husband. He was almost too easy to read, but she liked his looks and his strong hands with their long straight fingers and square nails.

Back at Goldney Villa in the more prosperous part of North End she parked the car and stroked the bonnet. It was right to keep the Bentley against all advice to sell it. It set her apart. At the wheel she was a queen, a lady, or at the very least a rich widow. She walked away, down the basement steps of the house and let herself in. On her front door was the number 29^A but Eleanor had never felt it necessary to amend her card. The postman knew where she was.

'You might just have struck lucky,' she said to her reflection, narrowing her eyes in approval at how she looked and lifting off her hat. 'Goodbye, Mrs Archibald Thorne, hallo, Mrs Harry Fairweather.' She made a face at the photograph of Archie she still kept on the table for appearances' sake.

Eleanor was careful in her preparations for the cocktail party. She chose a discreet black dress and took a new pair of silk stockings out of their tissue paper. Since Archie's death she had been saving these for a special occasion. The silver cigarette case, her ebony cigarette holder and a lace-edged square of fine lawn went into her evening bag which had a design of peacocks embroidered in silver and coloured threads. She checked herself one last time in the hall mirror, stuck her tongue out at Archie's photo and left the flat.

*

'No more Thorne in my flesh,' hissed Eleanor to the lady in the green overall who brought her lunch.

She thought she saw Ricky Thomas shambling off through the gate and called his name. He looked back but ran away.

'Never mind about 'im, he just showed me where you live,' said a deep voice behind her.

'Who on earth are you and what are you doing skulking about here?'

'Not skulking, madam. I do apologise if I caused you fright. I was just about to knock on the door when you appeared from nowhere.'

The man was tall and heavily built and wearing a dark formal overcoat. He looked uncannily like a bailiff but without the bowler hat. He held out his hand. 'Albert Goode, Mrs Thorne. I was a friend of your late husband. I don't think we've had the pleasure.'

Eleanor ignored the proffered hand. 'What do you want with me?'

'First of all I would like to offer my rather belated condolences on the death of your respected husband…'

'Mr Goode, I doubt you took the trouble to seek me out for that reason. I have an appointment and I am in a hurry.'

'Saturday evening, a lovely lady like yourself, of course. I understand. In that case you will not want to delay over our little bit of business. On your late husband's behalf. I represent some others of his acquaintance.'

'If you want money, I don't have any.'

Albert Goode made a ponderous half-turn and looked up at the house.

'I live in the basement.' Eleanor instantly regretted her indiscretion as she saw the man's eyebrows rise. She saw him appraise her easy windows, take in that there could be no room for a servant.

'That's as maybe. But as a widow you have certain obligations. Your husband left debts.'

'I tell you, I have no money.'

This time Goode turned to the car. 'This your vehicle? I thought so. Beautiful. Put it this way, Mrs Thorne. You may not have money, but you do have what we call assets. I'm sure we could come to some arrangement.'

'You've taken long enough coming up with these so-called debts.'

'I would not want to have disturbed a lady in her time of grief.'

'You mean you did not want to risk coming to the notice of the police, I suppose.'

'I see, Mrs Thorne, that you appreciate the situation. As to the debts. I have proof. I have a number of IOU notes that are commonly exchanged when gentlemen run short of cash at awkward moments.'

He pulled out a bundle of dog-eared scraps of paper.

'Anybody could have written those!'

'No, madam. If you care to take a closer look you will find each one is signed by your late husband.' Goode took a step towards her and held them out one by one. It was as he said.

'I need to think about this, take advice. I haven't time now.'

'Of course madam is in a hurry. But it would be unwise to take advice, very unwise. And the matter is pressing. As you can see these notes represent a very considerable sum of money. I speak on behalf of the people who are owed and in need of being repaid.'

'Give me the notes. I'll see what I can do.'

Goode laughed, a short, harsh bark. 'That would indeed be foolish of me, would it not, madam? I will leave the matter for your urgent consideration and I will call again. Meanwhile I will use my good offices to make sure you are not troubled. I would not wish for things to turn ugly. I will not divulge this address.'

He turned on his heel and walked away.

Eleanor was shaking as she climbed into the car and held onto the wheel. That bastard Archie was still persecuting her from the grave. How dare he drag her into his sordid little world. She could not possibly pay the money without selling her beloved Bentley. No! Of course. She must take the problem to Archie's father, let his family sort it out. It was the least they could do. Meanwhile she must not be late for the cocktail party. She talked herself into a better frame of mind as she drove.

'This is important, far more important than sordid debts. This is how I leave all that behind. Eleanor, my girl, you can do it. Walk in believing you're a queen and everyone else believes it too. That's what Archie used to say. He had a point, poor old Archie.'

*

'Eleanor Thorne, men will fall at your feet!' announced Eleanor to the ward in general.

The sight of Harry waiting at the gate was unexpectedly comforting.

'I'm sorry your husband was unable to come. I hope to meet him another time.'

Eleanor smiled inwardly at how unconvincing he managed to sound. 'That will not be possible. My husband is dead,' she said, sounding more vehement than she intended. 'I couldn't put that in my acceptance letter. Not quite the done thing.'

Harry was distraught.

'Let's put that behind us,' Eleanor said after a pause. 'I don't want to start the evening being sad. I want to enjoy myself.' She slipped her hand into Harry's and squeezed it gently.

The evening on board was such a success that Eleanor forgot all about the visit of Mr Goode until she turned into her road. She clutched her key as she hurried past the bushes in the drive, glaring into the shadows on the steps to her front door. Was there someone waiting down there? There was not. But on the mat inside she found an envelope addressed to 'Mrs A Thorne' in careful copperplate script. 'By Hand' was inscribed in the top corner. The letter summarised in formal language the situation regarding Archie's debts, stated the total sum involved and gave instructions for handing over the money. It was signed 'Albert Goode'.

Presenting this letter to Archie's father the next day, Eleanor was confident her troubles were over. But he took the line that as a widow, her husband's debts were her responsibility. She had the Bentley to sell which was fortunate.

'Any road, how do you know these debts are real? It could be plain blackmail and he'd keep coming back.'

'I saw the chits, the IOUs made out to different people he was representing. It was Archie's signature all right.'

'It'd be paying money to our son's murderer, like as not. I'm surprised the man risked it. You could have gone to the police.'

'I thought about that. They must have counted on me not wanting to rake it all up again.'

'Well, nobody wants that. Sell the car, lass, and have done with it.'

Eleanor changed tack. 'Maybe I should go to the police.'

Mrs Thorne came into the room. 'Police? What's this all about? Grim faces! Eleanor dear, you look right upset!'

Mrs Thorne was indignant her husband was being so mean. 'It's the least we can do, Percy! He got her into enough trouble when he was alive. And anyway, that car was a present.'

And so the matter was settled.

'He didn't stand a chance,' said Eleanor happily to the nurse who was taking her temperature.

'Men rarely do.' The nurse entered a figure on Eleanor's record sheet. 'You have to start as you mean to go on, mind.'

'Yes, you do,' replied Eleanor. 'You certainly do.'

27

Eleanor fingered the fabric of her nightdress under the stiff sheets. The child, Francesca, brought her a new one today. Good of her. Said it was only polyester, not silk, but it felt nice. Said the peach was the best colour there was. Always so apologetic, Francesca. It was better than the harsh hospital gown open down the back with its missing ties. *Just because I'm old and ill they think I don't notice, that these things don't matter. But I do notice and they do matter. I have always known that these things matter.*

Eleanor let the silky stuff slither between her finger and thumb and rubbed it against her thigh. Once it would have hatched on the rough skin round her nails but now her hands were soft from doing nothing. No weeding. No washing up in hard water. No peeling potatoes. The everyday currency of her life had fallen away, not just since being in this place but for a long time. Why weed a garden when no one will see it? Why cook potatoes to eat alone? No potatoes, no point. She lifted a fold of the fabric onto the top of her thigh and let it slip down again. It felt like another time, before potatoes and weeding. Delicious, floating, giddy. She kept it sliding up and down her thigh.

It was black and heavy, and she was dropping it over her head, feeling the beads on the bodice cold against the inside of her arms. She shook it down over her slim hips and reached behind to raise the zip fastener, wriggling to get it as far up her back as she could. Then she reached down behind her head and pulled it up the last few inches.

She was getting ready to meet Harry. He had asked her to wear this dress because she wore it on their first date, the cocktail party on board his ship. He had booked a table at The Keppel's Head and was more nervous than she had ever seen him. She looked across the table as he struggled with the wine list, blushing at his own ignorance and at the patronising manner of the wine waiter. She even began to wonder if she'd made a mistake, pursuing this relationship with a man who was so gauche. He was the sort Archie would have fleeced, except Harry never had enough money to be of interest to the Archies of this world. What Harry had in his favour was honesty, loyalty and stability alongside his good looks. And Eleanor's experience with Archie had taught her that these might be worth more than money in the long run.

She knew this must be a special evening. Harry couldn't afford to bring her here, let alone to buy good claret. So she was not surprised when he took her hand, looked steadily into her eyes and asked her to marry him. No faltering or stumbling. Not even a blush. He brought out a little box and placed it on the table beside his plate. He didn't open it. He was not there to seduce her with jewels. It might be from Cartier or Woolworths. She would not find out unless she accepted.

She withdrew her hand. 'You take my breath away.'

She cast her eyes down across the dark red box and watched her lacquered nails rotating the base of her wine glass smoothly on the white linen tablecloth. The other hand was clenching and unclenching on her lap, the nails pressing into the flesh of her palm. She excused herself on grounds of feeling flustered and, in the powder room, was amused to find this was true. She considered playing for time, spinning out the decision, making him wait. That would be her style. But he was off on sea trials tomorrow and in these uncertain times it would be unwise to let this opportunity slip away.

She returned to the table with a light step and moved silently behind Harry, covering his eyes with her hands. 'Guess who?'

'I can't possibly guess.'

'Your fiancée,' and she held him down firmly by the shoulders to stop him leaping up and knocking the glasses over. Her eyes shone down at him and he pressed her fingers to his lips.

The ring was made of sapphires, a large one and two smaller ones set in a row on a platinum band. It didn't come from Cartier or Woolworths, but from Harry's grandmother. He'd spoken of his grandmother before and Eleanor knew how much the ring must mean to him. She could also recognise its quality. The stones sparkled with an inner light and so did her eyes as Harry slipped the ring on her finger. It fitted perfectly.

Now Eleanor turned it on the middle finger of her right hand where she moved it as her hands grew thinner. She worried it might slip off or be stolen in the hospital. Maybe it was time for her to pass it on. But she couldn't see Francesca valuing it. The little one perhaps. Zoë. She had spirit. Announced once she was going to be famous. Always wondered who the father was. Nothing to do with that toad of a husband of hers, that was always quite clear. Neither of them looked anything like him. The boy had the Fairweather redness in his hair, but a dark red. He was going to be a handsome lad.

She moved the ring up and down, checking her knuckle was still big enough to stop it slipping off the finger. She was rash, that night, inviting Harry back to her mean little flat. She never meant him to see it. But she had to be sure of him.

She noticed the little grunt of surprise from Harry when they turned away from the front door of the villa and down the basement steps.

'My husband – dying so suddenly – his affairs were not in order. So it seemed best to let out the main house for some income. Just while I get it sorted out.'

Did she imagine it, or was Harry smiling to himself in the dark?

'I admire your courage,' he said as she let him in.

Later she was surprised at his assurance in unzipping her dress, enjoyed the slide of it over her body, shivered at his hands on her shoulders.

'You are beautiful in that dress, but more beautiful without it.' It was a cliché but Eleanor heard the sincerity, the awe, in his voice.

'So we've got a new nightdress, I see.' The brisk nurse voice floated into Eleanor's consciousness from a great distance. 'Pretty, that peach.'

'Black silk,' she said. 'You can't go wrong with black silk.'

28

Eleanor drifted in and out of awareness of the activities of the ward. Nurses did what they had to do and Eleanor was left with her memories.

She was back once again in the basement flat at Mayfield Avenue. She and Harry married hastily before Harry went to sea, a long posting this time. The Far East probably, but he wasn't allowed to say. She'd made sure of the wedding by telling Harry she was pregnant. Otherwise, he'd have been content to let the engagement drag on until his first leave. And who knew when, or indeed if, that would be. Now that he'd gone it would be easy enough to write to him and tell him she had miscarried.

She was considering how to word the letter when Goldie turned up on her doorstep. As she stood there with her hair shimmering in the evening sunlight, Eleanor was reminded of that other time when Goldie shimmered. It was the first time she took Harry to meet her family.

As she and Harry had come through the front door, the door of the front room had opened. Goldie was stepping forward, introducing herself. There was such a strange look on Harry's face. As if he'd seen a ghost. Her sister stood there, a vision of light in the dark hallway, her crazy halo of yellow hair shining like she was an angel or something. She, Eleanor, had to move Harry quickly along to find their mother.

Because of the memory she was sharper with her sister than usual when she saw her standing in the porch.

'You gave me a fright! What do you want, standing there like the ghost of Christmas past?'

At which Goldie burst into tears in a most uncharacteristic way.

'Come on in. Come on. What's up with you?'

'Nell,' and Eleanor sighed because Goldie would never learn to stop calling her that. 'Nell, promise me you won't tell Mother?' And then, 'Nell, I'm in trouble.'

'What sort of trouble?'

'*Trouble* trouble. I've got meself in trouble.'

Eleanor's stomach clutched at the realisation that her precious little sister, this innocent child for whom she'd always felt responsible, was somehow pregnant. What monster had done this? Was she sure? The questions followed faster than Goldie could answer them. The picture gradually emerged. On the days when Eleanor was working late, Goldie had been going to the tea dances on her own, not with her friend from down the road as Eleanor had assumed. She got friendly with a boy; they went walking on the beach to throw stones in the water and look for shells.

'Oh, Goldie! How can you be so naïve! I thought you could look after yourself!'

Eleanor scolded and Goldie wept and denied all knowledge of the boy and his whereabouts. She didn't even know his name and might not even recognise him again. She sobbed into Eleanor's shoulder. 'Promise you won't tell Mother?'

'As if! She'd flay me alive. She trusted me to look after you.' Eleanor suspected Goldie was lying about the name, but questions only made her sob harder.

'What shall I do? There's places you can go, aren't there?'

This was what had been going through Eleanor's mind throughout the whole conversation. If there was one thing worse than the thought of Goldie being virtually raped by a stranger, it was the idea of her being messed about with dirty needles by some sordid backstreet abortionist.

'It's not safe, not unless you go to a proper doctor. And you have to have money, a lot of money, and you have to know people, because it's illegal.'

She thought of the Bentley sitting outside in the drive. It was the only way. 'I'll sort something out,' she said. 'I'll see to it tomorrow. I know where to ask and I'll raise the cash somehow. Don't you worry, Gold. It'll be all right.'

Goldie still looked sad, but calmer. 'It would have been nice to keep it.'

'But hardly practical.' And to change the subject while her mind still raced on what she must do tomorrow, Eleanor added, 'I've got a problem too. In fact, it's ironic that you should be in this state. Because I've got to stage a miscarriage.'

This certainly grabbed Goldie's attention. 'What do you mean?'

'Well, I thought Harry would never get on with it. Get married, I mean. And you know I have to get out of here, they're going to sell the house? So I told him I was pregnant. I mean, it makes no difference. He was going to marry me anyway. I just thought it was better sooner rather than later. So now I have to tell him I lost the baby.'

Goldie was outraged. 'How could you? Do that to someone like Harry? That's so mean – he'd never dream you would lie to him.'

'Only a little white lie. No harm done. Just a letter and we'll be back to square one.'

Goldie was silent. Her expression gradually changed. Suddenly she said, 'I've got an idea. It might just suit us both. How about you *have* the baby?'

'What are you talking about? I haven't got a baby to have. I can't just make one!'

'But you can! You can have mine! Then I don't have to go to some horrid doctor and your lie will turn into truth.'

'You're crazy! You just can't hand over babies like that.'

'Why not? Who would know? I could come and live with you, keep you company.'

'But you couldn't live just round the corner without Mum seeing you getting bigger and bigger!'

'We could go away. The word is they're going to bomb Portsmouth again – so we go and stay in the country to get away from the bombs.'

'Hold on, hold on! Who says I even *want* a baby anyway? It's a mad idea.'

'Well you're bound to have one anyway when Harry comes home. Like you said, sooner rather than later.'

The idea was planted. All night Eleanor tossed and turned, tempted by the neatness of it, the risk, the secret they would share. No need to sell the car. No need to invent a miscarriage. But the fact that there would be no need for Goldie to have an abortion was the thing that weighed with her most. She knew there were risks involved, even with a reputable doctor. She would never forgive herself if anything happened to Goldie and already she felt a huge burden of guilt for not keeping a closer eye on her sister. It was the least she could do, as a respectable married woman. It would save Goldie's reputation and it might even save her life. And it wouldn't make that much difference to her. As Goldie had said, sooner rather than later.

Hardly aware she had made the critical decision, Eleanor started working on the logistics of the plan with typical thoroughness and attention to detail. Goldie must move in with her at once in case she started suffering from morning sickness. She remembered hearing Archie's parents talk of some people with a farm in Dorset. She'd find out whether they could go there later on, but before Goldie started to show her condition. She'd heard farmers were short of labour and were thankful for any help they could get. She'd take Goldie there and settle her in and then come back and carry on working. She couldn't afford not to on the allowance she was getting from Harry. It would be easy enough to start wearing loose dresses and pad herself out a bit. Then she could join Goldie when her time was near. When would be the best time to tell them at work?

'We'll have to go soon,' Eleanor said to the girl who brought her lunch. 'Before the bombs. Before the baby comes. We're going to the country, you know.'

'That will be nice,' said the girl.

29

Eleanor was sleeping when the priest arrived. He had been warned to keep his distance in case she tried to hit him. So after saying her name and announcing himself, he stepped round the bed and walked up and down by the window. After a few turns he heard a low moan and saw her lifting her nose in the air like a dog about to howl. As he leaned towards her she opened one eye.

'You smell,' she said, which was not what he expected.

When he backed off, making the sign of the cross, she told him to come closer and she sniffed and frowned, sniffed some more. Somewhat at a loss, he asked her permission to say a prayer.

'Do what you like. But keep waving your arms about.'

She still looked puzzled, which reflected how he was feeling. He did as she asked and was rewarded when, halfway through the prayer, she sank back on the pillow with a half-smile on her face.

Eleanor was drifting on tides of consciousness like a boat swinging on a mooring, tethered to her shrunken physical frame. One swing brought a tantalising whiff of a long-forgotten odour. Her nose flared for more of it as she struggled to bring her wavering mind and memory to bear on this scant piece of information. There it was again – but gone before she could breathe it in. She sensed a presence and opened an eye, reluctant to engage another sense when her nose needed all her energy.

A figure loomed, a bush of grey hair, blue eyes. Had to be the source of the smell. How odd. She tried to pull the person towards her but at that moment he lifted his arm. What he did with it looked suspiciously like the sign of the cross. So they really did think she was on the way out. How dare they! She was about to give him the same treatment as the impertinent child who called himself a doctor when the fragrance wafted over her. She breathed in and something stirred deep inside her and a long way off. Words she didn't understand were pulsing over her in soothing cadences, stepping up, swooping down. He had a fine voice. As the arm went up again, she made a grab for it and pulled it towards her, gripping the sleeve. It took him by surprise and he fell forward so that her nose was momentarily plunged into the stuff of his jacket. It was enough.

'Yes!' said Eleanor and saw the blue eyes widen as the figure returned to an upright position. 'Patrick,' she added softly.

'I'm sorry,' said the voice. 'I am Father O'Donoghue. And my name is not Patrick.'

But Eleanor had already closed her eyes and as he walked away she was back in a barn in Dorset inhaling the sweet smell of hay mixed with the spice of the incense that clung to her lover's clothes. She was lying in the nest they'd made in the hayloft and Patrick was carefully undoing the buttons of her blouse, one by one, and gently kissing each inch of newly exposed flesh. Eleanor had never experienced anything like the passion she felt for this man. It was both fiery and gentle and it gave her a feeling of joy and peace which tingled to the tip of every extremity in her body. For the first time in her life Eleanor trusted someone other than herself.

Patrick hushed her and their lovemaking continued in silence except for the soft groans and sighs which escaped with the rustle of clothes, the squeak of the hay and little explosions of flesh on flesh. *Ah, Patrick, I wonder where you are now? How would it have been if Harry had not come home?*

Eleanor was positively mellow when the nurse came in with her medication.

'How did you get on with the priest?'

Eleanor looked startled.

'With Father O'Donoghue?' said the nurse.

'Oh, him. He was far too old. But he smelt just right. So he did very nicely. Yes, very nicely, thank you.'

30

A blackbird was singing outside Eleanor's window. It was deafening. Its orange beak threatened like a toucan's bill. Its unblinking eye drilled into hers.

'Shoo! Shoo!' yelled Eleanor.

The nurse was indignant and charmed by the bird. 'Singing just for you,' she cooed.

'Frighten it off. Send it away.'

The nurse went to the window and flapped a hand, humouring her. The bird hopped onto the next branch and continued to sing. As soon as the nurse had gone it returned to its perch by the window. It puffed up its feathers and became a vulture. It lifted a wing to preen and shut out the light.

'Go away! Shoo!' Eleanor continued to shout until another nurse appeared.

'Shoot the thing!'

'It's only a blackbird. Lovely song.'

'It's come to get me. Send it away!'

Eleanor was clutching the sheet to her face, peering over the top with wild eyes. The nurse rapped on the glass. The bird flew off. Eleanor sank back exhausted and closed her eyes.

In her half-waking dreams she still heard the dreadful ring at her doorbell, saw the dark figures of death standing on the step with their badges of office and childlike voices. She looked over their shoulders to avoid their fearful eyes as they spoke, bringing the news that was unspeakable. All the time she was watching the blackbird singing its heart out in the cherry tree. Trills of a nauseous sweetness that drowned the words she did not want to hear. So eventually she shouted, 'I can't hear you, shut up!' as much to the bird as to the little girl dressed up as a policewoman, who glanced at her male colleague and took her arm gently and ushered her into her own house and into the drawing room with the pale green brocade curtains and tried to sit her down in Harry's chair with the Sanderson chintz cover they chose together, so that she shouted again, 'No! Not that one. That is my husband's chair'. She extricated herself from the young woman and sat in the chair opposite with its identical loose cover, just back from the cleaner's last week, and composed herself. Then she said, 'What was that you were telling me?' And they started all over again on the story of a man falling down in the street. She couldn't grasp what it had to do with her, except that, deep down, she knew Harry would never sit in his armchair again.

Why was it, Eleanor wondered in her lucid moments, that the images of this event were so clear-cut and enduring, while other memories of happier times kept dissolving and sliding off the canvas of her mind like so much rainbow jelly paint?

31

Words kept sliding off their hooks in Eleanor's mind. Her visitor was Goldie. She knew that. Goldie stayed solid; her voice, her eyes, her warm, soft hands. Goldie didn't shift into anyone else. And she was trying to tell her something.

'Our Nell will go far,' Mother used to say. *But I had my nose in the air and fell down a snake, slither, slither all the way to the bottom. Clawed my way up the ladder again, though. Made it up to her, covered everything over, nice and smooth, nice and pretty.*

Francesca. Funny child. Never knew what to do with her. Used to huddle in a corner and watch. Never came and asked for a cuddle. Thought that's what children did. But not this one. With her pale skin and that hair! All red and gold. Impossible to paint. Always came out looking like snakes. Mistake having a baby really. Never seemed to get much painting done after that. But Harry wanted her. He got through to her too. They matched. The sandy head and the tawny head always close together, bent over a book, playing a game, laughing. I had no place, right from the beginning.

Eleanor clawed her face. 'Go away. No! No!' She beat the air to push away the image of Goldie taking the baby from her, scarlet and screaming, Goldie soothing her, feeding her and settling her.

Goldie kept telling her the maternal feelings would come. Before the birth she said, 'When you hold the baby in your arms.' When that didn't happen she said, 'When you feed her.' Next came, 'When you watch her sleeping,' and, 'When you recognise her cry.' But none of it worked. Goldie left. Thought she was getting in the way.

As the child grew older I was frightened. Frightened all the time. Frightened she'd consume me. I was used to being in control, using materials that did what I wanted them to do – fabrics, paint. I never dreamed how hard it would be. Like being given a plank of wood and being told to make a gown with it. The child would not bend or fold or pleat or take a shape. She blunted my scissors, frustrated my every attempt to tweak her into place, pin her down.

Strange that Goldie should be such a natural, being the youngest. Never had to look after a baby like me and Lil and Vi. She was the selfish one who always wanted things – dolls, sweets, then beads and fancy clothes. Now Lil's long gone. Never see Vi. Never spoke to me after the Archie business. Thought I betrayed the family. Shan't be sorry to die. What's the point of it all anymore?

Where was I? Yes, Harry. Now there was another surprise. A natural father. More maternal feeling in his little finger than I ever had. Always so aware of the child. Even when she wasn't in the room. Never forgot she existed like I used to. Like I used to want to. Knew her moods. It was like the plank of wood turned to velvet in his hands.

It worked both ways. She could wrap him round her little finger. Nothing was too good for her. Dear Harry. There were times when he got things all upside down.

Goldie. Her golden sister. She'd loved her so much, right from the moment she looked into the crib when she was newborn. Her very own living doll. But something had gone wrong there too. Something about a boy on the beach. She'd never believed her. She was hiding something. But she didn't want to know. There are some things it's better not to know. She couldn't remember it all. Too tired. It had all been all right until Harry went. He had loved her. He protected her. From the child, from the world.

PART THREE
Fran

32

Fran is woken by the storm, rain rattling so fiercely against the window that she holds her breath and waits for the sound of shattering glass. But the noise of the elements stays outside, merging with the mad crescendo of a herring gull bleating into the gale. It's a luxury to be contained, safe in a cottage that has withstood this kind of weather for centuries, and she burrows deeper into the bed, ready to drift back into sleep. It takes her a while to recognise the strident note that joins the trio of wind, rain and gulls. The telephone is ringing.

Fran rolls over onto one elbow and grabs the receiver, head spinning.

Clipped, formal words announce a hospital that sounds familiar, that she can't place. Please not Zoë or Dan. She manages a questioning noise and the voice repeats, 'Queen Alexandra Hospital, Portsmouth.' QA, of course. The voice is asking her if she is Francesca Fairweather. She agrees, impatient.

'We have a Mrs Eleanor Fairweather. We believe you are next of kin?'

Relief floods in. Followed by guilt. She is listening as if from a great distance. *Found unconscious. Intensive care.* She takes in the facts, wonders about the gaps. She is being advised to come at once.

'Is she dying?' Her own voice sounds strange.

A hesitation at the other end, then a more human tone. 'It could go either way.'

'It'll take me all night to get to Portsmouth. What's the time?'

'Three am.'

'I should make it by nine or ten.'

'I hope that will be soon enough.'

'I can't get there any fucking faster.' She's already replaced the receiver but surprises herself with the f-word and notices she is shaking, not just from the cold. The still-sleeping part of her needs to dive back down into the slow warmth of her bed to take in the situation, but she is already in the bathroom brushing her teeth. She looks for stars through the roof light designed to let the moon shine down on the bath. No glimmer from the clouded sky tonight. She grabs the novel beside the bath, Marge Piercy's *Woman on the Edge of Time*, bookmarked with Dale's postcard of Notre Dame, and heads back to the bedroom. The deep ochre walls and the garnets and crimsons of the Indian blanket warm her. Her red cocoon, her haven she can still hardly bear to leave.

She pulls on yesterday's clothes – jeans, black polo neck and a loose red jumper recently bought in Penzance market to clash with her hair, which she flicks back into an elastic band. It's been a good winter, making a new home, shaping a new life. It must be more than four months since she saw Dale and they've rarely spoken. She can't afford phone calls to Paris. He has always had the ability to vanish into his music. Sometimes she's craved him, but mostly she's been too busy to mind.

Her brain gets into gear, ticking off the things she will miss – her singing lesson, showing Zelda the snaps of her birthday party, a gig with Patch on Saturday. Must let Patch know. How can she be so preoccupied while Mother apparently lies dying? Mother dying? Where are the feelings? Just this ridiculous shaking. She drags a bag from under fallen clothes and hangers at the bottom of the wardrobe. Knickers, how many? Big jersey, warm socks – that house is like a morgue. Better get going. Down the stairs into the smell of wood ash, the stove still giving off a faint heat.

Driving, empty stomach. Must have something. A quick piece of bread: banana sandwich, just the job. Potassium keeps you going, Zelda says. Nice green one. Mother hates unripe bananas. Among other things.

Oh, yes. The lyrics she was writing last night. Not bad. She pushes aside her notebook which is still on the kitchen table and saws off thick slices of nutty bread – Zelda's homemade – and constructs a sandwich. She bites into the bread, presses it with her tongue to the roof of her mouth, savouring the texture of the soft fruit on the cold slab of butter. It feels wicked to be enjoying it, a last luxury in the privacy of her kitchen.

The heavy front door is swollen with the damp. She slams it to engage the lock and turns into the weather, lifting her face to the soft rain, a lull in the storm. She sidesteps unseen puddles, hearing the pines wheeze in the wind and the hush and grind of the sea on the beach below.

The elderly estate car responds at her second attempt to start it. Revving the engine she reverses, and the headlights swing across the cottage and its garden fringed with tamarisk. Changing gear, she turns into the lane, dodging potholes, coaxing the cold engine up the steep gradient.

Driving steadies her and she has the roads to herself. What happened to Mother? Was it a stroke? Why didn't she ask? Where's the horror she felt when Dad dropped dead? That tug of war where she tried to pull him back, and it felt as if he were pulling her after him. She should have visited Mother more. It must be months. Christmas, in fact. But, hell, she needed the space, the distance.

Time keeps turning itself inside out. Winding through the deep Cornish lanes, she feels like an animal coming out of hibernation. Once on the A30 she's able to cruise along to the steady swish and flap of the windscreen wipers. But the Portsmouth rush hour hurtles her out of her rural time warp and scatters all thought.

In the hospital world the bustle of coded professional activity collides with the uncertain wandering of anxious visitors. Her mother is already out of intensive care. She makes her way to the ward along corridors of scurrying black tights and shuffling dressing gowns. Urgent trolleys with drips held high over supine bodies issue from lifts and everyone avoids eye contact.

Fran stands at the foot of the bed indicated, peering towards the occupant whose body scarcely disturbs the line of the hospital-tidy sheets. A gaunt, dark face lies on the pillow framed by white hair. A beak of a nose points to the ceiling and an egg-sized lump protrudes from the forehead. No, certainly not Mother.

She moves on to the next bed where a grey-haired woman with a round pink face looks up and smiles. Then comes a young girl with one leg in a hoist, reading. On the other side of the ward are an empty bed, an Indian woman sleeping and a freckle-faced middle-aged woman. Fran turns back to the first bed. It simply cannot be. She reads the name over the bed. It is indeed Mother.

She gazes down at the face, trying to breathe into it some likeness, some familiarity. The hands are not to be held. They seek each other, fingers clawed inwards, and twitch from time to time. The skin round the eye sockets is tissue-purple, thin as onion paper. She catches a feather of recognition in the flutter of an eyelid, the beat of a vein in the temple, but it quickly vanishes. She strokes a stick of an arm.

A tube leading up to a drip is strapped to the other arm; another tube emerges from the sheets and connects to a bag hanging under the bed. The bag contains a small amount of dark brown liquid. It must be urine. On the bedside cabinet is a child's plastic cup with a spout in the lid.

Nothing that clipped voice said on the phone conveyed the state of this stranger in the bed.

33

Fran lets herself into the house with the spare back door key which has hung on a nail in the shed for as long as she can remember.

Her hand goes straight to the light switch. Her feet feel the broken tile just inside the door and, as she turns the oversized key in the lock on the inside, she remembers how it always used to stick out and snag her cardigan.

She leans heavily against the door, relieved there is no sign of Eleanor's fall, no blood or breakages, just a couple of supermarket carrier bags on the table.

She closes tired eyes and sees the kitchen as it used to be.

On the far side, the cooker prancing on oddly curved legs with its faint smell of gas and old bacon fat. Then the beastly Beeston, the black-bellied boiler with its rituals: newspaper, buckets of clinker, riddling and curses. Firelighters made with rolled-up newspaper; the careful adding of coke from the two-handled hod – one false move and too much would slide in and put the fire out and you'd have to start all over again. And Mother would get so mad.

Next to the boiler came the porcelain sink with its wooden drainer and the plate rack on the wall. She can feel the wet sleeve of her jumper as the water ran up her arm with each plate she slotted in. And the mop. A stringy thing with a wooden handle which must be squeezed out while still hot – bang, bang, bang on the edge of the sink to fluff out the grey strands and stop it going slimy.

She opens her eyes. There it stands, the mop in its milk bottle, a grey, dejected flower, ready for next time. Except there won't be a next time. Mother will never recover enough to return home. Tears flood over. She will never again hear her drumming with the mop, the signal that washing up was over. The sink is stainless steel nowadays, the boiler a white metal rectangle, the cooker another white rectangle with a wipe-over top. No more pop and hiss of gas, no more saucer of spent matches. All cleaner and easier.

She pushes herself away from the door. She ought to ring Goldie. Telling Zoë and Dan was difficult. More difficult than she had expected. She can't face another call tonight. If only she could talk to Dale, but is he still in Paris? Too late to risk disturbing the concierge for nothing, too tired to speak French. Sleep is all she can cope with.

She fills the kettle, no longer the proper-shaped copper one which puffed like a train out of its narrow spout, but jug-shaped, plastic. Mother's hot water bottle is hanging, as always, on the back of the door.

Zoë was alarmed at the news. They'd been close. Mother always encouraged Zoë's ambitions and took her shopping for clothes. Things she would have liked to do with me, thinks Fran. Dan was tearful, his grief at losing his grandfather triggered all over again.

She fills the bottle, bending it to expel the air, dries the top with a tea towel and hugs the warmth to her.

The morning sun falls on the two carrier bags on the kitchen table. In one, a bottle of Gordon's gin and two large bottles of tonic water. In the other, a tin of Spam, a tin of baked beans, a tin of Ambrosia creamed rice and half a dozen eggs. How odd. Not Mother's usual choices at all. The sunlight also shows up the grimy state of the Formica tabletop and the sink. Not like Mother.

There is very little in the fridge and most of it is well past its sell-by date. Two cooked sausages on a saucer turning green, yoghurt dated six months earlier, mouldy cheddar and a pack of butter frozen into the ice that bulges, inches thick, on the rear wall. Fran shudders and slams the door. Maybe there's bread in the larder. She opens the door and stares.

The white and blue enamel bread bin sits facing her on the shelf under the window. The two shelves on either side are lined with empty Gordon's gin bottles. Each is placed at an angle with the label facing the door as if some sergeant major has just given the order to stand at attention. Fran feels as if she should walk along the rows with her hands clasped behind her back inspecting each bottle.

She is startled by a knocking on the back door and emerges to find a tall white-haired gentleman in a tweed jacket and baggy flannel trousers already peering round the kitchen door. Eleanor's old friend, John Penfold. Fran pulls the larder door shut behind her. She can't bear the thought of him describing the contents to his wife Maude or chuckling about it at the next bridge party.

'So sorry to intrude, but I thought you might be here. Anything I can do?' He makes an expansive gesture with large red hands.

'That's kind, John. I haven't really had time...'

'No, no of course not. I wondered how Eleanor...?'

'Out of intensive care. But not good. Not at all good yesterday.'

'You see, it was me that found her. Broken hip, they thought, the ambulance crew. I did wonder how...'

'I wondered if it was you. They didn't have the name. How did you...?'

John Penfold expands into his story of how Eleanor failed to turn up for bridge two nights ago and how the group didn't think too much of it.

'She'd been known to er...um...be too tired, you know.' John looks sideways at Fran, gets no reaction and continues. 'I was on my way home. Come quite close to here. I just acted on a hunch.' He purses his lips and twinkles in self-congratulation.

John found Eleanor's car unlocked in the drive and the back door open. 'She must have tripped on those steps as she carried in the shopping. Hit her head on the table it seems. Damn bad luck.'

Fran thanks him for acting on his hunch, thanks him again for clearing up and wonders whether he looked inside the larder.

John nods towards the bottles and tins on the table. 'I see you found the shopping.' He coughs a little laugh. 'Essential supplies.'

Fran nods. 'Yes, well...'

John places fingertips on her arm. They weigh like lead. 'As you're here, I suppose I should tell you. Eleanor did knock it back a bit. Since Harry went. Understandable. Damn lonely for her. But we have been a little worried.'

'I see. When I came to stay she certainly had a few. But I didn't think it was serious.'

'No.' John scratched his chin. 'Clever woman. Wouldn't have wanted you to know.'

'Come to think of it, there have been a few strange phone calls. Wandering, you know.'

'We had to take her home a few times. Fetch her car for her in the morning. That sort of thing.'

'I'm so sorry.' And so guilty.

'Not a problem. Everyone's very fond of her you know. Happy to rally round. Damn fine woman.'

Fran tells him which ward Eleanor is in so that he and Maude can visit. She listens to his car drive away and bursts into tears.

Why is she crying? She's more guilty than sad for Mother and her loneliness. How distraught Dad would be – his beloved Eleanor going to pieces. And not quite a year since he died. She still misses him. Why did he have to leave her to deal with this? To cope with Mother in this state? The house no longer feels like home, she's hungry, and there's nothing to eat. If only Zelda's mother was still round the corner. She could always rely on her. But Gaye Turner moved last year to live with Zelda's brother and his family in Sussex. She pulls her coat off the back of a chair and slams the door on it all. She needs to talk to Harry.

The graveyard is deserted. She sits on the bench near Harry's grave where a few daffodils are collapsing into the grass. There are no words for the sludge of feelings inside her. She pulls up her collar and hugs herself, staring out over the headstones. They're like seats on a bus; ghostly passengers facing forward, being taken to their destination. The oldest ones are up front, some from the last century. They must surely have arrived by now. And Dad way behind in the back row. They're facing east, and in front of them is a stone wall covered with plaques in memory of those who have been cremated. It's as if those chosen few have stolen a march, gone up in smoke and taken a shortcut to heaven. Ridiculous thoughts. But she smiles at how Dad would have enjoyed the fantasy and elaborated on it with some reference to compost.

Graveyards remind her of Verity and of Dale. Not that he's ever far from her thoughts. Where exactly is he? Probably back from Paris by now. She's tried ringing his London number. No reply. No one to leave a message with. Odd that he hasn't been in touch. Away from her home, the sea and her singing, the need for him is urgent.

She looks up into the branches above her. Ash tree possibly, like the one on Cadbury Hill. Fat buds are buttoning the black twigs to the blue of the sky. Not long before the leaves come. She stares back at the grave but Harry appears to have nothing to say about any of this. All that comes is a reminder to ring Goldie and she knew that anyway.

Back in the garden, she follows the paths of her childhood and puts a hand on the furrowed bark of the locust tree. The swing is long gone, but there are still celandines among the roots. What an odd child she used to be, straining to see over the wall that no longer seems very high. It's a relief to know she has finally achieved the ambition of that anxious little girl. She smiles to herself. It's been quite a journey but she's found her independence – she's playing in the street at last.

On the way back to the house she spots a tangle of magenta and green hellebores, their heads heavy on pale stems. She fetches scissors from the kitchen and carefully extracts a handful, finds a jug and sets them on the table in the sitting room. A shower of creamy stamens falls on the polished wood. She laughs. Mother always said they were too messy to bring into the house.

34

The hospital doctor makes it clear: Eleanor will never return home. He's amazed she's pulled through at all. At best she will be discharged to a nursing home, but that is unlikely. So the house will have to be cleared. Fortunately Eleanor was not a hoarder and the box room is not a huge space. Nevertheless, the task is daunting.

Fran begins to fill black bin bags but is easily distracted – first by a box of old photographs. Most of them are tiny black-and-white snaps which have begun to fade into sepia. She recognises various aunts, and her grandmother posed on a garden seat in her best dress.

Then she finds one that has been enlarged and shock streams through her body. A young woman is standing in a vegetable garden in front of a bed of tomatoes. An open smiling face, shoulders thrown back. She is carrying a trug of the fruit in one hand and a trowel in the other. Fran can feel her energy and confidence, proud of her harvest, bursting with life. It is Eleanor, but it doesn't look anything like Mother.

She takes the box downstairs and props the photo against the pepper mill as she eats her supper. It delights and puzzles her. She cannot help warming to this person in her garden. She wants to talk to her, to take a tomato, to pinch out the pungent green starfish of a stalk and taste the sweet red flesh. She can hear her laugh, but it isn't Mother's laugh. That is the puzzle. What happened after that photo was taken? What changed that vibrant personality into the person she knows?

Back in the box room Fran tackles a large trunk in the corner. Puffs of dust explode off the heap of carrier bags on top. One contains a disintegrating straw hat with a wide brim and tall crooked crown. Instant memories. Auntie Goldie wore it all the days of Fran's childhood summers. Somewhere there is a photo of the two of them – Goldie in the hat and a sundress and herself, aged five, eating a peach with juice running down her chin.

It was fun when Goldie was there. When did it all change?

Goldie often came to stay, but then she and Mother fell out and Fran never understood what that was all about.

Fran turns back to checking the carrier bags. One is full of old handbags. They smell of stale perfume from tiny lace handkerchiefs and loose powder that cakes, dry and pink, under her fingernails. There are gold-embossed invitations, lipsticks by Max Factor and Coty, pieces of tissue paper bearing the faded red imprint of her mother's lips.

She puts one bag aside – the velvet clutch evening bag with the peacocks embroidered in silver and gold and indigo threads which she always loved as a child. Into it go the lipsticks and the best lace handkerchief. The nostalgia bag. The last bag is of battered black leather, coming away from its frame. Fran glances inside and is about to lob it into the black sack when she spots the corner of an envelope in an inside pocket.

A George VI stamp and rounded handwriting that is vaguely familiar. She pulls out the letter and a photograph falls into her lap. Another of the small black-and-white snaps showing her mother and one of her sisters with their arms across each other's shoulders. Is it Auntie Goldie? It looks like her but somehow different. On the back is written *Longfield Farm, Bridport 1942* in the same rounded script. The letter is a scribbled note.

> *Couldn't resist sending you this. It's up to you of course, but I reckon it's time you came down here permanently. Don't want to spoil our little secret!*
> *Love and kisses,*
> *G*

Of course. Goldie with her young girl's handwriting. She used to talk of a farm in Dorset; stories of spending time there during the war, the luxury of fresh eggs. Probably Goldie was advising Mother to get away from the air-raids. As to their little secret – probably something trivial. Goldie always liked to dramatize everything. It would be fun to ask her about it sometime. She tucks the letter and photo back into the envelope and slips it inside the peacock evening bag.

The trunk itself is full of Eleanor's clothes: her cocktail and dinner dresses. Fran strokes the smooth satin of a crimson ball gown, folds it back to reveal the garment underneath and goes on, fingering each fabric and folding it back until she reaches the bottom of the trunk. Fine wool, slithering silk, velvet, with sequinned sleeves, beadwork bodices, all in rusting black, rich cream or the jewel colours that suited Eleanor so well. A Pandora's box of memories.

The phone interrupts and she races downstairs wondering what on earth to do with the dresses. Vintage shop? Local drama group? She jumps the last three steps and grabs the receiver. It's Zelda, not Dale.

'You okay? You sound strange, miles away.'

'Yes, I suppose I am.' Fran peers into the mirror on the wall and rubs a cobweb off her nose. 'Years away, actually.' She explains about the contents of the trunk.

'I've been trying to get you for ages.'

'It's weird, Zel. I found this photo and she looked like someone I never knew.'

'Who? Your mum? How is she?'

'Maybe she wasn't who I thought she was.' Fran draws an E outlined with a furrow of dust on the polished surface of the hall table. 'Oh, she's still hanging on, but I don't think it can last. They don't give her long.'

'Well, I guess that's just as well – for her as well as you.'

'Yes, I suppose so. But it's funny – just now I want a bit more time. Does that make sense?'

'But what for, Fran? Isn't it too late?'

'Probably.'

'But if you can't talk to her? You said she doesn't respond.'

'She was lonely, Zel, and drinking too much. I should have come more often.' Fran picks up the body of the phone and settles with it on her lap on the bottom tread of the stairs.

'Jesus, Fran, come on. You've made a life for yourself. Don't let her get to you! She might be ill, but she's no saint. Think what she used to put you through. I was there, remember? She was a nightmare.'

256

Fran changes the subject, asks about the children, and Zelda chats on about local gossip. Fran leans back against the banisters, remembering how she tried to push her head through them when she was small. At the end of the call she replaces the phone and fingers her mother's silver-backed clothes brush. Mother always checked the mirror before going out. Head on one side, eyes narrowed and two quick brushes to her coat collar on either side.

Next morning feels like the time to dismantle Mother's Installation, as she has come to think of the display in the larder. Sooner or later the twins will be coming to visit their grandmother. She doesn't want their last memory of her to be associated with gin bottles. She finds some empty cardboard boxes in the garage. It should be the work of a few minutes.

There are sixty bottles in all. How long did it take Mother to drink sixty bottles of gin? Did the installation just happen? Or did she plan it from the first bottle? She imagines Mother placing the bottles with the same precision that she placed ornaments or invitation cards on the mantelpiece. She can picture her stepping back and appraising the effect, then shifting one bottle a degree or two, just as she did with her flower arrangements.

Why? Perhaps Mother took up painting again and became obsessed with this strange still-life study, but her search of the house shows no evidence of paints or brushes. 'There's something I'm not seeing,' she says aloud, surveying the ranks of green glass. As if in answer to her question a shaft of pale sunlight falls through the window grille, lighting up the bottles on the right-hand shelf. They gleam, pristine and clear. What she is not seeing is dust, cobwebs, dead flies, spiders. Mother must have kept her bottles clean. It explains the presence of the yellow feather duster on the back of the door.

Why? Why? Why? Fran wanders upstairs into the room Eleanor insisted on calling the drawing room. Here everything looks as it always has, apart from the untidiness she has created herself.

The carriage clock stands unwound and silent on the mantelpiece and the shepherd and shepherdess incline their delicate heads on either side. The marble fireplace is flanked by two matching tables: one for Eleanor, one for Harry. On one is a white porcelain lamp. Its pair stands on Eleanor's table alongside a silver inkstand which Eleanor always used as her secret ashtray. The cream silk lampshade with its tasselled trim shows some discolouration. Only Eleanor smoked.

Fran sits down in Eleanor's chair with its chintz loose cover of faded pink roses. Here Mother used to sit, upright, alert, entertaining friends, her drink in a cut-glass tumbler on the table, queen of her kingdom. But how did the queen manage without her consort to refresh her glass on lonely evenings when she wasn't playing bridge? How many times did she cross to the cupboard to refill her glass? For Mother would never have brought the bottle to her chair.

She surveys the formation of Redouté rose prints by the door, their frames exactly aligned. By contrast with this elegance, the installation in the larder is a secret life, like Dorian Gray's portrait in the attic. Did Mother remember it, a private drawer in her mind, when chatting to John and Maude Penfold? Maybe that was its appeal.

She wanders back to the kitchen. Why is she making such a meal of this task? She certainly has no energy for it. Zelda's voice sounds in her ear. *It's no big deal!* Zelda reckoned the 'ginstallation' was Eleanor's idea of a joke and didn't think it mattered whether the twins saw it or not. *Why are you always trying to protect them? And from what?*

Fran is readily distracted by the box of photos and the photograph of Eleanor with the tomatoes. She wonders idly who took it. The eyes are not tranquil. Defiant almost. Happy? Aggressively so. Triumphant comes closest. She sifts through the rest of the snaps, spreading them out on the table, looking for more of her mother and people she knows. Eventually she tips the whole box onto the table. A small piece of folded newspaper flutters out after the snaps.

It must have been cut from the *Portsmouth Evening News* judging from the adverts – one for Handleys and another for Bulpitts, the drapers in Commercial Road. Alongside a thirties-style fashion plate is a short news item headed 'Local Gambler Meets Untimely End'. It has been dated neatly in ink, 12th January, and reports a street killing, of all things. She reads that 'the deceased was identified as Mr Archie Thorne of North End.' A name that rings no bells.

She decides to add it to the nostalgia bag and take it to Goldie's. She's promised to call in on the way home from the hospital. It'll be something to talk about, a light relief.

35

It's a few years since Fran saw Goldie. As her natural shades have faded she's coloured herself in, liberal with the paint to match the generosity of her big features. The result is a caricature of her former self. Fran is reminded of a picture she drew of her aunt as a child: crude crayons exaggerating the blonde hair, blue eyes and red lips. But Goldie's vibrant personality remains the same.

She opens the door with a prepared face, careful eyebrows raised, mouth severe. As soon as she recognises Fran her smile breaks open, false eyelashes fluttering excitedly.

'Sweetie, my love! I thought it was someone selling things. We get so many, such polite young gentlemen, but you have to be firm. Come in, come in. Don't trip over this doo-dah.'

She pats her Zimmer frame affectionately. 'I only use it to come down the hall. Stops me tearing along and landing on my sit-upon. That's how I broke the hip.'

Fran has forgotten about Goldie's hip replacement but her concerns are waved aside. 'I'll soon be dancing the gay fandango again!' Goldie parks the frame beside the coat stand. 'A cast-iron excuse not to go near a hospital. Well, aluminium at least. But otherwise I manage very well.'

'I reckon you could get up to the ward if I drove you to the hospital,' Fran teases.

'Oh no you don't. Can't stand them places. With all the old folk looking more dead than alive.'

'That's a bit how Mother looks.'

Fran tells Goldie about Eleanor as she unwraps the roses she's brought.

'Fetch me a vase from the doo-dah in the sitting room.'

'Which doo-dah is that then?'

Goldie laughs, deep and throaty. 'On the sideboard, sweetie, the cut-glass one.'

Fran fills the vase at the sink.

'Poor Nell. There! They look just the ticket. Speak for themselves, as they say. Luckily. I never was any great shakes at arranging flowers. Not like Nell.'

'Yet she's still got that knowing look. When she surfaces. Watching, you know, to see how you're reacting.'

'Yes, I know. Always playing some game or other. We never could keep up with her. Lil used to say, "Nellie's got that look on her face. She's got something up her sleeve." And she was nearly always right. Cuppa tea?'

Fran nods acceptance of the tea. 'I've started turning out. Up in the box room. I brought some things that might amuse you. Snaps and so on.'

'What fun. That'll be a good laugh.' Goldie warms the pot. 'Let's have mugs. I can't cope with diddly saucers these days. And I found these very nice bone china mugs, nice for tea. Biscuits in the tin.'

When they're settled Fran gets out the peacock bag.

'Oh, I always used to covet that.' Goldie runs a finger over the embroidery.

'Anyway, I found this photo. She looks so happy, and so, well, different from how she's always been. Where was it? Who took it?'

Goldie takes the photo and fumbles for her reading glasses which hang on a gold chain round her neck.

'Well, well! That takes me back, I'll say. But that's another story. Another story entirely. That was in the war, that was. We were staying in the country, lovely garden. The place where you were born. She must have told you about it? Yes, I thought so.'

'She does look different, don't you think?'

'Yes, she looks as she used to look. Our hearts were young and gay and all that jazz. Before it all happened.'

'Before what all happened?'

'Life, the war. She took fright, hardened up.'

'What frightened her?'

'Life, sweetie, just life.' Goldie turns away and reaches for a custard cream.

Fran peers into the bag, fingering the newspaper cutting. 'I don't expect this is anything, but I wondered why she kept it. It's about someone who got killed. Was there anyone you used to know called Archie?'

'Archie?' Goldie freezes, her mug in mid-air.

'What have I said? Who was this Archie?'

'Fran, sweetie...' Goldie takes a gulp of tea. 'Your mother is a very private person, as you know. She had her reasons back then. Well, I've never liked secrets. I mean, I'll keep a confidence for anyone. You can rely on me, absolutely watertight in that department. But I like to be out in the open about things generally. I don't suppose she's told you much about her life before she married your father?'

'No. Nothing. I never asked.'

'She wouldn't like me to tell you this, but I've never seen any reason for you not to know. She was married to Archie.'

'Married? To someone before Dad?'

Goldie pats her hair and nods.

'So how long were they married? What was he like? How come he got killed?'

'Luckily for her they weren't married very long. He was a bad lot, was Archie. In with a bad crowd, rogues and villains they were – that's what got him killed.'

Fran passes Goldie the newspaper cutting. Goldie reads it and sighs. 'Yes, that was how it ended. A sordid little end for a sordid individual, I have to say.'

'How on earth did someone like Mother get involved with someone like that?'

'She was taken in by his flash ways. Gold watch, good suits, champagne, all that sort of thing. He must've been leading quite a double life in those days, kept his lowlife friends very quiet. He was rich while it lasted and he splashed out, liked people to know. Oh, he could give a good party and I lived it up with the best of them, took advantage. We weren't used to luxury and it was such fun! Such a treat! Dressing up in our finery, all ossy-dossy with the perfume he used to give your mother! Treated like a lady, having things to eat we didn't even know the names of.'

Goldie pauses and pours them both more tea. 'But your mother, she took it seriously. She didn't just enjoy it, she *studied* it. She learned all the etiquette and which fork to use and so on. It was what she was supposed to have been born to – her time had come at last! Yes, she got very la-di-dah, your mother, with her cigarette holders and her posh accent. She got better at it than he was. Because he was a fraud – he was no more posh than we were.'

Goldie draws breath and snorts. 'It was just as well our mother had a sense of humour. It was very hard for her, getting dragged in his dirt. But she used to say, "It's rich! Our Nell always looked down on her family, wanted to better herself. Then she goes and marries beneath her. She never thought that was possible, but our Nellie managed it." Mum would nearly wet herself.'

'It's not like Mother to be taken in.'

'She wanted to be taken in. Our mum didn't trust Archie, she saw through him. But Nell saw her chance, thought she might never get another one.'

'So how long were they married?'

'Oh, not that long, let me see…don't remember dates, but it all fell apart. He started to lose at cards, blamed her, used to beat her. Said she was unlucky for him. It was out of the frying pan and into the fire and no mistake. It got very ugly, but she wouldn't run home. She'd too much pride for that. Then he was killed and we all got dragged through the mud with her.'

'What did she do then?'

'His family were very good, but then she met your father.' Goldie smiles and pats her hair. 'He was a lovely young man. Went on being a lovely man all his life, never stopped loving her. Though how he put up with her ways I'll never know.'

'How did they meet?'

'Oh, it was at some party with a set of posh friends she'd managed to keep in touch with.'

'Was it love at first sight?'

'Something like that.'

'And they got married and lived happily ever after.'

Goldie falls silent, examining her empty mug. When she looks up she eyes the peacock bag. 'What else have you got in there?'

'This letter. It was in one of Mother's old handbags. I think it's from you. And a lovely snap.'

Goldie peers at the photo and the note. She changes colour. 'My Lord! She never kept this. What in heaven's name was she thinking of?'

'Why? What's wrong? That is you two, isn't it?'

'Oh, nothing wrong, dear. Yes it's us. In the place I was telling you about in the country. Silly woman, to keep such things.'

'What was the secret you talk about? Is there a story...?'

'Good heavens, sweetie! I don't remember. I was always setting up surprises for folk and so on. You know me. Some silly thing I expect. Let's go in the sitting room and be comfortable.' She gets to her feet and moves stiffly away from the table. 'Sweetie, I think it's time for a drink. Not too early is it? You know where it is, on the doo-dah over there. Mine's a gin and orange. Help yourself to what you want.'

Fran frowns. What's going on? She picks up the snaps and the note and follows. After pouring Goldie her drink she returns to the first photograph.

She holds it up. 'Was it Dad who made her that happy?'

'He did make her happy, sweetie,' says Goldie evenly. 'But it wasn't your father took that photograph. He was away at sea at the time.'

'You didn't take it though, did you?'

Goldie laughs. 'No. It was a man – you can see that, can't you!'

Fran grins back at her. 'There's a quality about it I can't put my finger on. In the eyes. Or the smile. D'you see what I mean? It doesn't look like Mother.'

'It was a man she loved very much.'

'So, this wasn't Archie. It was after him, before she got together with Dad?'

'No, she was already married to your father.'

'You mean she was unfaithful?' Fran hears the indignant edge on her voice.

'Well, yes and no. You see, things were different in the war. Nothing was quite black and white. The only certain thing was that you were alive today and you might not be tomorrow.'

'All very well for her. But awful for Dad, miles away at sea, in danger and...'

'It was dangerous at home too. We went to live in the country to get away from the bombs. It was a young man—'

'So it *was* an affair!'

'Hold your horses, sweetie! You have to understand the circumstances. She'd not had a letter from Harry for weeks, months. Then she just received a package, all water-damaged, a whole batch of letters. She thought he was dead.'

'She hadn't heard, though? For certain? From the Navy, I mean. Or the War Office, or whoever let people know. I mean, she can't have done. He wasn't dead.'

'There wasn't any such thing as certain. You didn't always get to hear, it wasn't that straightforward. She was in a terrible state. She wrote, but she heard nothing.'

'How could she bear not to know? She must have phoned them?'

'It wasn't like nowadays with everyone on the phone. Not many houses had a telephone. And you couldn't get through. You had to queue up at the box in the village and put pennies in. Then they ran out before you got through.'

'That's awful.'

'As I said, she was in a bad way. And the local priest supported her. It was the priest who took the photo.'

'Priest? You mean a Roman Catholic priest?'

'Oh yes. She took to going into his church in Bridport, that was the local town, because it was peaceful and she liked the statue of the Virgin Mary. Said she could talk to her. And young Father Patrick befriended her. Well, sweetie, I'm afraid they fell in love. It was the real thing, no doubt about it. It was lovely to be around the pair of them.'

Fran is silent.

'Your mother was very beautiful, you know. Men used to fall in love with her all the time.'

Fran still says nothing, struggling to imagine Mother 'in love' with anybody.

'But this was the first time she'd fallen herself.'

'You mean she wasn't in love with Dad?'

'She thought so at the time. Especially after Archie, I guess it felt like the real thing. But then later, when Patrick came along... You could tell that was different.'

'I can't believe what you're saying.'

This time Goldie is silent.

'And did they...? I mean, was it – platonic? Him being a priest?'

Goldie snorts. 'Platonic? What do you think? They were both human beings, young and passionate. Wild horses couldn't have stopped them.'

'But you didn't try and stop them? You didn't care about Dad!'

'Fran, it just happened. It was how it was. As to your father, I cared about him all right. But I couldn't have stopped them even if I'd wanted to.'

'Which you didn't.' Fran walks to the window and looks out at the lights of the passenger ferry crossing the harbour to the Gosport side.

'Fran sweetie, you know me. I'm not that sort and I never was. I don't have a moral high horse. Live and let live, that's me.'

Fran knows in some faraway part of herself that this is true, knows it is one of the things she has always liked in Goldie. But that childhood knowing floats out of reach. It has no power against the rage in her throat.

Goldie is speaking again. 'It didn't last long of course. He had a terrible conscience about his calling and his vows. Whether he should go to his bishop and confess, whether he should leave the church. Your mother thought he'd leave the church for her.' Goldie pauses. 'Then came that awful day. He told her his conscience wouldn't allow him to give up on his vocation. The next day a letter came from Harry. It turned out the mail boat had been torpedoed but his ship was okay. He wanted to know why she'd stopped writing.'

'Good timing.'

'It was awful. She never got over it.'

'Awful that Dad was still alive and well?'

'No. Not that. She was just beside herself. I think she thought she could have persuaded Patrick if she'd had the time.'

Fran glares at Goldie. 'And Dad went and spoiled it all by being alive.'

'I shouldn't have told you.'

'Oh, I think it is just as well you did.' Fran puts on her coat and storms towards the door. Then she stops sharply and turns. 'What year was it?'

'1942. It was the summer, late summer and autumn of '42.'

'So, I was on the way? She was pregnant when she had this affair!'

Goldie says nothing.

'Are you sure it was the summer?' Fran walks slowly back into the room, counting on her fingers. She stops in front of Goldie. 'Just tell me this one last thing. Was I his child? This Patrick priest person?'

'No, you were not. You don't need to worry about your father. Trust me.'

The phone is ringing as she enters the house.

'Dale!' At last. 'Where have you been? When did you get back from Paris? I rang Mike – he had no idea. I so need to…'

'Sorry. I couldn't get you either. And sorry about your mother. I rang Zelda. She told me.'

He sounds strange, as if his voice has rusted. Fears race. There's someone else in Paris. Has been all along. It's all over.

'What's wrong, Dale? Are you all right?'

'Woods died. That's why…'

'Oh, Dale, that's awful. I didn't realise…'

'Me neither. I knew she wasn't well, but I was kidding myself. And all the time she was dying. The fags got her at last. Shrivelled up to nothing – but she never lost her sense of humour.'

Her loneliness is suddenly insignificant. And the fact that Mother was married twice or unfaithful during the war is really not momentous news. As to who her father is, well, paternity might still be too sensitive a subject for a time like this. She lets Dale talk.

36

Fran lies awake wondering when she'll actually see Dale, going over and over the things Goldie told her and finally falling into a troubled sleep. She wakes suddenly in the early hours. Moonlight is falling on the end of the bed and shedding light on a puzzle. She knows what is bothering her. Goldie has been lying. She's convinced of it. From the moment of revealing those photographs, there was something hanging in the atmosphere. Goldie was agitated, thrown off course by Fran's questions, trying to conceal it.

On an impulse Fran leaps out of bed, dresses and stuffs a few things into her bag. It's exciting to be starting a journey at night, an unplanned journey with an unknown destination which is so far only a name on the back of a photo. No one knows where she is and she's escaping from visiting the hospital. Once on the road her mind frees itself, unravelling her feelings as she drives.

Mostly they're about being let down by Goldie. She's been her rock, always there for her, utterly reliable. So *honest*. And now she's not being honest. And yet she said, 'You don't have to worry about your father.' Goldie is scared. Fran saw it when she turned from the window, saw it in her eyes. So Mother had a love affair. That isn't so terrible. So Mother betrayed Dad. A passing affair. But to think he might not be her father? That special connection? That is unthinkable. She has to know.

But in spite of that, little bubbles, thin poppings of excitement rise through the swampy feeling in her stomach. There's a promise of escape, a chance to rewrite her own history. Maybe she isn't forever trapped in that uncomfortable family triangle. She dismisses a twinge of guilt at this disloyalty.

By now the road is swooping along the coast in the grey dawn and she feels suddenly cold and hungry. She pulls off at a transport café. Her mission seems bizarre in the workaday atmosphere and she's tempted to enjoy her breakfast and go back the way she's come. Bacon, egg and sausages never tasted so good and the coffee is strong and hot. She's conspicuous among the truck drivers, but they are intent on their breakfast and only throw the odd glance and pointed comment in her direction.

It's mean to be abandoning Mother in order to spy on her past. She thinks of Zoë and Dan and the lie she wrapped around their upbringing. At least they didn't have to wait this long to discover the truth. Maybe she's about to discover for herself just how painful the truth can be. Painful but necessary. 'It's a question of identity,' she says to the sky as she walks to the car. 'I have to know.'

The Roman Catholic church in Bridport is up a side road off the High Street. The building is modern with a structure like a ship's prow above the main door, while inside it's laid out in the round. It must have been very different in Eleanor's day. A woman appears with a mop and duster and says the priest is often around in the afternoon.

Fran returns to the High Street and finds the post office and enquires about Longfield Farm.

'That'll be Peg Barnes's place.' The woman behind the grille calls a gentleman out of the back room. 'Here's George. He used to deliver over that way. He'll tell you.'

George nods. 'B&B you'll be wanting, then. But I'm not too sure she opens before Easter.'

Fran leaves the queue and takes down involved directions from George.

Sure enough, the approach to the farm is marked by a B&B sign. On the slate slab where milk churns once stood is a chicken cut-out advertising eggs, a stack of cartons and an honesty box. The bigger potholes in the rutted track to the farmhouse have been filled in with rubble and an attempt has been made to soften the concrete of the farmyard with tubs of geraniums, now withered and brown.

The whole place has a run-down air and some of the barns have roofs patched with corrugated iron. The farmhouse is a long stone building with small windows, probably unchanged since it was built. Two Welsh collies bound out of a big porch, knocking over a number of muddy gumboots.

Peg Barnes takes it in her stride when Fran introduces herself. Of course she remembers the sisters. She invites Fran in with the air of someone who has something to tell.

As Fran crosses the room she hesitates in mid-step as if some finger has pressed the pause button. Is it the shaft of sunlight hitting the corner of the mantelshelf? A sensation of warmth from the vanished range? A déjà-vu with no image? A whiff of some long-forgotten smell? She stands, nostrils flaring like a Bisto kid, but all she detects is wet dog and bacon fat. A violent sneeze jolts her and the tape moves on.

'Bless you!' says Peg over her shoulder. She is busy with the kettle and has noticed nothing. Fran feels sad enough to weep. 'No, no sugar, thank you,' she says.

Peg was only ten years old back then when Eleanor and Goldie came to stay, so Fran is not optimistic. But when she asks about a priest Peg flushes and beams. She disappears into a back room and comes back with a dog-eared black-and-white photograph of a wiry young man with rampant hair.

'Bright red it was,' says Peg, appraising Fran. 'A good bit brighter than yours.'

'Did he come here then?'

'Oh yes. Oh yes, indeed. I reckon he came in the first place looking for fresh eggs and cream. Mother used to get mad at the townsfolk wanting to be so friendly once rationing came in, when they never wanted to know us before.'

Fran nods and waits.

'After that, of course, he came to see her.'

'Her?'

'The dark one.'

'How did you come to have the photograph?'

Peg blushes again, more deeply.

'I used to clean their room. It had fallen under the bed. Didn't think it would be missed. After all, Nell she was called, she had a husband coming home from the war. What would she want with it then?'

'So was she friendly with the priest?'

'I'd call it more than friendly! I used to see them together. In the barn. Having a roll in the hay.' Peg smirks and stares away. 'I knew what they was doing right enough. Grew up on the farm, didn't I? Seen animals doing it since I was small.' She pauses. 'But humans, people I knew. That was different. And a priest… They aren't meant to, are they? It upset me at the time.'

But you got a kick out of watching them, thinks Fran, staring at the photograph, taking in what Peg has said. How dare this woman eavesdrop on her mother, even if she *was* only a little girl back then? 'How long were they here?'

Peg sniffs, collecting herself. 'Let me see now. Summer it was. That Nell used to come and go with that posh car of hers.'

'So they didn't both stay all the time?'

'No. I remember she kept coming and going even after the petrol rationing started. Pa was always on about that, how she must be getting it on the black market.'

'Do you remember which month they first came?'

'Can't say I do. They stayed through the autumn. Lambing time they went. Yes, that's right – they were here for Christmas. We thought it odd they didn't see any family at Christmas. But folk have their reasons. That's what Ma said. They left when the baby was big enough to travel. It was still very wee, though. But no, they weren't both here all that time. The dark one stayed on after my birthday. I know because she made a dress for my doll.'

Peg produces more snaps. 'My parents,' she offers.

Fran sees a couple in overalls standing at the farmhouse door with a collie at their feet.

'Only last year, Ma died. The other lady came to the funeral. That was nice of her. Can't remember her name. The one who had the baby.'

'Well, that would be the one you call Nell.' Fran is getting confused. She's amazed Mother bothered with such a trip, Mother who usually avoided funerals.

'No, no. The other one. Silly name she had, like her silly hair. Pretending to be blonde. No hair could be that colour and natural.'

'Goldie?'

'Yes! Goldilocks we used to call her. Not to her face, mind.'

'But it wasn't Goldie who had the baby.'

'She certainly did.'

'I don't think so.'

Peg raises her eyebrows and looks away. She sips her Nescafé.

Now I've offended her, thinks Fran. 'Goldie had the baby? You're sure about that?'

'Oh yes. It was her all right.'

'Peg, this is really important. You were only a little girl. Could you have got it wrong?'

'Little girl! I was ten. We grew up fast in them days. I should know. I was the one who fetched and carried for them. Ma was busy with the pigs. Said she hadn't got time to be a midwife too. I knew which one was doing the hollering. That Nell was useless. Had to come out the room in the end. Then Mrs Mullins came, she was the midwife, and she sent me packing. But I was doing everything for that Goldie up until then.'

'I see,' says Fran although she sees nothing at all.

'She was lovely with the baby. Ma used to say that for all her fancy hair she was a lovely mother. But if that Nell held the baby it would yell blue murder. She never could get it off like Goldilocks.'

'What did she call the baby?'

'Oh, it were a fancy name. Whatever was it? No, I don't remember that.'

Fran tears a page out of her diary. 'Here's my number. If you do remember, perhaps you'd give me a call. I'll be back there tomorrow.'

Peg takes the piece of paper and puts it on the mantelpiece.

Fran gestures with the photograph of the priest. 'May I?'

Peg hesitates, then nods and watches as Fran tucks it into her bag.

'By the way, for the record, Goldie's hair, it was absolutely natural.'

'Oh my,' says Peg, covering her mouth with her hand. 'Fancy that!'

Fran goes back into Bridport and checks into the more homely-looking of the hotels in the High Street. She cannot straighten out the dates and new information swirling in her mind. The fact Goldie had a baby at all is news, let alone one that must have been nearly her twin. But where is she, Francesca, in all this? The one called Nell came and went. So presumably Mother gave birth to her during one of those absences. Can a ten-year-old be relied upon? But what about the priest? How long did Mother know him?

Her parents were married in August. It occurs to her for the first time that she must have been conceived before they were married. Why has she never noticed that before? Just like the twins. History repeating itself. But it doesn't make her any wiser about whether Harry was actually her father.

By this time Fran has a pounding headache. She washes down aspirin with tea in a fish and chip café and walks slowly back to the church.

The priest is a brisk, sharp-eyed man with a somewhat impatient manner. He has explored the history of the church for personal interest. No, there is no record of a Father Patrick in the early forties. But yes, he has heard of a young priest who left under a cloud at that time, probably assistant to the incumbent. He isn't one to listen to rumours, but there is a story that he got a local girl into trouble. Who knows? There was a war on.

37

Fran sleeps badly in the overheated hotel room, tossing in a twist of sheets and feverish dreams.

It's late when she finally wakes. Sitting on the edge of the tangled bed, she takes the photo of the priest from her bag. A steady gaze. A warm smile. Where would he be now?

She no longer feels angry about the betrayal of her father. She can even understand how Mother might have wished Harry would not come home, shocking though that thought is.

There's plenty to think about as she drives back. She hasn't succeeded in tracing Patrick, but is less obsessed about whether or not he was her father. If he was, it would be exciting, romantic even; a good story. But it wouldn't alter anything with Harry. He brought her up and nothing could change that. Patrick was part of Mother's life. He's no more significant than that. Not really. Mother made mistakes. So has she.

The Dorset countryside falls to the sea on the far side of the road, and rolls into downland to the north, spreading away to west and east. She sees the sweep of limbs, the curve of a breast or a buttock in the intimate knolls and wooded valleys. Ever since Zelda first pointed it out to her, way back when the twins were babies, she has always seen this landscape as female, alive.

She pulls into a lay-by and leans on a gate. Cars and lorries are whipping past only yards away, but the view is timeless. The shadow of clouds, the ripple of wind in grass makes it seem that this earth woman is stirring. The land rolls in from under the sea, stretching under her feet, a giant earth mother protecting the coast. It's the same feeling of connection she's had a few times on Cadbury Hill and on the cliffs in Cornwall. Fleeting moments of knowing she belongs to the earth, that it holds and supports her. At such moments searching for identity becomes irrelevant, but they are rare and don't last.

As she starts up the car, she longs to be driving the other way, heading back west to her cottage, her haven. The sun is warm on her shoulder and she winds down the window to feel the wind in her hair. She puts thinking aside and speeds towards Portsmouth singing along to Zoë's Abba tape and beating a rhythm on the steering wheel.

At the hospital Eleanor is in a state of agitation. She's clinging to the sheet, grabbing at Fran's hand, then dropping it and muttering to herself. Her eyes are closed. Does she even know Fran is there? After a while she seems to fall asleep and Fran makes to leave. The woman in the next bed raises her hand and beckons.

'She had a visitor. They had the curtains round, whispering. Not that your mother takes much in. But she's been in a palaver ever since, talking to Jesus and so on. Blonde lady she was.'

Fran thanks the woman. By now it is getting late but she knows she won't sleep until she sees Goldie. Why visit Mother? Goldie who hates hospitals and hasn't been on good terms with her sister anyway? She diverts past Goldie's flat and sees the lights are on.

Goldie is on the sofa with her feet up and a half-bottle of whisky on the table beside her. She's sipping it neat from a shot glass. 'Well sweetie, it's good to see you. Have you come down off your high horse? Are we friends again? Or am I more in the doghouse than ever?'

Fran has forgotten she left Goldie's in anger – was that only the day before yesterday? 'I was out of order. I'm sorry, Goldie. I got in a real state, got things all out of proportion – took off to Dorset. You look all in. I thought you only drank whisky when you were ill.'

'I had a little excursion, too. Took it out of me, that's all.'

'You visited Mother. She was in quite a two and eight.'

'I had to let her know. Let her know you were finding things out.'

'About her priest you mean? Did she understand?'

'I don't know. Probably not. But then again it sounds as if something got through. I hadn't realised how bad she was. Oh, I know you told me, but it's not the same as seeing for yourself. So you've been sleuthing in Dorset have you?'

'I didn't get very far, more questions than answers. But the journey was good, getting away, soaking up the landscape.'

'The country never did much for me. But if it's calmed you down, that's a relief. Where did you go?'

Goldie listens and nods as Fran tells of her visit to the Catholic church, then refills her little glass. 'You've gone quiet. What are you thinking?'

'Well that's not all.'

'Go on then.' Goldie shifts. Uneasily, Fran thinks.

'Well, I did find out that a priest got a girl into trouble.'

'Rumours! Gossip flies round in a small place like that.'

'Well, yes. That's what the current priest said. He wasn't very helpful. But then – well, I went to the farm. I met Peg Barnes.'

'Oh! Marjorie's daughter you mean? You *did* get about. Well?'

'She had some first-hand information. Like the fact that he and Mother carried on in the barn. The fact that he had red hair, like me.'

Goldie sips her whisky.

'You see, it did begin to stack up. I mean, I'd like to believe it's not that important. But equally, I'm thinking, who on earth am I?'

Goldie is silent, nodding slowly.

'There is something odd, something particular I want to ask you. It's probably none of my business…' Fran breaks off, leans forward. 'You sure you're okay?'

Goldie nods, impatient. 'Yes, yes.'

'Well, that Peg said nothing about me being born. She said it was you who had a baby there, not Mother.'

'Ah.'

'Well? Was it?'

'Yes. Yes, it was. I thought that might come to light.'

'I don't understand. Why didn't you say?'

'Well, it's complicated.'

'You see, I thought that was when *I* was born. You said so yourself. And Mother always told me I was born in the country. But what I wanted to ask was, what happened to *your* baby, Goldie? Did it die?'

Goldie is nursing her shot glass and rocking slightly. 'No, she didn't die. It *is* your business as it happens. Much more your business than poor Patrick. Here, you'd better have some of this. Yes, I know you're not drinking. Medicinal. Believe me, sweetie, you'll need it. Get yourself a glass.'

Fran fetches a glass. She still drinks occasionally but she does get impatient with the rituals that say you can't hear bad news without needing a drink or celebrate good news without having another drink, of a different kind. She just wants to hear the news.

'I've kept this secret for so long, it's hard to know what the words are.'

'Any words'll do.'

'No they won't. This may be the most important thing I'll ever say to you. Oh my, oh dear. Try to understand, won't you?'

'Goldie, just tell me.'

'Fran, that baby, my baby. My baby was you.'

Silence. Words spinning, the world spinning.

'Me? You mean...?'

'Yes. I'm not your aunt. I'm your mother. Biological mother, that is. Yes.'

'But...why? What about Mother? How...?'

'Here, drink it.' Goldie pours into both glasses. 'I need it if you don't.'

Fran sips and feels the fire grab her throat and burn into her. It brings her back to her body.

'We planned it together, your mother and me, from the time I found I'd fallen for you. I had the baby and she went and registered you in her name.'

'You didn't want me.' Fran grips a finger between the finger and thumb of her other hand, moving the flesh over the joint, feeling the bone inside, reminding herself of her frame, the skeleton that holds her together.

'Wait.' Goldie's earrings rattle as she shakes her head. 'You see, in those days it was a terrible thing to be an unmarried mother. Added to that, our mum, she would have stood by me, but she was only just making ends meet as it was. But then, when I had you... Oh, dear.' Goldie pauses and sips the whisky. 'Once I had you, I found it was a terrible thing to give your baby away. It broke my heart. I had no idea what it would be like, how I would feel. How could I?'

'Couldn't you have changed your mind?'

'It was all arranged, Nell had told Harry she was expecting...'

'You mean Dad didn't know? It wasn't a proper adoption?'

'Oh, no. You know your mother. You see, she'd already—'

'But how did you get away with it? I mean it isn't legal, it can't have been.'

'Nobody knew. Marjorie Barnes wasn't to know what happened when we went home. Things happened in wartime and people weren't that concerned. They had worse things to worry about.'

'I can't believe you could do that.'

'Well, the long and the short of it was, I had a baby, Nell wanted one. Well, she...'

Fran stares. 'Mother *wanted* a baby? I never thought Mother wanted me. I always thought Dad must have persuaded her – or that it was a mistake.'

Goldie shook her head. 'It all made so much sense. Oh, but it was hard to feel as I did and to see Nell didn't.'

'So she didn't want me once she had me?'

'No, that's not true. But she had no idea about caring for you. And of course we hadn't allowed for the hormones. She had none, of course – and I had more than I could cope with.'

'And Dad never questioned it all?'

'Why should he? Whoever would have imagined such a thing!'

'So who was my actual father?'

'Sorry, love, that's the thing I can't tell you.'

'What! After all this, you can't tell me that critical thing? So was he someone famous? Who's still alive?'

'Don't waste your energy, sweetie. Don't press me. One day I'll tell you. At least you know it wasn't that tearaway priest!'

Fran crosses the room and stares out across the dark harbour to the lights on the Gosport side. She can hear the water slapping on the wall and wishes it could wash away the confusion in her head.

'Just one more thing I want to say.'

Fran looks round. She really can't take any more.

'When you had the twins. Do you remember you asked me to come and help? I *so* wanted to come. But it stirred it all up – all too close to home. Reminded me of how Nell needed help with you. Plus, I didn't trust myself to be close to you at a time like that. Afraid I'd go to pieces and tell you everything.'

'Oh, Goldie.' If only she had, thinks Fran, and squeezes Goldie's hand.

'I just wanted you to know. It wasn't because I didn't care. It used to keep me awake at night, feeling bad that I was keeping you in the dark all those years. And then I was letting you down some more by not helping out with your babies. I made such feeble excuses, but I just couldn't risk it.'

Goldie's shoulders are shaking and Fran puts an arm round her.

'And, Fran? Don't ever live someone else's life. That's what I ended up doing. You've done it too, I know. Live your own life, sweetie.'

Fran gives Goldie a long look. 'Yes,' she says slowly. 'Yes. I will.'

Goldie swings her legs to the floor. 'Just limbering up to go to bed. I won't see you out.'

Fran drives back on automatic pilot. What if Goldie had decided not to have her? Well, nothing. That's a strange thought in itself. She can't manage to think herself out of existence. What if Mother had had her own child? What if Goldie had kept her and brought her up herself?

She falls into a deep exhausted sleep and wakes at dawn still with this thought. A ghost of a moon hangs in the sky scribbled over by twigs of sycamore. What would it have been like to have Goldie as a mother? She's loved her and confided in her all her life as an aunt. But a mother? That would be different. She imagines being cared for by Goldie on that farm, sitting under an apple tree in an orchard full of spring flowers, playing with sticks while Goldie reads to her. As she grows older she builds dens in the barns, collects eggs and comes back to tell her adventures to Goldie, still sitting under the apple tree doing a pile of mending.

She shakes her head. What a crazy image for Goldie, who has never mended anything if she could help it. Who would be bored beyond belief by sitting under an apple tree for more than ten minutes and who is only happy walking on pavements with an off-licence on the corner and the main line to London not far away. Fran stretches and swings out of bed. The moon has faded into the ordinary day and she is left feeling unreal.

How on earth did Mother manage? Fran knows only too well about the business of bonding with your baby; how vital it is, and how hard it was with the twins – and she didn't have anything to get in the way. Except her own terror. Zelda rescued her, but for Mother, having Goldie around would only have made it harder.

Later she rings Dale, gripping the receiver and holding on to her confusion. The phone rings and rings in his London flat until she remembers it is the day of the funeral. Dale will be burying Woods. He could probably do with her support as much as she needs his. But they are having to go it alone.

As soon as she hangs up, Peg Barnes calls. She's remembered the name of the baby, she says.

'I bin thinking about it all after you went and it all come back. They were sitting round the fire in the kitchen folding nappies. Francesca, it was. Nellie chose it, said it was after some Eyetie painter. Didn't seem right, what with Mussolini and all that, Ma said.'

As she listens to Peg chatting on, Fran sees her name glow with a new aura. Why did Mother never tell her? An Italian painter. It makes all the difference.

'Goldilocks thought it was a bit la-di-dah, you could tell. But she just accepted it as if it wasn't up to her. I remember Ma remarking on it to Pa, but he just said posh folks have different ways. Funny though, that you should be called Fran. What's that short for?'

'Not funny really, Peg. The baby was me.'

Silence. 'Oh, well I never. I'm sorry if I've spoken out of turn.'

'Not at all, Peg. You've been really helpful. All's well that ends well.'

'Well, I'm glad it's all turned out. Give your ma my best. She was a lovely lady and she cared for my ma. We was touched she came to the funeral.'

Fran is glad it was Goldie who broke the news to her. She wouldn't have wanted to hear it for the first time, unprepared, over the phone from Peg Barnes.

38

The doctor has told Fran her mother is fading. She must fetch the twins from school.

She pauses in the kitchen and opens the larder door. So much has changed since she last looked in there. The bottles still stand in serried ranks. She is no clearer about why Mother set them up but she does understand why she took to drinking so heavily. She wasn't just lonely after Dad died, but isolated with her secret, holding on to it day by day, frightened about what Goldie would do next.

Fran gives a last look at the larder shelves. She never could see the installation as a joke and now she finds it sad. It catches at her throat and she shuts the door. At least this was a secret Mother had under her control.

At the hospital Zoë can't bring herself to look at Eleanor after the first glance at the bed. She stands by the window looking into the car park. Dan sits by the bed and takes Eleanor's hand in one of his, stroking it gently with the other as if it were a small furry animal. Fran notices how big his hands are and gets a lump in her throat.

She bends over Eleanor, tells her Dan and Zoë have come to see her. The message seems to take several minutes to percolate into Eleanor's consciousness. Then she opens her eyes, extracts her left hand from Dan's and starts grasping her other hand, pulling at her fingers. This takes more energy than she has. She closes her eyes again and flaps her right hand weakly on the bed cover.

Dan leans towards her. 'You want to take your ring off?'

The eyelids lift again and Eleanor gives a crooked smile.

Dan nods towards Fran on the other side of the bed. 'Can you take her ring off, Mum?'

'For Zoë,' says Eleanor, suddenly clear.

Fran hesitates with the ring in her fingers, the clear depths of the sapphire catching the light, then puts it into Eleanor's hand. 'Zo, Gran has something she wants to give you.'

Zoë drags her feet towards the bed and puts her hand out. Eleanor drops the ring into it and Zoë manages to squeeze her grandmother's fingertips. Fran resists the urge to tell her 'kiss Gran thank you' like she did when they were little. But Dan gestures impatiently and Zoë begins to lean forward, then turns away quickly and leaves the ward.

On the drive home Dan is angry. At least Zoë might have made an effort, given Gran a kiss.

'Poor Gran, lying there in that state. She'd hate to be seen like that.'

Fran feels for both of them. It's unfair that Dan made all the effort, while Zoë not only got the reward but seems ungrateful. Zoë tried her best. When she found her in the hospital lobby she was in tears and shaking. 'Gran looked like a dead person. I couldn't bear to touch her.'

Will Zoë want to sell the ring? Hopefully not, but it's old-fashioned and it's hers to do what she wants with. It was a surprise to see Dan so easy with her sick mother. He seemed to know just what to do.

Back at the house, the twins take their duffel bags upstairs while Fran starts peeling potatoes. She's surprised to find Dan at her elbow almost immediately.

'Here, Mum. For you. I meant to get it finished for your birthday but it took longer than I expected.' Dan thrusts towards her a small package wrapped in shiny purple paper.

Fran wipes her hands on her jeans and tears it open. She pulls out a tiny hare, minutely carved in honey-coloured wood with a soft sheen.

'Dan! It's beautiful!' She turns it over and fondles it in the palm of her hand. 'It feels wonderful. Oh, Dan!' She hugs him. 'I can't believe you made this. Made it for me.'

'Well, I thought you were really upset when you lost that one you had on a chain. Couldn't afford a silver one, so I thought this might do instead.'

The silver hare had gone missing during the packing up of Pseud's Corner after a particularly strenuous session at the local tip. She'd been distraught.

'*Might do*? It's wonderful, Dan.' Fran makes to hug him again but he lurches sideways.

'Made it at Mike's.' He picks two oranges out of the fruit bowl on the table and starts juggling them. 'Got a bit of help.'

'Oh, who was that?' Fran tries to sound casual.

'Certainly not Mike. He's only any good at shelves. Rubbish at carving.' He grins slyly.

He's teasing me, thinks Fran. That has to be a good sign.

'Did you tell him? About the silver hare, I mean?'

'No. Why?'

'No matter.' How bizarre that Dale should have helped Dan make a replacement hare. And why not tell Dan? 'Well, actually, it's just… It was Dale gave me the silver one. Years ago. Before he went to America.'

'That's weird.' Dan slouches out of the door and takes the stairs two at a time.

Fran cuts up the potatoes and puts them on to boil. Since Mother gave Zoë the ring she's been wondering what she can do for Dan. Now she knows what would be right. She fetches Harry's toolbox from the shed and puts it on the kitchen table. It's the first thing Dan sees when he comes down for supper.

'What's Gramps's toolbox doing there?'

'It's for you, Dan. I know Gramps would have wanted you to have it.'

'But those tools are worth a fortune, Mum.'

'So is Zoë's ring. But that's not the point. You'll use them, and that's what Gramps would have wanted.'

Fran sighs and rips another page out of her notebook and screws it up. Here she is trying to write a tribute for Mother and she wasn't her mother at all. Her mind refuses to run on Eleanor and she's worried about Zoë and Dan who are back once again for their grandmother's funeral. It's not the right time to tell them about the whole mother saga. Zoë would be upset. But that's not the problem. It's more about Dan. On the drive from the station Zoë was indignant.

*

'Miss Evans said to me, how many *grand*parents have you got, with the emphasis on grand.'

'Meaning?'

'Well, the whole school seems to have sussed that our real father just turned up, that we've got a surplus of parents.'

There came a grunt from the back seat. 'Shut it, Zo.'

Zoë ignored this. 'She's a cow, Miss Evans. Except that's tough on the cow.'

'What did you say to her?'

'I said, just the normal number, *thank* you. And I gave her one of my looks.'

Fran grins as she reruns the conversation. She likes her daughter a lot more lately, and enjoys her spirit. The prima donna behaviour has evaporated with the disappearance of Geoffrey and the influence of Zelda's family.

Zoë has her own agenda. That evening she comes and sits on Fran's bed.

'Dan's watching TV.'

Fran wonders what girlie subject Zoë doesn't want Dan to overhear. Maybe her periods are giving her trouble.

'Why don't you and Dale get it together?'

Her directness takes Fran's breath away. 'Just because he's your father – it doesn't mean we have to…'

'But you're both potty about each other…'

'What makes you say that?'

Zoë rolls her eyes. 'It's *obvious*. You both moon about and jump on the phone the moment it rings and all that stuff.'

'He does that?'

Zoë nods. 'Well?'

'We don't want to rush into things. I need some space.'

'*Space?* You hardly ever see each other.'

'You two need time to get to know him.'

'We've *done* that.'

'Well, it's okay for you. But I'm not so sure Dan…'

'I tell you, you'd be doing Dan a favour. There's this girl at school, right? She like quizzes people the whole time? She asks Dan, "Are your parents coming to open evening?" And he says, "My mum is, but I don't know about Dale." And she says, "Who *is* this Dale person?" Like everyone's been discussing it. And Dan says, "He's my father." And she says, "But I thought you only just met him, and who was the other guy who used to come?" And Dan loses it and smacks her in the face. And then Dan's in detention and so you see he'd find it a lot easier if you got together and he could just say "my parents" again.'

Fran is blown away by the simplicity of this argument. She's also shocked by the news that Dan, her gentle son, hit a girl in the face. So much going on under the surface that he hasn't talked about.

'But does Dan even *like* Dale?'

'Oh, Mum!'

'I don't know why "Oh, Mum". When he gave me my hare he did imply Dale helped with the wood carving, but you can't just assume…'

'The wood carving makes me *so* mad! I went to find Dan one time and there was Dale carving. I was *so* cross with him!'

Zoë sounds so possessive.

'Why?'

'His hands, of course! He might damage them and not be able to play. He's *so* casual.'

'What did he say?' Fran hears an echo of Verity making the same protest at the kitchen table in Fremantle Square. Still the same Dale.

'He *said*, "There's more to life than playing the cello." I ask you!'

Fran raises an eyebrow. *That* is a very different Dale.

'Dan says Dale's "okay". He doesn't hassle him.' Zoë twiddles her hair round her index finger. 'Actually I think it's great they get on. Dan hated Geoffrey.'

'I guess "okay" is high praise from Dan.'

Zoë sighs impatiently. 'Anyway it's not us marrying him, or whatever. But we'd know where we were if you did.'

Fran looks into the dark garden and wishes she could as readily know where she is herself. She smiles at her daughter, remembering that Dale used a similar argument himself. 'You are so alike, you know.'

Zoë grins back. 'I know. After all, he is my dad.'

39

On the eve of the funeral Goldie phones to announce she will be arriving early.

'There's something special I have to say. I want to be sure we can have a private conversation. Don't worry, sweetie, I'll get the ferry and take a taxi.'

Fran has had enough of mysteries and surprises and her feelings for Goldie are complicated. She can't be angry with her, but she doesn't respect her as she did. This is the hardest part to deal with. Zelda said, 'You must be so confused about your feelings for Eleanor.' But no. There's no confusion there. The confusion is all around Goldie, who has always seemed so honest and forthright and yet carried such an extraordinary secret – and still hasn't told the whole story.

Goldie duly appears next morning leaning heavily on two sticks, a black feathered pillbox perched on her outrageous pink and orange hair.

'I'm sorry if this is inconvenient, sweetie, but you'll understand. I've been worrying all night.'

'Where's your Zimmer frame?' is all Fran can think to reply.

'Oh, it's so awkward. Not making a fool of myself with that. Not today. Nell wouldn't have liked it.'

Fran smiles in spite of herself. Goldie is so right.

'I should have done it before today, but I knew you weren't really wanting to see me for a while.'

Fran cannot deny it. 'Come into Dad's study,' she says.

'I'm not sure...' begins Goldie. Then she adds, 'I suppose it's just the place.'

Goldie sinks heavily into an armchair by the window. 'There's a time and a place. And this is it.'

The morning sunlight falls on Goldie's face and the harsh tints of her scant hair. The skin around her eyes is puffy, the lids swollen and red, and her face, usually so full of life and laughter, is grey and drawn. Her body caves in on itself as she slumps in the chair. Her hands clench and unclench, naked against the black fabric of her skirt.

'Goldie, you're ill.' Fran grasps her hands. 'I should have come...' Fran holds Goldie's hands, stroking the backs with her thumbs. She is surprised at the fall of a tear.

Goldie pulls her hands free, gropes up her sleeve for a handkerchief and blows her nose, dabbing at her eyes in an attempt not to disturb the mascara that is already smudged on her cheeks.

'I'm just a silly old woman. You see...' She draws herself up and attempts a factual tone. 'All those years I had a fantasy that one day I'd tell you...' She swallowed hard. 'You know, what I told you. And you'd give me a big hug and call me Mother.' She blows her nose again. 'Life's not like that. I was living in a movie.'

'I'm sorry, Goldie. I still can't get used to it. But you're still my Goldie.'

'Don't get carried away now. I haven't finished yet...' She gropes in her bag for a packet of cigarettes, lights up with a shaking hand and exhales long and hard.

Fran passes her the brass ashtray off the desk. 'The thing I couldn't get over was that you'd been lying all these years.'

'That was no lie. That was my life. Oh dear, there goes the drama queen. But it's true, Fran. It *was* my life. I had to believe it in a way. Most of the time I forgot it was a lie. Otherwise I couldn't have survived. We were such fools. Young girls who thought we could mess with nature. Just to suit ourselves. Because it was convenient. We didn't reckon with the feelings. Great big stonking feelings. I had too many of them and Nell didn't have enough. And it did for both of us.'

Fran stares bleakly at her. 'You see, you were the one I always trusted. You and Dad.' She stops, remembering. 'Except he wasn't.'

'Which is why I've come today.' Goldie sounds almost brisk. 'Now this isn't going to be easy. You see, Fran sweetheart, Harry *was* your father, like I always said.'

Fran wants Harry to be her father, but that means... No, she can't follow that thought.

Into the silence she says, 'What are you saying?' and hears her voice falter.

'That Harry was your father.'

Fran feels outrage, disgust, a flash of indignation for Mother. 'But that's horrible!'

'It is not horrible at all. Just wait.'

Goldie ignores Fran's wide-eyed stare and raised eyebrows. 'So, he was your father. And for most of your life he knew how. But Nell never knew and that's why I haven't been able to tell you until now. I promised Harry solemnly I wouldn't tell you while Nell was alive.'

'What do you mean, for most of my life he knew how? Surely... You said he didn't know I wasn't Mother's child.'

'Just wait. I'm not telling it well. I began in the wrong place. Let me unravel it in my own way.'

Goldie pulls a dog-eared photo out of her handbag. 'I've always carried this round with me, romantic old fool that I am. That's how much he meant to me, your father. I'd have done anything for him. And I did. I fell in love with him at first sight. You were not the result of some fly-by-night affair. He might not have been in love with me, but he cared about me. He was gentle and wonderful. He was just like that. He cared about people. You know that.'

Fran takes the photo and gazes at the faded and familiar face. 'So how...?'

'Nell and I used to go to the tea dances on the pier in Southsea. Very respectable, they were. The way nice girls could meet young men. I met him there. Nell had to work late one week. A big wedding and there was a rush on to complete all the bridesmaids' dresses. So I went along to the tea dance on my own. We got friendly immediately. Harry was such a boy, he'd blush as soon as look at you, but he forgot to be self-conscious with me. And I fell for those grey eyes of his.' Goldie stops and draws on her cigarette, staring into the middle distance.

'Go on.'

'He was so gentle. And naïve! He had no idea what to do with a girl. And I didn't know much better, only from things Nell told me. I was so young! And I'd fallen for him completely by then. We were like a couple of kids. I think he thought of me a bit like a sister. Which was what I became, of course.'

'But I don't understand…'

Goldie holds up her hand. 'Well, sweetie, we got carried away, Harry and me. It started with just going walking – by the sea, walking and talking. And one evening we got cuddling. We went too far. I never dreamt… I mean I knew how you made babies, but I never connected it with what we ended up doing. That time, the time you were conceived, was at the end of the week. We arranged to meet again on Monday. I remember Nell didn't want to come. I didn't think anything of it at the time. Anyway, Harry turns up and he's half solemn and half excited. He's sorry he won't be seeing me again, but he's fallen in love. Just like that. Doesn't occur to him for a minute that I have too – with him. I tease him a bit and we have a laugh and a dance and say we'll be friends and I go home and cry for a week. Then I get on with my life – good old Goldie, always one for a good time.' Goldie dabs her eyes again.

'And then?'

'He'd met Nell, you see, sweetie. Over the weekend. Of all the unlikely coincidences.' Goldie plugs in her cigarette, exhales long and hard.

Fran watches the trail of smoke, attempting to rearrange the facts of her origins in yet another pattern.

'She'd given him a lift. I told you the story. I was nothing compared with her. Of course I had no idea of who he'd fallen for and he had no idea I was Nell's sister. Why should he? You should have seen his face when Nell brought him round to meet Mum. I'm looking out for them in the front room. Twitching the net curtains. I thought, who's this young man Nell's got in tow now? And there he was! Harry!'

Goldie pauses for effect and to inhale again. Fran stares intently at her, impatient for her to continue.

'Harry, he's gazing down at her like she's a goddess. And as they get to the gate, she looks up at him, and I can see, you can tell. This is it. This is the one she's going for. He's going to get her a new life. I tell you, I'm standing behind that door, and I'm going, Marigold Wilkins, you have never set eyes on this fellow before. Never! Because you know that's the only way you can cope.' Goldie stops to draw breath.

'You mean, you didn't say anything?'

'Not a word. I knew how jealous Nell was. Didn't want her getting the slightest whiff with that sharp nose of hers. So I walk out into the hall and hold out my hand and say, "I don't think I've had the pleasure," very firm, looking him in the eye. Even Harry got the message. But I'm thinking, what a lie, what are you saying? Pleasure is exactly what I did have. And as Nell went to find Mum, Harry looks at me kind of puzzled and hurt, and I just shake my head and he follows Nell.'

'Did you know then...?'

'That I'd fallen for you? Oh no, this was only a week or so after. So you see now, why I suggested to Nell what I did.'

Fran frowns.

'Don't you see, sweetie? When I realised I was expecting, my first thought was that Harry must never know I was having a child – because he'd guess it was his. And he'd be torn in pieces over it. He'd want to do the right thing by me. And then what would happen to him and Nell? And Nell would never forgive me, and I'd lose a sister into the bargain. Either that, or he'd marry Nell and poison their marriage with feeling guilty about me. You see what a hole I was in?'

Fran nods thoughtfully. It's hard enough to keep up with the facts, let alone with the emotions.

'When Nell said she had to fake a miscarriage... Well, it seemed the obvious answer. I didn't give you away so I could go on having a good time. If it hadn't been for Harry turning up with Nell, I'd have kept you. Even though it was tough in those days and Mum would have given me hell.' Goldie sucks the last from the cigarette and stubs it out.

'Would you really?'

Goldie nods. 'I think that's what they call irony. And of course, the other reason was that Harry could bring up his own child and the two of them would give you a much better chance in life than I ever could.'

'It's beginning to make sense.' Fran looks out over the lawn to the tree where she used to swing as a child. Now she has the whole story. The picture is falling into place. 'You said Nell – Mother – had to fake a miscarriage?'

'Oh, she told Harry she was pregnant to hurry him along a bit into getting married.'

'That figures.'

'Nell wasn't a bad mother, sweetie. It was just too much for her. If she'd thought too much about it she'd have felt a failure. I know. I did.'

'No, she wasn't a bad mother. I've come to realise that. And you've been incredibly brave. I didn't make it easy.'

'I was afraid you'd think it was sordid. Just a grope on the beach.'

'You were on the beach?'

'Well, yes. You could get under the wire.'

'Wire?'

'Barbed wire, sweetie. All the beaches… It was wartime, remember. Anyway, under the breakwaters, once it got dark, you couldn't be seen. The smell of seaweed always reminds me of him. He was so considerate – worried the stones would hurt me. And all the time there were other things he should have been worrying about. We were so naïve, thank God, as it happens.'

Fran stares and Goldie frowns. 'I've gone too far, saying all that.'

But Fran starts to laugh. 'On the beach! On the beach at Southsea! What a wonderful place to be conceived. How unlikely, how romantic and funny and different. No wonder I'm so drawn to the sea. That's the best thing you've told me.'

'Well, you're a funny one.' She pauses, shaking her head. 'And, you know, I'd do it again! I wouldn't not have you. Not for all the tea in bloody China. But if I could have another chance, I'd keep you and let the others sort their own damn selves out.' She sighs. 'How about a drink, sweetheart? I didn't dare have one last night. I wouldn't have been able to stop, I was that anxious. But I'd kill for a gin now, or whatever else you've got.'

As Fran pours Goldie's drink she tries to picture the scene in the narrow hallway. She feels suddenly indignant on behalf of Mother. Goldie and Harry were the first conspirators. At that moment in the hallway Mother became an outsider. However much she was loved and adored by Harry, however much she conspired with Goldie, Mother was the one shut out from the whole truth. Goldie always knew the whole story, for years the only one who did. But Mother lived with an unknown. No wonder she was always so frightened.

'Did you ever consider telling Mother the truth?'

Goldie shakes her head emphatically. 'Well, actually, in the early days I was tempted several times. But it would have been for all the wrong reasons. Nell was so smug when she got engaged to Harry. Once or twice I thought, I could wipe that smug look off your face. But I wouldn't have done. I wasn't that mean. And it would have ruined everything.'

'You were in a very powerful position.'

'I suppose I was. But it didn't feel like that.' Goldie sighs and takes a gulp of gin. 'I used to cry myself to sleep grieving over you. And then I'd visit. How strange that was! There I was with the three people I loved most in the world, and seeing you grow up. But knotted up with jealousy, all at the same time. Jealous of Nell for having you. Jealous of Nell for having Harry. And me working my socks off and going home to an empty place.'

After several more sips of her gin, Goldie hands over two envelopes. 'They're both from your father. One to me years ago. One to you to give to you when Nell died. Don't read them now. We're going to have to get moving, mustn't be late for Nell.'

'But you haven't explained how Dad found out.'

'Nell had problems, women's problems. Went to a gynaecologist. He decided she needed a hysterectomy. I expect you remember that.'

Fran nods. 'It was when I had glandular fever. I came to you.'

'That's right. Anyway, in those days the husband had to give consent. They knew each other anyway. You know how they're all like a club those medical types. And the doctor says, "I never knew Francesca was adopted." Of course, Harry told him you weren't. Turns out the gyny man could tell Nell had never had a child. Harry's absolutely stunned. It didn't take him long to put two and two together. Then he came to me and asked me straight out.'

'Poor Dad.' So that explained the whisky, his moods at that time.

'Poor Dad is right. Harry never really got over it. He so believed you were a love child – him and his queen. You were a love child, of course. I loved him to bits. And if he hadn't met Nell, who knows. He might have gone on to love me.'

'You've carried so much.' Fran smiles wryly.

'Including you. In a way I was lucky. I stayed in touch with you. I saw Harry all the time. But, as I say, in a way that made it harder. I couldn't get him out of my system. Lord knows I tried hard enough. But with all the individuals in the world, not one of them came in a hundred miles of your father.'

'Poor Gold.'

'One thing I have learnt. If you have the chance of love in this life, you take it. Don't waste the opportunity.' She gave Fran a knowing look.

'Is there no keeping anything from you?'

'I know there's something going on. I do know you quite well by now, sweetie.'

'I don't know whether to laugh or cry.'

'Oh, you've got to laugh. It's all a mess, but life goes on.'

And so they proceed to Eleanor's funeral, Fran shaken and in shock, Goldie shaky with relief.

40

Fran is hardly aware of the progress of her mother's funeral. She reads out what she has written about Eleanor's life in what seems to her like a monotone, lacking all conviction.

Back at the house she makes tea and listens politely to her mother's friends. She registers how grown up Dan seems, acting as wine waiter. The phone goes and Zoë answers. She comes to tell her it was Dale, who's away doing a series of master classes. He said not to bring her to the phone, he just wanted to know how she was, sent his love.

'He's just leaving Birmingham. I told him you weren't good.'
'I'm fine.'
'Who do you think you're kidding, Mum?'

Fran wishes Dale was here, is glad he is not. *If he was here I wouldn't be able to hold it together.*

When she drives Goldie to the ferry they hardly talk, and it's a relief to wave her goodbye. Something inside her is stretched to the limit. She's touched that the twins have done all the clearing up by the time she gets back. She shuts up the house and drives them back to school. Another silent journey with both of them sleeping and her own thoughts churning. She's angry with Goldie, but she has to admire her, too. And she has to admit that Goldie was probably right to believe that if she'd confessed the truth, Mother's jealousy would have destroyed everything. One of these days she must tell Zoë and Dan the whole story, but now she can't wait to be alone. Let the dust settle. She'll tell them in the holidays.

She'd intended to go back, to carry on clearing the house, but it will have to wait. The longing for her cottage and the sound of the sea is intense, so she keeps heading west, on automatic pilot towards Cornwall. If only she can get inside her cottage, she will be all right. She cannot bear to speak to another person. She focuses on her home and how it will wrap itself around her.

But the cottage is chill after the warmth of the car. She'd be welcome at Zelda's, but her teeming family would be too much. She sets about creating warmth: a hot drink, a fire, the immersion heater. She huddles over blazing logs in the cold living room, waiting for the moment when she can melt into a deep bath. It's wonderful to peel off her clothes which smell of death, and to slide into the hot water. She shakes off the image of the coffin sinking into the earth and feels the tension leave her. But when she wakes the water is lukewarm and the fire downstairs has gone out. She remembers the letters and takes them to bed with a hot water bottle.

She starts with the dog-eared pages her father wrote to Goldie. They smell of Goldie's perfume.

My dear G

I have been in great turmoil since I saw you. It is difficult to balance the needs of the three women in my life who are dear to my heart.

As I explained to you, ever since I discovered the secret you and Eleanor have carried, I have faced a dilemma about what would be best for Francesca. It seems too much to burden her with at university.

So I have kept my counsel and urge you to do the same. For there is also Eleanor to consider. She might just cope with my knowing about her, but as to the other part of the secret – I do feel it would destroy her to know about you and me. She takes things hard, finds it difficult to forgive. It seems to me that would lead to suffering for everybody. You can lodge a letter explaining everything, to be given to Francesca on Eleanor's death. I think I may do the same. It seems only right that eventually she, and any children she may have, should know the truth about their heritage.

Does this make me a coward? I fear so. I hope you can forgive me for this and that eventually Francesca will too.
Yours affectionately,
H

Next she tears open the envelope with her name on it.

Dearest Frazzle

It is strange to think your dear mother will be dead when you read this letter. And I don't know whether or not I will be here to read it to you. That would be my preference. I never wanted to take the coward's way out. But I think when you read what I have to say, and knowing your mother as you do, you will agree it is better not to have involved her in the truth.

The truth is, you are not her child. Although you are mine, and I give thanks every day for that. You were the result of a meeting between me and Goldie. If I hadn't met your mother immediately afterwards, Goldie and I would probably have been regular parents to you and there would never have been a bizarre story to tell. But I fell head over heels in love with your mother and was committed to her before I had any idea she and Goldie were sisters. Imagine my shock when I discovered it. Goldie made it clear she didn't want it known we had already met, and I admit I was relieved to go along with that. She also decided not to tell me when she realised she was pregnant with you.

Now the story gets complicated. Your mother sadly lied to me that she was pregnant, as she was anxious to get married quickly. This coincided with Goldie confiding about her pregnancy, and the two of them cooked up a plan for Eleanor to pass off Goldie's baby as her own.

The original lie was understandable in wartime. I was a pedestrian sort who might have taken a long time to get round to tying the knot, so I quite forgive your mother for bringing that forward. What I have found harder to forgive is that she so lightly took you on as her child, deceiving us both. We will never know just what her motives were, but I do believe she was concerned for her sister's fate, and the decision was therefore not simply one of convenience to herself.

It was only by accident of your mother's needing a hysterectomy that I discovered the truth. Her consultant confided to me that Eleanor had never given birth. After I got over my shock and disbelief and thought back over the years, I guessed the rest, and this was confirmed by Goldie.

Eleanor has never known I found out her secret. It is my belief she could not cope with the exposure. She also has no inkling I am your father. It is odd that she was never curious to know who was. Never pressed Goldie on the subject of his identity. I think it would be intolerable for her to know that Goldie and I had, to some extent, fallen for each other before she herself met me, even though my feelings for Goldie and for your mother were, and are, not comparable.

Whatever you or I may think about the plan she and Goldie hatched, we must remember how vulnerable they were – to social ostracism, poverty and of course the dangers of war. They were sisters protecting each other and doing the best they could in difficult times. They also have to be admired for carrying it through so thoroughly. I truly believe your mother has forgotten there is any lie involved. She came to believe her story. She has always been able to carry situations off with style. For Goldie, it has been much harder and I have deep admiration for her courage in keeping her end of the bargain. It broke her heart not to bring you up, and to see her sister being a very different sort of mother, someone who found it hard to express her love for you, a mother who didn't have Goldie's warmth and generosity of spirit. She has shown an extraordinary strength and depth of love over the years – for you, for me and for her sister.

At the end of the day, love is what it is all about. It surprises me sometimes that my love for Eleanor has never faltered in spite of being severely shaken over all this. Love cuts through all the complications and it's the only thing in life that really matters. My love for you has never been challenged and has been a steady source of joy to me. I hope it has seemed so to you. I am deeply sorry if you are hurt by all this, and I understand if you think

me a coward. But I did what I could and hope you will come to forgive me and to let go of any bitterness you may feel.
Your ever loving dad

Finally, finally the tears flow. If only he were here to comfort her, to tell her who she is. All her life she's been masked as someone she's not, someone who didn't exist. *I am the woman with no existence. No wonder I felt invisible. I was never there. The person I was does not exist. And I never was the person I am.* It's impossible, a frightening conundrum. She can't laugh it away and carry on as Goldie does. And the whole thing makes her feel guilty all over again for what she's done to the twins, *their* crisis of identity. The sins of the fathers, or in this case the mothers, shall be visited on the children unto the third and fourth generation, or something like that. Awful how those sayings come back to haunt you.

It's suddenly very lonely. She has an urgent need to communicate with another human being. Zelda, strangely, won't do. Dan comes to mind, but it would be unfair and anyway, he'll be in bed. Dale is the person she really wants to talk to now. She phones his number, but there's no reply. He must have been delayed, or he's gone to the pub for a meal. She's lost track of time.

She must have slept, for she wakes shivering and clutching an almost cold rubber bottle. She switches on the lamp and rereads the last paragraph of her father's letter. 'Love is all that matters,' she says aloud and dials Dale's number again. It rings and rings.

'Oh, bugger! Oh, Dale!'

'Yes?'

'Dale?' She stares into the receiver, still hearing the ringtone.

'I'm here,' says Dale, replacing the receiver and putting his arm around her shoulders.

'Dale!' She twists around and hugs him to her. 'How come…?'

'I was planning to go to your mother's house. Then Zoë rang from school, said you were coming on here. Said she was worried about you. So I came.'

'Zoë phoned you? She *is* trying hard. Yesterday she—'

'Never mind about all that. When did you last eat anything?'

'I'm not sure I did. I can't remember. But never mind about *that*. I need to tell you so much. Best read this. That's what I was ringing you about.'

Dale reads her father's letter while Fran grips his hand and watches his face.

'Blimey,' he says as he comes to the end. 'No wonder you're in a state.' He kisses her gently. 'So what were you going to say to me?'

'Like he says, love is all that matters. That's what I was going to say.'

Fran wakes early as the darkness is thinning and huddles on the window seat in her jumper, looking over the bay to the far headland. The shoreline and the horizon are barely discernible in the grey dawn. She needs a revelation, one of those rare shifts of perspective to give her insight, clarity. But the sea is just there, neither rough nor smooth, spreading its ruffled surface between land and sky. And she is just Fran watching the sea.

The events of the day before seem to belong in another world: Goldie and her final revelation; her own churning anger and confusion; the fact that even Dad chose to go along with it all. Everything seemed to change. But this morning she is still the same Fran. Goldie is still her Goldie. Mother was Mother. People doing the best they could. The past is the past. The future is what matters now. Her turn to do the best she can.

She can let the emotions burn and destroy her, or she can use their energy to move on. What was that word Maggie once used? Alchemy. She talked about the alchemy of the body. Fran's not sure what it means, but does that matter? 'Just listen to your body,' Maggie said. 'It will tell you what to do.' And, strangely, her body feels at peace.

Remembering what Zoë did yesterday, she smiles: ringing Dale to get him to drive for three hours, rather than Zelda who is a ten-minute walk away. Dale who simply held her until she slept and who is now dead to the world, stretched out across the bed behind her.

She slides down the sash window. Dale's even breathing is matched by the sound of wind in the tamarisks and the steady surge of the sea.

Lightning Source UK Ltd.
Milton Keynes UK
UKOW02f0055270116

267132UK00003B/62/P